THE
NIGHT
SHE
LIED

BOOKS BY LUCY DAWSON

LUCY DAWSON

THE NIGHT SHE LIED

bookouture

Published by Bookouture in 2023

An imprint of Storyfire Ltd.
Carmelite House
50 Victoria Embankment
London EC4Y 0DZ

www.bookouture.com

ISBN: 978-1-83525-319-9
eBook ISBN: 978-1-83525-318-2

For Ness

PROLOGUE

The cell door opens and an usher appears. 'Jury's back in.'

'What? Already?' Johnnie is unable to hide his astonishment. 'OK, don't panic.' He twists around to me. 'I've never believed there's a correlation between speed of deliberation and which way the verdict will go. All it really says when twelve people don't take long to agree unanimously, is that they felt strongly either way. You ready?'

I take a deep breath. 'Yes, I am.' Of course I'm not. I am not ready at all. Anyone who says otherwise in a situation like this, is a liar.

'I'll see you in there. Everything is going to be all right. I promise.' He forces a smile, before hurrying off.

I try to breathe normally as we begin the now familiar walk up the several flights of stone steps that lead to Court 14; but I'm puffing by the time we get to the top and have to ask the two officers flanking me if we can pause for a moment. I don't want to face them all appearing to be in the middle of another panic attack – expecting to be found guilty. I close my eyes and try to compose myself, holding onto Johnnie's assurances.

Everything is going to be all right.

One of the guards clears his throat. 'We need to go in now.'

I can't put this off any longer. I have no choices left.

The murmurs in the too bright and artificially lit court are thrumming, like a low-level single note, as I take my place in the dock. I don't look at the packed public and press galleries to see who has come to watch this bit. I don't look at the empty jury box to my right either, which is about to fill with the handful of men and women who have decided the course the rest of my life will take.

Instead I gaze to the front, at the same empty spot I've focused on since the start, between the two barristers who have their backs to me. One creamy-white horse-hair wig to my right – and on the other side, the Crown's much grubbier, almost tea-stained version.

'All rise,' the clerk facing the court commands and, obediently, everyone stands as the judge takes her seat. If Her Honour Judge Caroline Silverton KC is as astonished as the rest of us to be back here after only three hours, she does not show it.

The jury is recalled, and as they troop silently back in, the white noise pitch in my head rises another notch. I concentrate on amplifying it, drowning out everything else around me.

Everything is going to be all right.

The clerk's voice remains clear and steady. 'Will the defendant and the foreman please stand?'

I do as I'm told, fixing my gaze on the royal coat of arms above the judge's head. Higher powers have decided. I stare at the red cap of the crown, but as I close my eyes, all I see is a spreading pool of blood. My mouth feels dry, my breathing shallow. That single low note is sliding up and up. Louder and sharper. Impossible to ignore. Everything is *not* going to be all right. Guilty.

'Mr Foreman,' says the clerk, barely audible now above the noisy panic in my head, 'answer my question: yes or no. Have you reached a verdict in respect of the defendant upon which you are all agreed?'

'Yes.'

I swallow at the crescendo of shrill alarm. Guilty.

'On the count of murder...'

This is it. I start to breathe, deeply and quickly, in preparation for the moment of pain and shock that have finally arrived and are going to hurt. It's going to *hurt*. I close my eyes and brace for the verdict to slam into me. Guilty, guilty, guilty. I can smell it.

'STOP!' shouts a voice, and my eyes snap open.

What just happened?

PART ONE

NOVEMBER 2021

ONE

JUDE

It was midnight and I'd taken my hot chocolate to the window seat in the corner of the almost empty hospital café. There was, of course, no view, only the dark path and the shrubs hiding the swirling deep River Thames that lay on the other side of the walkway, but I didn't care. I slumped down, exhausted, took a mouthful of drink and immediately burnt my mouth because it was lava temperature. A comparatively pathetic straw to break the camel's back, but tears finally started to slip down my cheeks.

I'd managed to not react while I was dressing the lacerated hand of a drunk, besuited, late-fifties bloke and he called me a useless slut for no reason whatsoever. But when he noisily sucked the contents of the back of his throat into his mouth and flobbed the mucus and saliva onto my chest, I immediately jumped back away from him in the small A&E bay, and became entangled in the curtain. 'Spit on your tits,' he slurred, in case I hadn't noticed, before promptly vomiting on the floor.

'Slut' was quite a retro insult to have picked, and I'd had plenty worse said to me over the years, but he still managed to push me over the edge.

'Look – the patients are angrier and more frightened than they've ever been, you're burnt out, and to cap it all, you've just switched to permanent nights,' said my boss, Trina, when she found me tearfully cleaning myself up in the toilets. 'For some people, it just doesn't work. I was like I had constant jet lag. I was just this big jelly rolling around, cocking things up, angry and crying all the time. I'm not saying you're cocking up by the way,' she added, 'yet – but when you're *really* tired, stuff that would normally be water off a duck's back feels nasty. You sure you want to stick with it? Because you don't have to. I can change the rota?'

I shook my head. I didn't want to tell her my sleep had become so bad that I was only now able to drop off during the day and for a couple of hours here and there, so it was out of desperation that I'd asked to go on nights in the first place. My eyes were constantly heavy in my head, like snooker balls in dry pockets. I often couldn't find the right word I was looking for when talking and rarely felt as if I was 'in' the moment, rather as if my body was playing catch-up on physical reactions that ought to be instant. 'I honestly do feel like I'm starting to come out the other side of this transition bit,' I lied.

She eyed me sceptically. 'Yeah. Looks like it.'

'It's also the first anniversary of Dom's death today,' I added, my voice wavering. 'So...'

Trina stared at me. 'Oh love! I'm sorry. Come here!' She drew me into a hug and it was so nice of her, but the problem was, when anyone was kind to me, I immediately found myself on the verge of breaking down in floods of tears. I didn't want to embarrass her, or worse – have her sign me off work. The thought of being stuck in the flat on my own, staring at the four walls, or out of desperation having to go back to Mum's, was horrendous. I needed to keep busy. I could feel I was tense in her embrace and drew back after waiting another socially acceptable moment or two.

'You get yourself downstairs for a proper break and a hot drink.' She shook her head. 'It doesn't occur to them that we've got lives and problems too. They're only thinking of themselves once they're in this place.'

I blew my nose. 'I don't think Mr Spitty is thinking about much to be honest. He's pissed... I know it's not personal.' I started to feel embarrassed for making a fuss. 'Honestly – I'll be all right, I just—'

Trina straightened up. 'You can't look after other people if you don't look after yourself first, pet. I'm not saying pop out for an hour, just have a twenty-minute breather.'

But twenty minutes was plenty long enough for me to log on to my Insta and see the responses to my: 'Can't believe one year has passed since I last saw this smile. Love you Dom' post. Lots of people had written kind messages.

We miss you Dom! He loved you so much! Big love sweetheart!

Thinking of you and sending you all the hugs today xxx

Such a lovely photo of him! x

All the love to you darling xxx

Love goes on forever! x

Thank you for sharing these photos xx

I'd had plenty of nice WhatsApps too, and it was lovely that so many people had remembered without my social media prompt. But I also couldn't help feeling jealous that after they'd sent their messages, they'd gone back to their day, untroubled.

Except, that was unfair; everyone had their shit going on. We were all just doing the best we could. I wiped the tears from my eyes, tucked away at my corner table in the café, but it was quite hard to get them to stop, and I didn't actually see who shoved the small plate towards me at first.

'You look like you need this.'

I blinked and a doughnut swam into view. I looked up in confusion to see a sweaty male runner, dressed in T-shirt and shorts, despite it being November and the middle of the night. Breathing heavily, he put livid-scarlet hands on his hips and stared down at me. 'I saw you' – he thumbed over his shoulder at the path – 'while I was on my run. I'm not sure that's the best doughnut in the world' – he was right about that, the café didn't permanently smell of stale pastry and sadness for nothing – 'but even a bad doughnut is better than no doughnut at all. I'm not hitting on you by the way.'

I didn't even have the energy to raise my eyebrows at that.

'It's just you're a nurse.' He nodded at my scrubs. 'My mother was a nurse and I think you're all doing an amazing job.'

He hesitated and, sweeping his damp, curly hair off of his face, sat down without being asked, which focused my attention. While he was good-looking in a reality-TV identikit sort of way and wasn't obviously off his head on something, I instinctively edged back. He seemed almost hyper-alert and was giving off pretty intense vibes, already drumming the tabletop lightly with his fingers.

'I'm Rik,' he said.

'Hi Rik.' I forced a smile as I flipped into professional mode, quickly assessing him, working out what I was dealing with. Mental health issues? He wasn't carrying or holding anything that could be used as a weapon, was he? 'Thanks for the doughnut, but I don't want to keep you from your run.' I waited for him to take the hint and leave.

'It's OK, I'm in no rush. I'm pretty much done anyway.' He started jiggling his leg restlessly. 'This is only my second lunchbreak run this week, and my knees are already starting to protest. Annoyingly' – he frowned – 'because I really wanted to make it five.'

'Lunchbreak?' I repeated. 'It's midnight.'

'Yeah,' he agreed and ruffled his hair again. 'I'm nocturnal.'

'Oh right?' I said politely, glancing around to see if there was anyone who could help if I was going to need it. 'So while everyone else is fast asleep you're up and about, going for a run, working, popping to the shops – just at night?'

'Pretty much,' Rik agreed. 'Now loads of people work from home it's easy. You can get everything online and delivered whenever. It's becoming much more common a lifestyle choice than people think. It's still niche. I'm not going to lie. But more and more people are seeing the benefits.' He looked down at his feet, briefly. 'These things just take time.'

The penny dropped. He was lonely. Everyone had become so soul-crushingly isolated that we'd reached the desperate stage of offering a stranger cake in exchange for a five-minute real-life interaction.

I hesitated. There was always enough time to be kind. 'Well, give me some quick tips then because I've got to say, I'm not finding it a walk in the park. I've just started working permanent nights,' I said and felt sad when he sat forward eagerly.

'Are you through the first bit? When you're awake you feel like you're dreaming – and when you *do* sleep, you jolt awake feeling like you should be up and about?' He didn't wait for my answer. 'The next stage is the hyper-manic one where mentally you're more alert but emotionally you're all over the shop – it starts to settle after that.'

'I might be heading into the hyper stage.' I gestured at my obvious tear stains.

'Ah well then,' he sat back. 'Hang tough, Jude. It'll get better in a day or two.'

An unpleasant chill stole over the skin on the back of my neck, like being touched when you didn't realise someone was standing behind you, and I tensed again. 'How do you know my name?'

He looked confused. 'It's on your badge?' He nodded at my lanyard. 'I've got really good eyesight. It's all the carrots I eat.'

I glanced down at the terrible picture of me and felt really stupid. 'Sorry.'

'I should be apologising for my rubbish joke.' He cleared his throat. 'It's a myth anyway, but you'd know that being a nurse. I'd be actually orange if I ate enough carrots to affect my eyesight. I do use a sun lamp at this time of year though... if you're not going to eat that?' Rik paused briefly in his mono-logue and nodded at the doughnut.

I pushed the plate gently to him.

'You sure? Thanks... I do get actual sunlight on my skin – it's just at either end of the day and sometimes that's not enough. There are people in parts of the world who go from November to January without the sun rising at all.' He took a large bite. 'Then the days start getting longer and longer until between May and July it never sets.' He chewed. 'Which is why, rubbish though it is, I live in the UK. Yeah, that doughnut wasn't the best. I'm glad I took one for the team to be honest.' He sat back and scratched his head, frowning at the plate as I waited to see if he'd concluded his conversation with himself. He obviously spent a lot of time alone.

'You also need decent blackout blinds, a white, brown or pink noise machine and your phone on silent during the day,' he continued, 'but the good news is that living in London makes it easy. There are a tonne of places open all night. I don't think it would be so straightforward to be nocturnal in a tiny village in

Suffolk or somewhere. Sorry I freaked you out by using your name, by the way. I didn't mean to.'

'Please don't worry. It's my issue, not yours.' I felt bad for being so jumpy. One of the results of how aggressive we'd all noticed patients become over the recent months was how 'on alert' we now were, as health care professionals, in response. I was suspicious of everyone and everything, including small random acts of kindness it seemed. 'What's pink and brown noise?' I asked, trying to be normal and talk to this man without worrying he was about to leap forward and stab me.

He frowned with concentration. 'Pink noise is lower-frequency – like steady rainfall. It's not as full-on as white noise. Brown noise is even lower still like – I don't know – a rushing river. I'm a white noise person myself.' He shrugged and licked the sugar from his fingers. 'What else do you want to know?'

'Why did you start living nocturnally?' In spite of myself I was becoming intrigued.

'I've not slept well my whole life, but I had a particularly bad bout of insomnia about three years ago. I was working in the City. It was a lot of people and noise; queues, rushing, other people's music from their headphones on the Tube, phones everywhere, which was like – pow!' He lifted his hands up and mimed his head exploding. 'I was with people all day, every day, hearing them talk and finding it harder and harder to switch off. I stopped sleeping at night and in the end I gave up fighting my body. I wasn't going to win so there was no point. Now I live a fully reverse life.'

'But don't you get – lonely?' I addressed the elephant in the café.

He looked genuinely surprised. 'No. I still meet up with friends, I just do it at either end of the day for their breakfast and my dinner, or vice versa. Am I giving off a sad, lonely, talk-to-anyone vibe then?' He laughed. 'Shit! I just wanted to make sure you were OK. You looked a bit... broken.'

I flushed as I realised that all along he'd been pitying *me*. 'I have another question – so if you meet some friends for what's their evening meal and they hit the wine,' I moved us on hurriedly, 'do you join in, even though it's breakfast for you?'

Rik shook his head. 'I don't drink any more. It doesn't work when you're nocturnal. The timings are all wrong and it's actually a great excuse not to have to do it. You just say "no thank you – it'd be like you having a glass of wine with your corn-flakes" and people get it. It's not a big deal. I was in the army for a while and I got all of that out of my system while being a soldier.'

'I thought you said you worked in the City?' I reached for my hot chocolate.

He nodded, putting his hands in his lap. 'I *did* work in the City, but before that it was the army. I joined up when I was sixteen and loved it. They wipe you clean and reprogramme you – but I broke my back when I was twenty-three, and they discharged me.'

I put my cup down. 'You broke your *back*?'

'Sounds worse than it was. I'm fine.' For the first time, he pointedly changed the subject. 'So do they force you to work nights here then? Or did you choose to do it?'

I hesitated and was surprised to hear myself say: 'I've been finding it hard to switch off from work recently. My partner died a year ago – today – and I'm the opposite to you... I don't like it when it's really quiet at night any more. I sleep better when I can hear other people are up and around me, getting on with their day.'

'I'm sorry to hear about your other half.'

'Thanks. Well, this has all been really interesting, thank you.' I changed the subject again. 'I mean, obviously *I* won't be able to go fully nocturnal but—'

'Why not?' He interrupted, puzzled.

'Women don't have the same luxury of walking around

when it's dark without—' I began as my phone suddenly lit up on the table, brightly displaying the word MUM. I sighed and grabbed for it to shove in my pocket.

'You're not going to answer that?' Rik looked surprised. 'Does she usually ring you in the middle of the night?'

'At the moment, yes, a fair bit.' I dismissed the call. '*Her* husband died six months ago. We're all about the bereavement right now in my family!' I tried to smile. 'She's a bit up and down and some days it's easier to be a support than others.'

'Yeah, I get that.' Rik agreed. 'My mother died suddenly when I was thirteen and my dad and I were lost. Everything felt the wrong size. Literally, because neither of us could so much as work a washing machine. We learnt quickly though.'

I pictured Rik as a confused young boy, forced to grow up too fast overnight, and my heart hurt. Life was so incredibly fragile. 'So you know then,' I said.

'Oh yeah,' he agreed. 'I know... and I can promise you, it won't always feel like it does now. Trust in time.'

'Thank you.' I swallowed and managed a smile at him just as my phone lit up again. My mother was ringing back.

'Go for it – it's cool.' He stood up. 'Nice speaking with you!'
'You too.'

I watched, a little stunned, as he passed through the other side of the glass double doors and jogged off. I wasn't sure I believed in signs or messages, but I couldn't help feeling there was something more than coincidence about a man Dom's age passing outside, today of all days, and stopping to tell me that it wouldn't always be like this.

Mum was still hanging on in there. 'Hey Mum.' I cleared my throat and wiped my eyes again as I picked up. 'I'm at work. You OK?'

There was a silence down the phone. 'Mum?' I repeated. 'Are you there?' Excellent, so now she'd started pocket calling me in the middle of the night? What had she done, rolled on her phone in her sleep? 'Mum! Can you hear me? You've called me by mistake!'

Sure enough I heard a soft rustling and imagined the phone somehow having worked its way under the duvet. I closed my eyes, instantly exhausted again. 'Mum? Can you hear me? Fuck's sake...'

'You don't have to swear!' came the immediate reply, and I jumped.

'Mum? You *are* there?'

'Yes,' she whispered. 'I'm here.' There was a pause and I realised the sound was actually her crying.

I sat up in alarm. I had only seen my mother cry once, when I was fifteen years old. She was not the crying kind. 'What's happened?'

'Something terrible. Something so terrible' – she paused and gulped – 'that I don't even know how to tell you!'

'Where are you?' I demanded.

'At home! I can't even... oh God!'

The line went dead.

'Mum?' My heart began to thump and I called her back instantly – but she didn't pick up. I tried again but it just rang and rang. What should I do? Tim was away... they were all away. I made a split-second decision and dialled 999.

'Police, please.' I could hear the fear in my voice. 'My mother has just called me in a state of distress. I don't know if she's hurt. She's seventy-four and she said something terrible had just happened. She's alone at home and she's never done anything like this before. I tried to call her back but she's not answering. She uses a stick and I don't know if she might have had a fall, but I'm worried it could also be something like an intruder. The line cut off before she could tell me what was wrong... I'm over an hour away at work at St Guy's hospital, and my cousin and his family, who she's living with, are away too and there isn't anyone I can think of who could get to her quickly. I'm so sorry, but could someone go to the property? Her name is Lady Margaret Fawkes and the address is Highcombe Hall, Berkshire.'

TWO

JUDE

'I can't talk now, Mum, I'm just arriving at work.' I paused
outside the hospital. 'But I'll say it *again* if it helps – I'm sorry,
OK? Where are you now?'

'At home! Where else would I be?'

'Highcombe home, or the cottage?' I risked and there was a
dangerous pause.

'My drawing room *at home.*'

I closed my eyes. She was still in the main house. I could see
her now, sitting on the faded pink sofa, persistent puffs of smoke
from the ineffectual open fire dispersing into the air and
clinging to the chintz curtains. 'You're supposed to be moving
into the cottage, Mum.'

'I'm still recovering from my ordeal last night,' she retorted,
'waking up terrified to hear a hammering at the main door and
the police yelling that they were going to break it down – on a
Grade 1 property! That door is hand-carved black walnut!
What on earth were you thinking?'

'Me?' I exclaimed, clamping the phone to my ear as I began
to pace about in front of the entrance to A&E. 'I'll tell you
exactly what I was thinking! Last night you rang at midnight in

tears, telling me something horrible had just happened, then the line went dead! I knew you were on your own so I thought you were in life-threatening danger of some kind. I didn't know if you'd had an accident, if there was a burglar in the house, if you'd just witnessed something horrendous... take your pick! So I phoned the police!' I threw my hand up incredulously, and an approaching trio of teenage boys smirked at my obvious anima-tion, and one of them did an impression of me in a high squeaky voice, to the laughter of the others. I gave them a filthy look as they passed, which made them laugh even more. Turning to watch them saunter off carelessly to enjoy their evening, I managed to resist sticking up a finger at their retreating backs. One of them might see and they'd all double back. It wasn't worth it.

'I did *not* call you in tears,' Mum insisted. 'That is just total fabrication and I most certainly did not say something terrible had happened either. Now Timothy is coming back from South Africa early, Mr and Mrs Brooks are returning from their holiday tomorrow... all because of you. You have got to step out of this permanent high-alert mode you're in!'

I felt the blood beginning to bubble in my head. 'Yesterday was a difficult day for me.' I waited for her to remember why.

'It's *always* a difficult day,' she retorted. 'That's exactly my point!'

'OK, look – I didn't imagine what you said.' I struggled to keep my voice even in case any of my colleagues were about to arrive and were within earshot. 'The call registered on my phone. I can send you a screenshot of it if you like? Fourteen minutes past midnight. We've already been over this several times today, haven't we? Mostly when I should have been asleep *because I've got to work now!*' I tried to calm down again. 'But like I said then too, if something demonstrably happens, if there is proof that it happened, you can't make it un-happen because it doesn't suit your narrative any more.'

'"My narrative"?' she repeated. 'Oh God – which self-help book are you gurgling back at me now? I never said I didn't call you, sweetie pie—'

I stopped pacing immediately as I fought with the overwhelming need to hang up on her. Never had the term 'sweetie pie' been used to mean the exact opposite quite as effectively as when it came from the mouth of my mother.

'—I simply said that I wasn't crying. *Nothing terrible happened!*'

'Except that's exactly what you said!' I hissed. 'Why the fuck else would I have phoned the police?'

'Er, that's quite enough, thank you!' She raised her voice. 'You can stop swearing. You are forty-two years old. You don't need to speak to anyone like that to try and make a point.'

That actually made me briefly crouch down on the walkway in as close to the foetal position as possible, closing my free arm around my head before I exhaled and staggered up again, fixing my sights on the lit-up buildings on the other side of the dark Thames. She was unbelievable.

'Are you still there?' she asked when I didn't say anything. 'Maybe I was having some sort of nightmare, I don't know.' I imagined her dipping the word 'patronising' in a giant jar of honey. 'Perhaps that's the answer, darling? Hmmm?'

I saw myself flinging the handset over the bushes right in front of me, watching it slip into the water and disappear forever. 'OK,' I said tonelessly. 'If that's the way you want to play this, that's fine. But you know it happened.'

'No,' she shouted, suddenly pushing the jar of honey off the side so that it shattered everywhere. 'It did not happen! You are very overtired, very emotional at the moment and quite frankly bloody impossible! I'm going to hang up now before one of us says something we regret!'

She was gone. I stood in the middle of the walkway breathing clouds of stressed breath into the cold air as I

clutched my phone and waited for the adrenalin to dissipate.
Hot tears pricked my sandpaper-dry eyes as I stared blankly
across the water at the back of The Savoy and ignored the
people on their way home from work having to make their way
around me, shooting curious glances at the madwoman standing
rock-still in her scrubs, outside the hospital, rather than in it.

I would give anything to be opening the door to an anonymous luxury hotel room, padding over thick carpets and just
climbing into bed beneath crisp, clean covers, where no one
would find me, turning the lights off and simply going to *sleep*.

I put my head down, turned around and went in through
the glass double doors to start the long shift ahead.

* * *

It wasn't – I don't think – a conscious thing that at midnight I
found myself back down in the café. There had been some
surprise when I said I was going for a quick break.

'You all right?' Trina frowned at me from behind the nurses'
station.

'I just feel a bit lightheaded,' I mumbled truthfully. 'Didn't
you say yesterday I ought to look after myself better?'

'Yes, but no one normally listens to me, so...' She looked
pleased though. 'Good girl! Get some food while you're there.
Something green... a mint Aero doesn't count,' she called
after me.

I felt guilty as I walked through the waiting room, where at
least two fitful children were among the assortment of adults.
An elderly lady, eyes fluttering as she drifted in and out of sleep,
awareness and a shadowy no-man's land in between, gripped
the arm of her wheelchair. They'd all been there for ages. I
almost ditched my break to turn back and get them seen, but I
also really wanted five seconds to check my phone in case Mum
had messaged me. I hated it when we argued. It was also

genuinely worrying that she was apparently still holed up at Highcombe, completely alone.

Despite it being my childhood home, I wouldn't sleep there overnight with no one else in the house for all the money in the world. I pictured the long dark corridors, the vast empty attics, the still, silent chapel with its tombstones in the floor, beneath which some of my distant ancestors' bones were interred, and shuddered before sending her a text.

> Just checking you're OK. I'm not actually working tomorrow or Friday so I could get a train and help you sort the cottage? Help you unpack properly. I know this is hard for you. Love you xxx

I sighed and put my phone away, looking up just in time to see Rik running past the window.

He waved and I smiled back. Just as I was realising I was a little bit disappointed that he'd kept on going – which made me feel uncomfortable – he pushed in through the door, panting slightly.

'You've got it to three runs then?' I said, having already stood up to go back to work. 'Well done!'

'Cheers,' he gasped. 'I know it looks like I've come back to say hi but it's actually just an excuse to hide the fact that I've got the mother of all stitches.' He bent over and put his hands on his knees. 'Talking of which, how's yours?'

'My stitch?' I frowned.

'Your mother. She was ringing you last night, remember?' He straightened up and flicked his foot behind him, grabbing it so that he could stretch his quads.

'Oh she was fine, apparently.' I paused. 'Actually she kind of wasn't.' It turned out I was desperate to tell someone what had happened so they would agree that I'd been completely in the right and Mum had been unreasonable. 'She said she was on her own, something terrible had happened and then the line went dead.'

'Shit!' Rik gratifyingly let go of his leg and stared at me. 'You're kidding! You must have been terrified!'

'I was!' I agreed. 'I phoned the police. That's how frightened I was!'

Rik nodded. 'Very sensible. Did they go round?' He picked up the other leg.

'Yes,' I admitted. 'At which point Mum denied saying any such thing and insisted she was fine.'

Rik let go again and, legs planted wide, crossed his arms. I jolted slightly as it was a stance that Dom had often adopted. For a moment, it was oddly reminiscent of him. 'Why would she do that?'

I hesitated but alongside my confusion, the temptation of more sympathy and validation proved too much. 'My mother is supposed to have moved out of our old house by this weekend. Since my grandfather died, the estate passes to the next male heir – I know, proper Jane Austen stuff,' I agreed, a little embarrassed as Rik's eyebrows shot up, 'and she's not very happy about it. In fairness to her she's lived there all of her life and she's seventy-four now, so to have to get out and move into a small estate cottage when she doesn't want to is hard enough, but it's made worse by the fact that she doesn't like my cousin Timothy's wife, who is the new Lady Stratham. Why am I telling you this?' I stopped and scratched my head. He wasn't Dom. He was just a man who looked a little bit like him. 'I'm sorry.'

'Because you're stressed and worried about your mum.' He shrugged gently. 'It's fine. Go on.'

'OK.' I took my hairclip out, as it had started to slip, and let my hair loose so I could retwist it up as Rik raised his eyebrows again in surprise. 'I know. I'm borderline Rapunzel and it needs a cut,' I mumbled, 'but I've been busy. So anyway, she's had all of her things moved into the new cottage for over two weeks now. It's just sitting there in boxes she's refusing to unpack while she continues to stake her claim to the main house, except she doesn't have ownership of it any more.'

Rik nodded and waited for me to continue. Feeling compelled to fill the emerging silence, I blurted: 'Timothy's wife tried to flush her out by all of them going away, and she gave the housekeeper the week off too. Mum dug her heels in and stayed put only to apparently lose the plot last night when whatever the terrible thing was, happened. Everyone is now having to cut their first holiday in forever short because I raised the alarm, and Mum is furious with me, insisting that she was fine all along.'

'Is she though?' Rik put his head on one side. 'Furious I mean? Sounds like she's got exactly what she wanted – everyone coming back early so she won't be on her own *and* she's still in the big house.'

'Hmmm...' I said slowly. 'That hadn't actually occurred to me. You might be right.'

'People do strange shit when they're stressed. Anyway, I've got to go. Work is mental. Same time tomorrow if I haven't had a heart attack? I'll be happy to dispense more free advice then, if you need it?'

I smiled. 'I'm not working tomorrow or Friday, so no. You should rest up anyway. You really will knacker your knees.'

'Noted, thank you, nurse.' He hesitated. 'Do you by any chance want to grab breakfast tomorrow or Friday then? What time do you usually wake up?'

Wait – what? He'd said he wasn't hitting on me?

'Hey! At ease!' he laughed. 'You look terrified. I only meant I could show you somewhere that does really good all-day breakfasts, that's all! Friday would be better for me if that's cool with you? Say 8 p.m.?'

'You're not a journalist, are you?' I said, my skin tightening with fear. 'Is that why you've appeared out of nowhere and I'm suddenly telling you my life story without meaning to? My stepfather is *dead*. I get that he was a newspaper editor and an MP, but for the last time, there's no story there. Stop fishing around and leave us alone! What's wrong with you people?' Then I realised what I'd just said and, horrified, covered my mouth with my hands. 'I said stepfather and I really didn't mean to. I haven't even told my mother I know that yet. Please don't print it!'

Rik looked completely astonished. 'Journalist? I own a computer company called systemsRsolutions.' He edged backwards and put his hands up. 'Actually, you know what, Jude, don't worry. I'll save you the trouble. I thought you seemed nice. I enjoyed talking to you. I thought you might like breakfast, that's all, but you're being a bit weird...' His smile had gone. 'Why would *I* know anything about your parents? I really didn't mean to stress you out – I'm sorry. I'll leave you to it.' He stumbled back to the door, shooting me a last confused and frightened glance before he turned and hurried off into the night.

Shit! Had that really just happened? He was only trying to be kind.

My lone reflection in the window stared back at me before I glanced around the rest of the coffee shop in embarrassment. The only other couple in there were looking at me openmouthed, as if I'd just said something outrageous aloud, and for an utterly mad moment I wasn't even sure Rik had been there at all. Was I now so beyond tired I was hallucinating? Had I just been rambling to myself in front of this couple? 'You saw that man just then, talking to me – right?' I called over to them, genuinely worried.

The woman shrank back nervously and they both began to stand up. 'We don't really want to get involved,' the man said, gathering their belongings as they hurried out too.

'Wait, I'm sorry. I didn't mean to frighten you,' I began,

bewildered, but they'd gone. Had I shouted? All I'd wanted to know was if they'd seen Rik too...

The panic rose up my gullet so quickly I began to wobble on the spot. My head felt like it was full of wet candyfloss; I couldn't get the sticky thoughts to separate out clearly. I heard Mum crying down the phone, the man from the day before calling me a slut, and then Mum insisting she *hadn't* been in tears; I saw Dom's smiling face in the Insta picture I'd posted... and I started to breathe very fast. Someone else said something – the woman behind the counter I think – but I burst out of the coffee shop, pushing through the double doors into the sharp, dark air that was so cold it made me gasp as it hit the bare skin on my arms and drew the follicles into small bumps.

I looked frantically up and down the walkway and then I saw him, in his shorts and T-shirt, walking rather than running away, loping down the path. He even looked like Dom from the back, they were the same height and colouring.

'Rik!' I shouted and, to my huge relief, he turned back and I hurried towards him.

'I'm sorry, I'm so sorry!' I gabbled as he defensively reached out his hands and placed them on my arms to stop me crashing into him. I was shivering like mad, my teeth chattering in the cold. 'I didn't mean to be weird or rude! I'm just burnt out and I think I might have gone a bit strange from that and the sleep deprivation. I had a moment back there when I wasn't even sure you were real' – I heard the sound of my own desperate laughter as he let go of me – 'and I started thinking I'd been talking to myself. We can definitely say I'm in the hyper-manic stage of getting used to being awake at night, right?' And it was true, I was pin-sharp alert, but my tummy rumbled and I felt very lightheaded indeed.

'You wondered if I was *real*?' His eyes searched my face.

'Yes, I know how that sounds!' I tried to laugh. 'Like a grown-up version of an imaginary friend or something, I don't know. Or maybe I'm asleep right now? I'm joking obviously. I don't really think that.' I closed and opened my eyes. He was still there.

He frowned and started walking back in the direction of the coffee shop. 'Come on,' he called and I followed until he stopped outside the window, turning to face it. 'Tell me what you see.'

I stood alongside him. 'The coffee shop girl wiping tables and looking back at us like we're crazy.'

'Yeah, her,' he said. 'But I also see *us*. Our reflections, standing next to each other. You wouldn't see that if I wasn't real... and you wouldn't be able to feel this either.'

'Ow!' I exclaimed as he pinched me hard on the back of the hand.

He turned to face me. 'You need to come back inside, you're really shivering.'

We stepped into the foyer of the hospital, before moving off the mat as the confused glass doors began to repeatedly open and shut behind us like snapping jaws.

'I wonder, Jude,' he said, 'if you might talk to your boss about the possibility of you having post-traumatic stress disorder? I know what you're going to say,' he spoke gently over me as I started to protest, 'and I'm really not trying to mansplain PTSD to a nurse, but this looks familiar to me from my army days, and we can't always see it in ourselves. You must be dealing with a lot of really tough stuff at work at the moment and at the same time you're processing personal loss and grief. I'm sorry I said you were being weird, that wasn't OK.'

'No – it's fair,' I said. 'And maybe my mum was right too. Maybe I did imagine that whole conversation with her?'

He shrugged. 'One of the ways PTSD can affect you is a heightened sense of perceived threat to yourself or those you love.'

I rubbed my eyes. 'Not being funny though, but the threats

kind of *are* everywhere in nursing at the moment. People aren't very happy in general right now.'

'That's fair too,' he agreed. 'Just, put it on your back burner. Something to think about.'

He was probably right. Hadn't Trina said almost the exact same thing to me about self-care? 'I might just go back to see my mum tomorrow... help her unpack a bit... but' – I took a deep breath – 'if that offer of breakfast on Friday is still open?' I was amazed to hear myself ask him.

'Course it is,' he said. 'Give me your phone and I'll put my number in, then you can just let me know if you feel up to it.'

He watched me unlock it and pass it over. He tapped quickly then smiled. 'I've *really* got to get back to work now.' He stepped away, and the doors opened again letting in a blast of cold air. 'My lunchbreak is well over and it's only half four in the afternoon in San Francisco. My emails will be going crazy.'

I glanced at the clock and yelped. 'Oh my God – me too. My boss will be sending out a search party at this rate.'

'Well, when she finds you, talk to her. It's good to talk. See you Friday.'

I watched him head off into the dark again and looked at my phone. He'd put himself in my contacts list as 'Rik (real)'.

That was embarrassing, that gentle but teasing 'real'. I thought about him and the couple in the coffee shop drawing away from me... and then Mum insisting everything was all in my head. Was it possible that I could have simply imagined her saying something terrible had happened? I had to concede that perhaps it was.

THREE

Margaret finally managed to open the front door of the cottage and felt it as soon as she stepped over the threshold. The air was disturbed. Her skin prickled as she looked around the hallway. It seemed normal, boxes still piled high, bits of furniture shoved haphazardly against the walls by the moving men, but something was wrong. Timothy started gabbling away behind her, kicking off his boots in ignorant bliss, but she ignored him, walking slowly up the hall towards the light coming from the kitchen, at the end of the passage. The sitting room door was still closed and she continued past it, her palms starting to feel clammy.

The kitchen appeared, at first glance, exactly as she'd left it the night before, although it was arctic. Her eyes moved rapidly to the back door... which was very slightly open, just a sliver.

Leaning on her stick, she limped over to it, her ankle starting to throb as she pushed herself to move faster than she could cope with. Up close she carefully inspected the handle.

There were visible splinters where the catch had been forced and the screws had come away from the plates, loosening enough so that the door had opened. She swallowed giddily and shoved it closed, spinning around as Timothy appeared behind her.

'Oh dear – it's not very warm in here, is it?' He stepped over to the old Rayburn, feeling the lids. 'That's odd – they're hot. It hasn't gone out. Shall I crank it up a bit?'

'It smelt fusty in here,' Margaret lied hastily, 'so I opened the door. And it's not cold at all. You're not in Kansas any more, Dorothy,' she added, hanging a tea towel over the doorknob to hide the loosely hanging fittings.

Timothy glanced at her and gave a hearty laugh. 'Good point! South Africa and Berkshire isn't really a fair comparison temperature wise. I'm still adjusting. You'll have to indulge me until I get my thick British skin back.'

Margaret gave him a stare that indicated she didn't feel she had to do anything of the sort and waited until he was absorbed in fiddling with the innards of the Rayburn before moving to investigate the rest of the cottage. She didn't have to go far. The floorboards creaked as she cautiously approached the sitting room, afraid of what she was going to find on the other side of the closed door.

Forcing herself to seize the nettle, she flung it open with a gasp. The low-ceilinged room was naturally a dull space in any case, and she had to wait for her eyes to adjust to the gloom before her brain could make sense of the sight in front of her.

The destruction and chaos was absolute. Cardboard packing boxes, neatly stacked at the end of the room, had been toppled over and torn open, albums and albums of her photographs lay strewn on the floor, cellophane covers pulled back and images yanked from their long-held positions. Hundreds of black and white loose pictures of social gatherings, parties and events – glamorous people dressed up in elaborate costumes, laughing at the camera – appeared to have been tossed in the air and left scattered on the ground, as if a wilful child had been hurling great armfuls of autumnal leaves to catch on the wind. Stacked canvases had been flung around and all of the pictures in frames lacerated. Her self-portrait was sitting in the middle of the carpet like the centrepiece of a bizarre sacrificial ritual. The glass had been smashed and the painting itself slashed through the middle of her face. It might have appeared to someone else that targeting her features with the cuts was deliberate, a message perhaps, but Margaret knew it was simply methodical. They were looking for something.

She closed her eyes and tried to steady her breathing. She didn't need to see upstairs. She knew it would be in the same state.

'I've managed to – oh my God!' Timothy exclaimed, appearing behind her. 'What on earth?'

Margaret took a deep breath and turned to face him defiantly. 'I was angry, that's all. Don't make a fuss.'

His jaw went slack and he looked even more foolish than usual. '*You* did this? Deliberately?'

'I don't want to discuss it any further.' She shoved past him and collapsed into her sewing chair.

'It's as if you've been burgled!' He looked around. 'All this because I've asked you to move from the main house to here? This is a *nice* cottage, Margaret. It's not even really a cottage, it's a house. Most people would be thankful to have such a—'

'Let "most people" come here then,' Margaret shouted, jabbing her stick into the thin carpet. 'Oh wait, you already are, aren't you? Opening up Highcombe to the great unwashed; weddings, parties, Easter bunny bonnet parades, pumpkin trails, dogs carolling by candlelight.' Her voice rose naturally, as this was something she genuinely felt strongly about. 'I don't want people poking around my home!'

'Then we have to sell Highcombe,' Timothy insisted. 'You can't have it both ways. I'd be quite happy to do that, believe me. It's only because Annalise has her heart set on this major revamp.'

Margaret tutted in disgust at the thought of Timothy's dreadful perma-smile, spine-of-steel wife, but for once had no further comment to make as she looked at the devastation around her.

Timothy stared too, but once he'd finished scratching his head, he bent down and began to pick up some of the images that Margaret could see were from her fortieth birthday. Dickie had thrown her a surprise party, hired a big band and told all of their assembled family and friends how he owed everything to the woman he'd had the greatest of luck and sense to have married. They had all toasted her and sung 'for she's a jolly good fellow'.

Margaret watched as Timothy began to shove one of the happier moments of her life back into the nearest box.

'Just don't touch them. Leave them all alone!' Margaret wailed, and Timothy let go immediately, lifting his hands up to prove he wasn't still holding anything. He marched from the room, only to stride straight back in again.

'I'm sorry that you are upset,' his voice trembled. 'I'm sorry that you don't want to live here to the point that you did this' – he looked around at the chaos again in disbelief – 'and that you probably deliberately let the kitchen get cold on purpose because you want to stay in the main house, but you can't, Aunt Margaret. I've got a young family. You don't want them running around everywhere, annoying you.'

'I could get used to it!' Margaret exclaimed ungraciously. 'They go to school after all, don't they?'

Timothy shook his head. 'No. Annalise wants to start home schooling them.'

Margaret's mouth fell open. 'What? Oh how perfectly ridiculous! That's just cruel! "What school did you go to?" "The kitchen table – have you heard of it?" For God's sake, Timothy! This is too much!'

Timothy's expression deadpanned. 'I hated boarding and I won't make my children do it.'

'You don't know how lucky you were,' Margaret retorted. 'At least you learnt something. *We* had nuns who made it a priority to teach us to go to sleep on our backs with our hands crossed over our chests, so that if we died in our sleep, we'd be ready to meet God.'

Timothy blanched. 'Well, thank goodness times have changed then, hey?'

Oh he wasn't seriously trying to jolly her along, was he? Margaret fixed her eyes on him.

'Times *are* changing,' he insisted. 'So we need to get all of this properly sorted. Jude is already on her way. She caught the early train straight after work and—'

'Did you tell her to come up?' she demanded. 'Because she needs to sleep. She's burnt out, Timothy. On the edge of a nervous breakdown and already having to struggle with this horrendous switchover to working nights that they're making her do at the hospital. You shouldn't have called her to come and "help" with me, that was very selfish of you indeed.'

Timothy coloured. 'She said she wanted to come!'

'*She* actually has a proper job,' Margaret spoke over him. 'A very demanding one. Unlike some she doesn't have a wealthy father-in-law keen to splash his vulgar cash to buy himself some class, turning years of my family history into a theme park in the process.'

But that wasn't newly offensive enough to distract Timothy. He had started to look around the room again. 'I don't understand. I was here with you yesterday evening. We locked up together and it didn't look like this when we left. So – when did you do this?'

She watched him attempting to puzzle it out, wrinkling his brow with the effort.

'I came up here in the night,' Margaret lied. 'And stop trying to change the subject about Jude. I'm very cross that you've summoned her home when there was no need whatsoever. If she has some sort of total mental collapse, and I warn you Timothy – she's not far off the hearing voices stage – and I don't know... dies... on your head be it.'

Timothy looked horrified. 'Dies? What are you talking about? Of course she's not going to die! I—'

'And on the subject of death,' Margaret continued, 'while you were away in South Africa' – she curled her lip with distaste – 'I was unable to find your father's ashes. I expect Annalise has moved them. Would you ask her where she's put them, please?'

Timothy paled, swallowed and straightened up. 'We took them back with us and scattered them on Lissy's folks' farm.'

Margaret went very still. 'I'm sorry? You took my brother's ashes away without telling me and scattered them on the other side of the world at a location I will never be able to visit and honour? We were supposed to be interred in the chapel with Mummy and Daddy. All four of us together.'

Timothy took a deep breath. 'That was what his will said, yes, but he made it a long time ago. You know what Dad was like, not the most organised at keeping up with admin things, making changes, there was always something more fun to do. And I know he was your brother, but he was also my father, and just before he died he told me he wanted to be scattered in South Africa, like Mum will be when she dies. Annalise's family will show you where we did it, of course.'

'Oh they will? Oh how kind of them!' Margaret no longer needed to pretend to be angry. Standing up, she raised her stick and thwacked it down on a couple of already ruined canvases. Timothy jumped but stood still. Margaret pushed past him and stumped out of the cottage, her chest so tight she could hardly breathe.

Staggering down the nasty, twee little path and through the

gate, onto the drive that cut through the parkland and led to the main house, she looked around her wildly. As soon as Highcombe was within her sights, stoically sitting in the dip of the valley, she felt calmer... and as the mushroomy scent of nearby soggy ferns and grasses filled her nose she began to steady herself.

The air was dank, hanging over the bare trees like wet sheets, as if the day stood no chance of drying out and it wasn't going to bother with getting properly light either. It was miserable but somehow comforting in its familiarity. But oh God – this was all still utterly intolerable.

She exclaimed aloud with distress at the thought of Anthony's ashes catching on the wind, the last of him disappearing forever on the other side of the world without her, somewhere she couldn't even picture him being... and now *her* world was starting to implode; the police turning up in the middle of the night on Tuesday had damn near given her total heart failure.

She shouldn't, of course, have called Jude in the first place, but that was hardly the point. Jude hadn't needed to completely overreact in response. But then again, Margaret glanced fearfully over her shoulder back at the cottage and its ransacked contents – her extremely persistent daughter hadn't been that far away from the truth after all. Margaret tried to take the weight from her ankle, which was now starting to feel hot and prickle with pain.

Just the thought of fingers picking through her things, pulling her past apart... she started as a movement caught her eye. A handsome stag emerged through the fog across the drive on the edge of the wood. He was looking right at her. Margaret nodded in his direction, and he briefly shook his antlers, as if tipping his hat, before stalking off into the undergrowth. Margaret smiled faintly and realised she was going to have to go back into the cottage, before Timothy blundered into the kitchen and found the broken door handle.

But as she turned away from Highcombe again, the vibrant blue and yellow markings of a police car suddenly appeared against the whites and greys of the parkland, the beam of the headlights slicing through the low-lying mist. Still some way off but winding up the drive towards her. What were they doing back again?

Sweat began to pool at the base of Margaret's spine beneath her layers. Timothy had said nothing about a drama up at the main house. The grooms hadn't been chattering excitedly about anything at the stables when Margaret had gone down earlier either. Each of the girls had simply been going about their business mucking out and making up buckets of mash... But there were at least no flashing blue lights. Calm, Margaret. Stay calm.

She turned to face the car as it drew up alongside her. A couple of men – one uniformed, one not – smiled in greeting as the plain clothes wound down the window.

'My goodness,' she blurted defensively. 'Police officers, doctors and newsreaders simply get younger and younger. You two look about twelve!'

The plain clothes laughed. 'Flattery will get you everywhere. I'm looking for a Lady Margaret Fawkes. I assume she lives...' He pointed at Highcombe.

Margaret turned from hot to very cold indeed and, placing her hand in the small of her back as if it was tight, she pressed her clothes into the skin to absorb the damp. 'I'm Lady Fawkes.' She watched as the two men looked her up and down in surprise. 'I've been to the stables and haven't changed. I don't usually dress like this,' she explained. 'And no, I don't now live' – she pointed at Highcombe – 'I live...' She turned and gestured at the cottage behind them.

The plain clothes straightened up in his seat and somehow managed to look more official and yet blander at the same time. 'My mistake. I'm sorry. Might we have a quick word?'

Margaret gripped her stick more tightly. 'Of course, but no

one has been hurt, have they?' She swallowed visibly. 'I had a
son, Hilary, who died. I also lost my brother, elderly father and
husband in quick succession recently and this is all very' – she
waved her stick in the air at the police car – 'reminiscent of how
I found out about my husband.' She swayed on the spot and
thought she might fall over.

The plain clothes scrambled from the car to put a steadying
hand to her elbow. 'We're not here to notify you of anyone's
death, Lady Fawkes. Take a moment. We're in no rush.'

Margaret straightened up, her pale pink nail polish catching
in the car lights. 'Bless you for keeping me on my feet. Aren't
you kind?' She moved away from the policeman as Timothy
emerged curiously from the cottage.

'Hello there.' He extended a grubby paw. 'Timothy St John.'

Margaret rounded on him furiously.

'Sorry, Aunt Margaret,' he said quickly. 'Lord Stratham, I
mean. Still getting used to the new title, I'm afraid.' He gave
them all a tight, anxious smile. 'So there actually *was* a
burglary?' He turned to Margaret in confusion. 'Why didn't you
just tell me you'd called the police?'

'Because I didn't,' Margaret spoke through gritted teeth. He
was such a dim-witted earthworm of a boy, blindly wriggling
around eating things. 'They're here for some other reason,
Timothy.'

'A burglary? Here?' The plain clothes stepped forward and
offered Margaret his hand. 'DS Malin. When do you think the
disturbance occurred? Have you got any CCTV?'

'CCTV?' Timothy laughed bitterly. 'We don't even have a
working boiler in the main house!'

'How nice to meet you.' Margaret's smile was gracious but
she held onto her stick. 'My nephew is confused. There's been
no break-in. I'm moving house and everything is a little chaotic.
Frankly it does look like a bomb has gone off. But that hasn't
literally happened either.' She gave Timothy a withering stare,

silently ordering him to stay quiet, and turned back to the police. 'Now, you said you were looking for me?'

'I did' – DS Malin was rubbing his hands together briskly, pretending it was against the cold, having been left hanging – 'and I don't want to keep you standing around on a morning like this. Would you attend a voluntary interview instead, back at the station? We'd be able to take you there now, if that helps?' He stood to one side as the officer moved around to the passenger door and opened it like a chauffeur.

'You want me to go somewhere in that?' Margaret looked silently at Timothy, who leapt forward.

'It's quite all right, I can drive my aunt.' He hesitated. 'Is it – normal – to use a marked car for this sort of thing?'

'No,' admitted DS Malin. 'The pool car is in for an MOT. I asked a uniform friend for a favour, that's all.'

'I see' – Timothy grinned but with less certainty – 'because it does make something of a statement, doesn't it? Quite the talking point.'

DS Malin turned to look at it, as if surprised. 'Do you think so? Well, in any event we'd be very happy for you to drive yourselves, not a problem at all. You know where you're going? You can follow us now if not.'

'Oh, righto. Now? Gosh.' Timothy patted his pockets for his car keys, and Margaret began to feel rather unwell. Her armpits were sticky. She usually washed and dressed after her walk to the stables, but Timothy arriving unannounced to help her 'unpack' had completely thrown her routine and she was aware of a slightly sour smell catching in her nose. She clamped her arms tightly to her sides. 'I should like to change first before I do anything, thank you.'

'Of course.' DS Malin looked right at her. His eyes were very clear and pale. Insistent. She looked away first.

'What's the nature of the interview?' Timothy asked. 'Should my aunt have her solicitor present?'

'It's probably more helpful if we wait until we're at the station before we go into specifics, but I should stress, this really is voluntary.' He put his head on one side sympathetically, suggesting Timothy was completely overreacting.

'Yes, do stop fussing.' Margaret glared at him. 'I expect it's just about Jude unhelpfully crying wolf the other night.' She turned to the police. 'We'll be down shortly.'

DS Malin turned politely to Timothy. 'Lord Stratham.'

It was as if they had just been forced to agree a social engagement with a very pushy new-money neighbour. Margaret and Timothy watched the car turn around slowly, the tyres crunching on a loose stone before it crept away, back down the drive, slipping like a ghost into the thickening fog.

Red brake lights briefly illuminated, like two accusative eyes staring back at Margaret. They were almost at the main gates already. Fear sidled up and started to whisper in her ear. She closed her eyes but only saw writhing limbs twisted in bed sheets. 'Actually I *do* need a solicitor. Call Johnnie and tell him to come to Highcombe immediately.'

FOUR

JUDE

I yawned for the millionth time and stared out of the window. Everything normally looked much more interesting viewed from a train, but I was struggling to keep my eyes open as flooded field after flooded field began to blend into one. The reflection of the cloudy skies above made the ground appear white, dotted with random houses and bare trees. It was as if we were tracking over the surface of a giant, wetly iced Christmas cake. I yawned again, felt my head properly nod, jerked up and decided I'd eat instead. That would help keep me awake. Better to do that than nap badly now and not be able to sleep when I arrived at Highcombe. And in any case, it wasn't good to skip meals.

I reached into my bag and removed the Tupperware box containing my supper – chicken, hard-boiled chopped eggs and salad – and began to fork it into my mouth, wondering why I felt so cold when everyone else in the carriage seemed to have happily taken their coats off. I'd chosen the table right next to the carriage door, and while it was a bit draughty, I was the only one still huddled in my full-length puffy parka. If you weren't getting enough sleep, did it affect your body's ability to regulate temperature? I googled and discovered it did. I sighed. Surely I'd start adapting to working nights soon? I thought about Rik telling me this bit was just a phase and googled his company page again. Frustratingly, he wasn't on any social media platforms at all, and while his company info was uber informal (all first names and casual dress in their head shots... I'd put money on their offices having fake grass, deckchairs and inside putting green 'think space') it actually told me very little about him other than he was the CEO. I was about to start sniffing around Companies House, when a voice across the aisle said, 'You a body builder then?'

I looked up in surprise. A man in his mid-forties, laptop open, leaning back on the greasy headrest, wedding ring clearly visible on his left hand, was watching me. 'That's a very protein-packed breakfast.'

I just smiled politely and went back to eating. I wasn't getting into the whole it actually being my dinner and why thing. He could just think I was weird, that was fine with me.

'Or is it that – what's it called? Keto?' He tried again. 'You really don't need to lose weight, for what it's worth.'

Urgh. I would have put my headphones in – the universal language for 'I don't want to talk' but I'd forgotten them in the confused rush to get home and shove some stuff in a bag to make the earlier train so I could maximise my impromptu visit. 'Thanks,' I said, again keeping it polite. He didn't look like the type who'd persist with: 'I'm just trying to talk to you! Why are you being so snotty?' but my Spidey-sense had started to tingle.

Or had it? I thought about my perceiving threat everywhere and tried to calm myself down. Raising my eyes heavenward, I exhaled deeply and was just starting to feel a bit better when he chipped in with a faux amused: 'Oh sorry! Am I boring you?'

'No! No!' I forced a smile. 'Not at all. I'm just—' I was what? Deep breathing? I hardly wanted to encourage him. I made a snap decision and stood up, clasping the lid to the box and grabbing my bag.

'I *am* boring you!' He laughed. 'Don't worry, love, I was only trying to be nice. You don't have to move, I'm really not that bothered!'

'I'm going to the next carriage because I think my friend is in there, that's all,' I lied.

He chuckled again. 'Course she is. Off you trot then.' He closed his eyes, dismissing me.

I hauled my bag on my shoulder and was making sure I'd not left anything behind, when I distinctly heard him mutter 'silly bitch' under his breath. I stared at him in amazement, his eyes still smugly closed, and my heart began to thump, my body preparing for fight or flight. Really? All I'd wanted to do was eat my fucking food... and then the train lurched. I lost my grip on the box, the lid flew off and the contents spewed all over him, in his hair, lap, on his keyboard...

'What the...?' he gasped, his eyes snapping open as he felt it land. He immediately reared up to a half-stand, penned in by the table, dripping lettuce and dressing from his fingertips, trying to brush egg from his shirt front. 'You're off your head!' he roared. 'What d'you think you're playing at?'

Other passengers were twisting around to see what the fuss was about as he began to wriggle free from behind the table.

I gasped as he reached out, thinking he was about to grab my hair with his oily hands, but instead he reached past me and sharply pulled down on the emergency handle.

* * *

'I really am sorry,' I apologised to Timothy for the hundredth time as we rattled down the drive in the old Land Rover. 'I feel so bad that you had to drive all of that extra way to come and get me. And that you had to give that wanker the cash to get his suit cleaned. I swear, whatever he said, I did not deliberately throw it over him.'

'It's honestly fine,' Tim insisted. 'Flashing money at it was just the quickest way to defuse everything. You could see the transport police thought he was being a prick too, and they didn't want to have to press charges for assault.'

'Who even tries to have someone arrested for spilling a *salad*? My fork was in the box because I'd been trying to eat. I didn't attack him with it. But I really am sorry.' I paused. 'Do you also think we could not tell my mum about this? She's already convinced that I—'

'She's not here.' Timothy glanced across at me nervously as we pulled up in front of the cottage. 'I wanted to wait until we got back before bringing you up to speed, but it's been some-what of a busy day for the Highcombe ladies and the police.' He tried a laugh but it didn't quite come off. 'Your mum is down at the station now, helping them out with something.'

I drew back in my seat and stared at him. 'This isn't to do with me calling them the other night? She's going to be furious with me. I'm just messing up left, right and centre at the moment!'

'You're not at all. And that's not what she's most angry about anyway. Come and look at this.'

* * *

I surveyed the scattered photographs and pulled-over boxes littering the cottage sitting room as Tim bent and picked up another ripped canvas. 'It was like this when you arrived this morning?' I asked.

Tim nodded. 'She said she came up last night and did it because she's so angry at having to live here.'

'Wow.' I took off my coat, put it on the sofa and righted a box, opening the cardboard flaps. Weren't people only supposed to chuck their stuff around in films? I scooped a handful of images up to put them back in the box, feeling the slipperiness of the photos slide through my fingers. 'I knew moving was affecting her but...' I trailed off and looked around the room again.

Timothy cleared his throat. 'There's something else,' he blurted. 'I asked her to dismantle Hilary's room.'

I stopped what I was doing and turned to face him. 'Ah... I see.'

'I know,' Timothy said miserably. 'It's just I was getting heat from Lissy to have everything sorted by the time she gets back from South Africa with the kids next week. That room has been locked since we moved in and your mum has refused to give me the key... until yesterday.' He took an urgent step towards me and his voice lowered to a whisper. 'I had no idea the whole place was essentially a shrine.'

I sighed. 'It's quite something, isn't it?'

'It's *so* sad! It literally broke my heart.' Sure enough his eyes filled with tears. Tim was the deepest of feelers. Adverts for animal rescue centres could reduce him to a sobbing mess almost instantly. I reached out and squeezed his arm.

'The thing is she's refused to dismantle it. I can't just preserve it like that. What on earth would I tell *my* kids when they ask what's behind the locked door? "Nothing, darling, just all of the things that belonged to a little boy that lived here, but we don't go in there because he died".'

'It's OK,' I said. 'I'll do it. In fact let's go and do it now while Mum's not here.' I looked around the sitting room. 'This'll have to wait until later.'

* * *

The key was tight in the lock but with a little effort Timothy was able to open the door.

We fell silent as we walked into my forever little/big brother's bedroom.

The wardrobe door was partially open, revealing a selection of small clothes neatly on hangers. The covers on the bed were unmade and turned back as if the occupant had just got up. Lego pieces in primary colours were scattered over the floor, and the curtains were closed. I took a deep breath and drew them back, smiling faintly at the Thundercats design.

Timothy was looking at the toys on the floor: a He-Man, Battle Cat, Skeletor and Castle Grayskull. The Star Wars X-Wing was no longer white plastic, but had yellowed with age. There was a copy of an Andy Pandy book open on the carpet. All of the colours faded. He shook his head. 'I can't... you know, I think I might just need to go and make a coffee?' He looked up at me, his voice trembling.

'Come here.' I dropped the binbag and stepped over to him, drawing him into a hug. 'It *is* really sad but this is not Isaac's room.' I felt Tim tense as I referenced his own son and drew back to look at him. 'This will never happen to Isaac. It was a terrible, tragic accident.'

'I know.' He wiped his eyes. 'And I'm sorry. I should be comforting *you*. He was your brother.'

'You know what? I only remember good things about him, little bits and pieces,' I said. 'Smiles and smells, hugs and laughs... rather than him as an actual person, if that makes sense? And it's nice to have that. Plus I also still have you.'

He took a deep breath. 'Yes. You do. Do you want a coffee?' He looked at his watch. 'Or actually, something to eat?'

I let him go and picked up my binbag. 'No thanks. This is the middle of the night for me. I'm already feeling a bit punch drunk. A coffee might just finish me off. I'll crack on. Do we know when Mum's back?'

Tim shook his head. 'Johnnie's going to ring me.'

I straightened up in surprise. 'Johnnie's with her? Since when?'

Tim rubbed the back of his neck as if the muscles were tight. 'She asked me to call him this morning, so I did as I was told. He came straight up from London.'

'Oh, that's so kind of him!' I exclaimed. 'He's a good deed.' I felt better already. Johnnie would sort out whatever this was... minor clashes with local hunt protestors through to Mum's bad-tempered on the spot firing of a groom that had almost ended up in a tribunal, he always looked after us. 'I feel dreadful that he must have just dropped everything though,' I reflected. 'Bloody Mum!'

'Don't worry about it. He wouldn't have done it if he didn't want to. Put it this way – I don't think he offers this service to all of his old friends.' Tim glanced at me.

'I should hope not!' I said. 'He'd never get anything done. It's like when people message me random pictures of cuts and swellings, asking if I think they should go to A&E... You are one of Johnnie's *best* school friends though – that's different.'

Tim nodded slowly. 'Yes, he's very loyal to the people who are important to him.'

'He certainly is,' I agreed, picturing Johnnie in his suit, ready smile on his open, kind face. 'Right – I'd better get a wriggle on if we're not sure how long I've got until Mum's back.' I blinked and slapped my face. 'Come on! Get with the programme!'

'I hate to mention it...' Tim added, 'but there's your old room to clear too...'

* * *

I didn't really know where to start with my stuff. It was more of an accidental archive of my life rather than a bedroom. Some Topshop dresses in the wardrobe with improbably tiny waists, an old exercise bike, a suspiciously pink and floral duvet cover on the single bed – all swags and posies – a copy of *The Road Less Travelled* with various mortifying sections underlined that I'd written THIS!!! alongside... I hurled that in a binbag immediately. Peeling down a Cranberries poster that was still clinging to the wall behind the door, I respectfully folded Dolores O'Riordan before placing it in the binbag too, but selected 'Linger' on my phone in her honour. It had only just started to play when I heard someone say 'hello' behind me, and I turned to see Johnnie leaning in the doorway, hands in the pockets of his suit trousers, looking just as I'd pictured him earlier.

'Hello yourself!' Delighted to see him, I put my bag down and crossed the room to give him a warm hug and quick kiss on the cheek. He looked tired but smiled, the laughter lines crinkling at the corners of his eyes, as I resumed my tidying.

'Well, this is bit... weird.' He looked around. 'Finding you in here, listening to this. I've suddenly stepped into 1994 again.'

I immediately blushed scarlet, thinking of the kiss we had once shared, up by Highcombe's Great Pond, age fifteen and then again, in this very room, to this exact song.

He realised immediately what he'd just said too. 'Sorry! I didn't mean that precise moment in 1994.'

We held each other's gaze as the years vanished like the brief blinding flash of sunlight catching in a mirror... and then we were back to ourselves again.

He grinned and looked down at his feet. 'Anyway!'

'Yes, anyway...' I laughed. 'Tell me what my bloody mother has done this time? And Johnnie?'

He looked up again.

'Thank you for coming straight up. I'm really grateful.'

'I know you are. So... I've got to head back to London in a bit, but,' he paused and exhaled. 'Your mum has finished her questioning for today. Mrs Brooks is just putting her to bed.'

'Bed?' I sat back on my heels in surprise. 'It's not even 6 p.m.! What's the matter with her? Hang on' – the other bit registered with me – 'Questioning? About what?'

'She's—'

But before he could continue, a sharp, shrill scream pierced the air.

Mum had discovered what I'd done in Hilary's room.

* * *

In spite of the fact that I'd stripped it of everything bar the furniture, she'd managed to climb into the child-sized bed, fully dressed, and was tightly hugging a ragged soft toy – it looked like a rabbit – that I didn't recognise. She wasn't making a sound or moving. Her eyes were wide and staring straight ahead as I approached cautiously.

'Mum?'

'How could you? How could you take it all apart?'

Johnnie began to turn away respectfully to leave me to it.

Admittedly the timing had turned out to be pretty awful, but Mum didn't even lift her head from the mattress when she shrieked again, as loudly as she could. The sound was so raw and full of pain that I winced and stared back at Johnnie, who was as stunned as me. Timothy and Mrs Brooks appeared behind us, and Mrs Brooks started to shake her head lightly as she fixed her gaze on the floor.

'Mummy?' I moved closer until I was standing right over her. 'I'm sorry. No one meant to upset you. I did this so you wouldn't have to. Won't you come and get into your own bed?'

'Just go away, Jude,' she breathed.

'You can't stay in here,' I reasoned. 'Come on.' Some of my training began to seep back into my brain and I changed my tone of voice. 'Let's get you up and—'

'I don't want to.' Her voice had dropped to little more than a whisper, and I should have known better. You corner a cat and its tail will start softly swishing before it pounces, claws and teeth out.

'I know that losing a child is—'

She didn't let me finish before she furiously rounded on me. 'If you are about to compare your miscarriage with that selfish, feckless smear of a human, Dominic, to my losing Hilary who was *seven years old*,' her words were sharp and precise with rage, 'then I urge you to stop right now before I say something we won't be able to come back from. Hilary had things he liked and disliked. He had friends, clothes he would and wouldn't wear. Hair that curled if I didn't cut it often enough. He could tell me a joke, write me a birthday card, swim half a length, hug me... he was a *person*, not a collection of cells.' Her voice rose to a shout. 'What happened to you was a blessing. God's way of telling you to make a better fucking choice of man next time!'

I was so shocked I felt as if I'd been plunged into deep water. Everything distorted around me. I was aware of someone saying 'Margaret!' but the voice sounded distant and above the surface. I stared at Mum as she suddenly rose from the bed, throwing back the covers as if she was climbing out of a pool. 'If indeed you were ever pregnant in the first place,' she continued. 'Plenty of women have played *that* particular card!'

'What are you talking about?' I found my voice. 'Dom saw the positive pregnancy test for himself!'

'Says the nurse who had access to plenty of *other people's* positive tests at work,' Mum retorted, gasping aloud as she put her bad foot to the ground, wobbling without her stick. I automatically reached out a hand to steady her, but she shoved me away, briefly glancing at me, appalled. 'You need to wash your hair,' she said. 'It's all greasy at the ends and smells revolting.'

Was it? How mortifying that I hadn't realised.

'A man on the train tried to attack me and—' I began, but she didn't stop to listen, just staggered from the room.

I picked up the rabbit that was now lying on the floor and placed it back on the bed.

Mrs Brooks had already disappeared, presumably to go after Mum, and as the boys moved out of my way, I closed the door, twisted the key, double-checking, before handing it to Timothy. 'Don't let her have it back again.'

* * *

I made sure I was sitting bolt upright in the car as we passed the edge of the wooded part of the parkland, the pale tree trunks illuminated by the headlight beam as a ghostly owl drifted over us and disappeared into the forest. 'I'm so sorry about the smell of egg and oil in my hair. I didn't even realise until Mum said something. I'll make sure I don't get anything on the seat, I promise.'

'I can't smell anything and I honestly didn't notice the oil. Please don't worry – lean back if you want to.' Johnnie shifted in his seat uncomfortably. 'The other stuff she said to you in Hilary's room... I'm very sorry to hear that. I had no idea...' He glanced at me in the dark.

I caught my breath for a moment as the grief washed in again. It was like waves – some were easier to stand up in than others. I shivered and cautiously wriggled a little deeper into the seat as I touched my hair self-consciously, although there really was hardly anything in it at all.

Johnnie must have thought I was chilly because my seat began to warm around me like a hug. 'I wouldn't mind,' I said, 'but it was actually Mum who set me up with Dominic in the first place: *I've met this charming artist, darling!* so it's pretty rich her doing the selfish, feckless bit.'

Johnnie nodded sympathetically and waited for me to continue.

'I was eleven weeks pregnant,' I added after another

moment's pause. 'It was a total surprise. As you know, we'd made a conscious decision to be child-free. *Everyone* knew, because Dom told anyone who would stand still long enough. The only trouble was, I found out I was expecting *after* he'd left me and went back to Lydia. I don't think you knew that bit either?' I glanced at him. 'Unless Tim told you?'

'No, I didn't.'

'Lydia, if you remember, was his childhood sweetheart?' I glanced at Johnnie. 'They'd been on and off for years.'

'Yes, that I remember.'

'Do you want to hear something funny?' I glanced back at him. 'Well actually it's not funny at all, but when Dom walked out he said he was going to his mother's but I knew that wasn't true. I drove to Lydia's house the next day and our car was there. I was so shocked I just sat there for a bit – I'd taken Tim's Land Rover because I'd gone back to Highcombe rather than stay in the flat on my own – and Lydia called the police. When they searched the car, they found a rope, a saw and a load of old plastic sheeting in the boot. It properly looked like I'd been going there to do them both in!' I tried a laugh but it didn't quite come off.

Johnnie wasn't smiling. 'The police searched your car? They can't just do that! They have to have a good reason. Driving to your ex's home to see if he's there or not isn't illegal. Why didn't you just ring me? I'd have come and sorted it all out for you?'

'I know you would but I was... humiliated. And I did sit outside for a couple of hours, to be fair,' I admitted. 'I don't remember how long for exactly, I was in a bit of a state. Anyway, I told Dom I was pregnant and he came back with me straight away. But after he died a week later, I miscarried. The shock I think.'

We fell silent.

'I wouldn't have let the police anywhere near your car, let

alone search it,' Johnnie said a moment later. 'I'm so sorry you had to go through that, it must have been horrible for you. Always just call me.'

I glanced sideways at him and thought briefly about the note I tucked in a book he'd lent me, after our teenage kiss, saying I knew it might be weird, but if he actually wanted to go out with me, I'd be up for that, but if he didn't and was worried it might ruin our friendship, that was OK too and if he didn't say anything *at all*, I'd never mention it again. I'd put the book outside his bedroom door and went to a friend's house in Wales the next morning and waited. Nothing happened or was said and shortly after that he got the first in the long line of his very leggy, sporty blonde girlfriends. So always call – unless he was hiking up some mountain with Georgie or doing a marathon with Hattie. I smiled briefly in the dark. 'Well, thank you for taking me home now. It wouldn't have done me or Mum any good if I'd stayed. Plus I'm pretty tired at the moment. I'll be better off getting a proper sleep back at mine... as long as I can just hang on until about 6 a.m. when I can go to bed.' I yawned.

'Really? You'll have to do that? How long have you been up for now?'

'Since about 5 p.m. yesterday, so twenty-four... twenty-seven hours so far?'

'You can't possibly stay awake until 6 a.m. then?' He looked appalled. 'That'll mean you've been up for about thirty-seven hours!'

'Well, I'll see how I go.' I yawned again. My melatonin was obviously starting to kick in. That was the problem with staying awake at night; as soon as it got dark my body started trying to make me sleep – even though my mind had other ideas. 'It's my own fault. I just wanted to sort the rooms out for Tim. Oh, it's all a bit bloody bleak at the moment, isn't it?' I stretched. 'I just want to get Christmas out of the way and then... roll on the good weather and hopefully some happier days.'

Johnnie hesitated. 'Can I just say one more thing? I'm very much *not* religious, as you know, but what your mum said about the miscarriage being "God's will"? was just...' He trailed off. 'I don't know anyone who believes in a God like that and I know some pretty shit and fucked-up people.'

'Thanks. How is Flue?' I asked.

He laughed. 'I meant my clients, as well you know. But *Flo* and I broke up and since then *Selina* and I have broken up too. Thanks for asking.'

I grinned. 'Just as well, Selina Saunders sounds like the kind of woman who would scare the shit out of your kid's teachers.'

Johnnie grimaced. 'And me. Listen, I feel really bad having to do this now, but I actually do need to talk to you about why your mum was at the police station today.'

I sat up a bit. 'Of course. Sorry. So, I only called them on Tuesday night because I thought she was in danger and—'

He frowned. 'Oh don't worry about that – you ringing them is nothing to do with it. I can't tell you much because I'm now your mother's solicitor and I'm bound by all that entails, but some very serious allegations have been made about her. That's what they wanted to talk about.'

'I *knew* there was a problem when she called me on Tuesday and told me something terrible had happened!' I exclaimed. 'Why didn't she say so instead of making out I was knackered and had imagined the whole thing?'

Johnnie hesitated. 'It would actually be a great idea to get some rest when you get home, because I think you're going to need to come back to Highcombe tomorrow evening.'

'Really?' I was dismayed. 'That sounds ominous, and I was supposed to... meet someone... but sure. I'll cancel it.'

Johnnie looked away. 'Oh right! I see. Well, no, *definitely* don't cancel. You deserve some fun.'

'It's very early days,' I pointed out, 'but he seems nice.'

'Glad to hear it!' Johnnie said heartily. 'Well, I can always ring you if it looks like things are progressing faster than expected. It might not happen until Saturday in any case.'

'I don't understand. What's going to happen?'

He cleared his throat. 'I think it's highly likely that the police are going to arrest her.'

FIVE

JUDE

Rik was already waiting for me when I arrived at bang on 8 p.m. 'Hello!' he grinned. 'Hungry for breakfast?' He pushed open the door to the busy restaurant. It was buzzing with a noisy evening vibe of excitement and possibility, and I saw immediately that I'd made the wrong call clothes wise.

Normally, meeting someone for breakfast would mean jeans and a jumper – or a sweatshirt and smarter joggers. Definitely nothing involving heels and heavy make-up... so I'd gone with the former and was now surrounded by couples dressed up for a Friday night out. While the restaurant certainly did appear to serve all-day breakfasts, there were also candles on the tables and lots of people drinking wine and eating proper main meals. Rik was dressed in a white shirt and smart-casual trousers.

I sat down feeling like the kid who'd been allowed to stay up with the grown-ups, while also oddly glad that I wasn't obviously dressed as if we were on a date... because we weren't... and nervously set my phone on the table, which Rik side-eyed immediately.

'Sorry.' I tried to smile. 'I know it's rude but I'm on stand-by to have to go back up to Berkshire at short notice.' As soon as the words were out of my mouth I realised it sounded as if I was laying the ground for receiving an 'emergency' phone call if whatever this was started going south and I wanted to escape. Rik looked down at the table, gently moved his knife, and smiled.

'No, really!' I insisted. 'I'm not making this up.' I leant forward. 'OK, so look,' I lowered my voice as much as I could over the hum of chatter around us. 'It's my mum again. The police came round and took her in for questioning yesterday. She's been there most of today too. Her solicitor thinks they might arrest her. If they do, I'll obviously have to go back home again.' I sat back. 'See? I'm really not making it up.'

'Arrest her?' Rik's eyebrows had shot up. 'What's she done?'

'Johnnie – that's her solicitor, he's also a family friend – can't tell me yet. There are "allegations" about her. That's all I know.'

He sipped his water. 'Wow. That must be tough, having all of the worry without any of the information?'

'That's exactly it.' I hesitated. 'And she's not handling it very well, whatever it is. She trashed her cottage in the middle of the night on Wednesday.'

Rik was astonished. 'She wrecked her own house?'

I nodded. 'I arrived to find the whole place in chaos.' I smiled at Rik's slack jaw and picked up a menu. 'I know, right? So whatever it is that's going on, it's really got to her. Anyway, I'm not planning to fake SOS call you.' I nodded at my phone. 'I really am waiting for an update and you've got to admit, that's all so crazy it couldn't be anything *but* true, right?'

Just as I reached for my water, I realised the song that had started up in the background was one Dom had particularly liked and had played a lot. My heart began to thump. It didn't mean anything, good or bad. It was just a song.

Nonetheless the glass shook in my hand and I spilt a little of the liquid, which instantly made a large mark on my light grey jumper. If I'd been wearing the right clothes, a black dress or something, it wouldn't have been visible at all. In my haste to put the glass back down, I managed to knock the water carafe off the table with my elbow, which smashed everywhere into a million tiny, glittering shards.

* * *

'I'm sorry,' I said for the millionth time as we walked into Chinatown. 'I'm so sorry. You must think I'm insane.'

'I don't at all,' Rik said as we passed beneath the strings of red and gold paper lanterns above our heads, bobbing and swaying in the dark. The smell of cooking food twisted enticingly around us as we passed the welcoming, open doors of restaurants, and my tummy rumbled with confusion.

'We should have stayed and eaten,' I said. 'I can't apologise enough... but I do feel better for the fresh air, you were right.'

He turned to face me. 'Jude, it's OK. Your mum has some shit going on and you're trying to deal with it while completely reversing your sleeping pattern, handling a really tough job and grieving.' He shrugged. 'No wonder you're literally losing your grip from time to time.'

I instantly felt a bit better and smiled gratefully at him.

'It's actually normal to be clumsy when your sleep is messed up, just so you know. I was covered in bruises from walking into things when I was in my insomniac stage. So you knocked over some water.' He shrugged. 'Big deal. Bigger picture though – look, how beautiful is that?' He nodded upwards, and I followed his gaze to the moon. 'Can't stare right at the sun, can you? It'll be worth coming over to the dark side.' He grinned at me. 'I promise. And I honestly couldn't give a crap about missing breakfast. I'd much rather be out here taking all of this in.'

He looked up again and dug his hands in his pockets. 'There's a festival in Japan called Tsukimi which honours the harvest moon,' he continued. 'Viewing events take place all over the country in temples, gardens, shrines... you can take boat rides at night. There's music and dancing... I really want to go.'

'Who wouldn't? That sounds amazing!'

'Doesn't it?' he agreed. 'I've been over there for work and just missed it twice now, which is really annoying. I need to stop waiting for it to happen and *make* it happen. It's a waxing crescent at the moment.' He pointed at the slice of silver glinting like a scythe.

'I should know this,' I said, 'but what does "waxing" actually mean?'

'The moonlight is becoming brighter because it's moving towards fullness. Symbolically it's meant to be a time for new intentions, gathering information and momentum – acting boldly. You can only see about twenty-five percent of it at the moment,' Rik continued, 'but in about nine days' time, when it's directly opposite the sun, it'll be fully illuminated. Yin and Yang facing each other... but also an ending of cycles and letting go.'

'Where did you learn all of that?' I asked.

'My dad. He's into astronomy, navigation, charts, compasses – that sort of thing.' He kept looking up. 'It was something for us to talk about after my mum died. A shared hobby.'

I imagined the heartbroken small boy again, searching among the endless stars of a vast night sky, and fell guiltily silent as I thought about Mum flinging her photos around before huddling into Hilary's bed. She was dealing with a lifelong grief and massive change as well as whatever these allegations were. I ought to be showing a little bit more compassion. I sighed.

'Penny for them ?'

I turned to look at him and smiled. 'My thoughts? They're not worth that much, trust me.'

He hesitated as his eyes searched my face, then he leant forward. My eyes closed and I felt him very gently kiss me. For a brief moment it was perfect and then I heard someone shout 'Hey!'

Rik pulled back immediately and I turned to see a woman approaching us, dragging a very glamorous man in her wake. Was it the high heels she was wearing that were making her stagger or was she a bit drunk? I peered more closely in the dark and realised she was actually a good deal younger than me. Twenty-seven, twenty-eight? And wearing much more make-up than her beautiful skin needed. Heavily drawn eyebrows lifted as she gave me a shameless up and down. 'Who is this?' she demanded, pointing at me, tears flooding her eyes.

Rik looked at the girl, completely bemused. 'More to the point, who are you?'

The girl blinked and stumbled. Her male friend had to reach out and take her arm.

'Wait. What?' Her voice was slurring. 'You know who I am! I am appearing in that theatre up *there*.' She pointed loosely in the direction of Shaftesbury Avenue. 'And I wasn't needed tonight so I've been drinking in that pub round *that* corner' – she waved her other arm vaguely – 'where I very first met you.' She stumbled again and both men went to steady her.

'Don't you fucking touch me!' she suddenly hissed at Rik like a cat, who threw his hands right up in the air, alarmed.

'Woah!' he exclaimed. 'I was just trying to help you stay on your feet. I'm really sorry, I think you have me confused with someone else. We've actually never met?'

The girl stared at him, trying to focus. 'But, you're—' She tried to break free from her friend and lurched towards Rik, heaved, and was promptly sick at his feet.

'Oh my God!' Her male friend gasped. 'Soph! Mate!'

'Jesus!' Rik exclaimed as 'Soph', not done yet, turned and retched again, the vomit splashing down onto the street. I stepped forward and in a practised move whipped her hair back. She heaved again a couple of times and then hung there, spit trailing from her mouth as she started to cry.

'You're OK, Sophie,' I said. 'Well done. Hold her hair for a second, will you?' I turned to her friend. 'But don't let go of her.' I reached into my bag and pulled out my water bottle. I unscrewed it and handed it to Sophie. 'It's clean. Just swill your mouth out, sweetheart. Get rid of the taste.' But Sophie was having problems getting her mouth even close to the neck of the bottle. Her head was hanging right forward and she was starting to feel heavy in our arms. She was on the verge of passing out.

I looked more closely at her and placed my hand on her cheek. Her skin was clammy and cool. 'Sophie?' I said loudly. 'Can you hear me?' I watched her eyes flicker as she tried to lift her head up again.

'How much has she had?'

Her friend looked embarrassed. 'A few vodka doubles. She was a bit upset.'

'A few? There's nothing of her.' I sighed. 'She needs to go to hospital.'

'I can do that,' the younger man said immediately, and I looked at him sceptically. I hated having to think it but had he selflessly been her shoulder to cry on while she drank, or was there an ulterior motive at play here? 'We'll come with you,' I said firmly. 'I work at the hospital.' I turned to Rik. 'Won't we?'

'Um, fine, but how? I'm not sure we can exactly put her in a cab,' Rik said.

He had a point. Sophie had begun to vomit violently again, her body heaving as if she was exorcising her very soul. She needed an ambulance.

* * *

'Just let them take over now,' Rik said as the paramedics loaded Sophie up. 'You've got enough to deal with. You don't need to save the rest of the world too. Come on. She's safe.' He tugged my sleeve gently. 'This is a jumper, not a cape.'

I half smiled as I got what he meant and stepped back so the paramedics could shut the doors, the blue lights starting to turn silently as they began to inch off down the street, waiting for pedestrians to get out of the way... just as my phone began to ring. The timing was ridiculous. I scrabbled around in my bag. Sure enough, it was Johnnie.

'I'm sorry, but things are moving a little faster than expected. You don't have to come up tonight but you might want to. I thought I'd better let you know, as it's only nine o'clock and you can still probably get a train home. Or I'll pay for a cab if you like?'

'That's very kind, but a cab would cost a fortune. I'll get a train,' I said, and Rik glanced across at me, listening intently. 'Has she been arrested then? Is there anything more you can tell me now?'

'Not quite yet, but as soon as I can, I will.'

I hung up and looked at Rik. 'I don't know what to say. You got the gist of that, I'm guessing?'

'I did.' He nodded. 'And you're right – a cab all that way on a Friday night is a crazy idea. I'll drive you.'

* * *

He wouldn't take no for an answer. He immediately made a plan with all of the efficiency of the successful soldier it was easy to see he'd once been. We'd take a quick fifteen-minute cab ride to his flat to collect his car keys, then he'd drive me to my place to grab an overnight bag – it turned out we lived less than a mile apart – and then he'd take me to Highcombe.

'Look, I'm invested now and it can't be much more than a three-hour round trip.' He shrugged off my protestations in the back of a black cab as we crossed the Thames. 'Seriously though, I want to help. I'd be very happy to drive you.'

I concentrated on two boats chugging in opposite directions to each other, slicing up the reflection of the cloudless moon on the water like a sushi roll, as we crossed the bridge. 'Then thank you,' I admitted, relaxing my clenched fists as we reached the other side. 'I can't pretend I'm not glad that I don't have to get a late train on a Friday night.'

The taxi pulled up outside Waterloo Station and I looked around me. 'Aren't we going back to your flat?'

He nodded and once we were out on the street, took my arm, steering me through the traffic as we hurried towards the bright pink London Eye looming over us, partially obscured by a clutch of swanky developments rising up into the sky. I frowned in confusion as we ducked between the towers, before coming to a stop outside one of them. 'You live *here*?'

Rik was already holding a door open for me, leading into a mostly marble lobby that wouldn't have looked out of place in a luxury hotel in the UAE. A night porter glanced up from behind a vast desk. Rik nodded to him politely as we walked briskly past. 'Good evening.'

I managed not to say anything when he pushed a button for floor thirty-one once we were in the lift. That appeared to be the highest floor – so he lived in the penthouse? When the doors opened I stepped out into a windowless corridor, and automatic lights switched on, sensing our movement.

'My place is just... down here.' Rik edged past me, turned right and, head down, led the way. The corridor did not smell of other people's cooking, like most communal buildings, but rather of deep carpets and cool air-conditioning. The walls were papered in a textured bronze, and it was utterly quiet. If there was life beyond the thick, anonymous doors we passed, I couldn't hear it.

Rik was standing by a front door waiting for me. I stepped

past him into a hallway that opened out immediately into a vast kitchen and living space, ceiling-to-floor glass walls running around what was the corner of the building. Uninterrupted London-by-night spread out in front of us, so postcard perfect it was almost too surreal to look at.

'Two seconds while I find my car keys and grab a couple of things,' Rik said, disappearing off for a moment, leaving me standing alone to scan the glittering lights of the panorama, stunned.

The Thames and the City were framed in the left-hand wall of glass. I turned away from the bridge we'd just crossed towards The Shard instead, which sat to the right, shining needle sharp alongside the hospital where we'd first met. Right now my colleagues would be down there somewhere chasing scans, checking drips, giving pain relief. Wandering further into the room, movement caught my eye and I dropped my gaze down to the last trains snaking in and out of Waterloo, the tracks like criss-cross arteries and veins... late-night London operating without drama.

'This is a very nice flat,' I called out.

'I'm very lucky!' He shouted back from another room.

Who wouldn't stay up all night with a view like this?

My eyes widened as I noticed glass doors by the kitchen area leading out onto a balcony with a barrier that had to be waist height at most, to protect against a drop that was thirty-one floors down to the bottom. I turned back to him in amazement as he reappeared. 'Do you ever sit out there?'

'Yes. I occasionally smoke and I don't like to do it in the flat.' He hastened over to the kitchen and pulled two plastic water bottles from a cupboard that he began to fill. 'You're going to say what everyone says now, which is don't I feel compelled to jump?'

I stayed diplomatically silent.

'It's really common, that urge. The French call it *L'Appel du Vide...* the call of the void.'

My body turned completely cold.

'But the interesting thing is,' Rik continued, his back to me, 'it's not actually an urge at all. You step back from the edge as a safety reflex, and your brain then tries to make sense of the situation and assumes you must have been going to jump, when you weren't.' He turned and opened a drawer, slipping a small silver tin into his coat pocket. 'I'll just go to the bathroom – and then we'll go.'

He disappeared again, and I walked a couple of steps into the living area. The place was like a show home. Huge curved cream sofas with plumped scarlet cushions in front of a ridiculously large TV; a fresh-flower arrangement of poker-like fronds that appeared to be on steroids; a geometric design on the enormous rug that delineated the living space; but no books, no photos. I sat down on the sofa and briefly checked my phone. No messages.

'Ready!' He returned as I was slipping it back into my bag. 'There's a bathroom just through here if you'd like to use it before we head off?' Moving over to a wall of what appeared to be sleek cupboards with no handles, he ran his fingers over a discreet join and pushed. A secret door pressure-opened on to a plush bedroom with yet another astounding view of The Shard at the far end, through more floor-to-ceiling glass.

'The one in there is the door on the left.'

I did actually need the loo. I put my bag down and obediently did as I was told but turned right by mistake, finding myself in a walk-in dressing room instead of a bathroom. A selection of pressed white shirts hung on two rails, identical to the one Rik was wearing, like a uniform.

Turning left instead, I finally discovered a grey and white marble bathroom, all shiny lines and hard edges. A single toothbrush in a mug was the only personal effect. After I'd washed my hands and re-emerged, I found Rik standing next to my bag, holding my mobile and staring intently at it.

'Oh hey!' he said, frowning back at me. 'I know – I'm so sorry – I tripped over your bag on the floor, everything fell out and I was worried your phone had smashed. I've had a really good look and I can't see any cracks in the screen, but here – you tell me what you think?' He held it out to me. 'If I've damaged it even slightly, just say and I'll get you a new one.'

I hesitated. 'No damage. Thanks for telling me, though.'

He looked relieved. 'Phew. That's the last thing you need when you're waiting for a call – some clumsy twat like me breaking it. Let's go then.'

* * *

Ten minutes later we pulled up outside my Victorian terraced house, now converted into flats. 'This is nice,' he sounded surprised.

'I'm a single nurse so I should be in something way beyond Zone 4 that I share with four other people I met via a website, you mean?' I teased.

He looked embarrassed.

'It's owned by my family, not me,' I admitted. 'I just get to live here at the current Lord Stratham's behest, but I'm pretty sure my cousin Timothy has no plans to sell up and leave the country. Come in while I grab my stuff.'

* * *

I left him in the sitting room looking at my old photos while I hurriedly shoved some bits in a bag. 'You have a *lot* of plants,' he observed as I came back. 'And is this your partner?' he turned to look at me, holding a photo of me and Dom taken on our first holiday together.

I caught my breath and nodded.

'You look happy.'

'Thank you.' We were – at that point. I think.

He gave me a kind smile. 'Sure you've got everything? Keys? Phone charger? OK – let's hit the road.'

* * *

It was a nice and *fast* car. The seats were comfy. Or at least I thought so. Rik seemed to be fidgeting around a bit.

'You OK?' I asked as we approached the M25.

He nodded, his eyes gleaming in the reflection of headlights on the other side of the carriageway. 'I told you I broke my back? It was during a tour of Afghanistan. No, wait' – he held up a hand – 'I fell off a watchtower wankered. No glory in that and I have no complaints, believe me, but every now and then it properly pulls.'

'I'm sorry. I should have got the train. The last thing you need if your back is playing up, is a long car journey!' I protested.

'I'm happy to do it. I like being useful, and the good thing about working from home is I can just make up the hours as and when. I also like having the opportunity to drive outside London, it's fun!' He put his foot down for a moment, and I caught my breath, thrilled as we shot forward before dropping back down to a normal cruising speed.

'You know you said I looked happy in that picture?' I glanced across at him. 'I was, but just before he died, Dom actually left me for someone else. He came back again, but we were only together for another week after that. I just don't want to make out it was all perfect and... golden... because it wasn't.' I trailed off, not sure why I'd just said that.

Rik nodded. 'Life rarely is.'

It was my turn to nod and then yawn. The car was dark and

very warm. I didn't like to ask him if I could turn the heat down, as he was the one driving. I yawned again and sank back into the seat, blinking as I tried to keep my eyes open.

'It's OK.' He laughed. 'You don't have to fight it. Get some sleep. I'll wake you up when we get there.'

'I'll just close my eyes for a moment, if you're sure you don't mind?' I said. 'But I won't sleep the whole way, I promise.'

* * *

'Jude?'

I jolted and began to stir. The car wasn't moving any more. The engine was off and a cold draught was creeping through from the open window on Rik's side, but bringing with it a very familiar sweet smell. I blinked and the glowing end of a spliff swam into focus. Rik was smoking. 'We're here,' he said as I sat up stiffly, a crick in my neck.

I twisted to look around me. Sure enough, we were outside Mum's darkened cottage.

'I assume you're staying here and not down there.' He nodded down the drive towards the outline of Highcombe, silent and sleeping but for one or two still-lit windows. 'That's a big old place, isn't it?'

'Yes, it is.' I stared at the spliff again in confusion, and he noticed.

'Sorry. Does this bother you?' He quickly opened the door, stubbed it out and removed the silver tin from his pocket that I'd noticed earlier. 'It's medicinal.' He put the remains of the joint away. 'Pain relief for my back, that's all. Paracetamol doesn't touch the sides any more, unfortunately.' He smiled easily as if it was no big deal. 'Shall I help you in with your stuff? I might also just use your loo if that's OK, then I'm going to be on my way again, leave you to it.'

I sat up and rubbed my face. My phone was sitting on the top of my bag. One new message. I'd missed a call from Johnnie.

Without thinking I grabbed it and dialled the voicemail. I pressed it close to my ear but it was quiet in the car and Johnnie had a loud voice.

'Hi, it's me.' He sounded exhausted. 'Sorry to miss you – I expect you're going through a tunnel or something. It's just to say your mum was arrested and charged shortly after we last spoke. They've released her on bail and I've taken her back to Highcombe. She's very distressed but went straight to bed. I'm on my way back to London, but call me as soon as you're free and I'll chat you through everything and what happens next.' He hesitated. 'Just to give you a bit of a heads up so you have time to digest this before we speak, the charges relate to a historic event and are sexual in nature.'

My eyes widened, and Rik frowned out of the window.

Historic sex charges?

I hung up quickly and shoved the phone back in my bag. 'Thank you so much for bringing me back,' I began to gabble brightly, gathering up the rest of my belongings and reaching for the door in shock.

I had no idea what to say as we pushed up the moonlit path, my eyes gradually adjusting to the much blacker night. Historic sex charges? My mother? That had to be a mistake, surely?

'You forget how much impact the light pollution in cities makes.' Rik cleared his throat behind me. 'These stars are incredible!' He looked up as we reached the front door, and I rummaged around in my bag. I'd lost interest in the night sky, I just wanted to get inside. Except I couldn't find my bloody keys.

'I don't understand.' I went through the bag again and patted my pockets. 'I know I had them.'

Rik waited as I pointlessly tried the locked front door and glanced down at Highcombe. Only the outline of the building was now visible. All but one of the main lights had gone off. 'I'm going to wake everyone up if I go crashing down there and I really don't want to do that.' Especially not if they'd only recently got Mum to bed.

'Well, hang on here and I'll pop round the back and have a quick look,' Rik offered. 'See if that's unlocked.'

I gratefully waited on the step, clutching my bag, eventually starting to shiver in the considerably chillier countryside night air. He was taking his time. 'Rik?' I whispered after a moment or two. 'Any luck?'

There was no response and I'd just started to pick my way around the front of the cottage to go and find him, when the hall light clicked on from inside.

I hurried back to the step and waited. The bolts began to rattle and the door creaked open to reveal him looking a bit awkward. 'I'm not going to lie,' he said. 'The back door wasn't strictly speaking unlocked, but I barely had to give it a nudge. Your mother might want to get that seen to. Anyone could just walk in.' He gestured between us to make his point.

'Thank you,' I said, although I wasn't particularly liking the sound of being left with an unsecured door. I stepped inside, still shivering, and wiped my feet.

Rik looked around him curiously, sticking his head round the sitting room door. 'I have to say, it looks pretty good for a cottage you said she trashed?'

He was right. Someone – I suspected poor Mrs Brooks – had done an incredible job. The boxes, scattered images and scored canvases of my last visit had vanished, and my mother's furniture had been carefully arranged to mimic the drawing room layout at Highcombe, only on a smaller, more squashed-in scale. Plants sat on corner tables, paintings hung on the wall, cards were on the mantelpiece. It looked as if someone had been living there for a while. I felt a little like Alice in the Looking Glass. 'It really was nothing like this yesterday.' I stared at it.

'And that's her – your mother, I mean,' Rik said from the

hall. I found him bent over a photograph of her in her late twenties which had been placed on a small sideboard. 'How old was she in this picture? It looks like it was taken a while ago. That's quite some necklace!'

He was studying her closely, his eyes roaming over her beautiful aloof features and the fat jewels around her smooth neck.

'That was a borrowed piece, she doesn't own it,' I said.

A muscle in his jaw flexed and he straightened up suddenly. 'But she was quite the mover and shaker back in the day? An original socialite!' He was smiling but his voice had tightened with something that sounded like dislike.

'Not really original,' I replied, confused. 'The earliest socialites date back to the eighteenth century, I think, when you were just seen as the wife of someone important. Not so much a fun thing, more a mode of survival I imagine.'

'Yeah, it does look like she's had it tough.' He glared at the photo before turning to look at me, a strange expression passing over his face.

I paused, completely thrown. 'Rik, why are you being—'

But before I could finish he stepped forward quickly and pulled me to him. It was such a sudden movement I lost my balance and, gasping, stumbled into a raw, fierce kiss, nothing like the moment we'd shared earlier. For a second my body responded, but then my mind caught up and I pulled back, touching my fingers to my mouth. I could taste blood where he'd bruised my lip. 'What are you doing? Why—'

He pushed past me out of the house. I watched in astonishment as he jumped into his car and spun it round with a squeal of tyres before roaring off down the main drive.

As I was trying to make sense of what had just happened, a set of headlights suddenly appeared from the *opposite* direction, coming up behind me from Highcombe. It was Tim in the Land Rover.

'Jude? Thank God!' He jumped down and panted over to me in the doorway. 'You scared me half to death – I saw lights on up here and thought it really was burglars this time. Who was that I saw hurtling off at a hundred miles an hour?' He nodded in the direction of the gates.

'He's...' I trailed off. What *was* the answer to that question? 'He's someone I've been sort of seeing.'

Timothy said nothing, just eyed the tyre tracks in the muddy grass verge. 'Does he often make an exit like that?'

'No,' I said. 'He heard a voicemail from Johnnie as we arrived saying that Mum has just been charged with historic sex offences. Not something he fancied getting tangled up in by the look of it.'

'Oh. I see.' Tim wrinkled his nose. 'I'm sorry.'

I shrugged helplessly. 'Do you know anything more than that? Johnnie didn't leave any details.'

Tim cleared his throat. 'The next step is that she has to appear in front of a magistrate who will set all of the trial dates and—'

'There's going to be an actual trial?' I was astonished. 'She's a seventy-four-year-old woman! She can't walk without a stick!' I couldn't believe what I was hearing. 'Who's even made these allegations? Is it someone we know?'

Timothy looked back at me, frightened, and nodded. 'You remember the day after your mum had her accident and she threw my mum out of Highcombe for saying she'd made a fool of herself over the new groom at the stables, and we thought it was gross because he was the same age as us?' Timothy swallowed. 'It's him. He's the person who has gone to the police.'

'But that was nearly thirty years ago! What's he saying Mum did to him?'

'I don't know exactly what the charges are, but Johnnie says they're serious. He thinks she's going to be sent to prison.' He swallowed. 'Funnily enough, Richard Shand was only here a—'

I stepped forward immediately. 'Wait – that's his name? Richard Shand?'

Tim nodded again.

Richard.

Rik.

I looked down at the tyre marks on the grass and it was as if a hard lump of mud had caught in my throat. I saw Rik staring at the picture of my mother, heard the anger in his voice again: *'An original socialite.'*

He found me at the hospital.

I gave him information about her.

I let him into her house.

I'd dated my mother's accuser?

PART TWO

TEN MONTHS LATER

SIX

JUDE

I shoved the cottage door open and hurried down the passage into the kitchen to find Johnnie working at Mum's kitchen table. 'Thank you so much for turning straight round and coming back here!' I didn't even bother with hello as I hugged him quickly. 'I'm so sorry that I had to ring you, but as soon as I listened to Mum's voicemail I knew she was in a bad way and you'd be able to get here faster than anyone else given you'd just finished a meeting with her. How is she?'

'It's quite a deep cut to her thumb but then trying to pick up shards of glass when you're pissed is never a good idea.' He kept his fingers resting on the laptop keyboard, obviously in the middle of something. 'She's in her bedroom.'

I sighed. 'Right. I'll just go and check on her. I know it's twenty-four degrees outside, but could you put the kettle on? I'm desperate for a cup of tea.'

'Sure.' He'd already started typing again. 'Take your time. I'm in no rush to get back now.'

I puffed upstairs fanning myself and found Mum lying on her bed. The room was airless but tinged tartly with the Cox's Orange Pippin room spray Mum had long used that always sat at odds with her much heavier, dramatic perfumes. She looked like an elegantly dressed corpse, wearing a tight green silk full-length cocktail number that I knew from photographs was her engagement outfit. Emeralds sat at her neck and ears, and there was a bright red lipstick print on the empty tumbler next to the bed. I crossed the room and picked it up, sniffing it worriedly: whisky. All of this at only three o'clock in the afternoon.

'Mum?' I whispered, and her paper-thin eyelids moved as if marbles were rolling around beneath them. She forced them open and glanced exhaustedly at me.

'What's happened here then?' I found myself slipping into work mode as I put my hands on my hips, before impulsively crossing the room to throw the small, leaded windows open. I could hardly think straight the room was so warm, but it was such a stultifying late-August afternoon that the temperature outside was barely any different, with no hint of a breeze. The heavy drooping leaves on the trees in the parkland beyond were utterly still.

'That stupid new barrister Johnnie wants to use – Yasmin,' she mumbled. 'He brought her here and she had the audacity to take me through what to wear in court. It needs to be something suitable – "mature dignity". No bright colours. Nothing low cut, no jewellery unless they are pearls. As if I'm an imbecile.' She winced and tried to sit up a bit. 'We really are still no further on in this pitiful country than telling women even of *my* age that how they're dressed might give someone the wrong idea.' She gave up and slumped back down again. 'Apparently this Yasmin has plenty of tricks up her sleeve. I put this on after they left, I was so incensed' – she gestured weakly at herself – 'but then the door went' – Mum winced as if in pain – 'I thought it was Johnnie or Yasmin back again because they'd forgotten something.'

'But it was a photographer?' I prompted as she trailed off. 'Johnnie told me on the phone. Mum?'

'What?' She blinked and tried to focus on me.

'There was a photographer there? At the door?'

'Oh yes!' she exclaimed, remembering, and grabbed my wrist tightly. 'I was holding my drink and I opened the door dressed like *this*' – she motioned down at herself – 'he shoved a camera in my face then walked off. He wasn't in the least embarrassed or shamed. I just wanted *one* moment to feel like myself again, but now I'll be all over the papers just before my trial looking like some dreadful old whore!'

'How did you get the cut on your thumb?' I nodded at it. There was a plaster clumsily attached to the skin but I could see the dark outline of blood beneath.

'I threw my door keys at the hall mirror and it smashed. I tried to pick the pieces up and then I called you.' She made another attempt to sit up and this time managed it. 'I *told* Timothy if he let that stupid wife of his open Highcombe up to the public we would lose our privacy completely! "They won't come to the cottage," he said. Well, they bloody have, haven't they? None of this would have happened if your father were still here. He'd have called someone and had it sorted all out in a heartbeat. I didn't even have a bra on.' She glanced down at her clavicles and the top of her ribcage bobbing beneath her skin. 'They'll crucify me.' She rubbed her face bleakly, spreading wet tears across her skin as she did, although she didn't actually appear to be crying.

'Johnnie is still here,' I said. 'He's making some tea. Do you want to get up and come down?'

'No,' she retorted. 'Of course I don't.'

'I know you're upset, but there's no need to speak to me like that. I'll bring you one up instead.' I picked up her glass to carry it from the room as she slumped back down onto her pillow with a moan.

'Look I'm sorry – but ten months of this utter limbo! You can all bleat on that's positively quick at the moment, but I can promise you, it doesn't feel like it. Everyone whines about broken systems and backlogs as if that's an excuse – as if it hasn't broken MY back – and then without a word of warning, there they all are again, barging back in, taking over completely and one immediately swings from not being able to bear the waiting to dreading the arrival.' She closed her eyes again. 'How can this be right? I can't be the only innocent person who is having their life utterly destroyed by a lie? Why aren't more people talking about this flaw in the system? Because I tell you this, when this is all over, *I* will. I'll make it my life's work to ensure no one has to go through this sort of thing ever again! Because I won't go to prison, Jude,' she insisted, her voice shaking as her eyes snapped open and she looked right at me. 'I simply can't, and that's all there is to it!'

* * *

'Yes, the slice on her thumb is quite deep,' I confirmed as I went back into the kitchen. 'But she'll be OK. She cut herself with the breadknife the other day too.'

Johnnie looked up from his screen again worriedly. 'You don't think she's—'

'—self-harming?' I finished. 'Er, no. Mum's got pretty robust coping strategies.' I set the glass down and looked around but could see no evidence of the tea he'd said he'd make. He'd obviously become distracted.

Johnnie sighed. 'It's such a deeply shitty thing to do, doorstepping someone like that out of the blue. I don't know how these people sleep at night.'

'They don't,' I said, for a moment thinking very uncomfortably of Rik.

I'd managed to convince myself quite successfully – over the last ten months – that Richard really was a very common name and the man I'd briefly been involved with was not the same person who had made very serious allegations against Mum. My original theory that Rik was revolted when he overheard that my mother had been arrested for historic sex offences and had simply walked away was, after all, totally plausible.

I'd not called him after that night and he'd not called me, but that was, of course, normal when a relationship didn't work out.

I'd also carefully checked with Mum once she'd been released on bail that nothing had been taken during the break-in. I'd been over everything I'd said to Rik again and again and I couldn't think of anything we'd discussed that might be incriminating.

So even if he was *that* Richard, what real damage had been done – apart from to my ego?

Because when I did allow myself to consider the possibility that my mother's 'victim' had deliberately duped me, I felt very foolish indeed and deeply, deeply humiliated... I could practically hear Mum, her tone incredulous: *'a man turned up at the hospital on a "run" in the middle of the night and you seriously thought he was just interested in you?'*

I cried. Quite a lot at first and then I did the angry bit... but I'd worked through it – two dates hardly constituted a huge commitment, after all – and ultimately burying my head in the sand had served me well most of my life... so I just kept quiet.

The only thing that would have forced the issue in the lead-up to the trial would have been my being confronted with an image of Richard Shand that was also clearly Rik. Having suspicions was one thing, I wasn't prepared to outright lie – but there were no pictures of Richard Shand in the press because he was a victim of sexual offences so qualified for anonymity. I didn't search for Rik online because we'd broken up and I'd moved on, and I didn't look for Shand online either because I didn't want to leave a trail that the police might find should they want to investigate *me* at some point, although I couldn't see why they would... but I also didn't know how these things worked so I wasn't prepared to risk it. I'd already nearly compromised Mum enough as it was.

So all of that just left the very real possibility that once the trial actually started, I might be confronted with the nightmare of Richard Shand standing to give evidence while simultaneously realising he was indeed the man I'd dated, but Johnnie seemed to be under the impression Shand would be appearing in court behind a screen... so in that instance I could continue to legitimately tell myself that my briefly dating a Rik was of no relevance whatsoever. Just a coincidence. A very common name. No harm done.

'Can I just say, you're dealing with all of this very well,' Johnnie said as I glanced down at Mum's horrible new rescue cat which had just pushed in through the cat flap. I'd got it for her thinking it would be good for Mum to have a focus while waiting for her court date to arrive, but once it had settled in, it had turned out to be the most territorially aggressive cat in the world, hostile to everyone except Mum.

'Thanks.' I reached into the cupboard below and began to spoon the contents of a grim tin into a small china bowl. 'I'm not going to lie, it's been a very weird few months, but oddly, I'm in pretty good headspace, considering.'

'Well I'm really impressed,' Johnnie continued, moving his ankle hastily out of biting range as Perdu rushed past him, swishing her tail. 'It's not easy supporting someone bailed and pending trial like this. They've been charged with a crime but they're allowed to live what was their normal life for a bit while they wait for the courts to decide whether they can keep living it or they have to go off and get locked up. Excuse my language, but it's a headfuck.'

I put the dish down for Perdu and made a face at her as she made a very credible attempt to bypass the food and sink her teeth into my thumb. 'Especially given that a three to five year sentence is a lifetime at her age. I'd probably be pissed in the afternoon and trying to pretend I was still someone else too.'

'And things always become more heightened when you reach end game territory.' Johnnie rubbed his face tiredly. 'I knew being assigned a new barrister with only a couple of days to go was going to spin your mother out, although it's *really* not uncommon, but I hadn't realised how much it was going to bother her. Does she not talk to anyone but you?' He glanced at me. 'I always saw Margaret as very social, but...'

'Some of her friends have tried, in fairness, but since the court date came through she hasn't called them back, she's refused invitations... so yes, it's just me. I probably shouldn't be as responsive to her as I am,' I admitted. 'It doesn't encourage her to reach out to other people – but it's hard when I know she needs me. It's not for much longer now anyway.' I smiled at him. 'I'm going to make that tea, do you want one?'

'Oh sorry. I was going to do that, wasn't I? Another email came in and I forgot.' Johnnie shut the laptop lid and pushed it away to give me his full attention. 'Margaret mentioned you've just gone back on nights again? How come?'

I hesitated. 'Don't tell her but it's partly so she can't ring me as much. Well, she rings, but I don't have to pick up because I can say I'm asleep during the day. I've also really missed being awake at night recently. Maybe it's because it's been so hot, you know?' I looked out at the almost plastic and relentless blue sky. 'Once it's cooler at night you can get on with things properly. Although you can't tell people you're at your most productive at 11 p.m, they think you're weird.' I started to rinse the teapot out. 'Our whole society is geared towards "the early bird catches the worm.".'

'I hadn't really ever thought of that but you're right,' Johnnie agreed. 'Being the first one in the office used to be a badge of honour when I was a trainee.'

'Exactly. Which is hard if you're a night owl and not a lark.

Left to my own devices I'd go to bed around 3 a.m. and get up at
midday... that sort of "odd" timekeeping notices far less when I
work nights.'

'But how are you coping with also being up now?'

'It's short-term disruption. Once the trial is over, hopefully
things will become much clearer and, harsh as it sounds, either
way Mum is going to need me far less than she does now.' I
spotted a cardboard box on the windowsill, and peering over the
sides discovered the shards of mirror. 'There won't be lots more
of this kind of thing – you and me having to pop up what feels
like every five seconds.'

'I don't mind. I like your new haircut, too,' Johnnie said
suddenly. 'It suits you. It's quite a lot shorter, isn't it?'

I reached a hand up to the exposed nape of my neck.
'Opinion is divided. Trina, my boss, said, "what have you done
to your beautiful hair?" and someone else asked me if I'm
starting chemo soon so I've cut it in preparation?'

Johnnie wrinkled his nose. 'Rude.'

'I know. I just wanted to... feel a bit different. Have a
change. Live a little. Maybe I'm going full vampire – it's my
homage to Spike from Buffy! I loved him so much.' I sighed
before reaching for the teabags. 'By the way, if it sounds like I
have this whole new fascinating nocturnal life, I don't. I still
don't have time for anything but eat, work, sleep and call Mum
right now.'

'Well, like I said, you're amazing. When the trial is over, do
you think you might—?'

'Sorry, just quickly, before we move off the trial stuff,' I cut
across him, 'how *is* it going to affect her case that she is no doubt
going to be plastered, in every sense of the word, across all of the
weekend's papers in a green cocktail dress and jewels?' I peered
at the rather grubby cups I'd set next to the pot and hastily
decided to re-wash them. 'Could you also just grab the milk for
me?' I nodded at the fridge.

He got to his feet and opened it. 'There isn't any... as far as I can see?'

'OK – can you try the freezer? She usually keeps a small emergency carton in there. I'll stick it in some hot water. It won't take long to defrost.'

He bent a bit lower and glanced among the bags and packets, pulling out a drawer. 'In answer to your other question, I don't think it's *great* that she's going to appear exactly as the prosecution are going to paint her: Lady of the Manor determined to maintain her exalted position in society at any cost – selfish, morally compromised and greedy for attention, but...' Johnnie shrugged. 'What can we do?'

'And that's the defence talking,' I sighed.

'I know. And I still can't find any milk.'

I glanced over my shoulder. 'You're doing a boy look, that's why. You're going to have to actually lift some stuff up and search properly.' I grinned at him, but it faded quickly when he didn't smile back. 'You OK?'

Johnnie hesitated. 'Sorry. I can't discuss the details with you, but we have a troublesome witness statement that's bothering me. You're right – I *do* need to be doing more than scratching the surface right now.' He began to dig around in the freezer and roughly yanked a medium-sized clear bag out of the way, which promptly split, scattering frozen blueberries on the floor. 'Oh shit! What am I doing?'

'Don't worry.' I wiped my hands on a tea towel and bent to pick them up.

'Let me undo the bag properly and I'll – hang on...' he paused. 'Why has your mother got photographs in here?' He showed me the inside of the bag, which did indeed contain several images. *I* hadn't done anything wrong at all but nonetheless blood began to crash warningly in my ears. It was quite obviously not normal to have photographs stored in a bag of frozen fruit. No good was going to come of this.

'Shouldn't we maybe just...' I began nervously.

But he'd already reached in and pulled one out. 'Actually wait – I think it's a way of storing old images, isn't it? Or is that film, I'm not sure? Can you take these, I'll check.'

He passed me the bag, reached for his phone and began to google. 'It says you have to let them steadily get to room temperature first or they might be brittle. In that case maybe we should put this one straight back in then before we... oh!' He trailed off as he peered more closely at the image he was holding, and moved to the table, laying it down. 'So this is why it's in the freezer. That boy, the groom holding onto the horse your mother is sitting on, that's Richard Shand.'

Everything slowed right down, as if the back had sprung from a pocket watch and I was watching the cogs click to a halt. For a brief moment I considered dropping the blueberries in my hand on the floor just to create a diversion that might buy me another second or two thinking time, but it had run out. I swallowed and forced myself to look at the photograph.

A younger Rik stared back at me, and it felt as if my blood was thickening in my veins after a swift snake bite, the venom coagulating my thoughts too. I stared dumbly at the picture, unable to move.

'This must have been taken during that May or June of '94.' Johnnie squinted at the photo. 'It looks like Highcombe in the background to me, doesn't it you?'

'Yes,' I agreed, eventually, as calmly as I could manage. 'You're sure that's Shand?' It was such a desperate last clutch at a straw.

'Yes.' Johnnie leant in closer. 'I met him back then, didn't I? It's not the best photo, but it's definitely him.'

I took a deep breath and prepared myself mentally to lean in closer and then exclaim in 'shock'... only for the kitchen door to be thrown wide open, revealing my mother framed in the doorway, leaning on her stick and dressed in a more conventional linen shift dress.

'What are you both doing?'

She seemed to have sobered up remarkably and hobbled across the small space to snatch the bag Johnnie was holding, gripping it tightly in her own hand.

'Mum, what are *you* doing with photos in your freezer?' I asked, as there was a knock at the back door.

She glared across at it. 'If that's the bastard photographer back again, he's going to get a piece of my mind!' She limped over and flung it wide open – to reveal Timothy, his anxious smile tightening at the sight of us.

'Hello, all! Everything OK?' he tried, despite it very obviously not being all right.

'Wonderful, Timothy, I've never been better.' Mum shot a look of disbelief at him and then at Johnnie and me. 'The three amigos,' she remarked acidly and, still clutching the bag containing the remaining photos, she stumped from the room and thudded back upstairs before a door slammed, making us all jump.

'Well, this seems to have been a fun afternoon...' Timothy said, a moment later. 'I'm sorry I didn't pick up when you called, Johnnie... we were on a family day out. What's going on?' He turned to me. 'You look like you've swallowed something too big for your throat.'

That was about the size of it. I took a deep breath. 'I need to go and talk to Mum.'

SEVEN

So he HAD noticed her. She knew it. He had been eyeing her, circling around her, watching her having careless fun, laughing. She deliberately didn't look at him, standing at the centre of a group of notorious young men, many of whom had recently graced the pages of Tatler's *'Most Eligible Bachelor in Britain' feature. HE had been listed as apparently adoring skiing in Colorado and salmon fishing in Scotland, which was almost certainly him taking the pish not the fish, as he was clearly not the outdoorsy type at all. She watched him take a last drag of his cigarette, blow a cloud of smoke into the air like a spell, pluck two champagne glasses from the tray of a passing waiter and start to walk purposefully across the ballroom towards her.*

'He's coming,' she breathed to her brother. 'Take the others and bugger off.'

Anthony looked over his shoulder and whistled. 'Careful, Meg. You might have bitten off more than you can chew there.'

She narrowed her eyes, and Anthony laughed as he skilfully ushered their little group away. She stood taller, stuck out her chest, tossed her hair and turned at the last moment as if she was about to leave when she knew he was right behind her.

'Oh!' she gasped prettily, raising her hands as if surprised to find him there.

His eyebrows flickered and a slow smile spread over his face. He reached out and pushed the very cold flute against her décolletage, the glass touching the bare skin just above her heart, some of the liquid spilling between her breasts. She jumped for real and stared at him in shock.

'That's better,' he said, passing a glass to her and glancing around the rest of the room at the little knots of men and women flirting as he loosened his bow tie. 'You didn't pull it off the first time, I'm afraid to say.'

Tony Bennett was singing 'Alright, Okay, You Win' up on the stage with the Big Band, and the man laughed as Margaret glared at him furiously – her confusion giving way to outrage.

'Do I know you?' She cut him down witheringly, forgetting to be pretty.

His eyes travelled over her smooth skin, full lips, the curve of her neck, the diamonds at her wrist, the nip of her waist. His brief and brazenly cool appraisal made her involuntarily shiver.

'You will,' he said, taking a mouthful of his own drink; and handing it to her as if she was a waitress, he simply walked away, leaving her gaping at his elegantly retreating back while the band broke into 'Call Me Irresponsible'. He couldn't have scripted the moment more deliciously himself.

And he was, of course, right. The rest of the evening flew by in a blur where she was completely unable to concentrate on anything, until he returned to collect her, simply walking into the middle of a conversation she was having, taking her hand and drawing her onto the dancefloor.

Their bodies pressed together as she began to protest at his rudeness, just cutting in like that when she didn't even know his name.

'Oh shut up,' he murmured and looked down at her. 'You have far too beautiful a mouth – those lips are astonishing – to be *wasting it on telling me off.' He leant his head on hers for a moment or two as they swayed in perfect time to what would become the first song at their wedding: 'All The Things You Are'. He was a very good dancer and every word began to speak right to her... branding onto her skin, her heart and her soul... but something about the intensity of the moment spooked her.*

She pulled away. 'No,' she insisted. 'You jolly well don't just walk up and grab someone like that.' She turned to stalk off.

'Wait,' he called after her breathlessly.

She looked back and he was staring at her with a sweet boyish fear and vulnerability that speared right through her.

'My name is Benedict.'

EIGHT

JUDE

'Mum?'

She was lying on her bed again, eyes closed. There was no sign of the ziplock bag containing the pictures.

'I need to talk to you.' I tried again. 'I'm sorry to disturb you.'

She twisted her head on the pillow and glanced at me through narrowed eyes. 'I was just thinking about the first time I met your father. Trying to steady the buffs. It all seems like a lifetime ago now.' She exhaled.

By father I assumed she was talking about Benedict. That was a discussion about long-held secrets that I *didn't* intend to have today. One blast from the past at a time...

I made my way over to the window and sat down on the deep sill before swallowing nervously. 'You remember the night you called me at work to say something terrible had happened, just before your arrest?'

Mum tutted irritably. 'Oh, God – I'm not getting into all of that again now, Jude. I just want to sleep. My head is absolutely pounding.' She closed her eyes again as if to dismiss me.

'A man about my age came to the hospital that same night,' I persevered. 'We got chatting in the café, and we met in London once after that, but it didn't really go anywhere and I've not seen him since.'

'Bad luck.' Mum turned her back on me. 'Off you go now, please.'

'His name was Rik.' I watched her body stiffen. 'That picture of Richard Shand Johnnie and I just found in the freezer; Rik and Richard are the same person.'

Mum slowly rolled onto her back, hand resting on her brow, and stared up at the ceiling for a moment in silence. 'That was ten months ago,' she said eventually. 'My trial is in a handful of days and you're telling me this *now*?'

'I didn't know until a moment ago! I've never seen a picture of Shand before!' I said truthfully.

'But you knew you had dated a man called Richard and that I was being accused by a man called Richard. You knew that you met him around the time that I was arrested. And he just "came to find you"?' Her voice was soft. 'My Christ, Jude.'

I lowered my gaze.

'You say you met him in London. Where else did you go and what exactly did you discuss?' There was no trace of tiredness in her voice now.

'We met at the hospital a second night, too. I mentioned that you were still in the big house.' My voice wavered. 'And that you were alone.'

Mum said nothing. I could feel her staring as she waited for me to continue.

'After the break-in here, I met him in central London. That was the night you were arrested. I went to his flat... he came to *my* flat, and then...' I braced and looked at her. 'He drove me here.'

Mum began to drag herself up slowly to a seated position, grabbing onto the bedclothes for purchase. Her face was expressionless. 'You let him into this cottage?'

I nodded. 'I'm sorry.'

'Did you have *sex* with him in my house?'

It was so left-field and intrusive a comment that it was like being suddenly slapped, and I reacted defensively. 'No! *I'm* not the one that supposedly did something sexual with him!'

She didn't so much as flinch. 'But you let him into my home?'

'I didn't do it deliberately!' I tried to explain. 'I'd never do that! Of course I'd never have done that if I'd known who he was. He—'

'Stop talking,' she ordered. 'How long was he in here? Were you with him at all times? Concentrate! This is vitally important!'

'I lost my front door keys. He said he'd go round the back and see if it was unlocked. He got in and said he'd had to force the back door and—' I jumped as Mum shrieked aloud.

'You didn't lose your keys, you silly little fool! He would have taken them from you so that he had an excuse to "force" a door he'd already broken through two nights earlier. He put his DNA everywhere to cover his tracks and you *let* him do it!'

'What tracks?' I was bewildered.

'Oh, come on! How can you be so slow?' She leant back on the pillow. 'The very first thing Shand did when this whole thing started, was to come here out of the blue. That's when he threatened to go to the police and tell them I'd done those things to him – ghastly, horrible things – unless I paid him a large sum of money. That was indeed the night I rang you and said something terrible had happened. You obviously then told Shand, when he came to find you at the hospital, that no one was in the cottage. Did you tell him my belongings were here?'

'I don't know.' I struggled to think. 'Possibly?'

'You must have because the very next night it was burgled. I said I did it myself. I didn't, *he* did.' She sat back triumphantly. 'He was looking for something he didn't find!'

'But why didn't you just tell the police that at the time?' I exclaimed.

'Because at that point I didn't know Shand had already formally made his allegations; he was only threatening to. I hardly wanted the police here, poking around again, did I? I'd already had to send them packing once after you helpfully dragged them here in the middle of the night.'

'But Mum, if you'd only told me that someone called Richard had appeared in your life and was threatening you, I would have put two and two together when someone called Rik then turned up at the hospital!'

She snorted. 'Not by the sound of it! Did it not even occur to you that he might be something like a journalist?'

I coloured hotly. 'Of course it did! That's exactly what I thought, and he immediately proved that wasn't the case. If *you'd* said who you suspected of trashing your cottage, most of this could have been avoided, but you didn't; you lied to me.'

'*I* lied to *you*?' Mum repeated incredulously. 'Just to be clear, you told my accuser information that he used to ransack my house, and then you let him back into my house to eradicate any evidence that he'd broken in here in the first place. You didn't tell *me* any of this for the best part of a year, and now we're three days away from the trial and he might have God knows what he's either taken or you've inadvertently given him... but this is *my* fault?'

'What could he have?' I tried to defend myself. 'A moment ago you said he didn't find what he was looking for, and you've sworn blind from the start everything he's said is a pack of lies anyway.'

'Stop talking and let me think,' she closed her eyes.

'Is he looking for those photographs we just found? Where are they now, by the way?'

'*Shut up and let me think!*' she thundered so fiercely that I drew back in shock.

'Everything all right?' I heard Johnnie call worriedly up the stairs.

Mum didn't reply.

'We're OK,' I called back, 'but thank you.' I trailed off as Mum suddenly looked right at me.

'Well, who could have thought *you* would save the day?' she whispered. 'But in hindsight of course he targeted you. It's exactly his style.'

She propped herself up with a pillow. 'You said you went to his flat, yes? So you know where he lives? Go there and tell him that I'm fully prepared to do it. I *will* disclose it... it doesn't matter what,' she spoke over me as I opened my mouth, 'Just tell him. And you say that I have proof now that he was inside my house and that you'll say as much in court. No jury will believe his version of events after that, or anything that Tansy has to say. Johnnie's told you that she has come forward and said she witnessed me "assault" Shand, I suppose?' Mum snorted. 'Nothing to do with my having to fire her at the time for being a hopeless stable manager of course. It's outrageous. So Shand needs to drop the case now. No more lies. How can he have thought he'd get away with this?' She shook her head in disbe-lief and laughed. 'He's an idiot. You must go back to London and do it tonight.'

I stared at her. 'Mum, I just got here because you called me while you were very upset. You smashed a mirror and cut your hand up.'

'Johnnie can drive you. He's going anyway.'

'We should just tell Johnnie all of this.' I stood up to make for the door.

'You *want* people to know how gullible you were?' Mum looked at me incredulously. She reached for a tissue from her bedside table and blew her nose. 'You'll need to stay in a public place where people can see you with Shand at all times. As you've learnt the hard way, he's deeply manipulative and he will stop at nothing to get what he wants. He'll run rings around someone like you if you give him half the chance. Be on your guard.'

'Someone like me?' I repeated.

Mum sighed. 'Naïve, trusting, that's all I meant! Look, just empty your head of everything else and focus on the job in hand. I'm not cross with you, Jude, because I'm not surprised. You can't help it. It's just the way you are. You take things at face value. But I do expect you to play your part in putting this right. Is there anything else I should know? Because I do *not* want any more surprises.'

I closed my eyes briefly as I tried to make sense of everything she'd just said to me. 'Aunt Fan asked me if she could give my address to a man called Hugh in South Africa. She said he's my father and he wanted to get in touch. He's written to me and I've written back. That's all.'

'Oh God, I don't mean any of that crap! You really need to stop listening to people who have an agenda. Frances is a bitter half-wit who hates me and enjoys making trouble. Ignore her.'

I took a deep breath, opened my eyes again and looked right at my mother. 'I've done nothing but support you and be here for you since your arrest. I appreciate that the way you deal with feeling threatened is to come out fighting. It can make you appear rude and unkind. You say things that hurt the people around you.'

Mum drew back slightly in the bed.

'I'm not going to go and find Richard Shand.' I started to walk to the door. 'I'm going to tell Johnnie instead. It's the right thing to do.'

Mum reached out and grabbed my hand. 'They're no match for Shand. None of them. I will be sent to prison,' her eyes filled with tears. 'I swear to you on my life that Shand betrayed me every bit as duplicitously as he did you. I do not deserve what is going to happen to me because of him and you can stop it. You can help me. Please,' her voice cracked. She looked suddenly much older and frailer, her eyes desperate and wild as I stared back at her in shock. Until now I had not heard her sound genuinely afraid. Angry yes; ranting at the failures of the system that was allowing Shand a day in court at all, but not this naked fear. It was deeply unnerving to have the mother who had always been reliably unbreakable, if sometimes more deeply offensive than anyone else I'd ever met, suddenly start to fall apart in front of me... to need me.

'I'm frightened!' She pleaded. 'I'm sorry for the way that I spoke to you, but please don't let them send me to prison because of a *lie*.'

* * *

Johnnie and Tim looked up as I came back into the kitchen. 'Sorry about the shouting.' I tried to smile. 'Mum has now sobered up and would like to be left alone, as you probably heard, so I'll head back with you, Johnnie, if that's OK?'

He nodded and began to gather his things. I kept the smile on my face.

'You've remembered that I go to South Africa the day after tomorrow for a couple of weeks, I hope?' Tim looked worried. 'I don't want to leave you to deal with all of this alone – perhaps I should cancel?'

'Absolutely not!' I insisted. 'You need a break; I'll be fine.' All I could see in my mind was this new version of Mum in her bed like a baby bird, clutching at me, frightened and alone... while also insisting that she knew me better than I knew myself and everything I'd done when it came to Shand was entirely predictable and of no surprise to her... as if I had no right to any private feelings of my own. It was a confusing and uncomfortable sensation that made me feel very angry, yet also guilty. I was ashamed of my glib comment to Johnnie about her not needing me for much longer 'one way or the other'. Of course I didn't want her to go to prison! But she was also right – I did need to empty my head.

I was never going to let her – or anyone for that matter – inside it ever again.

NINE

JUDE

It was gone 8 p.m. by the time we arrived back in London. I changed and made my way over to the South Bank. The sun had just slipped from view, the sky was darkening and the London Eye glowed neon, towering over me as I walked towards what might still be his building.

Pushing my way into the lobby, I walked straight up to the night porter and took a deep breath. 'I'm here to see Richard Shand.'

He looked up. 'Floor and apartment number?'

'The penthouse.' I couldn't remember any exact details. 'My name is Jude Beauchamp.'

He picked up his phone. 'Mr Shand? It's the front desk.'

My world began to shrink in on me. So he *was* here...

'I have a Jude Beauchamp for you?' He put a hand over the phone. 'Mr Shand says would you like to go up?'

I actually laughed out loud, and the porter gave me a strange look. 'No thank you. I'd rather he came down to me.'

Shand was out of his mind if he thought I was going up to that noiseless, tomb-like apartment on my own.

The porter muttered into his phone before turning back to me. 'He'll just be a minute.'

I nodded my thanks and wandered over to the main doors, trying to keep calm, crossing my arms over my chest as I stared out over the square and thought about what I should say. I'd just deliver Mum's message and go.

'Morning, Jude.'

I turned around and there he was. A little thinner than I remembered, in a T-shirt, sweatpants and smiling. *Smiling?*

'Hi, Rik.'

He had the grace to look a little shamefaced. We held each other's gaze for a moment and he broke first. 'So, you look well. You look *different*. Nightlife is suiting you.'

I didn't say anything.

He shrugged. 'OK, so – do you want to come up for some breakfast?'

I slowly walked up to him. 'I was grieving and vulnerable. You took full advantage of both of those things. You should be ashamed of yourself.'

'I feel nothing but shame most of the time.'

I had no idea what that was supposed to mean and I didn't much care. 'Well, anyway, my mother says to tell you that she's fully prepared to do it – she'll disclose it. That's what I really came to say.'

I saw the fear flash across his face before he tucked his hands in his pockets. 'Your mother is a very damaged, cruel person.'

'You want me to tell her that?' I said tonelessly.

'She already knows.'

'She also wants you to know that I'll testify you were in her house, that you tricked me, and no one will believe your version of events after that. So you should drop the case.'

My job done, I turned and began to walk away.

'Jude?' I heard him call after me. 'You don't understand. Don't you want to know why I did it? Don't you want to know the truth?'

'No!' I shouted back and my voice echoed around the space before I pushed back out into the cool night air.

Done.

I messaged Mum and she immediately messaged back:

Has he agreed to drop it? You explained what would happen if he didn't?

Yes.

I quickly turned my phone off before she had chance to reply.

* * *

I barely slept a wink during the day on Friday however, even though a long shift lay ahead of me, because his stupid questions had worked. He'd tell me the truth about what? *What* didn't I understand?

It was a horrendous night at the hospital; three stabbings, one fatal – a fourteen-year-old girl. When I finally emerged through the main doors I felt like an empty shell that the already hot Saturday morning sunshine was never going to be able to fill. I closed my eyes briefly as the rays bounced off my greasy skin, and my low-bar plans to soak in a bath until my fingers turned wrinkly before climbing into bed and trying to shut everything out simply melted away. I opened my eyes and stared at the current of the fast-flowing river, trying to find some meaning in something, anything, as a breeze gusted off the

Thames making me shiver. My tummy rumbled and a tear ran down my face. My body didn't know what to do. I was just a jumble of confused and shocked physical reactions. That poor, poor girl.

'Jude?'

I turned around to see Richard sitting on the low wall dressed in a white T-shirt and linen trousers over trainers, legs wide and elbows resting on his knees as he waited, looking up at me.

'Not now,' I begged. 'Please.'

But he got up and started walking towards me anyway.

'I mean it,' I warned and, already exhausted, my voice cracked with the threat of more unshed tears.

'What's happened?' He looked at me searchingly.

'Nothing I want to share with you.' I turned away and looked out over the water again.

'Rough night at work?'

'Very.' I closed my eyes. 'So please, *really* don't do this.'

'Why don't you come and get a quick dinner with me? You've got to eat?'

'No!' I cried, spinning round to look at him as if he was mad. 'I've just come off a horrible shift, I'm meeting some friends later in town for one of their birthdays in a vague attempt to pretend that my life is still slightly normal and not completely... fucked up... then I'm going to try and get some sleep, in preparation for my mother's trial first thing on Monday, unless you're going to drop it, of course?'

'A quick coffee then?' He ignored my question.

I glared at him and started walking away, into the wind and the sun.

'She has a photograph,' he called out behind me. 'I wanted it back and I didn't think everything through. I never do!' His voice grew louder. 'I just wanted it back.'

I thought instantly about the freezer bag of images and,

although I forced myself to walk away, I knew he was telling me the truth.

* * *

But a photograph of what?

I was unable to stop thinking about it, all through heading home, trying to grab some sleep, going back into town for the birthday drinks, walking home and now staring up at the full moon, huddled on my sofa at 2 a.m., when my phone screen lit up beneath my face. A message from someone my phone recognised as being 'possibly Rik (real)'. He had kept my number?

> Please let me explain properly. I'll be at the Serpentine at 6 a.m. By the Diana memorial? Or the bridge? Loads of people around at that time. You'll be totally safe. Hope to see you x

The Serpentine? I closed my eyes and hugged my knees more tightly into my chest. The day before the trial? Of course I wasn't going to meet him. He was out of his tiny mind.

My phone buzzed again. Mum.

> I STILL HAVE NO NEWS THAT HE HAS DROPPED THIS. GO AND TELL HIM HE IS TO DROP THIS NOW! I'M SO FRIGHTENED!

I let the phone slip from my fingers and I wrapped my arms over my head as I started to cry. I thought about the girl who had been stabbed. How smooth and perfect so much of her skin had still been. I thought about the sound her mother had made when we told her she'd died. I looked up and Dom's photograph smiled back at me, then I saw my mum squashing herself into

Hilary's bed and I felt Rik... or Richard's... arms pulling me towards him that night in the cottage, the anger in his kiss... and I didn't understand.

I wanted to understand.

TEN

JUDE

He was sitting on a bench facing the water as I approached, one arm outstretched across the back of it.

I stopped walking and took a deep breath. The setting full moon was now very close to the horizon, its reflection a thumb smear of gold on the misty water. Deep indigos were blending up into lighter violets as the night sky prepared to bow out to the arrival of the sunrise waiting in the wings. Soon all of the waterfowl would begin their racket with proper intention, but right now there was no more than a lone goose call here and there and low murmurs of the first swimmers undressing, ready to glide into the cold of the Serpentine with a gasp; more beginning to arrive on their bikes. Just for a moment I saw into a magical half-light between night and day, where in some parallel universe he was simply waiting for me with all the possibility that held, but there were ghosts here, too. It could be Dom sitting there. I wasn't sure any more who I'd come to see and what answers I wanted.

I sighed, exhausted, and maybe he heard me because he turned around. Although I was determined not to be taken in by illusions this time, the genuine, weary relief that spread across his face at the sight of me stopped me in my tracks. He looked as if he hadn't slept a wink since I'd last seen him outside the hospital. I held his gaze for a second, and he looked so broken and afraid that the pieces of my heart exploded out with no warning, before sucking back in again, re-forming into something shaped differently by this whole experience we were being forced to share. I walked over and sat down next to him.

'Thank you for coming.' He pointed at the sky. 'Supposedly peak illumination will be about 8 a.m., when it's directly opposite the sun, but I'd say it was looking pretty amazing right now, wouldn't you?'

I frowned and looked down at the grass. He was nervous. That was new, too.

'You probably know this anyway, but I checked and the next time there will be two blue moons in a single year will be 2037, so worth noting, I think.'

'Richard.' My voice was quiet. 'What is it you want to tell me?'

He bent down and retrieved the morning's Sunday paper from beneath the bench. 'I picked this up just after midnight at Waterloo Station while I was out for a wander.' He passed it to me and there, on the front cover, was the picture of Mum in her green dress, squinting angrily at me from the front page, photographed, as she'd said, in the doorway of the cottage. The bright sun was shining in her eyes and illuminating the gobstopper ruby on her hand as she clutched her tumbler of whisky. Her ostentatious emerald necklace hung scratchily around her thin neck, catching on the green silk spaghetti straps. She was right that it was obvious she wasn't wearing a bra as she gripped the wall for support with the other hand. Her scarlet mouth was slightly open; captured in the middle of saying something furious to whomever had taken the picture. It was quite the image. My eyes moved to the headline:

Sex Trial of Socialite Begins Tomorrow

I peered at the accompanying text in the half-light.

The trial begins tomorrow at Reading Crown Court of Lady
Margaret Fawkes, Highcombe Hall, Berkshire. Lady Fawkes,
74, is charged with one count of indecent assault and two
counts of cruelty to a person under the age of 16 years in the
late 1990s. Lady Fawkes – the widow of former newspaper
editor Lord Benedict Fawkes and a once-regular fixture
within London's upper social circles – denies the historic
offences.

I passed it back to him wordlessly.

He cleared his throat. 'I went to her for help with something
when I was fifteen and working for her at Highcombe. You'd
left the morning I arrived. She called me a liar and she grabbed
my genitals to hurt me, not as a sexual thing; but that's the indecent assault bit of the charge. She slapped my face and then she
picked up a whip and she hit me so hard and so many times that
it cut right through the clothes I was wearing.' He turned his
back slightly towards me and lifted the base of his sweatshirt.
The moon illuminated several silver scars snaking up his spine,
out of sight, and I quickly looked away.

'That's the cruelty part that she's charged with. After your
stepfather died, I went to see her and she showed no remorse
whatsoever. In fact... she accused me of making everything up,
and she also said I was only doing it to extract money from her.
You've seen my flat, Jude. I don't need money. When someone
denies something happened, even though you know it did
because you were both there, it does something terrible to you as
a person.'

I turned my head to look at him. He was staring unseeingly
ahead at the setting moon.

'The anger you feel is just something else. It eats you up from within. You remember how you felt that morning when she insisted she hadn't said something terrible had happened and you knew she had?'

I nodded.

'Now imagine that feeling a million times over; hotter than the sun. All I wanted was for her to say three words: "please forgive me". If she had, we wouldn't be sitting here right now...' He motioned between us. 'But when it became clear that wasn't going to be something she felt able to do' – he looked down at the ground and began to jiggle his leg – 'that meant my going to the police. And *still* she doubled down. She says she has this photograph...'

'Go on,' I said.

He cleared his throat. 'I'm not going to tell you what it apparently shows... but if it were to be shared publicly it would annihilate me. My family would never get over it. But I truly believe she would do it. She despises me so much, that she'd rather destroy both of us than simply admit that what she did to me was wrong. I'm sorry that I used you to try and find it, but you can tell her she wins. I won't be in court tomorrow.'

I looked down at the newspaper image of my mother. 'I believe you, for what it's worth, that she did those things to you, and while it's not the public apology you deserve, on behalf of my family, I'm very sorry. She was taught to suppress all emotions from a very early age and that leaves some people with a sort of contained rage that bursts out of them with no warning, but it's still very wrong that she behaved that way. What did she think you'd done?'

His eyes clouded with tears that he made no attempt to hide. 'I can't tell you that but truly, thank you for saying sorry and acknowledging what really happened. I really did like talking to you.'

I hesitated before leaning forward to kiss him very gently,

which somehow managed to give me the last word. I got up and walked away, turning back briefly to see him staring out over the water as the sun rose. We were done.

My phone bleeped as I neared the gate to the road.

Well? Time is running out!!

I shoved it back in my pocket. She could stew a little longer.

* * *

I wasn't able to sleep. Instead I quietly waited all day in my stuffy flat for news from Johnnie that his hunch had been correct and Richard Shand was now refusing to give evidence and withdrawing his allegations... but none came. As the hours crept by I began to feel uneasy.

By 10 p.m. I was still on the sofa, having received approximately a million missed calls from Mum. I finally bit the bullet and called her back to admit I actually didn't know what was happening, but mercifully she didn't answer.

'Hi Mum, it's me. No news, I'm afraid. I'm at home so I'll try you again in a bit.'

I quickly hung up and thought about Richard alone on the bench after he'd announced that Mum had won. What would he have done after that? I imagined him returning to his flat, thirty-one floors up – knowing he was beaten... and then I remembered him telling me that he'd fallen from a watchtower, that was how he'd broken his back...

The French call it L'Appel du Vide... *the call of the void.*

It creates an anger and a sense of disbelief that eats you up from within.

I won't be in court tomorrow.

The ice that flushed through my veins made me gasp aloud.

My stupidity, of all people's, was utterly breathtaking. How had I not seen what had been staring me in the face for the last few hours while I'd been sitting like a fool, waiting for the phone to ring?

I jumped up and yanked my T-shirt off, snatching up a random dress and pulling it over my head, grabbing my phone and bag, shoving on my trainers and banging out of the house. I looked around desperately for a cab, but there was hardly any traffic on the road at all. I began to run but all I could think was I'm too late. I'm already too late.

* * *

I'd convinced myself of it by the time I arrived. I actually felt lightheaded with fear at the thought of what I was going to find when we pushed the door to his flat open. As the porter rang up to him all I could see in my head were horrible images of Richard dead by various means, having taken his own life, quietly, in the gap between my leaving him by the Serpentine and now, so when the night porter said – 'he says to go straight on up' – I stared stupidly at him.

'He's there?' I repeated. 'You just spoke to him?'

The porter raised an eyebrow. 'Unless it was someone pretending to be him?'

I shot him a sideways look of alarm that he wouldn't have understood and hurried to the lift.

Richard met me as the doors opened, in a T-shirt with his hands in the pockets of baggy grey jogging bottoms.

I exclaimed with sheer relief and burst into tears, flattening back onto the lift walls at the sight of him as my legs gave way beneath me.

'Hey, hey!' He pushed the closing doors open again, stepped in and helped me back onto my feet in amazement. 'What's wrong? What are you doing here?'

'I thought you'd... I thought I was going to find...' I sobbed, then forced myself to stop with a gulp.

He stared at me, utterly bemused. 'OK, so are you coming in or are you just going to go up and down in the lift?' He wedged a shoulder in the gap to stop the doors that were bossily trying to shut on him again.

'I was worried. I wanted to make sure you're OK.'

'That's kind of you. Thank you.'

We stared at each other and suddenly we were kissing. I hadn't planned it. I'd needed to know he was OK, but he was lifting me up, his mouth was on my neck, my hands were reaching around him. He was safe and he was carrying me into the flat, kicking the door shut behind us.

* * *

I woke with a start in his white impersonal bedroom a couple of hours later to find that he wasn't there. The air-con was whirring and I shivered. The blinds were wide open; I was looking out on to the London skyline and it was looking back in at me.

Glancing at the clock I saw that it was midnight and moaned. My sleep pattern was shot to shit. Immediately alert, as if I'd had a power nap, I gathered the sheet around me and slipped from the bed, grabbing my creased dress from the floor and darting into the bathroom.

I found him sitting on the balcony with the doors open, wearing nothing but his loose, grey jogging bottoms and smoking while staring out over the river and watching the traffic feed over Waterloo Bridge. I focused, instead, on the small silver tin open on the table, and he glanced up as I approached.

'Hey!' I waved shyly and awkwardly. I'd forgotten how weird the first post-sex bit was, when you'd been as intimate as it was possible to be but had none of the familiarity yet to make that fact comfortable.

'Hey yourself.' He smiled. 'Come and join me. It's going to storm.'

I walked across – but I couldn't step out over the threshold.

He offered me a hand. 'I've got you,' he said. 'You can do this.'

I hesitated but with a gasp of disbelief, I clutched his hand and eased out onto the small platform, before sinking immediately onto the chair, feeling better the second my line of sight was lower. He was right, the air felt heavy and still, but the hum of the switched-on night-time city... a million phones, washing machines, hotel air-con units, newsagent fridges, gallery security alarms, tube station lights... was comforting even if the air itself remained stale and full of fumes.

'Well done.' He passed me the joint. 'Here. It'll help.'

I swallowed as the roll-up slipped comfortably between my fingers with all of the inevitability of a bad ex, back again.

'Not too much at fi—' began Richard as I took a deep draw, then blew it out slowly and with all the control of a lot of practice.

He watched me, eyebrows raised. 'OK,' he said and laughed as I stared up at the heavy moon, dark clouds gathering and moving across it. 'You are full of surprises.'

'I'm really not actually,' I said and shivered.

'I think you are.' He looked at me tiredly and smiled again. 'This all suddenly got a bit art-house film, didn't it? Hopefully any second now a single red balloon is going to blow past symbolising all is not lost... although we're a bit high up for that.'

I suddenly wanted to go back in. 'You're right, the weather is going to break.' I stubbed out the joint, placing the unused half back in the tin. Heading back into the kitchen feeling slightly sick – it was strong gear – I reached into my bag for my phone and discovered another dozen missed calls from Mum in a frenzy that she'd been in the bathroom and missed my earlier call. Her last charming messages read:

> WHERE are you? I have NOT heard from that evil cunt. Is he dropping it or not? CALL ME BACK

followed by

> Your fucking selfishness astounds me. You are a deeply unpleasant, thoughtless BURDEN! I'm switching my phone OFF and going to bed. I don't want to talk to you tonight now. I just wanted it all to disappear. That's all you had to do.

> Make him disappear.

She was quite evidently very drunk indeed. Just for a brief moment my own anger surfaced and without thinking I messaged back:

> He's a person who you have hurt very badly and I don't know what to say to you right now I'm so ashamed.

I hit send and instantly regretted it. What good would it do, her reading that smashed out of her brains? It would only make matters worse and it was something that I needed to say to her face, calmly when she was sober. She and I were going to have to talk. Now that the court case wasn't going to happen and there was no risk of her going to prison, there was also no excuse for this kind of behaviour any more. Things were going to be different from now on. I jumped at a sudden flash: lightning. 'I'm sorry, I just have to call her back quickly.'

Richard frowned, confused, as I moved a step away from him while the phone rang out, but true to her word, she didn't answer, so I left a message. 'Hi, it's me.' I lowered my voice.

'Sorry I missed you earlier, I've been napping at home. Look – everything is *fine* – we'll talk in the morning.'

I hung up as there was another flash. Richard was still watching me, and I suddenly felt as if I was going to be sick. *Really* strong gear... 'One minute,' I swallowed, shoving my phone on the side, and rushed from the room.

In his clean-edged bathroom I waited, hanging over the loo, and eventually stuck my fingers down my throat to speed things up. I didn't actually puke, just gagged violently – but I felt better for it and returned to the sitting room to find him standing over my mobile, staring intently at the screen. He must have picked it up the very second I set it down.

'Old habits?' I couldn't help myself, and he blushed before holding it out to me.

'Thank you for what you messaged to her. That was brave. So why did you need to call her straight back to apologise for saying it?'

'I didn't. I apologised to you, not her?'

We both jumped as there was another flash and the thunder boomed right overhead, only a second or two of delay. Richard sighed and stretched his arms up before letting them fall heavily by his sides again. 'OK. Whatever you say.' He walked back over to the kitchen.

'She's pissed,' I explained. 'She wouldn't have put that nasty stuff otherwise.'

He glanced at me briefly then looked away.

'When you first came to the hospital, how did you know I was there?' I asked.

He picked up the lemon and reached for the knife, pausing the edge of the blade above the bright, taut, shiny skin. 'It's surprising how lax lawyers are with details. I just trailed you around a bit.' He put the knife back down. 'Jude, I heard you tell your mum you're at home. Why did you do that? Why not just tell her you're here with me?'

The laugh of disbelief escaped me before I could stop it.

'I'm serious,' he said. 'If I asked you to, would you ring her now and tell her you're here?'

I hesitated just a beat too long.

He frowned and looked out of the window, apparently deep in thought. There was another flash of lightning, and he opened a drawer of the island and pulled out a brown envelope. 'So I need to give you a couple of things back.' Opening it he removed a photograph. 'I took this from your flat.'

I moved closer to get a better look. It was a picture of a teenage me with Johnnie, both clutching bottles of Aftershock with our tongues out, Mum sitting in the background laughing and smoking a cigarette.

'And this one was obviously from today.' Richard's hand knocked the handle of the knife and made it spin so it pointed towards him as he laid a second image down. It was me kissing him on the bench by the Serpentine.

I stepped back from the images in shock. 'You had someone photograph us?' My heart began to thump. 'Why?'

'It was something one of my lawyers suggested...' Richard shrugged. 'That it would be helpful to have proof that we'd met and you'd threatened me.'

'So why have you chosen the one moment where I kissed you goodbye? It makes it look like we're involved with each other, which, when this was taken, we weren't?'

'I don't know.' He shrugged. 'Would it be a problem if, say... your mother saw this then?' He tapped the picture. 'Her daughter with *me*. The dirty secret.'

Everything started to blur in front of my eyes, the photographs, the blade of the knife. 'Richard, have you done this' – I motioned between us and then in the direction of his bedroom – 'to get back at her?' I could hardly breathe as I looked around the flat, suddenly terrified. 'Have you photographed us in here, too?'

Too late I remembered Mum's warning to stay in public, not to go out of sight with him.

'Oh my God,' he said. 'You think I'd do that? You really think I'd do that?' He brought his hands up to his temples. 'This is so fucked up. I'm sorry, I'm so sorry, Jude, I never meant to hurt you!'

'Shit! You *have* done it to get back at Mum, haven't you? I thought this was real. I thought we'd been honest with each other. I am so sick of always being caught in the middle of people's messed-up... shit... and lies... and being *used!*' I realised I was crying so hard I couldn't get the words out properly. My breath was coming in gasps.

'This isn't like that, I swear! I'm giving them back to you!' Richard reached out to grab my wrist, but I shook him off.

'Don't touch me! Don't fucking touch me. I trusted you! This is over!'

'No, please!' he said desperately. 'Not like this. Don't go like this!'

'It's over!' I was suddenly white-hot with fury. 'You disgust me. All of you!'

'You're right.' He suddenly straightened up. 'You are so right. It *is* over and I'm sorry.' I saw him eye the knife. 'Forgive me.'

'No!' I shouted, and we both lunged for it at the same time.

PART THREE
PRESENT DAY

ELEVEN

Where are you? Please call!

I need you. He's dead!

This is bad really bad. You need to get rid of your phone or they are going to think we had something to with this because really we did. Suicide stabbing is really rare. Tell them you didn't know I was meeting R. I will be OK.

Margaret stares at the screen in shock and blinks again as her head pounds. She sits up in bed and is nearly sick, her empty stomach churning. The nerve endings in her gut feel bruised and raw, burnt by the alcohol she consumed in great gulps the night before. She reads the messages again. Sent in the middle of the night. He's killed himself? And Jude found him? Or was there?

She tries to focus and think. Destroy the phone, Jude says. These messages were sent several hours ago. What if the police are already on their way? Margaret looks at the flashing light on the top of the phone and yelps in alarm. She might be sending out a signal that is being traced right now. She fumbles to turn it off immediately, stiffly climbs out of bed and dresses with more speed than she has been used to needing for a very long time.

Downstairs, she opens the back door and is about to step outside when she jumps to see that Perdu has left her a gift on the doormat, a slaughtered baby wood pigeon. There is no time to deal with it; she simply steps over the body and, having crossed the garden, slips the phone in her pocket and starts off over the uneven ground towards the dyke.

Panting a little with shock and haste, in the sweet-smelling early morning air that promises heat, she jabs her stick into the tufts of grass, leaning on it heavily. It is going to be *extremely* hot today; her bad ankle is already throbbing as she glances up in disbelief. The August sky is a clear, unforgiving Forget Me Not blue at only six thirty a.m. She reaches into her pocket just to check the phone is still there and hasn't fallen out. Jude is right. She needs to be properly rid of it *and* the messages she sent threatening 'what would happen' if he didn't drop the case... insisting Jude make him disappear...

Pausing for a moment to catch her breath, Margaret looks out across the parkland. It contains all of the bright wonder and quiet simplicity of natural beauty that feels so significant and poignant when someone dies and is no longer earthbound; but it's fear not profundity that is sharpening her senses like this. The deer are moving languorously around. She watches as a doe raises its head, aware of her presence even at this distance, considering her.

Luckily far too stupid an animal to make a decent witness. A few more strides and she's at the water's edge, staring down at the murky depths waiting to swallow the evidence. She draws out the phone as a few early autumn, crisp brown leaves blow across her feet and sit on the surface, floating like tiny boats. Margaret hesitates and looks behind her at the bent grasses; the trail her footprints have created in the dew. She might as well erect a sign. Frowning, she puts the phone back in her pocket. This isn't going to work. Yes, she walks up to the main house every day, but she doesn't usually take this route. It's suspicious.

She changes course to her left, the reassuring bulk of High-combe now firmly in her sights and silhouetted on the horizon as she reconsiders her options. She could walk to the Great Pond – slip the phone into *that* – but again, she has pointedly not set foot in the gardens since her disagreement with Timo-thy's bloody wife about the plans for the perfectly ridiculous 'Prairie adventure' space. It would be remarked on – noticed. In fact, Margaret realises, she needs to be witnessed doing exactly what she *normally* does. Nothing out of the ordinary. Even today.

Especially today.

So she heads to the stables. The radio is already tinnily chattering away as the yard girls move around talking to them-selves and the horses. Margaret breathes in the rich scent of hay as she stands outside Biscuit's box, for once not enjoying the play on words, and waits for someone to appear and see her. Normally the girls are like mice, scurrying all over the place, not missing a trick, but today when she actually needs one of them... Margaret tuts and glances at the yard clock as she absently strokes Biscuit's nose once he's put his head over the door. Time is getting on. Luckily, Clara, the large one, walks round the corner carrying a bucket, whistling tunelessly, and stops short to see Margaret there, right in front of her. She freezes, her cow-like eyes widening.

'Morning, Lady Fawkes,' she manages, eventually, remem-bering her manners, but then she just stands there – idiot girl – not knowing what else to say.

'Morning, Clara.' Margaret nods briskly at her. Job done. 'Going to be a lovely day, isn't it?'

Clara's foolish mouth falls wide open, and Margaret can practically hear what she will clump off to tell the other girls, the second Margaret is out of earshot: *'"Lovely day!" she said, like she was off to the shops or something and not actual court. Can you believe it? She's got some front, that one!'*

Margaret nods at Biscuit and makes her way off towards the main house without looking back at Clara. Her ankle is now on fire but she keeps going. Gripping the phone in her pocket she squeezes it savagely.

Dead. Actually dead!

And *suicide?*

Margaret has been to hell and back over the last ten months; her life ruined, her reputation destroyed, and now at the eleventh hour, when she has offered the lying little cockroach a quiet way out, still he must make noise and *fuss.* Margaret pauses and turns back, looking at the new barn where the former groom's cottage once stood, before the fire. She is physically shaking with anger.

'May you burn in hell.' The curse she utters is a hissed whisper but the strange moan that escapes her immediately afterwards catches her by surprise. She rounds over momentarily, leaning on her stick, and clamps her hand over her mouth.

Margaret imagines what she will have to say to everyone: *'You feel sorry for someone so mentally unstable that they take their own life, but that does not mean you allow them to bully you and tell lies about you.'*

And that would probably work, if it wasn't for the fact that *Jude* discovered the body?

She obviously fell right into some sort of trap – it was almost certainly the vindictively planned intention of an arch manipulator to make his melodramatic suicide really *count* – because if the last year has taught Margaret any lesson at all, it's that something can absolutely be made out of nothing.

And the complainant dying the night before the trial starts, with the body being called in by a member of the accused's immediate family, is most definitely something. The police are naturally going to want to establish if Margaret or Jude had something to do with the death... and the message exchange between the two of them is hardly going to help matters.

Margaret's phone must indeed disappear.

Mrs Brooks obviously sees Margaret coming down the drive, because when she reaches the family door to the big house it swings open before she rings the bell. Quite like old times.

'Good morning, Your Ladyship. How—'

'Mrs Brooks.' Margaret doesn't look up or wait to hear the end of the housekeeper's sentence, just walks into what used to be her neat boot room and now houses a jumble of wellingtons and brightly coloured coats belonging to Annalise and Timothy's various offspring.

'I've come from the stables. I'm afraid I'm rather grubby.' She kicks off her Hunters and looks around at the tangle of footwear options available to her, selecting a pair of dreadful fluffy sheepskin slippers, which must belong to Annalise. Slipping her socked feet in, she walks into the kitchen, treading Annalise's DNA around, not her own. Quiet and still. No buzzing children. The kitchen really is the most revolting colour now. Her duck-egg was so much nicer.

'How lovely and cool it is in here. An old-fashioned Indian summer. Although we probably can't call it that any more, can we? Now, I have a rather trying day ahead of me.' She throws all of this over her shoulder as she carries on walking. 'Literally of course. So I'm going to take a brief moment in the chapel.'

She glances back at a blushing Mrs Brooks, the woman's gaze lowered, embarrassed. 'I understand.'

Margaret stares at her, wondering if her old housekeeper is in fact thinking all sorts of insults and slurs, hurling them silently in her direction. 'Do you?' she says. 'How extraordinary.'

Mrs Brooks turns a deeper red. 'I apologise. I meant that—'

But Margaret has already turned and is leaving the room. 'I have my keys. I shan't require assistance.'

As she passes the family sitting room, she notices that for once the sofa cushions are plumped. They won't all be back for another two weeks, having decided to stay in South Africa until the trial is completely over and all of the 'unpleasantness', as Timothy so wetly put it, is done. Margaret smiles grimly. Well, poor little Timmy is in for a shock. She thinks happily of Annalise's face when the news reaches her that Margaret's trial has collapsed before it even began. She shall be sad to miss that.

Reaching the dividing door, she selects the correct key from the bunch in her other pocket, and feeling the reassuring weight slide into the old lock, turns it and steps into the hallway. Now on the newly public side of Highcombe, she closes the door behind her – glancing briefly back at the *private* sign – but not bothering to lock it. The house won't be open for hours yet, only the family staff are here. She will be left in peace. Taking care not to slip in her cheap new footwear, she makes her way down the corridor to the main entrance hall and, once in its airy, cool, familiar space, gives a sigh of relief.

Looking up the main staircase at the portraits lining the walls, she briefly sees her father standing at the top before his stroke, inspecting his waistcoat pocket watch. A man who knew he was in charge, about to clatter down to the dining room for breakfast. As he fades away, Margaret sighs again and fixes her gaze on the cameras in the corner – they aren't switched on until the house staff arrive at seven thirty, she has time yet – and begins to climb the stairs with some difficulty. She makes her way down the east corridor, through several more doors, up another staircase... As she climbs higher, the hallways notice-ably narrow. She remembers being told that was a particular feature of the cells beneath the Old Bailey. Narrowing spaces becoming tunnel-like, several arches getting smaller and smaller, leading down to the gallows. Deliberately designed to reflect the condemned prisoner's final journey to meet their maker, only briefly opening out into an area known as the bird-cage at the end; a small space with netting overhead. One last look at the sky before retribution.

Margaret pauses, gripping the bannister, feeling rather giddy, then continues to the attics.

She is going *up*, not down.

The boards creak as she walks into the cavernous space of the attic, across to the particular window where she would sit as a child, looking out over the park, scribbling her poems. Bending with a groan, she inspects the rough brickwork beneath the deep sill and pulls at it. It doesn't give; she simply breaks a nail. Even she can't distinguish the right one first time. That's reas-suring. Trying again, she finds the correct brick and slides it out to reveal the small, dark, metal, almost postbox-like door behind it. Fumbling with the tiny key she retrieves from the bunch in her pocket – the light is poor despite the bright skies on the other side of the window – it opens eventually. Margaret reaches into the space where she used to hide her treasures as a child and feels around; empty. She fumbles under her shirt and from her waistband untucks the plastic sandwich bag that contains the photograph; the two of them in bed together. Placing it carefully back into the cavity, she adds her phone and closes the door, locking it before returning the brick. She does as little else as she possibly can to disturb the dust and spider webs. Highcombe will keep her secrets, just as it has for count-less others before her.

Climbing to her feet, her blasted ankle snatching as she tries to straighten up, she pauses for a moment and stares out of the window. If she closes her eyes she can almost hear Anthony calling for her, ready to go and play. He was never an annoying little brother. He was nothing but a joy. Trees to climb, the park to explore. She takes a deep breath. She must go. It's no good to stay with the ghosts today.

* * *

She is sitting at the back of the chapel staring at the altar and Christ on the cross, waiting to be found and witnessed praying, when she finally hears Mrs Brooks tentatively coughing behind her.

'Lady Fawkes? The staff are arriving shortly. I wonder if you might like Mr Brooks to drive you home? We have a very large wedding this coming weekend, so it's going to get very busy with deliveries soon.'

People may see her and there might be a scene, the woman means. Unpleasantness. Margaret pauses. Just for a moment she sees Benedict at the end of the aisle, in morning dress, waiting for her, grinning. That was the thing with Dickie that made him so irresistible; the twinkle in his eye that promised fun. As if he was always on the verge of being caught doing something naughty. She glances around the empty pews. Anthony smiling, Fan gripping his hand, glaring furiously back at Margaret in that awful pea-green dress which didn't suit her. Her mother in the vast hat that blocked everyone else's view, unusually relaxed with the relief of finally having Margaret off the shelf. 'Once a broad never a bride'. She looks down at her muddied skirt and, just for a second, sees the slippery silk of her wedding dress. She feels it sliding over her body, remembers stepping out of it in front of Benedict, lying on the bed, smoking, in his loosened shirt and suit trousers, watching her.

'Those are nice new undies,' he'd remarked. 'I do like that you always wear such pretty little matching sets.'

She'd flushed delightedly at that – in spite of 'undies'. It was something of a trademark of hers, lots of beautiful, alluring and expensive bits of lace and silk intended to titillate. She had taken particular care choosing her wedding trousseau, and she felt beautiful as she walked towards him with a slow smile, climbing seductively onto the bed until she was straddling him, planting a languorous kiss on his mouth. He turned his head away to put his cigarette out as she waited excitedly.

Turning back, eyes heavy-lidded, he'd kissed the end of her nose. 'Not tonight, Josephine. I'm exhausted and far drunker than I look.' He yawned and moved her onto the bed next to him, leaning his head back on the pillow and closing his eyes.

She'd stared at him in astonishment, thinking he was joking. She had never had a man decline her in a state of undress, but his mouth had fallen open and his snores began to echo around the honeymoon suite. He'd passed out.

After she'd carefully unhooked the stockings, taken everything off, packed it away and put on her camisole and shorts set, she removed her make-up in the bathroom and dried her eyes which were oddly full of tears. It had been a long, emotional day, that was all. She had glared at herself fiercely and returned to a darkened room. He had apparently woken up enough to switch the lights off, undress and slip beneath the covers, his back turned to her.

'Lady Fawkes?'

Margaret jumps and catches sight first of the ghastly slippers that really are on her feet and then Mrs Brooks still expecting an answer to something, but what was the question?

'I'll ask Mr Brooks to bring the car round then?'

Margaret remembers. It is indeed time to go back to her house and get changed.

'Thank you, Mrs Brooks,' she says. 'That would do very well.'

* * *

In her own bedroom, her mind settling now she is rid of the phone, Margaret stands in her slip and looks at the outfit hanging on the back of the door: a modest Wedgwood blue. No jacket – only a fool would wear a coat in weather like this – but purchased for the dropped waist with pleats that will move while walking up steps but *not* lift in the event of a sudden gust. She smiles. Thank God she won't have to wear the ghastly thing in public after all. But she will put it on for now. Everyone will be here soon. Better get this pretend show on the road.

Margaret moves across the room to her dressing table, picking up her stiff bristle brush. Glancing absently in the mirror, she gives her carefully curated ash blonde hair another quick going-over, watching it habitually bounce back into the style it has held for the last forty years. She pauses briefly and puts down the brush, staring back at her reflection, lifting the hoods of skin that have fallen over her eyes before releasing them and drawing her jowls tight, watching the crepe disappear. She thinks briefly of the newspaper picture – her green cocktail dress wrapped around a dried-out old lizard – and has to close her eyes to force the image away.

Slipping the vile dress from the hanger, she climbs in. She has to wriggle and reach in the most uncomfortable way to try and do the zip up to the top. She will have to ask one of her legal team to do the last bit – the girl will do. She looks at herself, swears in disgust and leaves the room angrily, unable to look at herself a moment longer.

Perdu is, as ever, lying across the second to last stair, unrepentant and only stretching, arching her back and getting up once Margaret has already been forced to step over her. Yawning, she follows her mistress into the hall, where Margaret slips her feet into the new, mid-heel beige court shoes. Like a runny shit for each foot, revolting. In the kitchen, Perdu weaves around her legs and rasps a miaow every bit as scratchy as the small pink tongue in her delicate, lethal mouth. Margaret glowers down at her and softens slightly. 'What, you mean a squab isn't quite enough breakfast on its own, you horrid little cat?'

Perdu looks entirely unembarrassed about the mauled

remnants of the bloodied and feathered wood pigeon she dragged in through the cat flap while Margaret was at the chapel, and merely yowls again. Margaret does as she's told and heads to the cupboard for a tin.

'I don't know anything at all, I'm afraid. I was here all night. I didn't speak to anyone.' She practises while hunting around for lamb, Perdu's favourite. She lifts down the tin, and placing it carefully on the table, keeps it well away from her dress and peels back the lid. The smell of jelly-encased meat fills the room. That's all she has to do; tell the truth.

Reaching for a spoon, she cuts into the cat food and a large scoop comes away with a disgusting audible squelch, but it's not that which revolts Margaret. In the tin, buried within the mulched-up meat is an intact and perfectly smooth, rounded piece of gristle that looks very recognisable as coming from a dead animal; reminiscent of the knuckle of a bone, only in miniature, like the tibia of a child. With a bright flash in her head like a camera going off, Margaret sees the small body lying inert, tiny cold feet cradled in her hands. Sometimes, even all these years later, the shocking loss of darling Hilary will sneak up on her with a freshness of power and pain, as if it has all just happened and he was here only moments ago...

Hands trembling, she finishes spooning the cat food into the bowl, and Perdu crouches down next to it. The sound of her gobbling and gulping makes Margaret feel sick. She washes her hands then fills up a glass of water, standing over the sink to take small sips. She must focus and – dear God, what *is* that smell? It's fishy almost. She looks around her, confused, and sniffs again, putting the glass down and moving over to the larder. As she opens the door, she is assaulted by the smell of a trout she took out of the freezer last night and intended to put in the *fridge* to defrost in time for her supper. What on earth did she put it in here for?

She simply doesn't recall, but she also had far too much to

drink last night. She hesitantly touches the scales near the fin. The flesh gives plumply at her touch and deposits a slimy, clear mucus on her fingertip. She picks up the plate and puts it in the fridge anyway. She'll just have to cook it a little longer than usual tonight. It will be fine.

There is a knock at the front door, and she jumps nervously. Now, she must remember to look shocked when they tell her the 'news', but not say anything.

'Good morning!' The legal girl is on the doorstep. She is smiling. Why is she smiling? She ought to be looking stunned or at least grave.

'Margaret?' The girl says gently, and Margaret realises she is staring into space like a fool. 'Are you all right?'

Margaret blinks. The girl is probably too junior to have been told anything of importance. That's all it is. 'Of course I'm all right. And really, for the hundredth time, as I keep saying, I would like to be addressed as Lady Fawkes. Kindly also come in and fasten the top of my zip before the gentlemen arrive,' she adds. 'I can't reach it.'

The girl smiles, not intimidated, follows her into the drawing room and points at a silver-framed picture under the lamp on the side table. 'Is that you? You were so glamorous!'

Margaret glances sourly at the foolish young woman in the picture who ought to have made a much better set of decisions. 'Yes, that's me.'

'Such a tiny waist!'

Margaret looks away. The sum total of her achievements. 'I used to write poetry,' she announces and immediately wishes she hadn't as the girl looks back at her and opens her mouth to say something that Margaret knows with absolute certainty she will not want to hear.

Luckily Perdu rushes in and, distracted, the girl bends to tickle her head. For some reason Perdu does not bite her as she bites everyone else. 'Good morning Purr-dy,' the girl says.

'Perdu,' Margaret corrects, turning away but lifting her hair. 'It means soldier or lost one. It has nothing whatsoever to do with purring. Will you please do up my dress?'

'Have you taken your painkillers today, Margaret?' The girl's cool fingers briefly touch Margaret's skin as she fastens the zip. 'Is your ankle hurting very badly?'

Margaret whips round. 'Don't be impertinent. I have managed my injury perfectly successfully for many years, and I certainly don't need pain management strategies from someone completely unqualified to do so.' She glares at the girl. 'I'm *frightened.*'

This is not actually a lie. She wants them all in here *now* telling her that there has been a development; *I'm so sorry, Margaret, there has been a suicide...*

'Of course you are,' the girl agrees. 'But in my experience, emotional flare-ups can exacerbate physical symptoms. I see it a lot with clients.'

'In your experience!' scoffs Margaret. 'You're all of twelve.'

'I'm nearly forty, Margaret, and a partner.' The girl remains unruffled. 'It's going to be a long day in court,' she continues, 'so—'

Margaret pales. No it isn't! They should be telling her all charges against her have been dropped. Dear God, she is paying their firm thousands! Well, Timothy is. How can her legal team *not know* that her accuser died last night? This is absurd! How hopeless are they, for God's sake?

The girl is looking at her again. 'Have you had anything to eat or drink this morning, Margaret? You look a little lightheaded.'

'Where is Johnnie?' Margaret blurts desperately. '*He* will know what's going on! I want to see Johnnie!'

'Margaret?' This time the voice calling her name is male, and she looks up, faint with relief as Johnnie himself appears in the doorway, ducking under the low beam. 'What are you

THE NIGHT SHE LIED 129

shouting about now?' He flashes her a smile that she supposes is intended to be reassuring. 'I thought we discussed this? Number one rule: getting cross isn't going to make anyone sympathise with you. I don't need the jury to like you, but I *do* need them to feel sorry for you. So no voice raising, remember?'

Margaret is on the verge of total panic. 'Jury?' She looks at him like he's mad. What is he talking about – jury! How can there be a trial when the complainant is *dead*! Without his testimony there can be no trial!

'Let's also remind ourselves that Yasmin really is top-class, so let her do the heavy lifting,' Johnnie continues. 'I actually think it's a blessing that Michael had to return the case. Yasmin has an excellent track record with both trials and appeals. When she—'

'Appeals?' Margaret can hardly get the word out. 'You're already talking *appeals*?'

'Margaret, please!' Johnnie briefly holds a hand up in the manner of an old-fashioned traffic policeman. 'That was not a slip of the tongue. I don't make careless mistakes.'

He shoves both hands in the pockets of his beautifully cut trousers and holds his head up high. Just for a second Margaret sees the strong, stocky boy of his youth in hand-me-down clothes trying to hide the hem of his jeans floating on his ankle bone, the denim pulled tight across his thighs while his shorter, leaner and older brothers teased him mercilessly. Johnnie's mother was frugal to the point of lunacy after the full extent of her husband's fondness of gambling came to light and they struggled to keep the wheels from coming off completely.

'You're going to see Yasmin earn her money today,' Johnnie insists. 'Ready to face the enemy?'

He stands to the side, and Margaret looks at the narrow doorway, very bright light shining into the hall, illuminating one or two small, downy feathers lying on the floor that she must have missed during the clean-up earlier. The birdcage.

Her head begins to swim and her eyes flood with tears. 'No!' She starts to shake her head. 'There has been a mistake. I thought... this shouldn't be happening!'

Johnnie frowns as he watches her but then his voice becomes firm. 'Exactly. That's exactly the case we are going to establish. Come on. We need to leave now.' He draws out his phone and glances at the screen. 'Nothing annoys a court more than not turning up on time.'

Still, she can't move. She is rooted to the spot with fear. 'I said no.'

'Margaret,' Johnnie says in a voice one might use for someone else's child they'd like to shout at but can't. 'We *must* go.' The phone begins to ring and he gives a short exhalation, checking the number before raising it to his ear and speaking into it. 'We're about to leave so be quick.'

Margaret watches the blood pour from his face as he listens.

'Fuck,' he exclaims, most unlike him, and turns to look at Margaret in astonishment.

At last. The relief is extraordinary, calm spreading through her like the drugs she hasn't done for many, many years, washing through her veins. They have found the body. Thank God.

Johnnie closes his eyes and exhales deeply, phone still clamped to his ear. The only other sound is the rhythmic tick tock, tick tock of her father's carved clock and then the mechanism whirring in preparation. She is the only person in the room not to jump as the hour strikes, the tiny door snaps open and the cuckoo darts out.

'You're quite sure?' Johnnie glares at the wooden bird as it begins to call out the time, before spinning on the spot and marching from the room.

Margaret almost laughs. Silly boy. She opens her eyes. Snap! The cuckoo disappears back into his house, and she waits beatifically for Johnnie-come-lately to return and tell her what she already knows.

'I think I should like a cup of tea.' She turns to the girl. 'Now that we're not in a rush after all. Perhaps I do feel a little giddy.'

The girl opens her mouth to reply, but Johnnie is back and he stares right at Margaret. 'I've just been informed that Jude has been arrested and is requesting our legal representation.'

Margaret swallows her surprise but says nothing. 'Arrested?' she picks her words carefully. 'What for?'

'On suspicion of murder.'

The gasp of shock that escapes Margaret is real. 'Murder? Don't be ridiculous! Jude would never... it wasn't—' She stops herself just in time but she sees that, of course, Johnnie has noticed.

It wasn't what, Margaret?

Jude's a witness, not a suspect! Her ankle begins to throb. She wants very badly to sit down, but refuses to let her features betray her as she looks around for her stick which is propped against the sofa.

Murder. Oh, you bastard. You utter bastard. Even *dead* the final shots keep coming.

'Who has Jude allegedly murdered?' she asks quickly because, of course, she is not supposed to know anything about Jude's whereabouts last night.

Johnnie's eyebrows flicker and he crosses his arms and leans on the door frame. Running his tongue thoughtfully over his top lip, he makes a single, slow 'pop' noise with his mouth. 'Do you know what the chances are of a complainant dying from natural causes the night before a criminal trial begins?'

Margaret gasps again. She hopes it doesn't sound as theatrical as it feels. 'No! *That's* who has died?'

Johnnie nods – then waits.

Margaret's mind scrambles. 'The chances are small, I should think. But not impossible. Surely it was suicide?'

'What makes you say that?' His voice is sharp.

Margaret's blood cools a little. She does not like his tone. It calms her. She is still the client and he would do well to remember that. 'Well, it's one thing to tell lies about someone. It's quite another to swear it's the truth in a court of law. Perhaps it seemed the only way out – at the last minute – of the very unpleasant hole he'd dug himself.'

Johnnie frowns and looks at the floor. 'Well, he bled to death,' he says quietly. 'Jude was the last person to see him alive, and Jude was also next to the body – quite literally red-handed – when the police arrived.'

Margaret's breath begins to quicken. 'I really would like that tea.'

'Margaret,' the girl's voice is steady. 'Is there anything we should know?'

'Yes. I don't take sugar and I prefer it weak.'

She staggers over to her stick and grabs at it, sitting heavily in her sewing chair. Johnnie and the girl exchange a glance that needles Margaret and makes her feel very bad-tempered indeed.

'I have no more an idea of what happened last night than you do!' she shouts, thumping her stick down into the floor. 'For God's sake, can you not give me a moment to absorb what you've just told me? My child has been arrested for murder! Have you no compassion?'

'I'm afraid you'll have to absorb it in the car. We need to leave now.'

Her throat is husk dry. 'But I don't understand. You just said... I mean, how can my trial possibly go ahead if—'

'Your accuser is dead?' Johnnie finishes, his face impassive. 'There are provisions for a witness's statement to be read in court in the event of their unavailability. It's likely – although not a given – that Jude's arrest will lead to the trial being suspended, because the police are going to want to establish *you* didn't have anything to do with the death, so they'll send the jury home for now, I should think; but you still have to turn up and appear in front of the judge formally then hang around while they consider their options. Come on. Time to go.'

Margaret stares at Johnnie, stricken, her scrubbed-clean nails digging into the arms of the chair. No, no! This was not supposed to happen! She will not step through the Highcombe gates.

She will not give strangers, who understand nothing about what it *really* means to live a life like hers, the opportunity to shout abuse at her on the court steps as she gets out of the car; cameramen will *not* film her, and members of the gutter press will *not* call out their disgusting questions...

She will not allow them to beam her into the homes of the whole country for the cheap sport of jeering at the dirty old posh bird getting her comeuppance... while those who know her shake their heads as they watch her enter the court on their TV screens and exhale heavily. *'Ghastly business. My God it's aged her.'*

'His death would have needed to happen at least a week ago to be certain of an adjournment that would avoid a court appearance entirely,' Johnnie explains, still watching her care-fully. 'What was Jude doing in Shand's flat at midnight, Margaret? I wasn't even aware they knew each other. Were you?'

Margaret ignores him. 'I will not go.'

'You have no choice and, on the way, you can tell Daisy' – he nods at the girl – 'everything I need to know about last night, so that she can pass it on to me.'

'You're not even coming with us?' Margaret is outraged.

Johnnie shakes his head. 'I'm going to Jude.'

Margaret stands up with a wobble, leaning all of her body

weight on her stick. She looks at the antique rug; thin and unforgiving for older bones that are as brittle as dry spaghetti. They must have a duty of care to have her medically assessed in the event of her injuring herself? She steps forward, deliberately lets the stick catch the edge of the rug and comes crashing to the floor.

The pain is worth it as they set about calling an ambulance, to take her to hospital and *not* court.

TWELVE

Johnnie stands up in the small consultation room at the station as the door opens and Jude is escorted inside, dressed in a large sweatshirt and baggy joggers. There obviously wasn't much of a selection in the police cupboard and they were deemed close enough, size wise. She looks lost in them.

'Hello.' He tries a smile and pulls out a chair.

'I'm so sorry!' she whispers, her eyes filling with tears as she puts a hand on her head and rubs it in confusion, like she's bumped it and doesn't remember how. 'You should be with Mum in court. How's she coping?'

'She's doing OK.' Johnnie decides now is not the time to mention Margaret's 'fall'. 'You don't need to worry, she's with one of my very capable colleagues.' They both sit down and wait for the officer to leave. 'They will almost certainly suspend her trial in light of last night's events. She'll be fine.'

Once they're alone, he turns to face her over the table. 'Are *you* OK?'

'Um.' She gives a frightened little laugh and wipes her eye with her sleeve. 'I'm holding on, if that's what you mean by OK. Does Mum know? That I'm here, and why?'

'Yes. She was shocked, of course, but she took it in her stride.' That's all he can tell Jude because the truth is, Margaret didn't ask if Jude was all right, or even if she was injured. Instead, he opens his file. It seems the only thing to do. 'I'm sorry it's taken me this long to arrive. The traffic from High-combe wasn't kind, but we'll get started.' He picks up his pen.

'Are you all right?' she says suddenly. 'You're being very... impersonal? If that's the right word?'

He looks up immediately. He wants to say it. He wants to ask: '*Richard Shand*? You've been having a relationship with *him*?'

'Sorry,' he says instead. 'I don't mean to be. It's just the professional process. Certain things we have to do and say.' He clears his throat. 'A reminder of how this bit works, which you may or may not remember from your mother's arrest; the police make disclosures. That means they share the evidence they have with us and ask you questions about it. At this stage they don't have to tell us everything, so if they don't mention something, don't assume it's slipped under the radar.' Johnnie starts to find welcome direction in the words he's spoken numerous times before. 'I will then give you my recommendations about the strength of the evidence against you, but ultimately I act on your instructions. I can't and won't force you to do or say anything you don't want to.' He looks at Jude. 'Make sense so far?'

She nods. 'Yes. Johnnie, are you angry with me?'

He swallows. 'Have they provided you with the medication you asked for, by the way? I believe you requested the morning-after pill from the custody officer?' He looks up and holds her gaze as she flushes scarlet. He immediately regrets such a cheap shot. 'I should say that, although I'm representing your mother in her case and everyone would expect me to represent you both as it's so intertwined, if you don't want me, that is, of course, not a problem. I would understand completely.'

She sits forward urgently, suddenly animated. 'Of course I want it to be you!'

He looks at her hands, gripping her knees. There are remnants of dirt under the short nails as if she's been digging in a garden, but he knows it's dried blood. Her legs are starting to jiggle. Shock. She also looks utterly exhausted. She must have been up for hours by now.

'I'm sorry. I thought I should at least offer but... OK, look, let's start with the irrefutable bits.' He pulls himself together. 'A knife was recovered from next to Shand's body – which they have your prints on. Your dress was heavily bloodstained – no results back from that yet, but I don't think we doubt it's going to be Shand's blood, do we?'

Jude shakes her head silently, but holds his gaze.

'Shand sustained multiple stab wounds to his neck, throat and chest and a slash across his fingers.'

Jude says nothing as Johnnie continues. 'They have a witness who saw you leave the building at around ten past midnight, then return a few minutes later.'

'The night porter?' Jude interrupts. 'He didn't even look at me. He was too busy on his phone. I could have been anyone.'

'OK, well, they have security CCTV in the lobby that shows you holding a mobile phone when you're leaving, but nothing when you come back. There was also no mobile phone found in your belongings.'

Jude looks away.

'The 999 call was logged at nineteen minutes past midnight, but from Shand's number.'

'Can we call him Richard, please?' Jude shifts uncomfortably on her chair.

Johnnie glances briefly at her. 'Of course. You told the call handler that Richard severed the main artery and vein in his neck and you couldn't see any signs of life. You gave the address, but not your name and you hung up. The police have also disclosed two photographs found in Richard's flat. One is of you and me when we were younger, with your mother in the background – it's a regular-sized, domestic snap. The other is a larger image that looks more like something a paparazzo might take, in which you are kissing Richard Shand.'

He looks up. 'So, in bald terms, from the police point of view, they've got a violent stabbing, your prints on the knife, Shand's blood on your dress. You were having a relationship with Shand, who was also the main complainant in a trial due to start tomorrow in which your mother is the defendant. You didn't call 999 immediately and you only did it after you'd left the building with your mobile phone and returned without it. That's very obviously why they arrested you at the scene.'

'You *are* angry with me, aren't you?'

He hesitates. 'You and I found a photograph of Shand in the freezer and you asked if I was sure it was him, like you had no idea.'

She's right. He *is* angry and he can't do his best for her if his own feelings are going to influence his response to what she's telling him. He stands and snatches his file up. 'Jude, I'm sorry. We're going to have to get someone else to do this. I'm not—'

'No!' she exclaims so fiercely that he steps back in surprise. 'You and Timothy are the only people in the world who *know* I would never kill someone. I love Tim but he'd make an awful solicitor.' She tries to smile. 'I need you to help me!' She looks right at him, her eyes filling with tears. 'Please!' He can hear desperation in her voice. 'You said in the car that time you'd always sort everything out for me. I'm sorry that I didn't tell you about my dating Richard, but I genuinely didn't know the person in that photograph to be Richard Shand at that point. It's more complicated than it seems.'

'These things usually are.' He stays on his feet. 'But I'll tell you what else makes absolutely no sense to me at all...' He puts his file back down. 'You're a nurse... an A&E nurse... who sees someone stab himself violently in front of her. Surely the very first thing anyone does in that instance, but especially if you're a health care professional, is call for help?' He looks at her. 'Why didn't you immediately call 999?' He sits back down. 'What can you tell me about what *really* happened next?'

* * *

As the shock kicked in, I couldn't look at the knife lying on the floor by the stool. I fixed my gaze on the night skyline instead, something to orientate myself to, as I tried to process what had just happened.

The familiar smell of rust caught at the back of my throat, but in his space, rather than the hospital, it was all wrong and, jumping up, I staggered over to one of the balcony windows. Tugging the heavy handle, I hauled it open, but was too afraid to step out and when I glanced back into the room behind me, his gently cupped, bloodied hand was on the floor, poking out beyond the kitchen island, palm open and up to the sky like a tacky cast ashtray. Except those lifeless fingers were real. They would still be warm.

I tried to swallow; my breath was coming in fits and starts as I searched desperately around for my phone. An ambulance. I started to dial... I needed to ask for an ambulance, but they'd send the police too, of course they would. I was going to have to explain why I was here, that we'd had sex. *Everyone* was going to know... Mum was going to be— *Mum!*

I stopped and I thought about the messages on my phone from my mother. How they might now appear.

Has he agreed to drop it? You explained what would happen if he didn't? Make him disappear.

Oh shit. SHIT. I dialled her immediately in a panic... but her phone was still off. It went straight to voicemail.

My teeth started to chatter as I redialled. My whole body was beginning to jerk as if I was being controlled by some invisible strings, making me move to a beat that was growing louder and louder in my head. Shock. That was all. My brain trying to process what had just happened. A normal reaction. Calm down. I pictured Mum in the dark cottage bedroom, fast asleep, stick by the chair, window wide open as always, regardless of the time of year. It was so quiet the Highcombe owls occasionally piercing the stillness could be enough to jolt someone from sleep, or that horrible bark the foxes made, like children screaming, so why wasn't she picking up? Drunk to the point that she'd passed out? Not now, Mum. NOT NOW! I dialled again – three calls back-to-back. Our code for emergency.

As I waited for her response, I reached through the window to grab the small tin from the table. Retrieving the half-joint, I lit up and inhaled deeply, making the end glow violently as a small piece of black ash floated up into the air.

Staring at the moon, I tried very, very hard to stay in control and give Mum a moment to call back. She would call... I forced myself to think of something else as a distraction. Something – anything. Maybe it was the gear, being so frightened and thinking about her, but I suddenly vividly remembered Mum catching me, Johnnie and Tim lying flat on our fifteen-year-old backs smoking by the Great Pond at dusk, watching the returning swifts dip and dive through the sky, great clouds of sweet-smelling grass in the air around us, Tim giggling uncontrollably and Mum swaying slightly, poured into a tight black and white evening dress as she stood over us and immediately noted the soggy joint floating sadly on the surface of the water among the lilies, where we'd flicked it over our heads at the sound of her approaching footsteps. Nothing got past her, even slightly pissed.

'It's supper time,' she'd drawled. 'Everyone has been calling and calling you. Didn't you hear?' Her admonishment was slightly ruined by an impromptu hiccup and small burp which made Tim start to wheeze and rasp with laughter up his sleeve like Muttley. A brief smile broke across Mum's face before it was replaced with a stern: 'Clearly not. At least you'll all eat like horses I suppose. Come on, get up. That ground will be soggy by now, you'll all have damp bottoms.'

Tim snorted again but Mum just rolled her eyes.

'Timothy, your mother will be furious with me if she realises what you've been encouraged to get up to here. I'll get the blame for sabotaging your father's birthday, then your *father* will get all little brother sulky with me for upsetting your darling ma, and everything will turn into a bloody mess – so you jolly well get up now and come back before she gets a whiff of what's going on. You'll have to *run* to the house to clear the smell from your hair and clothes.' She clapped and hiccupped again. 'Chop, chop! What are you waiting for?'

Johnnie and Tim obediently set off down towards High-combe. Johnnie was already a renowned cross-country champion so powered off ahead, but Tim, a little podgy, wove a breathless and unusually wide arc behind him through the long grass. It was a bit like watching Johnnie attempting to get a piglet-shaped balloon airborne only for the balloon to drift off in a different direction altogether. Tim suddenly lost puff and collapsed out of sight in the grass as if his string had escaped from Johnnie's grasp. Johnnie, not noticing, carried on. Mum had laughed and, for once, slipped her arm around my shoulders – the last time I ever saw her that relaxed.

I pulled on the spliff again, wincing as it was so strong, and stared at the blank screen in my hands. Please ring... please, please ring.

That was the same night Johnnie had kissed me and I'd left the next morning... so Richard would have arrived at Highcombe only hours later, according to him. If I'd only stayed and not gone off to my friend's house, met him myself... would none of *this* have happened? I glanced over my shoulder back into the flat and almost passed out to see that the pool of blood was spreading on the floor. I whimpered aloud, making silent deals with God about what I would do, if he'd just make Mum ring me...

With fumbling fingers I sent a text.

Where are you? Please call!

I need you. He's dead!

He's dead. I thought about walking into the hospital morgue, where I'd formally identified Dom, and glanced over my shoulder again at the unmoving hand. I waited in the quiet for what felt like an eternity, even though I knew it was probably only seconds; but very suddenly I *felt* the temperature drop – there was a moment of pause and finally the rain arrived; big, fat drops gathering pace as the weather turned. I took another deep drag... and finally my mind began to calm. As I stubbed out the remainder of the joint, I felt as if I was stepping out of my body and getting much-needed clarity on the situation. It all became obvious in an instant. I couldn't call 999 yet because I had to get rid of my phone. I had to protect Mum from what appeared to be a plan to hurt Richard.

Not looking at the body, I moved past the kitchen island and out into the hall. Shoving my feet into my trainers, I put the door carefully on the latch before slipping out into the communal hallway. It was deserted and the quiet, long corridor felt claustrophobic, like it was narrowing in on me. I put my head down and hurried to the lift but as the doors closed I looked up at my reflection and my mouth fell open in horror. I had blood splatters all over my face and hair, on my clothes.

Well, if anyone saw me, I was just going to have to keep moving. I just needed to get the phone in the water. I was certain of that. I swayed slightly as the lift moved, then realised it was me. I hadn't actually pressed down. I corrected that oversight and returned to the task in hand, messaging Mum.

> This is bad really bad. You need to get rid of your phone or they are going to think we had something to with this because really we did. Suicide stabbing is really rare. Tell them you didn't know I was meeting R. I will be OK.

I hit send once the doors pinged open and rounded the corner sharply, looking down. I had to make it past the night porter behind his desk. He didn't even lift his head though, just his hand in acknowledgement, transfixed by something on his phone.

I pushed out of Casson Square into Southbank Place and the heavy summer rain. At first it was a huge relief, cleansing me. I lifted my face and let it wash me blessedly clean for a second or two, but then I looked around and began to panic because I was starting to feel sick. My head was pounding as I fixed my sights on the water and made my way up to the edge. The Thames was churning and glittering with reflected lights as I neared it. Up close it was violent with powerful currents and freezing waters... it felt malevolent and I immediately wanted to get away from it whispering at me. How I hated it! I drew my phone out of my pocket and tried Mum again but still fucking... nothing! I flung the phone away from me with all of my might.

It didn't make a sound as it arced through the rain and slipped beneath the water, but the second it had vanished, my wet skin turned cold.

But wait, I'd meant to do that anyway, hadn't I? It was the *right* thing to do. Get rid of the messages. Look after Mum. She warned me. She warned me about him and now look! I exhaled in confusion. The right thing to do. I stared up at Richard's building and the hundreds and hundreds of windows. Behind each one a story. *Richard* was behind one of them. I was going to have to go back. I needed to do the *right* thing and call for an ambulance. How long had I been down here already? I frowned, not sure. My head was all over the place. I made my way back towards the doors. The night porter saw me coming from a distance, buzzing the door open before I had to do anything.

'Thank you.' I pushed into the cool of the air-conditioned space, shivering like mad.

'No problem, coming back for an umbrella, hey?' His eyes were fixed down on his phone again. 'You got caught out!'

I glanced at him, horrified. How the fuck did he know? But he still wasn't looking at me, and I realised my mistake and that his world was about to be overrun with police, paramedics, forensics, concerned residents, press, and he seemed like a nice man... I felt so bad for him as I tucked right back into the corner of the lift but risked a glance at myself; my face and hair were soaked, less blood though. I closed my eyes as the doors shut again. I didn't want to go back up there, but I needed to call for help now that I'd taken care of the other stuff.

I padded back down the corridor and paused outside the front door, open an inch or two. That *was* how I'd left it? For a second I imagined the hand turning over in the silence of the apartment once I'd gone, pushing down onto the floor; Richard heaving himself up to sitting. I saw myself swinging the door open and a horrific drag of blood across the floor leaping out at me, but no body.

Squeezing my fists, feeling my nails digging into my palms until they hurt, I psyched myself to go in. That would not have happened. Nothing would have changed and I had to go back in. I *had* to.

I slipped off my shoes and pushed the door shut behind me. Tiptoeing back into the open-plan space, my hair dripping, I saw it immediately... because of course the body was still there. Of course nothing had moved. The only difference was the dark puddle of blood now opening out like a lake, mostly from the biggest wound on the neck. I still couldn't look at the knife, but I moved over to the kitchen, reached for Richard's mobile on the side and, as I told the 999 handler I needed an ambulance, I began to switch into professional mode; I felt it start to take over. One of the knife wounds had severed the main artery and vein and there were no signs of life. It was actually much easier to cope with everything like that, and I managed to give the address too before I hung up, because there was nothing more to say.

It occurred to me then that these were the last moments of peace Richard would have before they came for him. His body was no longer his own and that made me feel desperately sad, so I returned to take his hand in mine. I lay down next to him and closed my eyes as I reached out, because I was frightened. When I felt his skin I jumped and not just because it was already cooler to the touch. I forced myself to hold on quietly regardless and we waited together.

'I am so sorry,' I found myself whispering. 'I hope you didn't feel any pain.'

* * *

'Jude?' Johnnie tries again, as she doesn't seem to have heard him. 'Can you tell me exactly what happened after you realised Richard had died?'

She rubs her face and lifts her gaze to meet his. 'So this is what I can tell you... After what I saw him do to himself, I was completely overwhelmed and I had to get out of the flat. It was an instinctive thing. I just ran. I went downstairs and it was raining. It was actually a relief... I was covered in his blood and I wanted it off me. I walked to the riverside and I felt so... freaked out I guess... that I tried to call Mum. She didn't answer and I threw my phone in the water.' Jude doesn't look away as Johnnie feels himself staring at her in open disbelief. 'I realised what I'd done and immediately went back up, phoned the police from Richard's mobile and waited with Richard until the police arrived.'

Johnnie rubs his face. 'Right, so even if you hadn't just caveated that statement with "this is what I can tell you", I wouldn't have believed what you just said in any case, and neither will the police when they interview you in a minute. I can hear them now just repeating it over and over: "but you're a nurse".'

'So? I don't understand?' She seems confused. 'Harold Shipman was a doctor?'

Johnnie's eyes widen in alarm. 'Do *not* say that in there.'

'Sorry, I'm sorry! My point is... I'm just human. And if it's jobs that matter, what about the fact that Richard was a former soldier who had seen active duty? He knew what he was doing and how to do it.'

'But getting help would have been second nature to you – instinctive.'

Jude closes her eyes and shrugs helplessly. 'That's what I'm saying. You don't know how you'll react in a situation like that until it actually happens. You can't control that first reaction. And when you say: "getting help"' – she looks at Johnnie tremulously – 'to be completely clear, there was nothing anyone could have done to save him. It wouldn't have made any difference if I'd called for help immediately. He was beyond help.' She shifts in her chair. 'What is the "normal" response to something like that anyway?'

She waits for Johnnie to answer and, when he doesn't, she continues, 'I needed to get away from what I was looking at; it was too much to process. I wanted to speak to Mum and I can tell you that's really not unusual.' Her eyes flood with tears again. 'When people are hurt, or frightened, no matter what age they are, they call out for their mothers. I've heard little kids do it, I've heard people in their eighties do it – because mothers are supposed to make us feel safe.' She stops abruptly, wiping the tears with her sweatshirt sleeves.

Johnnie passes her a tissue.

'Take a break for a second,' he says. 'Gather your thoughts.'

'They *are* gathered,' she insists. 'Since Mum's arrest I've been there constantly for her, and I don't begrudge that, but it's been relentless. Calls at all times of day and night, so when she didn't pick up the *one* time I needed her, the whole stress of everything got the better of me. I flung the phone away. That's all.'

'The trouble is,' Johnnie persists more gently, 'it's going to look to the police like you had something on that phone you wanted to hide so badly, you dealt with it before calling 999. So they're going to ask you what it was. Instructions? Details of a plan? Confessions?'

'There was no plan, no confession.' She hesitates, bites her lip, looks up and holds his gaze. 'You know how sometimes you say something like "I wish the day would just end and get dark already"? and it does, but it would have done that anyway, even if you hadn't said anything?' She waits.

'Right, I see,' Johnnie says slowly. 'So you or Margaret have messaged something like "I wish he'd just die", and you don't want the police to be swayed by that?' He leans forward. 'Does Margaret still have her handset?'

'I don't know,' Jude admits but then she pauses and sits up a little straighter. 'Can't I just say "no comment" to everything, like they do on TV?'

Johnnie shakes his head. '*It may harm your defence if you do not mention when questioned something that you later rely on in court.* Your defence is that Shand – sorry, Richard – did this to himself. You're going to need to tell them that because – and this is going to sound blunt – plenty of people would happily prosecute you on this evidence.'

Her eyes widen but she doesn't respond.

'I still can't believe that you were...' Johnnie starts to blurt but manages to catch himself. 'I mean, Richard Shand? You had genuine feelings for him?'

'Yes,' says Jude. She refuses to look at him. 'I had genuine feelings for him.'

'He made some really shocking allegations against your mother,' Johnnie says. 'So how does that work? You'd have to believe *he* was telling the truth and your mother was lying?'

'I did, but—' Jude stops suddenly and shakes her head.

'But what?' Johnnie says.

Jude takes a deep breath and looks him straight in the eye. 'We got into a discussion about the photographs the police have shown you. Mostly the one of me and him kissing. Although I am actually kissing him goodbye in it, ironically. We both got upset but Richard was *really* upset.'

'What were you upset about?'

'I thought he'd used me to get back at Mum... but I didn't hurt or plan to hurt him, I swear! It just... might not appear that way.'

'Did you tell your mother to get rid of her phone?' Johnnie asks.

This time Jude doesn't lower her gaze. 'No comment.'

THIRTEEN

'So you've lost your handset?' Johnnie sits back and looks at Margaret. 'That's what you're saying?'

Her dark eyes move round the room like a crow's, the sharp gaze alighting on the scant items of functional furniture and then on him. 'This place isn't a patch on the Reading station. It smells disgusting in here and it's hotter than Hades. Can they at least open a window?'

Johnnie mentally counts to five as she ignores his question. 'I am very grateful to you both for coming straight here from the hospital.' He nods his thanks at Daisy, who smiles at him tiredly.

'Which was also pointless.' Margaret interjects. 'They didn't so much as X-ray me. This country is going to the dogs.'

'Well, even so. It's much appreciated—'

'Really, why?' Margaret rubs the top of her stick restlessly. 'As I imagine you're going to "no comment" me anyway?'

You bet your bloody life I am. Johnnie forces a smile. 'You know how this works now, Margaret. You've no doubt got quite a lot of pain relief on board. You might – through no fault of your own – misunderstand a question or give an answer that may be impaired or inaccurate, without meaning to. The investigating officer, DS Grade, is a pretty strong woman...'

Margaret rolls her eyes. 'When men say "strong" they mean difficult. At least be honest about it.'

'All right then, I will. She's tricky. She'll be provocative and deliberately try to goad you, get under your skin.'

Margaret snorts. 'You never met my mother, did you? Come on, let's get this over with.' She goes to stand and looks down at herself. 'Christ, I look like I'm about to host a garden party.'

She twists her good foot in what appears to him to be a perfectly reasonable beige shoe.

'Sorry, I'm not quite done yet. I still need you to tell *me* if you have that phone?'

Margaret waves a hand in irritation. 'I'm tired and now we know for certain that my trial has been suspended, I just want to go home. This whole thing is ridiculous and becoming more farcical by the second. Of course Jude didn't murder him! Have they actually met Jude? She couldn't say boo to a goose.'

Johnnie stays silent. How incredible to make your daughter's inability to hurt someone seem a failing in some way, but it is at least a genuine reaction, he's sure of it. It doesn't suggest a joint premeditated plan to kill Shand.

'I really am sorry to be a bore about this handset, Margaret.' Why does being in her presence make him feel the need to talk like he's head boy of a minor public school? He imagines, just for a minute, speaking to one of his section 18 GBH defendants in the same way, and nearly chokes on the water he's reached for. 'But the thing is, the police were banging on about this phone business in Jude's interview earlier. They're now convinced there is something deeply incriminating on your mobile. I'm equally convinced that whatever it is probably isn't anywhere near as bad as Jude thinks it is, and it's just her panicking and trying to protect you, because she loves you so much and would do anything to support and look after you.'

THE NIGHT SHE LIED 151

He waits for a reaction to that, but Margaret simply looks at him with bland disinterest. She seems utterly unmoved by the horrors that her daughter must have witnessed last night. While Margaret has always possessed the ability to be cold and aloof, he would never have had her down as psychopathic. You think you know someone... Perhaps she's got more in common with some of his organised, violent clients after all.

'The trouble is,' he tries again, 'it's going to wind up being a really serious stumbling block for her, I think. So do you still have it?'

'It's at home somewhere, I imagine.' Margaret is starting to lose her patience. 'I don't recall. I fell over and its whereabouts wasn't at the top of my priority list. Unless one of you picked it up? Is this your way of telling me it's been left at the hospital by mistake?'

Johnnie looks at Daisy worriedly. That can't have happened, can it?

'I didn't pick it up and I didn't take it to the hospital either,' Daisy confirms, unruffled.

'Well then I have no clue where it is. Can we please now get this over with?' Margaret bursts. 'I really must go home. I'm in a lot of pain.'

'I know, Margaret, but before we go in, I also need to talk to you about the nature of Jude and Shand's relationship—'

'Er, no, you certainly don't!' She retorts. 'Jude told me everything on Friday, after that photographer popped up like a jack in the box... I mean, what can one say? Her sheer stupidity is breathtaking, but,' she shrugs, 'what's done is done. Anyway... no comment, no comment, *no comment.*'

He is astonished. That's a totally unexpected reaction. 'You don't think that perhaps...'

'I don't want to think about it at all, thank you!' She exclaims. 'How did Jude get on in the first interview?'

'Fine. It was the preliminary stuff. You know.'

'The bare bones,' Margaret says. 'Yes, I do know. Well, as they start digging deeper don't let her talk too much. She prattles when she's nervous. She'll say something stupid that they'll read too much into. Have they given her some rest yet? Because it's not fair to question her in more depth now; it's the middle of the night to her. I assume you've explained that to the strong, difficult woman? Or shall I... and can we please now *get on with this*?'

'Yes! I'm sorry.' He turns to Daisy. 'Would you—'

'No,' Margaret interjects. 'Not her. You're coming with me. It's simply not possible to take anyone called Daisy seriously in a legal sense. Dear God, it really is unbearably hot in here! It's got to be some sort of human rights violation.'

Johnnie forces himself to bite his tongue. She doesn't need to belittle someone so personally unconnected to her openly and with no provocation whatsoever. Since receiving the news about Richard Shand's death, she seems to be becoming more strident by the second. This is more akin to the Margaret he recognises from his youth; single-minded and indefatigable... except, as the shell of older age and longstanding pain has tightened and shrunk around those qualities, they've malformed into irascibility – and apparently, sheer unchecked rudeness. But he needs her on side and Daisy places a brief hand on his arm to remind him as much.

They have already spoken privately about Margaret's double standards: determined to hold her own, yet completely dismissive of the opinion of other women around her, only seeming to take men seriously. They concluded that it must be a generational thing, but Johnnie is beginning to think it might just be a Margaret thing. He also knows that Daisy is not offended by Margaret's comments, but that's not the point.

'Come on then.' He stands up reluctantly. 'But please remember, no deviation from "no comment" whatsoever. Regardless of what they ask you.'

Margaret lifts her gaze and it settles dangerously on him. 'I heard you the first time, Master Saunders.'

* * *

'I am unable to tell you the exact whereabouts of my mobile phone, Meera, because I simply don't know where it is.' Margaret repeats slowly to DS Grade as if she is hard of hearing.

Johnnie tries to keep his breathing even and calm. So much for 'no comment' but, thus far, with the exception of deliberately using DS Grade's first name and being overall very patronising, Margaret has not said or done anything too offensive or damaging.

Her temper is only now beginning to fray as DS Grade is doggedly hanging onto the lost mobile, as Johnnie knew they would.

'It was a small, cheap, pay-as-you-go phone which *you* seem to think is a mark of subversive behaviour on my part. Quite the opposite. It was to protect *my* right to privacy,' Margaret snaps. 'I was married to a newspaper editor for many years, I know exactly what tricks the lower end of the industry uses. They don't call them hacks for nothing.' Margaret pushes herself to a stand. 'Hence the type of disposable phone that I have used for years, and I really could care less that I've lost. I'll just get another one. I don't sit around on a phone looking at other people's opinions that are of no interest whatsoever. I use it to make telephone calls and that's it. I want to go home now. I'm in a great deal of discomfort.'

'That's no problem.' DS Grade stands up too. 'Thank you for your time, Lady Fawkes.' She smiles politely. 'We can pick this up again when you're feeling better.'

Margaret ignores that, already making for the exit.

Well, that could have been a lot worse, thinks Johnnie, standing up too, immediately wary. *Why* wasn't it worse?

'Please, let me,' says DS Grade, rushing to open the door for her.

'Aren't you kind? And what pretty little nails you have!' Margaret fires a final parting shot to assert her dominance.

'Thank you, Lady Fawkes. My mother thinks I should have them shorter for work. More professional. Yet this also coming from the woman who pierced my ears when I was a baby. Go figure, right? I wasn't even allowed a boyfriend until I was eighteen.'

'Well, mothers usually have their reasons,' Margaret responds absently.

'You know I think you're remarkable.' DS Grade shakes her head with apparent admiration. 'If I'd told my mum I was in a relationship with the man who accused her publicly of a sex crime, she'd disown me completely!' DS Grade carefully places the image of Jude kissing Richard down on the table.

Margaret glances briefly at it then double-takes, moving closer to get a better look at the image.

It is such an obvious tactic – wait until they think it's over and their guard is down – but effective when used by someone experienced and good at their job and Johnnie, watching Margaret closely, can see something about this has hit home.

'I have shown Lady Fawkes a photograph of Jude Beauchamp kissing Richard Shand, taken yesterday, Sunday 22nd August—'

That's it! Thinks Johnnie as Margaret's eyebrows flicker. The fact that it was only yesterday. She didn't know that?

'—as verified by Jude Beauchamp,' DS Grade concludes. 'Lady Fawkes, would you like to sit back down? You look faint. Can I get you some water?'

Margaret picks up the photograph. Only her eyes move, taking in the park bench, the early morning light, the trees in full summery leaf... the kiss. Johnnie quickly looks at her fingers but her grip is loose and relaxed.

'I'm not surprised at Mr Shand, of course,' Margaret says eventually. 'He has a history of manipulating people, but I'm... astonished... that my daughter would fall for his... act.'

'You had no idea they were in love?'

Johnnie sucks in his breath. He wants Margaret out of here, now. There is something poisonous starting to swirl in the air. An energy building.

'Interview terminated.' Johnnie looks at DS Grade for confirmation, but she pretends not to hear him.

'Love?' Margaret repeats softly.

What do you want me to tell you, Margaret? That I loved him? Would that make it better or worse?

She sighs and lets the picture fall from her fingers. Johnnie watches her lift her gaze and let it settle on DS Grade. Her face is still and calm, but something sharp and dangerous is squatting just beneath the surface, as if her mouth might open in a snarl, her eyes narrow and with a movement that no one would see coming, she'd dart forward and tear teeth into the face of the other woman, biting and ripping at flesh and features. Johnnie steps back, unnerved by what he's sure he just witnessed in her expression, but just as quickly the threat seems to have slipped away.

'Jude has always had a complex relationship with men.' Margaret's voice is even, confident, the touch of a drawl to her cut-glass clarity. 'She puts them on a pedestal and becomes terribly sad when they let her down. It's probably my fault for sending her to an all-girls boarding school. You don't develop a balanced approach to the opposite sex. You don't develop healthy attachments full stop, but it's just what we all did.' She shrugs. 'We didn't question it. We were sent away to school too, except I had my brother, Anthony, whom I adored, as balance when I was at home. Jude, of course, was not so fortunate... it wasn't how it was supposed to be. The death of a sibling – any child – is something a family never recovers from.'

Johnnie looks at her, so astonished at the skill with which she has flipped the mirror that he doesn't tell Margaret to stop talking.

'Yes, in her earlier interview, Jude told us that you found the incident of your son's death very hard to recover from,' DS Grade says.

'Accident, not incident,' Margaret corrects. 'He fell from a horse and was trodden on. The wound became infected, he contracted sepsis and of *course* I found it hard to recover from. What an appallingly crass thing to say.'

'My apologies. I just meant it affected you to the extent that you changed your daughter's name from Rachel to Jude when she was five, cut her hair short and dressed her as a boy.'

Margaret sighs again. 'No, DS Grade, I did not do that, *Jude* did. We took advice from a leading child psychologist who told us that it was a normal reaction to the loss of her brother and to indulge it if we felt able, which we did. I was bereft when she didn't want to be my little girl any more, she didn't want hugs, she started furiously biting things – furniture, dolls, people – and she wanted to be called something completely different: "a boy's name". I suggested Jude, that's true, because it was a good compromise. Jude may recall events differently, but I can assure you, it was all her own doing. It stuck, so to avoid confusion when she went to school, we changed her name legally on her behalf. I now think we were rather ahead of our time, as it happens.' Margaret considers and regards DS Grace with a wide smile. 'You might also notice that Jude's hair is very short at the moment, also very much her own doing. I think it looks utterly repellent. But it's up to her. Nothing I can do.' She shrugs.

'Like her choice in men?' DS Grade persists. 'I mean,

Richard Shand, of all people? Do you think she did it deliberately to hurt you?'

Margaret exhales slowly. 'I'm saddened that she allowed herself to form such an unhealthy attachment to Richard Shand. I warned her what he was like and had I known she was romantically involved with him so *recently*' – she glances again at the images – 'I would have strongly discouraged her.'

She hesitates then adds: 'My daughter has been going through a very challenging time of it. Her partner Dominic died suddenly a year and a half ago. I introduced them.' She shrugs. 'I don't always get things right. I was with her the night it happened and she got the call. Anyway, since then she's relied on me a great deal; we speak every day. Her work is extraordinarily demanding, physically and mentally. It's my job to listen and I buy her little gifts; bags, clothes – that sort of thing – because she doesn't earn very much, her morale has needed a boost and it *is* the small things... the manicures, the haircuts' – she glances briefly at DS Grade as if suggesting she could do with one – 'that make a difference. It sounds trite but self-care is vital, it's what helps us bear periods of stress in our lives. And yes, maybe selfishly I'm making up for lost time now she *allows* me to buy her pretty things' – Margaret's eyes flash – 'but Jude has been very brave. I probably shouldn't say this because I don't want you to get the wrong idea, but she completed a private rehabilitation stay for cannabis addiction last year. She asked me to pay for it and I was very happy to do so. It took such courage for her to admit she had a dependency... so as you see, actually we do still share confidences, we are close, we support one another. She's also been experimenting with living nocturnally again in an attempt to overcome her debilitating sleep issues. She is a complex girl, I don't deny it, but I really am very proud of her!' Margaret's voice briefly chokes. 'So to hear that Shand exploited that vulnerability? Of course *that's* hard to bear. Oh Jude!' Margaret looks at the picture again and closes her eyes. 'What have you done?'

* * *

'What have *you* done?' Johnnie keeps his voice as low as he can while guiding Margaret back down the corridor. 'Sudden death of a former partner and *cannabis rehabilitation*? Since when?'

'No comment.' She refuses to look at him, just furiously jams her stick into the ground with each step.

'But Margaret, you weren't even asked about them – you volunteered the information!' He takes her arm, tries to make her stop and listen to him. 'Because the photograph made you angry? Did you not realise Jude was romantically involved with Shand right up to the point of his death?'

'No comment.' She shakes herself free.

'I understand how it must feel to discover the only person you trust has been keeping something like this from you, but you mustn't try to punish or hurt Jude back by telling the police that—'

'You understand nothing!' Margaret steps forward suddenly into his space.

He is much taller and stronger than her but it's such an oddly aggressive decision he instinctively moves away.

'He has deliberately taken *everything* from me... and to think she gave herself so willingly... to him of all people, him! It's *disgusting*.' She spits the word out with a curl of her lip. 'But nonetheless I protected her in there. I didn't punish her at all. You're a fool.' Margaret turns to walk off when DS Grade appears behind them.

'Sorry, Mr Saunders – just to confirm' – she smiles ingratiatingly – 'your colleague has been asking the custody officer again about Jude needing to have sleep during the day, because she's nocturnal, and I just wanted to assure you we are giving that every consideration we possibly can. She's also been checked over because she's vomited, but please rest assured that's a very normal reaction to the particular type of "emergency" medication she requested, and it's over three hours since she took it so all will be fine. She won't need to take it again. Nothing to worry about!' DS Grade places her hands either side of her tummy as if pregnant, while Margaret looks away, revolted.

'Do let me know if you have any other concerns though. We're here to help.' DS Grade's smile widens and, having left her deployed hand grenade gently rolling around at their feet, walks off down the corridor humming tunelessly under her breath.

'Do not let that little performance achieve what Grade hopes it will,' begs Johnnie in the god-awful silence that follows. 'I understand you're hurt and angry, but—'

Before he can finish, they both jump at a call of 'Mummy!' from the other end of the corridor.

Jude – being moved to another part of the station, standing frightened, cuffed and between two officers – has spied Margaret and is calling to her. There is unmistakable desperation and fear in her voice; the grown-up version of a child calling in the dark, in the middle of the night, to be rescued from a nightmare. 'I'm so sorry. You were right. I shouldn't have gone there alone.'

Johnnie watches as Margaret takes one step towards Jude, but then halts, scrunching her face up tightly as if she's in acute physical pain. She gasps aloud, then turns her back on her daughter and starts to walk away.

'Mum?' Jude calls out again, but Margaret keeps on going and does not look back.

FOURTEEN

'She's angry with me,' Jude repeats, her face tear-stained. 'That's why she didn't respond.'

Johnnie pretends to leaf through his notes. 'No. It's like I said; we've asked her not to speak to you, that's all. It's better that the police don't see any emotional interactions they could try and exploit.'

Jude wipes her eyes. 'But they seem all right, especially the female one. She reminds me of my boss Trina. No nonsense, says it like it is, but kind.'

'Kind? DS Grade?' Johnnie frowns. He hates to admit it, but Margaret might have a point about Jude being too trusting.

Detectives like DS Grade scare him. How women like her deal with what they are exposed to at work every day, only to go home and flip back into being partners, friends and *parents* takes a super-human strength he knows he doesn't have. The caseloads he deals with every day have unquestionably changed his perspective on the world, but... he glances at Jude while trying to recover his original train of thought... long before doing this for a job, he learnt that 'better to have loved and lost' is complete shit. Loving someone and losing them colours your world with a tint that you see through forever. The intensity might fade a little, but it's always there. He's nowhere near as robust and indefatigable as DS Grade, that's for sure.

'DS Grade is doing a job,' he reminds Jude. 'However nice she seems.'

'OK,' Jude accepts that without further question. 'Sorry.'

'It's fine, you don't need to apologise. There is something else they want to raise with you.'

He looks up to see Jude patiently waiting to hear what he has to say. She looks so tired now her skin is practically translu-cent. 'But it's getting late in the day and we've voiced concerns that you need to be given some time to sleep and rest. They agree, which probably also means they're waiting for a test result to come back for something and is why they're stalling. I think maybe tomorrow would be—'

He's interrupted by his phone ringing. 'Sorry – one second.' He picks up. 'Hi Mum. I'm really sorry but I can't talk, I'm still at work. It's OK... I've paid it for you, remember? So don't worry. Will do. Bye.'

'Is she OK?' Jude asks. The normal outside world reaching in to the small room is unsettling for both of them.

'She's fine.' Johnnie says, shifting uncomfortably. 'Well, she's not. Her memory is... anyway, look, that's for another day. But thank you. As I was saying, in the morning we'll—'

'No!' Jude pleads, shaking her head. 'I'd normally be waking up now anyway, so it's not a problem, let's get it all over with. What else do they want to ask me about?'

Johnnie takes a deep breath. 'It was something your mother brought up in her interview.'

* * *

'We recovered some illegal class B drugs from Mr Shand's property,' DC James is taking the lead this time. Johnnie can smell the aftershave heating up on the detective's body, he's excited. He must be portfolio building. 'Are we going to find your DNA on the partially smoked cannabis roll-up?'

'Yes,' Jude replies quietly.

'Were the drugs yours?'

'No. Richard was using it for pain management.' She reaches for her water.

'Was that the first time you'd smoked cannabis since completing your spell in rehab?'

DC James looks, thinks Johnnie, quietly triumphant, unable to prevent himself glancing at DS Grade like an enthusiastic spaniel that just brought a stick back to its master. Johnnie really hopes he wasn't this obvious when he was working his way up the ranks and trying to impress the senior partners.

Jude takes a sip then reaches a finger down and dips it into the water, breaking the surface tension. 'You've been talking to my mother.' She doesn't look up at them. 'The reason I know that is because I only told *her* I was going to a private treatment programme for cannabis addiction so that she would give me the money for it, partly because I was broke and also so I could have a break from her for three weeks. I *didn't* really go to rehab...'

No, no, no... Johnnie has a moment where all he can hear in his head is the now infamous song, and has to force himself to concentrate, while suppressing an exhausted yawn. It's late, he's been up since 5 a.m. They are all tired, they shouldn't be doing this now.

'I took a week off sick because I was grieving. My partner had died suddenly—'

'Yes, your mother confirmed she was with you that night,' DC James interrupts Jude impatiently. 'I'm talking about what happened *after* that, when you went into rehab?'

Jude stares at him. 'That's right,' she says after a moment's pause. 'Mum was with me that night and she was a great help when I subsequently miscarried, but I really wasn't coping. I tacked my sick leave onto two weeks' annual leave,' Jude continues, her voice trembling like the water surface she's dipping her finger in and out of, 'I caught a train to a friend's holiday cottage in the middle of nowhere for three weeks, undisturbed, and I watched movies, read books, walked, grieved and cried.' She puts the cup carefully back down on the table. 'That's why you won't find anything on my medical records, or see any payment going out of my account to any facility anywhere. I didn't go.'

'If it was private treatment, it wouldn't appear on your NHS medical records though, would it?' DC James has another throw. 'And you could have paid cash.'

'Your GP still has to provide referral information,' Jude points out. 'And I've never heard of any rehab that takes cash. It wouldn't be ethical. There would be a paper trail. There are no records because it didn't happen.'

DC James looks gutted, and Johnnie has to suppress a slight smirk, but DS Grade has had enough and takes the baton.

'If it's not one problem it's your mother, eh?' She smiles at Jude. 'Putting her foot in it! We asked her about changing your name when you were five and the boyish haircuts she gave you. It probably won't surprise you to learn she remembers things a little differently. She said it was your choice to do all of that.'

Jude shakes her head. 'If you're going to try and pit me against my mum – divide and rule – it won't work.'

'Look, you're not the first person to have a difficult relationship with their mother,' DS Grade soothes. 'I'd work nights to get away from mine calling all the time if I didn't have kids, it's an inspired idea!'

'I know you've told her about me and Richard,' Jude says suddenly. 'I could see it all over her face. I've had years and years of practice at interpreting my mother's moods. I expect you showed her the picture of us kissing and thought she'd be so angry with me she'd drop me in it? Except there's nothing to drop me in. There was no plan to hurt Richard. She wasn't involved.'

* * *

'So now they have "illegal class B drugs" too.' Jude looks at the ceiling of the small custody cell. 'With everything they've got, they're going to charge me, aren't they?'

'They won't do it tonight, but in the morning I think they will, yes.'

'What will happen then?' She looks at him anxiously.

'The Crown Prosecution Service will formally charge you with Richard's murder, but it's the police who hand you the charge sheet which will also give you the date of your first hearing. You'll be kept in custody because of the nature of the charge – that's normal, so please don't think that infers anything either way – and they'll transfer you out of here.'

'To prison?' Jude's voice is light with fear.

'Yes.'

'This is going to sound stupid, but I've never been in a real prison before. Is it like you see on TV?'

'Well, you'll go to the first night's unit for your induction, you'll be there for about a week, so it's not like TV in the sense that they don't just open a cell, put you in and expect you to work it all out for yourself, no.'

'Am I likely to get hurt?'

Johnnie hesitates. 'Self-harm is more of an issue in women's prisons than being attacked. These are people who don't have any control over what is happening to them, so self-harming is a way of reasserting that control. And given some of your former... issues...' he pauses, 'I'm going to need you to be kind to yourself, Jude. Please?' he begs, 'because drugs are widely available – a lot of the women come from backgrounds of extreme poverty, often violence. That also means they don't have much and there's a lot of theft, so you'll need to hang onto your stuff. It's very noisy, overwhelming, the food isn't great. I wouldn't ask people what they're in for, I wouldn't—'

'OK, thanks... Let's just – stop.' She swallows. 'How long am I likely to have to wait for my trial?'

'I would hope no more than a year,' Johnnie says. 'But there is a huge backlog of cases at the moment, even for the most serious ones.'

'A year,' she repeats to herself. 'He did this to *himself*!'

There is a sudden, random shout from outside the custody cell, and Jude jumps.

'I know how this is going to sound, but you need to try and rest,' Johnnie says. 'I know you're also going to say that you'd normally be awake now, but I need you to revert back to sleeping at night, for the time being at least. You are very plainly exhausted. I'll be back first thing,' he promises her.

'Wait. I need to tell you something,' she says suddenly. 'I *did* have a bit of an issue with smoking weed after Dom died, and it *was* getting out of hand, so I asked Mum for some money and I took myself off to my friend's cottage and I did a three-week rehab on myself. I haven't lied to the police – I didn't pay a facility – but Mum wasn't exactly wrong either. There's no way they can prove what I was doing in the cottage, and I did it for precisely this reason, I didn't want a paper trail. I'd be screwed work wise if they knew. I wouldn't be allowed to work again and I'm OK now. I really am.' She looks right at Johnnie.

'When you say "getting out of hand" are we talking hallucinations, paranoia?' He manages to keep his voice calm. 'Are you still smoking a lot?'

'No, no,' she says wearily. 'Nothing like that. It was a stress release thing but it mucked up my sleep and I was having a few mood swings. I stopped not long after Mum's arrest and I haven't smoked for ages now. Well, until I was with Richard this weekend. I just want to be straight with you about it, that's all... I smoked some of his gear while I was waiting for Mum to call me back just after he died. It was right there and...' She shrugs. 'I'm used to reaching for it when I'm *very* stressed out. My head was completely scrambled when I went down to the river. All I was thinking about was getting rid of the phone to protect Mum. I panicked, I threw it in the water. There!' She exhales. 'That's it. You know it all now.'

'Well, thanks, but I wish you'd told me earlier, and I'm still worried about your mum's phone,' Johnnie says. 'She didn't have to tell them about the drugs thing, but she did. What if—'

'She's really not going to hang me out to dry as punishment. She genuinely doesn't have anything to use against me, for a start. Like I said – the only thing they might have been able to read into were the messages on our phones, but Mum would have come off far worse than me, so there's no chance of her giving the phone to them. She shuts off her feelings completely when she needs to.'

'It's just I really hate having loose ends like this,' Johnnie explains. 'They make me uncomfortable. Could she not just "find" her mobile again because—'

'Johnnie,' Jude says. 'It's long gone. Trust me.'

FIFTEEN

Margaret sits on the deep windowsill holding the phone. It's such a huge relief to be home. After making a show of going to the stables, as she normally would, for the second day in a row, she has hurried back up to the attic to properly consider the situation.

Surrounded by various pieces of less significant furniture and oddities, breathing the reassuring odour of slightly damp and musty packing boxes, she cradles the mobile in her hands and thinks about Jude, picturing her lying on the thin, plastic, blue mattress in the custody cell which Margaret remembers only too well; crinkling and giving sad puffs of used air every time she turned over on it.

Jude won't have got any sleep.

Having that photograph of her daughter kissing Shand shoved under her nose by that ghastly, aggressive, cheap police-woman with such smugness was intolerable. The second time a picture of Shand has broken her heart – vile curse that he is. She reaches into the hole in the wall with one hand and draws out the photograph, studying it with equal contempt. Well this can finally be destroyed now that he's not coming back – she drops it carelessly on the sill beside her – burning will be best. But what to do with the phone?

She traces the shape of the buttons with her thumb. What would handing in this phone even achieve? Apart from serving herself up on a plate for the child who has lied to her.

Do you owe your offspring anything if they betray you so casually and heinously?

Sinking the handset in water is the obvious answer but – oh dear God! Margaret lurches with shock as a little envelope begins to flash on the screen. She seems somehow to have switched the bloody thing on! She hurriedly scrambles to turn it off again when she realises she simply has voicemail she has not listened to and the phone is letting her know.

'You have two new messages received Sunday, 22nd August 2022 at—'

It'll just be Jude telling her that she's woken up at home and she'll ring back later… when she was, in fact, with *him*. All of those desperate calls she made that Jude simply ignored because she was too busy f— Margaret's eyes snap open as she realises that is not all that has been left on her phone.

The shock of what she hears next, is like having her hands plunged into a bowl of water so hot that for a split second it feels icy cold. As it starts to burn – and she should snatch her hands away – she forces herself to grip the phone more tightly and listen. Her face pinks lividly, her breath quickens. When the torture finally stops, she hangs up feeling sick, shivery and giddy, quickly rubbing a circle in the grime on one of the thin panes of glass. A shaft of sunlight breaks through and she fixes her gaze on the reassuringly familiar sight of the Highcombe grounds as she gathers herself. Breathe, Margaret. Breathe.

She swallows, and in a flash sees her mother, of all people, advancing towards her clutching a wooden hairbrush; Margaret shrieking, her six-year-old skin tingling with powerless fear because the back of the brush is about to meet her bare buttocks with considerable force... being told to be quiet this instant or it really *will* hurt.

Margaret grips her fists tightly, silently. She knows how to absorb pain.

Oh you fucking, fucking abomination, Richard Shand!

She compels herself to look at the trees, breathe, but her gaze is distracted by the mummified, dangling remains of a woodlouse swinging into sharp focus as it twists within the binds of silk from a hiding spider. Margaret blows so hard it lifts and sticks to the bulk of the web rather than falling down into her lap.

She wipes a larger porthole with her finger. Watching the trees on the edge of the parkland blousing about in full leaf on the lively wind has always soothed her. She would like to be able to open the window and listen to their rustle and shimmer but it's welded shut with age and disuse. This is good, she is starting to calm. She MUST calm!

Despite the recent hot weather, the grounds are still lush and verdant rather than the displeasing dried-out tones that can accompany late summer. The hedges are fat and unkempt thanks to Annalise's ridiculous insistence that they ought not to be cut until September because birds might still be nesting, but otherwise the gardens themselves don't look too shabby.

Later on members of the public will be wandering about the place, but for now, she can pretend this is the Highcombe of yesteryear. It was such a relief to arrive back at home, Perdu crossly weaving around her legs, and today it is much cooler, the sort of August morning she remembers from numerous summer holidays as a child, when threatening, fast-moving skies would give way to rain. She and Anthony would be forced to sit inside watching droplets cascade down the glass while a sorry badminton net sagged; cat gut strings of discarded racquets lying in the grass would swell and grips begin to gummily peel away. The ground would be too slick to tack and the horses too

grumpy anyway... and yet there was something about that
particular weather, then and now, which Margaret finds deeply
comforting. Safety inside. Their parents would be abroad so
they would be allowed to run up and down the corridors breathless and laughing – a relaxed Nanny Harris turning a blind eye
– occasionally cannoning off one of the other staff when
rounding a corner too fast.

There, that's better. Much better. She feels contained again.
In control.

Margaret shifts her gaze to the parkland and the deep,
freshly dug trenches of disturbed earth alongside the partially
erected wooden skeleton which will form the *adventure playground*. The large flat pack barn alongside it will house the gift
shop and café. A blot on the landscape doesn't even come close.
She looks at the deep gouges in the earth... the perfect place to
conceal a phone... even a body. She swallows and wonders
where they will have taken him... if right now he is in a funeral
parlour somewhere or more likely, a hospital morgue because
they will have had to perform a post-mortem. She looks at the
photograph by her thigh and sighs at the thought of him laid
out, being lifelessly sliced and prodded ... but she *must* now
destroy the photograph. Immediately. The phone—

'Margaret? Is that you up there?'

She instinctively shoves both items behind her into the
corner of the window seat where the wall meets the glass,
before turning to face into the attic so that she is hiding everything with her body. When Timothy puffs up the steep stairs
into the space, she is looking back at him, composed.

'I thought I heard a scream? Are you all right?'

A scream? Did she? She blinks, momentarily thrown. 'I'm
fine. Aren't you supposed to be in South Africa!' she counters
with ungracious outrage.

He walks into the light. His pink face – either courtesy of
the Cape Town sun or the exertion of running to assist her –

clashes horribly with his orange and red checked shirt, unironed chinos and unbrushed hair. Every inch the rather eccentric lord he doesn't even want to be. Such an unattractive boy.

'I was,' he confirms. 'Annalise and the kids still are, but when Johnnie called to tell me about Jude, I flew straight home. I arrived very late last night.'

'Well Mrs Brooks might have mentioned that when she let me in!' Margaret flares again. 'I would have liked to have known.'

'Why, wouldn't you have come up here if you'd realised I was home?'

Margaret bristles at the use of 'home' and doesn't answer.

Timothy glances at the curiosities surrounding his aunt, wrinkling his nose at a dirty gilt cage containing a small bird on a perch. 'Ah – taxidermy. Every country house's interior decor accessory of choice. Might I ask you what you are doing up here, Aunt Margaret?' He tries to smile as he looks at her questioningly.

'It's an automaton,' Margaret corrects him, pushing her body more forcefully up against the glass, trying to squash the phone out of sight. 'You wind it up from underneath.'

Intrigued, Timothy does as he's told, placing it back down as the feathered bird begins to move its tail and head jerkily, chirruping and singing, the realistic sound echoing dustily in the space around them.

Timothy shivers. 'Well, that's even creepier than when I thought it was stuffed.' He turns back to face her. 'So, what are you doing up here?' he repeats.

'Well, as you can see, I've just been to the stables' – she nods down at her leggings tucked into thick walking socks and plucks at one of Benedict's thin old jumpers that she's wearing over a plaid shirt – 'and now I'm taking a moment to reflect.' It's her turn to force a smile.

Timothy nudges the edge of a sticking out packing box

with his foot, tucking it safely back in while not meeting her eye. 'This whole situation is...' He struggles to find the right word as Margaret regards him silently. 'Horrendous,' he decides. 'You must be going to hell and back with worry.' He glances at her. 'I mean, obviously there's been some sort of terrible mistake. Jude would never do something like that. Johnnie has actually already called' – he inspects his watch – 'at not even 8 a.m. He's on his way over to her now. I was looking for you anyway, before I heard the... scream... to let you know that, incredibly, they're gearing up to charge her.' He clears his throat. 'Johnnie also told me that there was some confusion as to the whereabouts of your mobile phone and some messages that might be on it, and I wonder if it might be the one I saw you put behind your back as I came up the stairs?' He clasps his hands and looks at the floor. 'Perhaps I could have it, please?'

Margaret's heart begins to thump.

Timothy looks up again and finally notices the opening in the wall. 'What on earth is that?' He squints at it. 'A sort of miniature priest's hole?' He glances at the bunch of keys on the other side of Margaret and his eyebrows lift. 'A hiding place?'

'Go away,' says Margaret. 'This is nothing to do with you! Nothing at all!'

Timothy looks confused. 'It's everything to do with me. I live here. Jude's my family.'

'Johnnie thinks he wants the phone, but he doesn't!' She glares at him. 'Trust me!'

Timothy gives a shocked laugh. 'You can't withhold evidence from a police investigation, Margaret! That's not your choice to make!'

Margaret holds his gaze. 'Oh really? What is on my phone proves without a doubt that Jude killed Richard. She rang me from Richard's flat and left me a message saying she'd call me back, but she didn't hang up properly. You hear her walk into the kitchen to find Richard. You hear them start arguing. They fight and then she kills him.'

Timothy actually reels, staggering backwards. 'You hear it happen?'

'Yes, Timothy! I've just listened to it myself.'

Timothy stares at her. 'So you did scream... I thought so.'

'I don't know if Jude's aware that the voicemail exists,' Margaret continues. 'But it *is* there. And if you give that evidence to the police, Jude will have no choice but to plead guilty. Murder carries a mandatory life sentence. She would serve at least twenty-five years.'

Timothy swallows. 'I can't—' he begins, visibly jumping as a mobile starts to ring, echoing around them. 'Oh shit, that's mine,' he realises, pulling his handset from his pocket.

'Johnnie is calling me now,' he whispers, looking at the screen in panic. 'I don't know what to do.'

'Just don't answer.' Margaret reaches behind her while he is distracted, beginning to surreptitiously wrap her fingers around the edge of the photograph, trying to edge it beneath her so that she is sitting on it. 'If they hear what is on that phone,' she warns, 'they will lock Jude up.'

'But I...' He looks at her desperately. 'Hang on. What else have you got back there?' He tries to look around her.

The phone is still ringing.

'Nothing,' hisses Margaret. 'Bugger off, Timothy!'

He glances at his mobile again, still shrilly demanding attention, then back at her. 'This is *my* house now, Aunt Margaret!' His phone finally falls silent and, apparently angry that he has missed the call, he shoves it into his pocket, darts forward and slides a hand behind Margaret, pulling at the edges of the curling photograph, grabbing it *and* her mobile, neatly sidestepping with surprising agility as Margaret tries to snatch them back. Moving to another window, he holds the photograph up to the light and stares at the captured image.

'Oh my God!' he gasps in horror. He turns to look at Margaret. 'Did you take this picture?'

Margaret doesn't say a thing, just presses her lips very tightly together.

'You did, didn't you?' He takes a step back, away from her.

His pocket begins to ring again, like an alarm going off and, *whimpering*, Timothy starts to shake, closing his eyes and inexplicably putting his hands above his head as if he's holding a bomb in one hand and the charger in the other, like an utter simpleton.

Margaret stares at him in disbelief as he appears to have some sort of mental collapse in front of her. 'Now Timothy!' She swallows her anger so that she can speak instead with the sort of firm authority Timothy has been trained to obey. She rises from her seat slowly. 'Calm down, stop fussing and give me the photograph and the phone.'

'But I can't just pretend I haven't seen this?' Timothy bleats, shaking the photograph like a sheep with a bell around its neck. 'I need to tell Johnnie what really happened!'

PART FOUR

MAY 1994

SIXTEEN

'You smell absolutely rank,' laughed Johnnie, distancing himself from a dripping wet Timothy, covered in pond slime, bits clinging to his hair as his trainers squelched.

'Why didn't they shove *you* in? I'm not their little brother, you are,' Timothy spluttered, wiping his lips, as they headed back towards Highcombe. 'I've got flies in my mouth.'

'Because they know if they so much as lay a finger on me, I will... fuck them up!' Johnnie kicked a stick on the ground like a rugby ball, sending it cannoning over the rhododendrons. 'Look, don't worry about it. They're leaving in an hour's time. You've actually survived.'

'How come you're not going home too?' Timothy grumbled. 'I can't wait to leave. I hate this place.'

'You don't want my scintillating company then? Fine, up yours.' Johnnie flicked him the v's. 'There's still a massive bit of gunk stuck to the top of your head by the way.'

Timothy's shoulders sagged. 'Urgh, thanks, man.' He paused, reached up and felt around his hair, before peeling the weed off and flinging it into the undergrowth with a shudder. Breaking out into a trot, his not inconsiderable belly rising and

falling as he moved so that he could rejoin a still-striding Johnnie, he glanced slyly at him. 'You staying around hasn't got
anything to do with a certain cousin of mine by any chance,
has it?'

Johnnie visibly turned cricket ball red, despite a blindingly
bright May sun shining right in Timothy's eyes. He pointed a
delighted, accusative finger. 'I knew it! You have so badly got it
for her.'

'No, I don't.' Johnnie looked away, the flush creeping
around the back of his neck.

'Yes, you do!' crowed Timothy. '*That's* why you've been
hanging around the stables since you got here, when I know you
hate horses as much as I do! You want to jump Jude in her jodhpurs, hump her in the hayloft and shag her on the saddles.
Oooh, Johnnie!'

'Hey!' Johnnie stopped immediately and turned round.
'Don't talk about her like that!' His good humour had
vanished, and Timothy's smile faded too as he shrank back
nervously and cringed in anticipation. 'I'm sorry! Don't
hurt me!'

Johnnie's face softened. 'I'm not going to hurt you, you
knob.' He turned and started off across the grass again. 'But you
need to stop reading your mum's Jilly Coopers... I don't want
you getting any ideas about playing tennis in the nude.'

'Ha! How do you know that bit's in there if you don't read
them too?' Timothy crowed.

'I found the book in your room and those were the pages
stuck together.'

'Shit. Seriously?' Timothy stopped. 'My mum will go nuts.'

Johnnie laughed. 'You're so gullible.'

Timothy turned scarlet. 'The only knob here is you,' he said,
putting his fist on his forehead and miming it pumping up and
down. 'A knob*head*.'

Johnnie let that one go. 'Keep a secret, though?' He cleared his throat as Timothy puffed back alongside him. 'We *might* have got off with each other last night.'

Timothy stopped immediately. 'You and Jude?'

'No, me and Jilly Cooper,' scoffed Johnnie. 'Of course me and Jude! It was after dinner.' He shrugged. 'We went back up to the Great Pond to finish that last spliff.'

Timothy's mouth fell open. 'Hey! You might have told me!'

'*Someone* fell asleep in the library, remember? Bit too much pudding.' He prodded Timothy's gut. 'Anyway, two's company...' He raised an eyebrow happily and shoved his hands in his pockets, starting to walk again but more slowly. 'Do *not* tell anyone but I think I'm going to ask her out.' A flash of worry passed across his face.

'Wait,' Timothy caught up. 'So it wasn't just getting off? How would that work when you both go back to different schools? And isn't it a bit... I don't know... weird? You're friends.'

'It would be weird if it was *you* and her,' Johnnie retorted, 'but I'm not her family, am I? And I think it's a good thing that we've been friends first. It means we'll have stuff to talk about. I know what she finds funny, what she likes doing, what she cares about... and OK, so I don't know what'll happen when we go back to school, but we can write, can't we?'

'You? Write a letter?' Timothy couldn't help himself.

'Shut up!' Johnnie looked hurt. 'I can do writing and stuff when I want to, and it's not that long until the summer hols anyway. I don't mind waiting. She was giggling a lot when we kissed.' He rubbed his nose with embarrassment. 'We both were. Do you think that means she likes me too, or—'

'She just snogged you because she was high?' Timothy finished unhelpfully.

Johnnie sighed. 'Yeah. That. But I didn't kiss her *because* she was high. I'd never, you know, take advantage.' He looked down at Highcombe, the house imposingly squat in front of them. 'I don't want to ask her out if she doesn't really like me though, in case it *does* get all weird. I thought I'd try and talk to her about it later when a few more guests have cleared off and it's quieter. Mate – girls are seriously complicated.'

Timothy shrugged. 'I wouldn't know. How was it?'

'How was what?'

'The kiss.'

Johnnie blushed. 'It was good. It was amazing actually.'

Timothy dry retched.

'Well don't ask then if you don't want details!'

'No' – Timothy was fishing around in his mouth – 'I just felt wings and legs.' He retched again. Johnnie stopped and frowned at him. 'I'm OK,' Timothy said, holding up a hand. 'False alarm.'

'She hasn't said anything to *you* about me then?' Johnnie asked casually as they resumed walking.

'No.'

Johnnie gave another sigh then glanced at Timothy. 'You need to go and get changed.' He nodded at the front of Timothy's shorts. 'You're drying out a bit but now it looks like you've pissed yourself. The others won't have finished breakfast yet so they might not even see you.'

But Timothy was already gloomily peering at the lawn in front of Highcombe. 'Nope. Looks like they've taken their coffees outside with the papers. Great. Here comes everyone teasing me.'

Johnnie ducked back behind a tree. 'Is Jude there too? I look a sweaty mess. I wanted to get showered first.'

'Doubt it. She's not usually up until past eleven.' Timothy squinted again. 'Can't see her. Anyway, won't she just be impressed you've already been for a run? Wasn't that the point? Hey Jude!' he sang. 'Check out my guns... grab these tight buns and make them *harder*...' He clutched his buttocks and gave a thrust only to squeal in alarm and leg it as a furious Johnnie gave chase after him.

'You've both got rather a lot of energy for such an ungodly hour on a Sunday morning,' Benedict drawled, looking over the top of his *Telegraph*, a circle of all of the Sunday papers at his feet as they skidded to a stop in front of the adults, Timothy panting in relief as Johnnie glared at him.

'Have you wet yourself, Timothy?' Margaret remarked, glancing at the front of his shorts.

Timothy flushed with embarrassment as Johnnie sniggered.

'No, Aunt Margaret. I haven't. I was pushed in the pond.'

'Well go and change, there's a chap.' Margaret had returned to the camera in her lap that she was fiddling with. 'And don't sit on anything on the way.'

Timothy nodded quickly and was about to make his escape when Benedict put his paper down. 'Wait a minute. Who pushed you in?' He turned an unblinking gaze on Johnnie and eyed the curve of the boy's biceps with distaste. 'Do you know, there's been quite the explosion of steroids... the sort of thing athletes and body builders use... among young men recently, just to look good. Is that what you do? Do *you* take steroids?'

Johnnie blushed and stepped forward. 'No, I—'

'Of course he doesn't take steroids!' Margaret peered at a button on the back of the camera. 'Don't be ridiculous, Dickie.'

'Nothing ridiculous about it,' Benedict shot back. 'It induces "'roid rage", testosterone surges that make you want to do odd things like shove people in ponds for no apparent reason...' He stared at Johnnie but just as quickly lost interest again, returning to his paper. 'I blame the schools and their obsession with sport, churning out nothing but meatheads. Ridiculous.'

Timothy looked at a crushed Johnnie and cleared his throat. 'He didn't shove me in; he was the only one who hauled me out. Aunt Margaret, has Jude come down yet?'

Johnnie shot him a grateful look.

'Come down?' Margaret said. 'She's gone. She left about ten minutes ago for some chum's place in Wales, in a terrible rush. Overslept as usual. Brooks had to fly like the wind to the station.'

'Gone? How long for?' Unable to help himself, the desperation in Johnnie's voice betrayed him, and Benedict looked up sharply, a slow smile spreading over his face as he folded the paper across his lap, reached for his cigarettes and lit up.

'Ah, I see. I take it she didn't say goodbye?'

Johnnie swallowed. 'I – lent her a book I hadn't quite finished reading myself, sir.'

Benedict's grin vanished. 'Oh well yes, that is very irritating.' He took a drag and blew out a cloud of smoke, resting his hands on the arms of his garden chair, legs still crossed as he regarded Johnnie again. 'What do you want to be when you grow up?' He tapped the side of his head. 'Mentally, I mean.'

'I...' Johnnie floundered like a landed fish under Benedict's penetrating gaze and glanced at a copy of John Grisham's *The Firm* lying on the ground at Margaret's feet. 'I want to be a lawyer.'

Benedict spied the book too and laughed. 'Oh do you? Solicitor or barrister? Obviously you'll know there's a significant difference between the two?' He wriggled back into his chair, beginning to enjoy himself.

'Don't be mean, Dickie,' Margaret rebuked, still fumbling with the back of the camera, which suddenly popped open. 'Ah! Done it! I think *I* found your book actually, Johnnie. It was on the floor outside your room. I assumed someone had dropped it. You'll find it in the library.'

'Whereabouts in Wales has Jude gone, Aunt Margaret?' Timothy persisted.

'No idea.' Margaret briefly glanced up and narrowed her eyes as her sister-in-law appeared, making a great show of pushing Margaret's father in his wheelchair. 'Don't park Daddy directly in the sun, please, Fan, he'll burn. Jude said she might be back the day after tomorrow, unless she's having fun in which case she'll stay. Oh now look, here comes everyone else all at once!' Margaret eyed Johnnie's older brothers ambling towards them, their arms slung around the shoulders of their various girlfriends. 'We'll need more coffee. I wonder where Mrs Brooks is?' She looked around vaguely. 'Ah and here's the birthday boy!' She lit up with delight as Anthony appeared still holding his cup from breakfast. 'Hello, darling!' she beamed. 'Not too hungover then? Sleep well?'

'Like the proverbial. Kicked off my party shoes, climbed straight into bed!' Anthony replied and glanced at his son. 'Timsy! Did you fall in the Great Pond again? That's the second time in two days!'

'Third actually,' Timothy corrected despondently as Johnnie's brothers grinned and the girls giggled.

'Timothy, you know I *do* have a telephone number for Jude somewhere if you want it?' Margaret began to search about her as Johnnie's parents and another couple of house guests drifted delicately out into the bright sunshine, blinking and wincing.

Johnnie watched Benedict scowl as Anthony sat down next to Margaret and stretched his legs out in the sun, leaning his head on the back of the chair and closing his eyes comfortably.

'Not South Africa, but it'll do.'

'Yes, when do you fly home?' Benedict said. 'Friday or Saturday?'

'Friday,' Anthony confirmed. 'Don't worry. Not long until we're out of your hair.'

'Wait – what about me?' Timothy asked quickly. 'You're not staying to drop me back at school?'

'I was going to ask your aunt Margaret to do it.' Anthony opened one eye and regarded his sister hopefully.

'But, Dad!' began Timothy.

'What's the prob, old chap?' Anthony looked at his son in concern. 'It's only a day or so?'

'OK.' Timothy lowered his head and started to pick at his fingers.

'Well I feel disinclined to say yes now seeing as my nephew is so clearly underwhelmed by the prospect of more time in my company, but fine. We'll take him back. You are a pest.' Margaret frowned at Anthony, mock annoyed, then began to look around her again. 'Ah. Here we are!' Margaret held a scrap of paper aloft triumphantly. 'The number for Jude. It's 01654 code, although I have not the foggiest where that is.'

'Don't talk like that for effect, Margaret.' Benedict took a vicious drag of his cigarette. 'Everyone will think we're terribly neglectful parents. Or at least you are. You'll get a reputation.'

Margaret looked up, bewildered, as Anthony, still sunbathing with his eyes closed, frowned. 'Steady on, Ben!'

'It was a *joke*.' Benedict uncrossed his legs and stubbed his fag out. 'No one thought I was talking about darling Hilary.'

An appalled hush fell across the group as Margaret's spine straightened and her body stiffened completely.

'Who is Hilary?' one of the girlfriends whispered, a little too loudly, to Johnnie.

Margaret heard, and with an icy gaze still fixed on Benedict, managed to say, 'He was my little boy, he died when he was seven.'

Benedict's eyes glittered. '*Our* little boy... "And only in death was he truly exalted and adored", Benedict 1, first verse, May 1994.'

Margaret continued to stare at him, her eyes wide with shock.

As their silent energy crackled – and for no more than a couple of seconds – it was as if something was visibly swirling in the air above all of them, dancing like a will-o'-the-wisp in a way that Johnnie didn't really understand but could see the adults were finding excruciatingly uncomfortable. It was his own mother who broke the silence.

'Oh look!' she blurted, relieved to announce a distraction heading up the long drive towards them. 'This must be your taxi for the train station, boys!' She turned to her older two sons.

'That can't be ours?' The same girlfriend checked her watch. 'We're not due to leave for another three quarters of an hour. I haven't finished packing yet.'

'There's someone in the back,' observed Fan. 'Are you OK, Daddy? Can I pass you some water?' She smiled winningly at her father-in-law and held a glass up to his mouth, helping him to sip.

'Maybe Jude missed her train?' Timothy suggested, and Johnnie stepped forward eagerly.

'No, I told you, Brooks drove her.' Margaret tore her eyes away from giving Fan a death stare and shielded her gaze from the sun. 'Who on earth is it?'

They all watched as the taxi slowed to a halt. The door opened and a long leg emerged, followed by the rest of the body of a tall boy with slim limbs and rather unruly curls, clutching a rucksack. A carefully chosen black suit jacket and trousers over a black shirt lent him some gravitas, emphasising his pale face and suggesting the appearance of a trainee priest; but with incongruous confidence, he reached into his back pocket, pulled out a couple of notes and fed them through the partially open window for the driver. Straightening up he realised everyone was staring at him in total silence. Giving a short, visible exhalation, he made the sign of the cross on his body and started bravely towards them, offering up a shy but devastating smile.

'Well, take me to church...' blurted the girlfriend, voicing the thoughts of more than one of the group, earning her a scowl from Johnnie's brother.

The boy arrived on the grass in front of them and let his bag slip from his broad shoulder with a friendly nod. 'Hello.'

Benedict got to his feet, slipping his free hand into his pocket. 'Well hello to you too.' He offered the boy a smile. 'Can we help?'

Mrs Brooks had appeared, carrying another laden tray, and stopped to stare at the stranger.

'I've come about your yard?' the boy said. 'I'd like to work here,' he added helpfully, when no one said anything, too astonished to answer him.

Only Johnnie's eyes widened in alarm, sensing the arrival of competition.

'I am sorry, Your Lordship!' Mrs Brooks put the tray down and marched over to the boy. 'You don't skip up to the main house! You go to the stables! Come with me!'

'It's all right, Mrs Brooks.' Benedict held up his hand, cigarette aloft. 'We don't mind! It's not the 1950s, we're all friends here. So what yard job are you after?' He looked the boy up and down. 'You're much too tall to jockey.'

'Eventually, I hope to be a dressage groom,' the boy replied.

'Plaiting horses and making them look pretty?' Benedict laughed. 'What fun.'

There were a few titters from Johnnie's older brothers, both unamused at the way their girlfriends were staring hungrily at the interloper like lionesses who hadn't eaten for several days. Johnnie could only continue to stare at this new threat to his fledgling relationship with Jude; tall, mysterious, good-looking *and* good with horses? Fuck that.

'I'll walk you down to the stables,' offered Timothy suddenly, stepping forward.

'You're soaking wet, remember?' Margaret stood up and gave the boy a dazzling social smile. 'I'll take you.'

'Thank you.' The boy nodded. 'I'd be very grateful. I believe the head groom is called Tansy? That's who I probably need to speak to, I'd imagine?'

He was trying to sound formal and smart but thanks to a

pedestrian, nondescript accent and lack of finish, wasn't really pulling it off.

'So Tansy isn't actually expecting you?' Margaret frowned.

He shook his head. 'No. But I'm a hard worker and I'll do whatever needs to be done.'

'You don't even know if there's an available job?' She looked at him incredulously. 'How old are you?'

'Fifteen,' he confessed. 'But I've got a letter from my father saying he's happy for me to be having a crack at this—'

'Oh, like Paddington!' One of the girls pouted. 'That's adorable!'

Johnnie rolled his eyes as the boy blushed.

'Legally I can leave school on the last Friday in June because I'll be sixteen by the end of the summer holidays... so I'm only a month early. I didn't get on with school. I tried but I couldn't concentrate. I'm better with my hands and being outside.'

Benedict inclined his head and drew on his cigarette again. 'Full-time education isn't for everyone. There's no shame in that.'

Johnnie's mouth fell open as he looked at Jude's father. Seconds ago he'd been moaning about meatheads.

The boy nodded gratefully. 'Thank you. I thought I'd show some initiative. Some friends said Tansy runs a good yard that's well invested in. The kind of place I need to be.' He squared his shoulders and held his head high.

'Well good for you,' Benedict remarked. 'Tell Tansy to find him something, Margaret.' He turned to his wife, who shot him another look of irritation. 'I like that kind of can-do attitude. We can always use a bit of that around Highcombe. What did you say your name was?'

'I'm Richard.' The boy nodded at all of them again. 'Richard Shand.'

SEVENTEEN

'So do your parents own horses?' Margaret asked, inspecting her Vamp nails as they crossed the gardens, heading in the direction of the stables.

Richard shook his head. 'A paper shop. The girls from the local hunt yard would come in for their crisps and Coke and talk to me if I was serving. They let me start to muck out. I loved it, I love horses. They have souls.'

Margaret glanced at him and flicked a small bug from the front of her crisp white shirt. 'I think you're probably right.'

'My mother died two years ago, and the horses helped me a lot when that happened. They were kind to me.'

Margaret frowned and looked out across the parkland. 'I'm sorry to hear that you lost your mother. You must miss her very much.' She turned back to the boy. 'Remind me how old you said you are?'

'Fifteen.'

'And are you quite sure your father is happy for you to be doing this?' Margaret asked. 'I had a son who would be about your age now and I'm not sure I'd have wanted him turning up at a place where he knew nobody, looking for a job?'

His face darkened. 'I can't work in that shop every day for the rest of my life, having the same conversations over and over with my dad. I love him, but I'll do myself in.'

Margaret put her hands in her pockets. 'Well I don't think that will be necessary.'

She turned the corner and walked into the yard. A radio was playing 'Love is All Around' to the horses in their boxes but there wasn't a groom in sight.

'Typical,' Margaret tutted, walking straight over to a handsome young horse waving his head at them.

'This is Drivetime, my baby.' She scratched the white flash on his nose. 'He's new here too and also like you – a bit impulsive. He's not a big fan of people, particularly men, so don't...' the words died on her lips as Richard simply walked straight up to Drivetime, who regarded the boy with liquid chocolate eyes before pushing his nose against the flat of Richard's outstretched hand, butting it gently.

'Reminding you he's boss... but he likes you.' She watched the horse and boy with interest.

'I like him too.' Richard looked at him in admiration. 'He's beautiful.'

'Right, let's be having you, you nasty little...' Tansy called out as she rounded the corner carrying a bucket. She stopped dead at the sight of her boss.

'Good morning, Lady Fawkes,' she stammered, her eyes widening as she took in Richard scratching Drivetime's nose.

'I know, no biting!' Margaret remarked. 'This is Richard, he's going to be working here now and, by the look of it, I suggest you hand over care of Drivetime to him – under your supervision, of course. Train him up to your high standards, please, Tansy, and I'll ask Mrs Brooks to send someone down to sort out where he's going to sleep.' She eyed Richard. 'We might put you in the separate cottage. We're a rather female-dominated yard at the moment and I don't think it'd be a good idea to put you in the coop with the girls.'

'Oh but I was next in line for the c—' began Tansy, falling quiet as Margaret looked right at her.

'Sorry, Lady Fawkes. I'll ask Mrs Brooks to make him comfortable.' She lowered her voice.

'Good.' Margaret turned her back on them. 'I'll leave you both to it then. Welcome to Highcombe, Mr Shand.'

* * *

'Hello! Richard, isn't it?' Johnnie stuck his head around the stable door to find the new boy wonder messing around with some sort of arrangement of leather straps and metal stirrups. The horse he was next to whickered and stamped a foot.

'I'd stay there if I were you,' Richard warned. 'Maybe on the other side of the door just to be safe.'

'Oh... well, all right.' Johnnie frowned at the horse and pulled a face at it when Richard turned his back. Unfriendly sod. 'What's wrong with it?'

'Nothing.' Richard glanced over his shoulder. 'Can I help you?'

'Yes!' Johnnie beamed. 'You can. I've been sent to ask you to join us all for dinner at seven. A welcome, if you will.'

Richard looked surprised then rubbed his face. 'Oh no, really? Do I have to?'

Johnnie shrugged. 'I suppose not. Refusing might be seen as a little gauche, but—'

'Gauche?' Richard gently shoved the horse away as he lowered his head and nudged him. 'I don't know what that means.'

'Um, unsophisticated... sort of bad mannered.' Johnnie straightened up. 'But I'll pass the message on.'

Richard hesitated. 'No. It's just one night, eh?'

'That's the right call I think,' Johnnie agreed. 'Excellent! See you at seven!' He turned to leave.

'Wait!' Richard called. 'What do I wear?' He ruffled his hair anxiously and looked down at his T-shirt and jodhpurs.

Now that Johnnie could actually see his physique he realised that Richard might be lean but he was strong. *Elegant*, he realised gloomily. That was the word. All Richard needed was a polo stick next to him and they'd all swoon themselves stupid.

'Well not that, obviously.' He nodded at Richard, who looked down at himself. 'Lovely though it smells down here' – he wrinkled his nose at the sweet, rich smell of hay and horse-shit – 'you don't want to bring it into the dining room. It's an informal thing though, so jeans, a top – you'll be fine.'

'Thank you.' Richard nodded. 'I appreciate it.'

Johnnie didn't reply, just for some reason best known to himself, he gave Richard a *salute* before heading back out into the sunshine. A rat flitted past him, scrabbly claws and thick scaly tail swishing before it vanished into an empty loose box. Johnnie dug his hands deeper into his pockets and tried to ignore his already nibbling conscience. He paused and almost turned back – but then he thought of Jude returning and ambling unawares into the stables to be greeted by Richard in his polo get-up. His resolve hardened and he headed back up to the house.

* * *

'Do you want to say a few words, darling, before we all go through to dinner?' Margaret flicked a piece of lint from Antho-ny's lapel. 'It's not every day you turn fifty.'

Her brother shook his head. 'I said something at the party yesterday. I know today is actually the day, but everyone will be sick of me.' He looked fondly around the room at his nearest and dearest enjoying a pre-dinner drink. 'Thank you though, Meg.' He bent and kissed his sister's cheek. 'It's been such a treat to spend time with you, and I'll be thinking of this grate-fully when I'm back in Cape Town this time next week.'

Margaret sighed. 'I'll miss you so much. The sun goes in when you're not here.'

'Come with us. All the horses you can shake a stick at. Mountains to photograph... and Hugh's wine estate is starting to do *very* well, apropos of nothing.' Anthony looked at her slyly.

'Shhh.' Margaret glanced over her shoulder. 'Dickie will hear you.'

'No, he won't!' Anthony scoffed, but moved closer and quietened his tone. 'Hugh's got real ambition, you know. He works hard.'

Margaret wrinkled her nose. 'He was one of the scholarship boys in your year, I seem to remember? They always felt they had just that little bit more to prove.'

'Oh don't be such a snob! Bring Pa, we'll sell this hideous carbuncle, sucking all of the money into it.' He glanced around the library and shivered. 'Have a life. Have a love.'

'Sell Highcombe?' Margaret was horrified. 'You wouldn't!'

Anthony frowned. 'I don't want it and I don't want it for Timothy either. I don't want it for you and Jude. Help me to persuade Pa to sell it and come with us. I know you think Fan has been trying to butter Pa up while we've been here, but she's genuinely very fond of him and wants to help.'

Margaret rolled her eyes.

'It's true!' protested Anthony. 'And I wouldn't oppose buying Dickie a nice flat in Soho, somewhere for him to tart about, pay him off. Or he can hike off back to his mother in that dreary Scottish glen of theirs.'

'No.' Margaret shook her head, tight-lipped. 'I don't want that either. I love him.'

Anthony sighed and drew Margaret into a more discreet

corner. 'That's not what love is and you know it. Fun and smiles one minute, rejection and insults the next, only returning to the fun when you start to pull away. A toxic—'

'That's straight from Fan's pop psychology mouth, not yours.'

'Well, she's right. She's got the measure of Dickie.'

'She's a silly bitch.'

Anthony sighed again. 'Be careful, Meg. She's right about how he plays you. That comment he made about Hilary earlier was appallingly unkind.'

Margaret pretended to look confused, as if she couldn't quite remember. 'About being *our* little boy, you mean?'

'Well, really the bit when he suggested that you weren't particularly interested in your own child until he died.'

Margaret inhaled sharply, her shoulders drawing up tightly around her ears, and then she tossed her head. 'I don't want to talk about it any more. I hate all men. They're all shits. Except you.'

'Hugh isn't a shit...'

'Stop it.' Margaret was starting to become cross. 'Hugh might be one of your gang, but he was never one of mine. He's dull—'

'Kind, handsome and loves you.' Anthony paused. 'And would love his daughter too if he was allowed.'

Margaret's skin blanched completely. 'Now that's quite enough. Someone will hear you. I was drunk.'

'You wanted some affection and there's nothing wrong with that.'

The memory of Hugh's disappointingly wet, eager kiss that completely spoilt the appeal of his taut, muscular body made Margaret's skin crawl, particularly because she'd been pathetically desperate enough to have allowed sex to happen anyway – and that made her as furious now as it had at the time. 'The briefest of extra-marital affairs does not a parent make.'

Anthony drained his drink sadly. 'And there she is, my little Venus de Milo back in her mausoleum. Lifeless, pale, cold stone.'

He looked at her pointedly and raised his voice again. 'You've really pushed the boat out and spoilt me. Such fun to be all actually dressing for dinner.' He looked down at his black tie and gestured at Margaret's column of scarlet silk. 'Mother would approve.' He raised his champagne glass.

Margaret had recovered herself and gave him a sardonic smile. 'You know perfectly well she'd be telling me I look common and red isn't my colour, she – oh!'

Anthony turned at the surprise in her voice, and a hush fell over the rest of the room as they noticed Richard standing in the doorway, hair brushed, hands in the back pockets of his black trousers, his black shirt a little creased and his eyes skittering about in panic as he clocked the bow ties, cocktail dresses, glittering jewels and waiters with trays of drinks.

Benedict stepped forward holding a glass. 'Everything all right, old chap?' His voice was light. 'Something we can do you for?'

Richard rubbed his jaw uneasily, all of his earlier confidence having evaporated. 'I... shouldn't be here. I'm sorry.' His silent gaze landed on Johnnie, gripping a champagne flute.

Margaret watched as Johnnie looked away guiltily and started to squirm.

'Oh now you mustn't worry a bit,' Benedict said. 'Never apologise for interrupting a party with horse alerts in *this* house.' He swung around and addressed the rest of the group. 'Margaret's new toy, a very expensive colt, has been a little unwell this afternoon.'

Margaret's mouth fell open and she stepped forward, alarmed. 'Drivetime? Why didn't you tell me sooner?'

'You were busy with vital seating arrangements, dearest. It's all under control. I asked our new groom Richard to keep me updated if there were developments. Thank you, Richard. Lady Fawkes will be right there. You can go now.' He gave Richard an almost imperceptible wink then turned back to the group. 'Let's all go through to dinner, shall we? Get our own nose bags on.'

* * *

A hurriedly changed Margaret dashed into the stables to find Richard brushing Drivetime furiously as the horse chewed a piece of hay and regarded his flurry of visitors with interest.

'I don't understand,' she said. 'He looks absolutely fine?'

'He is.' Richard looked at her, shamefaced. 'Your husband was just saving me, that's all. I was told' – he took a deep breath and blushed in the gloom of the box – 'that I'd been invited to dinner.'

'Ah!' It all dawned on Margaret. 'I'm sorry to hear that. Do you want to tell me the name of the prankster in question?'

Richard shook his head. 'If that's all right?' He rubbed at his eyes quickly, as if he had something in them, but Margaret had seen the hot gleam of humiliated tears.

She walked up to him and placed a light hand on his shoulder. 'There will always be people who play that particular card and it's an unkind one. I don't believe it should bother you, but if you want to learn how to get ahead... it's the little things that catch one out.' She moved her hand to the cuff of his cheap shirt. 'Never buttons, always links. Get yourself a "uniform" so that you're never caught out socially. A crisp white shirt never lets a man down. Lose all traces of a regional accent. It's grarse, not grass... barth not bath, all right has a "t" at the end of it. Your history starts with helping out at the local hunt, not your father's paper shop. You see? And don't trust anyone like Johnnie Saunders.' She smiled briskly. 'He's got a crush on my daughter Jude. He thinks she's coming home tomorrow – although she's actually decided not to – and he's worried she's going to fall for you like everyone else. You might also be interested to know that Johnnie's father is on the brink of financial ruin. Rumour has it one or two paintings have started disappearing from their lovely little farmhouse. It's all just sad discoloured squares on empty walls now, and Johnnie's mother has stopped wearing several of her favourite rings because they're "far too showy". Johnnie and his brothers haven't been told yet. People in glass houses, and all that. And I shan't be letting Jude and Johnnie get together anyway, of course,' she added, more to herself. 'Leaving foolish little notes in books. Jude needs to do far better than him.'

Richard straightened up. 'Please don't say anything to Johnnie, will you? I can fight my own battles.'

'Well, I shall if I want to, because this is my house and you are a member of my staff,' Margaret rebuked. 'Again, knowing your place in the pecking order and abiding by it means you won't stand out as an oddity.'

'I'm sorry, Lady Fawkes.' Richard hung his head.

'I should think so,' Margaret acknowledged, then ruffled his bouncy hair and kissed him briefly on the cheek. 'Go to bed now. It'll all be better in the morning.'

Richard's mouth fell open with astonishment as she turned and started walking back towards the house to change again and rejoin the party.

* * *

Johnnie was already panting as he approached the stables on his morning run, trying to blast away the excesses of the night before. He stopped for a second but decided he would keep going after all. He didn't want to cramp up. Sprinting, he reached the edge of the parkland before his conscience really bit in.

'Oh, for fuck's sake!' he swore aloud and turned back. He'd

just apologise and leave. It *had* been a cheap trick to pull, Timothy had been right. Tim had been really cross when Johnnie had confessed what he'd done. 'I expect the others to bully: isn't it hilarious to hang someone on a coat peg or shut someone in a cupboard and lock the door? I thought *you* were better than that.' He'd glared at Johnnie and stomped off to bed.

The accusation had stuck in Johnnie's throat and he'd really not felt good about the whole thing as a result.

Puffing as he walked into the stables, and wrinkling his nose while stepping round some shit of some kind, not wanting it to get in the tread of his new Nikes, he toyed with calling out hello. The place seemed deserted apart from a radio blaring out that piss-poor Wet Wet Wet song that really was all around now, when he heard a voice he recognised, prattling away nervously.

'I don't want to! I've changed my mind. Can we stop?' Timothy sounded scared.

'You don't have to do anything you're not comfortable with.' That was Richard.

Johnnie's eyebrows shot up and he crept to the edge of the box, peering over the stable door. Both boys were facing away from him as they stood in the straw, Richard with a comforting hand in the middle of the much shorter boy's back, Timothy tentatively reaching his hand out towards the nose of Drivetime.

'You promise he won't bite me?' Timothy stammered. 'Aunt Margaret says he doesn't like people.'

'He does, he's just learnt not to trust some of them, that's all. He knows you don't want to hurt him. Very slowly...'

'Oh fuck...' breathed Timothy. 'I'm doing it! I'm actually doing it! I have spent my whole life afraid of them and in *my* family, that's been hard, I can tell you! He's really soft!'

'There you go,' Richard's voice was kind and encouraging as he patted Timothy's back. 'Well done!'

Johnnie watched as Timothy glanced up at Richard and

shyly smiled. Johnnie drew back quietly out of sight, intending to slip away without being noticed, only for Tansy to appear round a corner, pushing a wheelbarrow full of manure.

'Hello! It's Johnnie, isn't it?' She lowered the barrow and wiped her hands on a nearby cloth. She gave him an incredulous up and down, fixing on his snow-white trainers. 'Have you lost your way?'

Johnnie raised a finger to his lips pleadingly and glanced behind him, but neither of the two boys emerged. Just maybe, they hadn't heard...

He gave a confused Tansy a silent thumbs up and started to edge around the back of the box Richard and Timothy were in, to make his escape via the opposite exit – only for a shovelful of fresh horseshit to come up and over the side of the partition wall, landing squarely on his head.

'Fucking hell!' he gasped, dung falling from his hair as he looked down at himself, unwittingly depositing small lumps of browny-yellow crap on his new Nikes.

Richard appeared, triumphantly holding the shovel, followed by Timothy, his mouth falling open at the sight of Johnnie.

'These were box fresh, you maniac!' Johnnie swallowed in fury as he kicked off some cloying remnants only to see stains on the virgin fabric mesh.

Richard shrugged. 'I'm sorry, but what can I say? You're not really dressed right, are you?' His stare hardened as he threw the shovel down and marched off back into the horsebox.

'Hey! I came down to apologise, actually!' Johnnie pushed past Timothy to follow him.

Richard swung round as Johnnie appeared in the now open doorway of the box. 'Oh, mate! You should have said! That would have made all the difference! Enjoy your nice new things while you can, won't you?' He nodded at Johnnie's feet. 'I hear there won't be much more where they came from.'

'What?' Johnnie frowned. 'What are you talking about?'

'Ask Daddy. Anyways, now you've said sorry and I can see what a nice dude you really are, maybe I won't make a beeline for your girl Jude, when she gets home? How about that? Or maybe I will?' he shrugged. 'Who knows?'

Johnnie's face washed out. 'You stay away from her.'

Richard stepped forward. 'Or you'll what? Challenge me to a duel? Slap my face with a white glove? Bet she's gagging for a proper ride.'

With a shout of fury, Johnnie put his head down and rugby tackled straight into a surprised Richard, lifting him off his feet and slamming him into the back of the stable as Drivetime began to whinny while the two boys tussled at his feet.

'Stop it!' pleaded Timothy, walking nervously into the box as Drivetime sidestepped back and forth, shaking his head as Johnnie and Richard scuffled, trying to land punches on each other. 'You're upsetting the horse. He doesn't like it.'

Johnnie scrambled to his feet eyeing Richard winded on the stable floor, having managed to get an elbow into his stomach. 'Keep your mouth shut about Lord Fawkes's daughter or I'll have you sacked.' He wiped his mouth, looking to see if he was bloodied.

'Because that's how people like you deal with stuff?' groaned Richard. 'Prick.'

Johnnie's resolve shattered and he bent down to grab Shand, drawing his other fist back only for the bloody horse to bite the bare skin on the back of his arm.

'Ow!' Johnnie howled and swung round, his temper completely exploding as he boxed the frightened animal on the nose. 'Get the fuck off me!'

The horse's eyes rolled right back and he reared up. Johnnie stepped away but a sharp hoof caught Timothy in the face and he screamed loudly, staggering and clutching his mouth.

'Leave him alone!' yelled Richard, jumping up. 'What kind of person hurts an animal?'

'He bit me first!' began Johnnie, only for Richard to finally find his target. The side of Johnnie's face and eyeball exploded with pain as he stumbled backwards, lost his footing and wound up sprawled on the filthy floor. He began to kick out desperately as Richard towered over him, pummelling into him with both hands, as hard as he could. He seemed to have lost control, and Johnnie began to feel genuinely frightened as he instinctively curled up in a ball to protect himself.

'Stop it!' someone bellowed and, suddenly, miraculously, Richard was being pulled off him. Johnnie hauled himself up onto one forearm. Margaret was holding onto a shaking Richard, her arms around him as he began to sob noisily onto her shoulder. 'Now, now.' She rubbed his back. 'You're all right.'

Johnnie managed to sit up with a gasp, and Margaret looked first at him, then a cowering Timothy, blood leaking through his fingers as he clutched his lip and tried to get away from a still pacing Drivetime. 'What on earth happened here?'

Richard drew back from her, his face tear-streaked and still weeping. 'I'm so sorry! I've not lost it like that since my mother died... I'm not making excuses, but...' He gasped and suddenly clutched at his side, in obvious pain.

Johnnie watched, feeling ashamed of himself in the face of the other boy's very real suffering.

With difficulty he hauled himself up to a stand. 'I apologise,' he said. 'I apologise to you too, Lady Fawkes. If you'll excuse me, I'll go and start packing. I think my mother and father were planning to leave this morning in any case. I was going to stay on to keep Timothy company but under the circumstances I'll go with them.'

Margaret nodded. 'I think that would be wise. You can take Timothy back up to the house with you as well, please, and as for you' – she turned to Richard – 'go back to the cottage for the rest of the day, take some paracetamol and tell someone if you start getting sharp pains when you breathe in and out.' She shook her head. 'You boys will be the death of me.'

* * *

By 10 p.m., once what was left of the house party had retired, worn out by the excesses of three nights of extended birthday parties and dinners, Margaret fell gratefully into bed. Finally alone in her room and with space to think, she began to worry about Richard and wondered if perhaps she ought to check on him. He had as good as collapsed onto her earlier. Never mind cracked ribs, what if an unintentionally hard kick had ruptured something, like a spleen? Or there was some internal bleeding, hidden away but catastrophically, silently leaking into his system? Benedict had popped down to check on him at supper time and hadn't seemed unduly worried.

'I dosed him up, gave him something a little stronger to take away the pain,' he'd assured her. 'At most I think it's a bruised back or the like. He said Johnnie scrummed him into the wall, nasty little rugger bugger. But he was fine. Don't let it trouble you.'

But that was what he'd said last time too and look what had happened then...

Margaret focused on the ceiling rose, lit up by the light shining through from her en-suite bathroom, and forced herself to breathe, but she could *smell* the hospital, hear the machinery bleeping, see the tubes carrying mysterious liquids in and out of Hilary's small body and feel the limp little hand in hers. It was no good – she threw back the covers. She was going to have to go down to the cottage and check on Richard again.

Slipping on her shoes by the back door she shushed the whining dogs who wanted to come with her, but would gallop off into the park barking, proving more stress than comfort.

Margaret reached for her wax jacket and pulled up the hood. She only hesitated when she actually opened the door. It was chilly for May but the night was a close inky black with little moon and Margaret did not like the dark. Years of burying herself beneath the covers because Nanny Harris always, always turned off the light *and shut the door* had taken its toll, and her childhood fear crept out from beneath the bed to bite her once again. But she would do it, because he needed her and she would not let him down.

Margaret took a deep breath, trying not to think about what animals were lurking in the gardens, looking back at her right now, still and watching. In fact, that was a good point... She doubled back to her study for her camera and slung the strap around her neck. Checking on the new, male, very attractive groom, alone and at this time of night would be gossiped about and chewed over if she was discovered. Better for her to have a proper excuse; she was doing a night shoot and had decided to check while she was out anyway... less contentious.

She was aware of the owls screeching and calling almost as soon as she began to walk up the drive, her heart pushing against her ribcage, only to almost die of fright as a torch beam bounced out of nowhere, right into her face. 'Who's that?' she breathed, 'Show yourself!'

'My apologies, Lady Fawkes.' The light shone upwards and rather eerily illuminated the ingratiating grin of Brooks doing his gamekeeper bit, the nosy old sod. 'I'd heard a bit of coming and going and thought I better check it wasn't anything untoward.'

'No, just me.' Margaret smiled tightly and lifted her camera, very glad of the excuse. 'Shooting the nocturnal side of Highcombe.'

Brooks frowned. 'Would you like me to come with you? You don't want to be out there alone, do you?' He nodded at the outline of the woods.

'Thank you, but I'm fine,' Margaret dismissed him. 'It's late and you need to go off duty. It's too bad I've disturbed you, but please be assured I'm quite all right. That will be all, thank you, Brooks.' She waited for him to sling his hook and, sure enough, even he got the message eventually and clicked off the torch.

''Night, Your Ladyship.'

Margaret strode off far more confidently than she felt, but as her eyes adjusted, it wasn't quite so bad. She lifted the camera and captured the dark sky for effect in case Brooks was still there watching, but began to pick up pace as she moved towards the stables. She would check on Richard and go straight back to bed. Tiptoeing past the horses coming to the edge of their boxes and looking at her curiously, she felt her way up to the dark yard desk, not wanting to alert any of the other grooms to her presence by switching on a light. She bumped into the edge of the table and felt for the ledge above it, into which the hooks were screwed – but there was no spare key to the cottage hanging where it ought to be. Frowning, she reached her fingers out and, feeling her way, counted the five hooks from left to right again, until she got to the second to last – empty. How very odd.

Someone else must have already taken it. Her heart began to thud a little faster and she hastened out of the stables and across the yard. The small but detached groom's cottage was set back further, next to the barn. No lights were on, although as Margaret peered closer she could see one upstairs window was lit. The smallest sliver of light was visible at the edge where the curtain had been very tightly tucked in but fallen a little loose.

Margaret walked across the grass and when she reached the front door, twisted the handle quietly. To her enormous surprise it yielded. Unlocked? She frowned and eased into the tiny downstairs hall space, pushing it gently shut behind her, only to freeze as she heard a low moan coming from upstairs. Her lips parted as she swallowed her fear. Oh God, he really *was* ill and she'd just sent him off to bed with paracetamol. Had she learnt nothing, *nothing*? And what did Benedict know either? She should have come here earlier and checked Richard for herself! She began to mentally scramble through the practicalities of this emergency. There was no telephone line in the groom cottage. How was she going to call for an ambulance? She'd have to leave him and rush back to the yard, wake up the girls. Another guttural cry from above her and she covered her mouth with her hand in guilty panic. What had she done? Just left him here suffering!

She began to hurry up the narrow, tight stairs. But wait – what was that? She froze halfway up. That was a male voice, someone talking quietly, making soothing noises. Someone else was up there. Moving as if in a dream, Margaret got to the top and very slowly pushed the bedroom door open. The lamp was on the floor to soften the glow, casting shadows of the two naked male bodies on the bed against the wall in front of her, neither party aware of her presence, very much otherwise engaged. Horrified, Margaret could only stare... before shock and outrage started to churn in her stomach, burn in her veins and her mind... she slowly lifted the camera around her neck and, breathing faster, finger over the button, she snapped.

* * *

Back in her darkroom at Highcombe, illuminated by the blood-red bulb, she pulled the photograph from the tray and hung it to dry, watching the grainy image emerge. Fixating on the two figures, Richard with her husband, both clearly visible, her anger began to sharpen too, pressing on her from the inside out, until the point of her fury ran her heart right through.

EIGHTEEN

PRESENT DAY

The phone eventually falls silent for a second time when Timothy does not answer Johnnie's call.

'Well done,' Margaret says. 'We can call him back in a moment when we've decided what we're going to say to him. Now, take a couple of deep breaths.'

Timothy tries to do as he's told, but as he looks at the photograph he's holding, he begins to shake. He remembers exactly how muscular Richard appeared to him at the time, yet through adult eyes, he now sees a boy's body delicately balanced on the cusp of adulthood. Broad but fragile shoulders, easily broken.

'This is Benedict, with Richard.' He looks up at Margaret, devastated. 'How can you have known this for all these years and said nothing?'

'Plenty of marriages survive affairs, Timothy.'

Timothy stares at his aunt and tears spring to his eyes. 'It's not an affair when one party is an adult and the other is a fifteen-year-old child. That's abuse.'

'Don't be absurd! It's nothing of the sort!' Margaret shifts the weight from her bad ankle, leaning on her stick. 'It's perfectly visible that he's enjoying it.' She gestures in disgust at the photograph.

Timothy tries to keep his voice even. 'It's a common misconception that when a male has a physical response to stimulation which is beyond his control, that means he is enjoying it.'

'Oh shut *up!*' Margaret gives him a look of revulsion.

'Whatever you think.' Timothy is starting to feel sick. He wants to put the photograph down, not be holding it any more, not be anywhere near it. 'Legally he had the mind of a child and he wasn't old enough to give consent for this' – Timothy holds the picture aloft – 'to happen to him.'

Margaret waves a hand. 'What rot! He most certainly did not have the mind of a child! He knew exactly what he wanted. You can play semantics with me as much as you like, I will continue to tell you that Richard Shand was sexually promiscuous and plenty of boys simply are at that age.'

Timothy closes his eyes.

'Oh stop it!' Margaret snaps. 'That is a body brimming with testosterone and his mind knew what it was doing, too. He seduced Benedict. My husband thought he was in love with Shand.'

'Men like Benedict often "fall in love" with vulnerable boys who just happen to be in their power in some way.'

'How dare you! Richard Shand was a devious, charming manipulator!' Margaret insists, talking over him. 'Jude fell for it too! He targeted her as well and duped her into a relationship. She doesn't want me to tell anyone but I'm telling *you* so that you understand what Shand is really like. He so successfully conned her that... incredibly,' Margaret pauses, 'she went back for more on Sunday and look what that led to.' She limps closer to Timothy. 'Shand is toxic and *that's* why I kept the photograph' – she glares at him – 'because I knew that one day he would come crawling back, wanting even more from this family and I would need to be ready for him. Now that he's dead and no longer a threat I'll destroy it... and you need to give me that phone back, too.' She nods at it in Timothy's hand. 'If anyone were to hear that message, Jude would have no option but to plead guilty immediately... no trial, no chance... all taken away by *you*.'

She straightens up and regards her nephew impassively. 'But by all means, if you think everything is black and white in life and you are convinced that Jude deserves to go to prison...' She drums her fingers on the top of her stick as his pocket begins to ring again.

'Heeerrreee's Johnnie!' Margaret quips. 'Go on then: answer the phone. Ruin Jude's life forever.'

NINETEEN

1994

'Excuse me? Please can I speak to you?'

Margaret could hear his footsteps quickening behind her, knew that he would reach her and that she couldn't outrun him. She turned and glared at Richard, the bats flitting around them as the July dusk gave way to night, and slammed the gate to the manège. 'You *can* speak to me, but you *may* not.' She flicked off the floodlights and started back towards the stables.

More footsteps and this time, *this time*, a hand on her arm! She spun around and shook him off. 'Don't you dare touch me!'

'I'm sorry, I'm sorry!' he begged. 'Are you angry with me? You were kind when I first arrived, but I've been trying to speak to you for nearly a month now and you just keep walking away. I need your help with something that only you will understand.'

Such manipulation! The fury began to twist within Margaret's fingers like sharp pieces of metal. She wanted to reach out and scratch him. 'He's my husband. What part of what you've done do you think I'd understand?'

Richard's eyes widened in shock. 'You already know? He's told you?'

'Oh, I know all right,' she hissed. 'I know *exactly* what you've done.'

'I haven't done anything! *He* came to see me and gave me that medicine that made me feel really weird, like I was drunk. I couldn't move. He hurt me.' Richard's eyes filled with tears and he looked at her pleadingly. 'And now it keeps happening. He keeps coming to my room at night. Please tell him to stop.'

Margaret began to understand what he was suggesting and at first her breathing sped up at the horror of it all, but as she stared at the stranger who had so innocently appeared out of thin air and walked right into their lives, intoxicating everyone, she realised that *they* had been the naïve and foolish ones, not him.

'Oh my God,' she whispered, a chill stealing over the skin of her bare arms. 'Who are you?' She took a step back from him. 'Who put you up to this? How much did they say they'd pay you, because it won't be enough. My husband *is* the papers and when he finds out what you're trying to do he'll annihilate you.' To think she'd allowed herself to be so enchanted by this man-child! This trojan horse!

'What? I don't want money – I just want to go home!' Richard exclaimed. 'But he says if I try to leave, he'll tell my dad what I've done with him. He can't do that.' The tears fell from his face. 'It would kill my family.'

'Oh really?' Margaret laughed harshly. 'You'd be amazed what families can survive when they have no choice.' Her voice shook as all of the pieces started to fall into place. 'So let me guess. You're going to need me to get you away from here and give you a nice little set-up to make you forget all of this ever happened, aren't you? You people disgust me. Fuck off back to wherever you came from!' Her voice began to rise.

Richard exclaimed aloud, his body visibly starting to tense and his fists gripping. 'I'm *fifteen!*' He shouted back at her, just as suddenly. 'You said you used to have a son my age and that was too young to be looking for a job on my own, but you've known all along what he's been doing! You're no mother!' His accusations echoed around the yard. 'You're evil!'

Margaret gasped as the words ripped through her skin, tissue and muscle, like a bullet lodging between her shoulder blades and exploding; another cavity created by a boy loved at first sight and lost. Staggering towards him, she reached out a hand and, confused, thinking she was about to fall, Richard instinctively offered his hands to her, but she grabbed for his genitals, squeezing hard, intending to hurt. Richard gasped in pain, his feet lifting up onto his tiptoes.

'Don't you dare mention my son with that filthy mouth of yours,' she breathed. 'You will not bring shame and embarrassment on me or my family when this was obviously what you intended all along.'

'I didn't, I don't!' cried Richard. 'I hate him. You know what he's been doing and you've just been pretending not to see it!'

Margaret released him but just as quickly slapped him hard across the face.

'Stop it!' Richard sobbed. 'Please.'

'You are disgusting and your vile plan will not work on *me*!' Margaret looked around wildly and spied a riding crop. Grabbing it from the table she began to hit his shoulders and his back, hard, hard, *hard* as he cowered in front of her and pretended to cry out for effect, as if she were actually hurting him, which only made her angrier, until she noticed Tansy out of the corner of her eye, watching, terrified.

'Get back to settling down everyone for the night!' Margaret shouted as Tansy turned tail and scuttled off.

Drivetime whickered, appearing in the doorway of his box.

'And you can fuck off too!' Margaret kicked the door.

The young horse rolled his eyes and disappeared back in alarm, vanishing into the gloom as Richard stared at her, scrabbled up and bolted in the direction of the cottage.

'Oh, so *now* you want to just run away?' Margaret called after him triumphantly. 'Don't need my help after all? You little bastard!' The rage that she had been squashing and poking into the deepest corners of her, packing and packing it in for years and years, had exploded, consuming her entire body in a rush, like petrol catching. With an energy she had never felt in her life, she tore after him in her leggings and trainers, stumbling on the uneven earth, soft and swollen with recent unseasonal rain. All she could hear was the sound of her own panting, the muscles in her legs beginning to scream as she sprinted towards the cottage and crashed in through the open front door, still clutching the whip.

'Where are you?' she shouted, rushing straight up the stairs, shoving the tiny bathroom door open and finding it empty, taking two strides across the square of landing into the bedroom; no one there either, curtains half pulled, bed unmade. No clothes, no sign of him, but as she looked down at the tiny bedside table, there was half a packet of cigarettes and one of Benedict's many silver lighters. Roaring aloud, she snatched it up and sparked the flame, holding it first to the covers on the bed, then three steps across to the cheap curtains, gasping in shock at how quickly they whooshed with flames, instinctively dropping the lighter and backing out of the room.

She half slipped down the wooden stairs in her haste to escape, glancing into the tiny sitting room and kitchen – both empty. Stepping out into the deepening dusk she saw him running in the direction of the stables, clutching a small bag.

'Stop!' she shouted and gave chase, but her body had already started to give up on her. Her legs were wobbling and as she reached the lumpy turf, they buckled and her foot caught a divot. She felt and heard something snap as she went over and, just for a blessed moment, she passed out, but when her eyes opened again, she realised she was still on the ground. The physical pain in her ankle was unlike anything she had ever experienced, including childbirth. She began to writhe and gasp, blinded by it, until Tansy loomed over her, hands covering her mouth.

Frightened, Margaret looked down to see what was so horrifying. A white shard of popped bone protruded through her skin, and the foot itself was at an impossibly grotesque angle. Tansy continued to stare at her but then lifted her gaze, something behind Margaret stealing her attention. The girl's mesmerised face began to glow a rosy pink like a child watching fireworks. Margaret twisted to see for herself that the cottage was completely ablaze.

'Don't just stand there!' she shouted at Tansy. 'Go and release the horses before they smell the smoke and try to kick their way out!'

The useless idiot finally came to her senses and did as she was told, but before she was even close, Margaret saw that *he'd* got there first; the dark shapes of frightened, fleeing horses were already galloping out across the parkland.

* * *

On her return from the hospital late the following morning, Margaret insisted on being taken to her study. She was sitting behind her desk, looking out over the estate, her eyes swollen and raw from crying, when the door opened and Benedict appeared, dressed in a suit and whistling jauntily. He stopped at the sight of her.

'Margaret! What are you doing down here? Mrs Brooks was supposed to have put you to bed to keep your foot up!'

'She tried to. I have some correspondence to chase.' She leafed loosely through some papers, the pages falling from her fingers, then looked out of the window again, her eyes filling with yet more tears.

'Darling, even you can't have an ankle pinned in the middle

of the night then the next morning simply behave as if nothing has happened!' Benedict looked at her carefully. 'You've got a lot of general anaesthetic swilling around your system, which always makes you feel blue. Admin can wait. Go to bed and rest. I'll have Mrs Brooks bring you some tea.'

Margaret turned her head to look at him. He was wearing his club tie like he was Bertie Wooster. 'You're going to London?'

'Yes.' He tightened the knot cheerfully. 'Last-minute thing. Afternoon meeting but I might stay on for supper and possibly overnight.'

The phone on her desk rang, and Benedict gratefully dived for it before she could lodge any objection.

'Lord Fawkes. No, Lady Fawkes is... oh. Have we?' He looked at his watch. 'Oh hell. No I can't, but... leave it with me for five minutes, please. Thank you.' He hung up and raised his eyebrows. 'You've forgotten to collect Jude from school. They've been crossly on the phone, apparently, wondering if we're stuck in traffic because it is, of course, the last day of term and everyone else has gone home.'

'Oh God!' gasped Margaret. 'You must ring them back now and charm them, explain about my accident. You'll have to drive, obviously.' She reached for her crutches. 'If I come at least they'll see we're not making it up.'

Benedict stared at her. 'Don't be ridiculous! You've just been discharged from hospital! You're not going anywhere and neither am I! I've said I'll be at this meeting now. Brooks can go and get her.'

'That makes it obvious we completely forgot to collect our own child – what will they think of us?' Margaret struggled to a stand.

Benedict shrugged. 'I couldn't give a shit.'

Margaret felt the blood rush to her head and the first prickles of pain in her leg. They had warned her to stay ahead of it rather than only take the medication once it had started to hurt again. Was she due some more now? She couldn't remember. 'That's as may be, but *I* care.' Her voice trembled. 'You must come and get her. Please.'

'No,' Benedict replied simply. 'Sorry.' He put his hands in his pockets and felt around for his keys. 'I'll let you know if I'm going to stay in town later though.'

'You don't need to go. You're not an editor any more, Benedict. You're a former, very mediocre MP who was given a job by a friend; it's not the nineteen fucking fifties and you *are* to come back after your "meeting".' Margaret's voice shook with energy. 'If you're not going to collect Jude, you can at least be here to have dinner with us later. I'm not asking you, I'm telling you.'

Benedict put his head on one side, regarded her thoughtfully then laughed very suddenly, making Margaret jump. 'I'll let you know what I decide to do.'

He turned to leave the room.

'Benedict – about the boy.' She watched her husband's body freeze and wished she could see his face, his first instinctive reaction, but as he turned back to look at her his expression was impassive.

'It's done. He's gone. Leave it, Margaret, there's nothing more to say.'

They watched each other, both assessing their next move, the silence only broken by the whir of cogs as the clock prepared to chime. The cuckoo emerged from its little door and Benedict glared at it, moving like a snake and striking at the switch so that the tiny bird froze, beak open mid-cry.

'"Nothing more to say?"' Margaret repeated in a whisper, her hands and fingers trembling, the ends having turned white with the pressure of gripping the crutches to maintain her balance as she tried to stay on her feet.

Benedict stepped forward, right up to her. 'What do you

want me to tell you? That I loved him? Would that make it better or worse?'

'Love?' She could barely breathe. 'That's not love!'

'Do not presume to tell me how I feel,' Benedict said. 'You know, perhaps you're right.' He looked at her searchingly, reached out and placed his hand lightly on her jaw, tipping her face up to his as if to kiss her. 'Maybe I should go and find him,' he whispered.

Margaret's trembling began to intensify as she looked into his cool, emotionless eyes. 'If you ever go near him again, I will ruin you. I have *pictures* that will ruin you. You will lose what little political credibility you have left. The papers will turn on you, and I will see you out of here without so much as a penny to your name.'

Benedict shook his head gently. 'You wouldn't do that in a million years! Have people pity and ridicule you? Humiliate yourself? Expose your own marriage as a sham?'

'It's not a sham! You made a mistake and I'm prepared to accept that, but—'

'Yes, we all make mistakes, don't we, Margaret?' He watched her carefully. 'Sometimes when we're in South Africa without our husbands...'

Margaret flushed. 'We're talking about you here. Not me. This must *never* happen again. In any case, I've paid him off. Bought his silence – because you know *that's* what it was about, right? Money? There's no fool like an old fool.'

A muscle in Benedict's jaw flickered as he held her in his hand and his grip tightened. 'You used to have such a beautiful mouth.' For a moment Margaret thought he might finally hit her... but he let her go.

She swallowed, the wet jelly around her exposed, soft heart beginning to harden into husk again. 'Is there anything that could incriminate you?'

Benedict looked sulky. 'No. Of course not.'

'You're sure? You didn't write him any of your dreadful mooning poetry, nothing like that?'

Her husband glanced at her with intense dislike. 'You are an appalling bitch sometimes, Margaret.' He whisked around on the spot and banged out of the room, the door slamming so hard that the frame reverberated, before Highcombe settled back into position.

Margaret gave way to tears that fell onto the old-fashioned blotter beneath her fingers, only wiping them hurriedly as a tentative knock announced Mrs Brooks's arrival.

'Ah, perfect timing,' Margaret managed. 'Could you ask Mr Brooks to get the car ready, please? I need him to drive me to collect Jude from school. We're rather late leaving already.'

Mrs Brooks eyed her employer's pallor and tear stains. 'You don't look well, Your Ladyship. You really shouldn't—'

Margaret lifted her head wearily. 'I will not have them thinking I forgot my own child. I will not have them saying anything about me at all.'

'But no one will think any the worse of you for having an...' Mrs Brooks paused, 'accident. You can't help—'

'Oh, will you stop bloody fussing?' Margaret exploded. 'Just for once, will someone do as I say?'

Mrs Brooks bit her lip and turned to leave the room.

'Wait!' Margaret called after her.

Mrs Brooks stopped and looked back over her shoulder. 'It's all right, Your Ladyship. You don't need to apologise.'

Margaret stared at her. 'I wasn't going to. Richard Shand...' She sat down again. 'After Mr Brooks found him walking to the station, he drove him where, exactly?'

'A pub in Manchester. Belonging to an uncle, I believe.'

Margaret snorted. That sounded about right. An 'uncle' indeed... 'And Shand was given the money?'

'Yes, Your Ladyship.'

'Well, while I'm *sorry*,' she spoke acidly, picking up her pen, 'that Mr Brooks will need to get back in the car again after spending so long in it already, I really do need to go, so tell him to be as quick as he can.'

'Yes, Your Ladyship. And *I'm* sorry that things ended between you and Richard so painfully.' Mrs Brooks's voice shook slightly at her own bravery. 'What do they call them in the papers? Toy boys, isn't it?'

Margaret looked up with sharp surprise at her employee. There was a moment of silence as the two women regarded each other.

'I will, of course, be making a generous extra payment to Mr Brooks this month, to thank him and you for your discretion,' Margaret said eventually. 'That'll be all.' She watched Mrs Brooks dart from the room and closed her eyes.

Fucking people. Every one of them a crushing, predictable disappointment. Every single one.

* * *

'Anyway, that was what the other teacher said, but I don't know if it was true.' Jude finally drew breath and stopped talking, nervously fiddling with the pendant necklace her parents had given her for her recent birthday.

Margaret put her knife and fork down. 'Why don't you go down to the stables and see the horses?' The incessant prattle was increasingly getting on her nerves.

Jude wrinkled her nose. 'Do I have to?'

'Well, go and see Tansy then.' Margaret's voice was flat.

'You'll meet the new horse boy,' her father added unexpectedly. 'Very good with your mother's one apparently.'

Margaret coughed and reached for her napkin. 'No, he's left actually, Daddy. Unfortunately, he burnt the groom's cottage down.'

'We had to "fire" him.' Benedict laughed, sitting back and

picking up his wine glass as he looked at Margaret. 'Didn't we, my love?'

'I didn't fire him, he absconded.' Margaret reached for her knife and fork again.

'He set the cottage on fire?' Her father mumbled in astonishment, slowly raising his hand to scratch the tight shell-pink skin of his liver-spotted head in confusion. 'I don't believe it! He seemed such a nice boy. Always said hello when he saw me being wheeled down the drive to the stables in this thing, getting some air.' He lightly tapped the arm of his chair. 'What have the police said? Have they caught him?'

Benedict put his glass down. 'It was no more than a careless accident, Henry. Cheeky cigarette. The police have got better things to do. But you should fire Tansy too.' He nodded at Margaret. 'Can't have a head groom who turns a blind eye to smoking at the stables.'

'What?' Jude's knife dropped to her plate with a heart-broken clatter. 'But she's been here forever. Oh Mummy, don't sack her!' She looked at her mother pleadingly, who ignored her and instead stared at Benedict.

'That's the stance we're taking, is it?' she asked. 'Because Anthony and Fan arrive tonight and I suggest that we—'

'Oh for God's sake,' Benedict groaned. 'So I could have stayed in London then, you'd have had plenty of help if you'd come off your crutches. Why are they here *again*?'

'They flew in this morning to collect Timothy for the holidays and take him home.'

'For two people that live in South Africa they spend a remarkable amount of time in England,' grumbled Benedict. 'Haven't they heard of hotels? Why do they have to come here and bring that vast pudding with them?'

'Because it's Anthony's home.' Her father's head shook as he tried to hold it up defiantly, his rheumy eyes fixing fiercely on Benedict. '*His* home.'

Benedict shoved his chair back from the table. 'Well, I think I shall pop back down to London now.'

Margaret gave a sharp, tight exhalation. 'It's half past seven. You'll have missed the dinner in any case.'

But Benedict was already rounding the table to kiss her goodbye. 'Darling heart, I shall be back before you know it. Never fear.' He bent and briefly touched the back of her neck coolly with his lips. 'Look after your mother, pip squeak.' He blew a kiss at Jude, shoved his hands in his suit pockets, and disappeared off whistling, without a care in the world.

* * *

The voices were rising in the library as Jude and Timothy sat in the small sitting room on the other side of the door, scrunched up on the old squashy sofa watching TV.

'My dad never yells.' Timothy glanced behind him as they both heard Anthony shout: 'But that's not the point, Margaret!'

'Wow. He full-named her. Do you know what it's all about?' Jude bit her nail worriedly. 'Did they say anything in the car after they picked you up from school?'

'Um.' Timothy squirmed uncomfortably. 'Sort of.' He darted a look at Jude. 'I'm not supposed to tell you.'

Jude leant forward and punched him gently on the arm. 'You have to! I'm your cousin, we have to stick together. You need to have my back. I've got yours.'

'OK.' Timothy wriggled round reluctantly to face her and took a deep breath. 'So my mum said your mum has fallen in love with Richard. He worked in the stables.'

'I think Grandpa was talking about him at supper?' Jude whispered. 'Seriously?'

Timothy nodded. 'He's *our* age, Jude.'

'What?' Jude exclaimed. 'That can't be right!'

'It is. I met him. He was really nice.' Timothy grabbed a

cushion and began to twist the corner of it anxiously, not meeting Jude's eye. 'He helped me to stop being afraid – of the horses,' he added quickly.

'But my mother would never do something like that. It's gross.'

Timothy wriggled a bit closer. Jude could smell a slightly sweaty and stale tang clinging to the school uniform he was still wearing. 'My mum said it wouldn't be the first time she's cheated,' he whispered. 'Obviously.'

Jude drew back and fanned her nose. 'What do you mean "Obviously"?'

Timothy looked at her, wounded. 'I don't smell. Don't be mean.' He lowered his eyes and muttered: 'My mum says that your dad is a "poof".'

Jude's heart began to beat a little faster. 'No, he isn't.'

'She says he's disgusting and because you and Hilary were born your mum has "obviously" had other boyfriends.' He swallowed and wouldn't look up. 'She says your real dad is in South Africa. He went to school with my dad.'

'What?' Jude exclaimed. 'That's not true at all! He—'

'Get out!' The library door was flung open before Jude could formulate her thoughts any further, and a white-faced Margaret appeared, leaning heavily on her crutches. 'Go on, get out of my house!'

'I will leave,' said Fan, her voice level, 'because I don't want to upset you any further when you had major surgery last night and are probably so full of drugs you don't know what you are saying, but this is not your house. You live here because Henry lets you. When he dies, it will unfortunately be my house, as Anthony's wife' – she glanced at her husband, caught miserably between the two women – 'and you will not be able to live here any more. There will have to be a way of maintaining this place financially and that means opening it up; weddings, conferences, shoots, so please – if you want the family to hold onto Highcombe, no more scandal and, particularly, no more arson.'

'Oh, just get out,' spat Margaret. 'I see you, Frances. You're a cheap fake... all of that grasping ambition and prejudice hidden beneath your simpering "kindness". Go back to South Africa where you belong.' Margaret felt she was about to faint. Her body was sinking lower and lower onto the arm supports of the crutches.

Fan's cheeks flushed. 'He wasn't interested in you, Meg! You're much too old for him. You've made a fool of yourself and a fool of us!'

Margaret froze and stared at her sister-in-law. 'You are disgusting,' she managed eventually.

'*I'm* disgusting? Everybody is talking about you. Everyone! You are a laughing stock.' Fan turned to Anthony. 'We're leaving.'

'Oh, he doesn't have to go,' said Margaret. 'Just you. It's just you that is no longer welcome here.'

Fan laughed bitterly. 'When will you learn, Margaret, that if you force people to choose, you will never win?'

'That's rich, you lecturing me about choice!' Margaret exclaimed. 'Who on earth would choose *you* unless they had to? A ghastly, uncouth, cheap and fat little blob with dreadful hair who bores everyone rigid... It was only because you were already pregnant that he felt he had to stand by you and go through with it!'

'Margaret,' breathed Anthony, his face rigid with shock.

Fan began to twist the wedding ring on her finger, looking at Anthony, her eyes wide. 'Ant?'

'Don't speak to my mother like that!' Timothy thundered, jumping up, scarlet in the face. 'She's good and kind and I love her! I'm sorry, Jude.' He turned wildly to his cousin. 'Dad, we need to leave. Now.'

He ran over to Fan, who had started to cry. 'You're horrible.'

He looked at Margaret, his own eyes filling up as he wrapped a stout arm around his mother's shoulders. 'DAD! NOW!'

Timothy led his mother from the room as Anthony, who had been staring silently at his sister, came to life and obediently followed his son, only pausing to hug a horrified Jude.

'I'm so sorry, darling. I didn't mean this to happen. You can come and live with us whenever you want. You've always got a home with us.'

'Oh no you don't! You can't have her. She stays with me.' Margaret inched closer on her crutches as Anthony let Jude go.

He shot one last wounded and much colder look at Margaret before he hurried from the room.

With a wail, Margaret fell to the sofa, her crutches splaying out beside her.

'Mummy!' Jude rushed over to her. 'Are you all right? Timothy said Aunt Fan called Daddy a "poof" and that he isn't my real father.'

'What on earth are you talking about?' Margaret gasped, covering her face with her hands. 'Can't you see how much pain I'm in?'

'I'm sorry. I didn't mean to upset you. I – oh Mummy!' Jude glanced down at her mother's leg to see a fresh, vivid scarlet blossoming, like the spreading petals of a peony, through her mother's bandages. 'I think you might have split your stitches. That's a lot of blood! Mummy! Look at me! What do I do? I should know what to do!'

'I'm fine,' gasped Margaret. 'I'm fine.' She grasped tightly at her daughter's wrist as the furnishings began to blur, her head became heavier and Jude started to scream, but Margaret felt strangely calm, as if she just wanted to go to sleep. Find Hilary.

She closed her eyes but it was *Richard's* tear-stained, reproachful face she saw staring back at her, holding out his arms, but just as quickly the image disappeared like the reflection of sunlight on water and he was gone.

TWENTY

PRESENT DAY

Timothy lets Johnnie's third call go and exclaims aloud in frustration at his own eternal, impotent inability to take control. He turns around just in time to see a small smile vanishing from Margaret's face.

'What could you possibly be finding amusing about this?' he asks incredulously. 'You've told me there's a recording of the violent death of someone I once knew on this phone that could send someone I love very much, to prison. How is that remotely *funny*? Are you lying to me?'

Margaret's mouth flattens out and her eyes harden. 'Don't be absurd! Listen to it for yourself then, but I warn you now, it's not something you will ever be able to un-hear... oh, just give them to me!' Margaret comes alive suddenly, tired of waiting, and thumps her stick on the floor, leaving a neat little circle on the dusty bare boards like a wax seal. 'Jude made a mistake, that's all. A brutal, terrible mistake... but he betrayed her very badly and you *know* she is a good person, Timothy. Should a life well-lived be defined by one act of madness? There is a very, very fine line between innocence and guilt.'

Margaret is right in front of Timothy now, at the top of the stairs. 'My dear boy' – she places a hand on his shoulder and he flinches as, clasping her stick in the other, she turns him gently so that the large, warped glass window is behind him – 'stand where I can actually see you and listen very carefully to what I am going to say, one last time. No, look at me, Timothy,' she instructs, waiting until he does as he's told. 'I have been very far from an example of the best mother, but Shand will destroy Jude from beyond the grave over my dead body. Give me the phone and the photograph.'

'But surely it's about doing what's *right*?'

Whatever he is expecting his aunt to do next, it is not what actually happens. She simply grips her stick as if his words have turned her to stone, her eyes close and she pitches backwards, like a statue knocked from a plinth, falling down the shallow flight of five stairs behind her, only becoming human again at the last moment and, instead of crumbling, splaying on the small landing between the second and the first flight of stairs, below him.

'Margaret?' he gasps and rushes down. What on earth just happened? Her stick has slithered away from her, her jumper has rucked up slightly and her legging-clad legs are grotesquely bent and folded in a way that doesn't look compatible with her ever getting up again. She is unconscious.

'Aunt Margaret?' He sets the phone and photograph down so that he can place his fingers on her cool wrist first to search for a pulse, and then under her nose to see if he can feel her breath on his skin. She was just talking to him a moment ago!

As panic begins to overwhelm him, the automaton up in the open space above comes to life out of nowhere. He looks up to see it moving its stiff wings, opening its beak and singing a couple of notes before stopping just as suddenly as it started. Timothy scrambles to his feet and pushes his back against the wall in terror, now barely in control of his sensibilities. He doesn't want to be in this space a second longer. God, how he hates this house!

'Mrs Brooks!' he shouts and practically falls down the next flight himself in his haste to get help and get away from whatever it is that just happened. 'Help! We need an ambulance! Quickly!'

* * *

It is only when he and Mr and Mrs Brooks are watching the remarkably prompt ambulance containing his aunt pull away... and the immediate shock of thinking she actually just died standing on her feet in front of him is dissipating... that Timothy pats his pockets to make sure he has his keys, wallet and phone to follow on in the car – and remembers.

'Mrs Brooks' – he spins on the spot, the gravel crunching under his feet – 'did you see anything on the landing next to Lady Fawkes when you attended to her? A phone maybe?'

The housekeeper shakes her head. 'It was just Her Ladyship out cold, not moving. I put the blanket straight over her and the pillow under her head and waited until you came back up and they put her on the stretcher.'

Timothy pictures the swathes of that very blanket being tucked around his aunt as she was carefully lifted into the ambulance – now disappearing up the drive.

'Shit!' he shouts out loud, making Mr and Mrs Brooks jump and stare first at him and then each other.

'She's got them in there with her!' he exclaims, turning to run to his car but he knows he's already too late.

* * *

When he's finally allowed onto the ward and is shown to the bay where Margaret is lying peacefully, he finds her fully clothed, bar her jumper which is hanging over the back of a chair alongside her thick socks. His eyes alight on his aunt's long-damaged ankle which he has never seen in the flesh. There is a large dip in the vein-threaded skin where something anatomical is missing, and a crude purple scar cuts into the crevice, all jagged joints and staple marks. A lump of misplaced bone sticks out at the side of the ankle, and Timothy swallows. How on earth she has managed to walk on *that* for all these years? It must plague her every single day.

Margaret's eyelids flutter and she regards him briefly before closing them again. 'Hello, Timothy.'

'What did you do with the photo and the phone?' he asks, putting down her boots he'd found by the back door, alongside an overnight bag Mrs Brooks packed 'just in case' on a chair.

'How nice to see you too.' She shifts uncomfortably. 'I put them in the bin somewhere here... but do you know, I can't remember which one? There must be hundreds of them. May I ask' – she turns her head to a nurse, who has just come into the bay to get a machine and has started to wheel it out – 'what happens to all of the rubbish in a hospital?'

'It's incinerated,' the nurse replies absently, trying not to run over Timothy's foot as she leaves.

Margaret looks at Timothy, gives a wan smile and closes her eyes. 'I win.'

'You *win*?' she hears him repeat, incredulously. 'It's not a game, Margaret. Jude has just been formally charged. I found out on my way over here. Margaret? Did you hear me? Do you even care?'

Margaret doesn't open her eyes. She refuses to cry in front of him.

* * *

When the curtain to the bay pulls back Margaret sits up in the hope that it's Timothy, back after all, because she wants some water, but it's a doctor, accompanied by a nurse. 'Finally.' She winces as she adjusts her position. 'I take it you've come to tell me I can now go home? I've been here for hours!'

The doctor smiles, unruffled. She reminds Margaret of the ditsy lawyer girl. Daisy? 'I'm sorry we've kept you,' she says. 'While it's great to have established you haven't broken any bones, we still needed to do a few other tests and the hospital is really busy at the moment. Is your son still here?' She looks around, presumably for Timothy, and Margaret waits for the 'son' sting to pass.

'He's my nephew, and I don't think so. He was cross with me. I expect he's gone home in a sulk.'

The doctor and nurse look between each other.

'Don't do that,' Margaret snaps. 'It makes me feel like a headmistress who wants to give you both detention for being annoying.'

'There's no one here with you at all? No one we can contact?'

'No. I have a daughter but we don't talk any more.' Margaret's tone is brisk. 'Whatever it is, you're going to have to tell just me, I'm afraid.' She gives them a brittle smile but her heart has started to flutter.

The doctor looks down at the papers in her hands. 'Obviously when someone has a couple of unexpected falls so close together, and one of them might have been caused by a loss of consciousness *before* falling, we have to consider what might be causing that—'

Oh, thank goodness! That's what they're on about. Obviously she can't tell these two teenagers that she staged both incidents and the numerous scans they did earlier were completely pointless; she purposefully tripped on the rug and threw herself down the stairs. It'll be interesting to see what they're about to incorrectly attribute that to, however. Margaret folds her hands in her lap and, out of nowhere, remembers a past boyfriend – one she rather liked, pre-Benedict – driving her back to High-combe too fast and running over one of the peacocks her mother had just grandly installed on the drive.

They'd both gone to announce their 'discovery' of the dead bird and found her parents having tea with a professor of medicine and his surgeon wife. All four adults had stood over the dead peacock on the tarmac, which practically had a tyre print down its back, and the professor of medicine had gravely nodded and said: 'Bird influenza, I shouldn't wonder, Henry. You might want to get your chap to keep the chickens in for a while.' Margaret rather lost her faith in the medical profession after that. She smiles at the memory of sharing an incredulous look with the boyfriend and wonders what became of him. Very good in bed as she remembers. And out of it. They did it pretty much everywhere, in fact. She sighs wistfully.

'Margaret?' The doctor's voice draws her back and Margaret blinks, about to ask her to refer to her as *Lady Fawkes, please*, when the doctor says, 'And it was during that general examination that one of my colleagues felt the hardness and the lump in your tummy.'

'Oh *that*.' Margaret grimaces. 'It's been there for a while. The start of something deeply glamorous like a hernia, I expect. I still ride often and muck out. I'll have just lifted something awkwardly.' She waves a vague hand.

The doctor and nurse look at each other again. Secret squirrels.

'Oh for God's sake, just stop it!' Margaret bursts. 'I don't know who told you this is an acceptable bedside manner but they were woefully misguided!'

'We've done some blood tests and scanned you,' the doctor hurriedly continues. 'Margaret, the news I have to give you now may be very hard to take in but you have advanced stomach cancer and—'

'Cancer?' Margaret interrupts incredulously. A beat passes as she stares at the doctor. 'Right, well, then I want to know' – she sits herself up – 'and don't give me the PC line you're no doubt told to trot out which talks about averages, variables and outcomes, because I shan't be having any treatment – exactly how long do I have left?'

* * *

'Here we are,' Timothy says as they pull up outside the prison gates. 'But I reiterate, they're not going to let you in to see her, so this has essentially been a pointless hour-long journey when you really should have gone straight home from the hospital.'

'I don't want to see her and I told you, there's nothing wrong with me, just a few bruises.' Margaret leans forward to look out of the window. 'I should have had something more sensible on my feet than just a pair of socks, then I wouldn't have slipped on the attic stairs, but *thank* you for coming back to get me and *thank* you for bringing me here. I just wanted to see for myself that she will be safe. One watches such ghastly images of prisons on TV. Overcrowded Victorian buildings not fit for purpose. You're a parent. You understand that, surely?'

Timothy stares straight ahead. 'I'm doing this for Jude, not you. She would want me to collect you from the hospital, and she would want you not to be worried about where she is. It was the right thing to do. That's all.'

Margaret rolls her eyes. Sanctimonious little shit. Sometimes he is very much his mother's son.

'Well, I think this is rather nice, Timothy!' She peers through the Land Rover window at the squat red-brick building in front of her. 'Modern double-glazing, well-tended gardens. It's got the look of a travel hotel about it, don't you think? Yes. I feel very much better now! Jude will be fine. Thank you. Let's go back to Highcombe.'

* * *

She hobbles into the gloomy kitchen, everything aching and really rather starting to hurt, but she feels calm, as one always does when one has decided upon a plan. She puts the overnight bag on the table and fills a glass, glancing into the garden in blowsy full bloom, sloping down towards Highcombe, glowing gloriously in the still-strong late-afternoon sun. She carries the glass over to the table, removes the phone from her bag and sets it down to stare at it as she gingerly takes a seat. She thinks about the photograph, sitting in one of the bins at the hospital waiting to be burnt and gone forever, but *this* still has a purpose to serve.

Taking a sip of water, she thinks about the pictures of Jude kissing Shand. That hurts almost more than the dull-coloured bruises starting to rise to the surface of her skin like fat in gravy. There was no end to the lengths he was prepared to go to, but Jude could have said no, she *should* have said no. She knew what Shand was like. She was warned and she did it anyway.

It was a breathtakingly heartless and deliberate act of betrayal.

Margaret looks at the phone again. The shocking revelations the small, cheap handset contains would start a firestorm of activity she has neither the time nor the energy for right now: questions, statements, solicitors. Her last six months would be entirely gobbled up... a waste of her time in every sense of the word and Jude owes her these six months. She is perfectly safe in the neat, ordered building Margaret saw earlier. The time will pass quickly and all Margaret wants is a lunch here and there; the theatre, a gallery, a few early morning hacks in the crisp coming autumn, her favourite time of year – nothing extravagant but a swan song, nonetheless.

Margaret has always liked the notion that swans start to sing just before their death because they have been silent for most of their life.

Yes. She will have this last moment and *then* she will hand the phone in.

PART FIVE

ONE YEAR LATER | AUGUST 2023

TWENTY-ONE

'Just remember – we don't have to prove you are innocent, we have to show them that there is reason to doubt your guilt.'

Johnnie feels as if he's repeating the same platitudes again and again as they wait in the tiny cell, little more the size of a horsebox, deep in the bowels of the Old Bailey. It had evidently shocked Jude to arrive in the blacked-out prison van to quite so many shadowy, shouting figures pressed up against the other side of the glass, random bangs of their fists to get her attention, cameras held up, as they called her name.

There is the immense interest in her case that accompanies all stories the desperate-for-content, twenty-four-hour-news outlets are hungry for these days. It will be a short trial at two weeks which they also like, as the case stays nice and fresh, but most of all, she's silver-standard clickbait; an attractive woman accused of a violent crime... bettered only by the gold medal *missing* attractive woman, probably the victim of a violent crime.

He warned her to expect the presence of the media, but the reality of their greeting will have felt very hostile and frightening.

The world is a different place to the one Jude stepped out of a year ago to go to prison; hotter, even angrier, the cost of everything is going up and up, everyone striking... What effect will that backdrop have on the jury though, if any? Will it make them more or less open-minded? He has no idea. He watches her, trembling and small, twisting her now longer, growing-out hair around her finger. She does at least look sympathetic. For a moment he imagines Margaret in her place. She would have been defiant in the dock, imperious, unable to accept being on the wrong side of the pomp, language and customs designed by their nature to be exclusive. It would have isolated her from everyone. She would have been the very definition of an unsympathetic defendant.

But as he looks at Jude, waiting to be called, he only sees a very frightened woman who has a year of experiences under her belt which have changed her forever. He's read her prison report: issues with sleeping, nightmares, anxiety, dietary problems, tends towards isolation, an inability to adapt to the prison environment, depression... Today has been a long time coming for her.

And now it's here, he has warned her as best he can that it's going to be the Crown's job to bring Richard back to life... show the jury that he was a living, breathing, feeling person. Richard's family, his friends and other important people to him will all be told that Jude brutally took his future away from him, with her bare hands.

He looks down at those hands, resting in her lap, the nails nervously bitten to the quick, her rough, raw skin that looks sore, probably because she keeps picking it. He knows she is dreading seeing Shand resurrected. Dreading having to talk about it. Dreading having to listen to the evidence, the experts, the barristers, the judge – all of them trying to apply the law to what only *she* knows happened that night. He tries to think of something to say that will reassure her, but before he manages it, a noise distracts him and he looks up to see Yasmin has come down to them, in her wig and gown.

He frowns. 'Problem?'

Yasmin smiles tightly. 'Lord Stratham has just arrived... with Lady Fawkes... who is about to make her way to the public gallery. Do you think you could go and have a word? She's giving off some pretty strong not-giving-a-damn vibes which I think we can probably do without.'

Jude's mouth has fallen open and it's a moment before she appears able to speak. 'My mother is here? No response to my letters, no visits, no contact for a year but she's here *now*?'

'Leave it with me.' Johnnie stands up quickly. 'I'll sort this out. It'll all be all right.'

* * *

He hurriedly takes the steep stairs two at a time, becoming angrier and more breathless with each leap. What the fuck is Margaret playing at? This eleventh-hour appearance can't just be a simple but pathological need for control and attention, nothing is simple with her... and the woman doesn't have a conscience either, so she won't have been drawn here because of a sense of parental responsibility.

He pauses for a second at the top of the steps and thinks about Timothy's tearful confession after Margaret's plunge down the stairs last year; Margaret's insistence that there was a recording of Jude killing Shand on her phone and *that's* why it had needed to be destroyed. Johnnie exclaims aloud with derision, just as he did at the time. Utter bullshit. She has never believed her daughter capable of such a crime. So what is it? Why is she here?

He turns the corner to see Margaret herself making her way towards security and swears under his breath in disbelief.

He hasn't seen her for a good few months. Margaret is

wearing an androgynous wide-legged black trouser suit which she's teamed with the palest of pink silk shirts. Her much longer, now silver-white hair hangs down past the middle of her back, but is drawn off her face in a half-ponytail secured with a thin black band to reveal pearl and diamond drop earrings. Vast sunglasses cover half of her face. She drums her fingers on her stick as she waits for Johnnie, causing a vast ruby on her finger to catch the sunlight and gleam like a glass heart. She is utterly mesmerising.

Fucking, *fucking* hell. Johnnie closes his eyes, takes a deep breath and hastens over to his former client and Timothy, who is standing several steps behind his aunt, also dressed in a new linen suit. He already appears Britishly crumpled in stark contrast to Margaret's sharpness.

Up close however, as Margaret removes her glasses, Johnnie sees tired eyes and skin that has a delicate rice-paper quality to it. Tiny beads of sweated make-up are clustering around her hairline. Her hands grip the stick but the ring has already slipped round, too big on her finger, so that the ruby is digging into her palm. The swathes of the suit can't quite hide her thin frame.

'I dare you to say it to my face,' she says as he stares. 'I dare you to tell me I don't look magnificent.'

'You do,' he says truthfully. 'And that's exactly both the point and the problem, Margaret.'

'I can't see why. Pastels and pearls, after all.' She gestures at her shirt and earrings. 'All I'm going to do is sit in the *public* gallery.'

'Why don't you—' begins Johnnie.

'They're going to find out that she's the *Honourable* Jude Beauchamp, you can't hide her background, and if I'm not here, people will read into it.' Margaret simply speaks across him. 'They will think it means Jude did it and I've washed my hands of her. For the purposes of this trial, I will not have everyone think that the family has fallen and this baseless mire of scandal is about to consume us. In any case, plenty of people's children have had rather public difficulties, I've come to discover. You're almost no one if you haven't.'

So that's it. At all costs maintain the façade... and the circus of trying to stop her will do more harm than good.

He stands to one side.

She is pleased, like a cat that has just stumbled upon a mouse she shall now play with. 'Thank you. Come along, Timothy.'

'No,' Tim says flatly behind her. 'I said I'd bring you here and I have, but I'm not going in. My phone's in the car. Johnnie can call me when you want picking up again.' He turns and simply walks out of the building.

Margaret tuts. 'He is becoming very disagreeable in his middle age.'

'You're sure you wouldn't rather join him?' Johnnie says. 'You're going to find some of the evidence very upsetting?'

Margaret raises a heavily drawn-on eyebrow. 'I'll be the judge of that.'

* * *

Johnnie is already seated behind Yasmin as Jude is led into the comparatively brightly lit courtroom – there are no windows – looking around as she's led to the dock, blinking, almost as if she is confused by where she finds herself. He smiles reassuringly, but she looks right through him and up to the gallery, where her mother is sitting.

Margaret stares resolutely ahead and refuses to meet Jude's eye. Jude's initial expression of disbelief, presumably at the shock of her mother's altered appearance as much as anything, begins to fade until her shoulders sag and she lowers her gaze, fixing it down at the ground and on her feet instead. Johnnie frowns. This is exactly the Jude he did *not* want the jury to see when they walk in and take their places in the currently empty box. Hunched over, miserable, looking like she is guilty. Damn you, Margaret!

They all stand for the judge – Her Honour Judge Caroline Silverton KC – to take her place and the court staff begin their practised routine. The jury is sworn in, and Jude doesn't look up once. She only raises her gaze when the barristers set to work, seeming to focus on the snowy, creamy tones of Yasmin's wig – in comparison with the sepia one perching on the formidable brain of the very experienced prosecution barrister, David Hamlin KC. David's glasses are balanced on the end of his sharp nose, having appeared to slip there because all of his spare flesh has been so efficiently burnt away by the sheer energy created by the pistons going double time in his mind. Johnnie observes the man's gown swamping his lean body as he practically jumps to his feet with a practised confidence.

'Members of the jury, I will shortly open the case for the prosecution that the Crown brings against the defendant. Almost exactly a year ago, Richard Shand died at his home at a little past midnight. There is no doubt that one of the twenty-two stab wounds inflicted upon Mr Shand was responsible for his death. There is no doubt that only Mr Shand and Jude Beauchamp were in the property when Mr Shand died. You will learn that an argument about betrayal ensued and Richard was stabbed multiple times with a knife from his own kitchen. Jude Beauchamp insists that Richard stabbed himself these *twenty-two times* in front of her. It is the Crown's case that Jude Beauchamp inflicted these wounds upon Richard Shand, that she killed him and that she intended to kill him from the very moment she arrived at his home. It was a hot, late-summer night... but make no mistake, this was a very cold-blooded murder indeed.'

Jude swallows and reaches for her water with a shaky hand.

Mr Hamlin says she did it; Jude's defence is simply that she was there, but she didn't do it.

These two positions will be added to, bit by bit; evidence, expert opinions. Like someone standing at the front of the courtroom pressing clay together to form a sculpture, they will shape it, take lumps off, remould it again – until it becomes something tangible. For a moment Johnnie imagines a time lapse film of someone building a bust from scratch, sees the eyes and face begin to form until they recognisably belong to Richard Shand. He pictures Richard opening his eyes and looking accusatively at all of them.

Johnnie shudders. Glancing at the gallery he sees Margaret watching David Hamlin intently. Jude, on the other hand, is looking at the floor again, her eyes already full of tears.

TWENTY-TWO

'If the members of the jury could please take a copy of the graphics bundle and pass it along until you all have one. Thank you,' David Hamlin begins, looking at his notes and waiting as an usher hands the files to the jury. Johnnie opens his copy and looks through the evidence: scene photographs, images of the knife and the empty slot in the wooden block, a pool of blood on the kitchen floor from which a body has been removed, the picture of Jude and Richard kissing, spliffs in the tin, her blood-splattered dress, CCTV stills of her arriving at the flat on foot and alone while the same dress was still crisp and clean... leaving again covered in blood clutching her phone... by the Thames, arm arching back while throwing something in the water... returning empty-handed with wet, dripping hair... At the back of the file is a photo of Jude's work lanyard. In the profile picture she looks tired and unsmiling in her uniform.

She looks uncaring, Johnnie thinks in dismay, the very last person you would want to nurse you if you were ill and vulnerable. In contrast, at the beginning of the file is a picture of a young Richard, smiling happily in his soldier's uniform. He looks proud, confident: an upstanding young man who fought for his country and was a credit to society.

David Hamlin is very obviously determined to make it clear to the jury straight out of the trap that the pictures they will see of pools of blood may look anonymous but it all flowed from a person with a life, someone who would have willingly given it to protect any one of them and keep them safe in their beds. A good man who had everything taken away from him the night before he was bravely preparing to stand up in a court *just like this one* and give damning evidence against the defendant's mother.

And just in case the jury has been left in any doubt about the nature of this man, Mr Hamlin begins by calling Richard's father to give evidence.

The man who takes the stand and looks back at the jury is the older version of Richard that he will now never become. The father and son share the same kind, clear eyes and dignified stature. Integrity is coming off Mr Shand in waves.

'We spoke at about six o'clock in the evening. Richard didn't want me to attend his trial the next day.' His father speaks with difficulty. 'He said *her* mother' – he points at Jude – 'Lady Fawkes' – he nods furiously up at Margaret in the gallery – 'was going to deny having ever whipped him as a child. He said she'd call him a liar.'

Johnnie winces and closes his eyes as the judge steps in to remind the jury which case is being considered here and what isn't, but the damage is already done; Richard has been successfully positioned as a victim and Jude, as one of *them*.

Remember, Mr Hamlin will remind the jury at every turn... *this woman in the dock is part of a dysfunctional family who believed themselves above the law. They had already hurt Richard before she even picked up the knife!*

Mr Shand clasps his hands behind his back as if ready to face a firing line, while he looks straight into an empty future ahead of him, and waits for the next question. Mr Hamlin pauses, letting the jury see for themselves the impact of this shocking crime on a devastated father.

'Your son was a very organised man, wasn't he?' Mr Hamlin speaks quietly. Respectfully.

Mr Shand nods. 'Yes. It was his army background.'

'You found his affairs were all in order, I believe, after his death?'

'Yes. He left everything to me.' Mr Shand quickly wipes his eyes. 'I've set up a charitable foundation in Richard's name, for children who haven't had the best of starts and need someone to help them get a second chance at life, which is what it said in his will that he wanted.' His lip trembles.

'That is very admirable,' Mr Hamlin says after a moment's pause. 'He was clearly a man of great compassion and empathy. So Mr Shand, you would have expected someone like that to leave a note if he was going to take his own life, wouldn't you? A last letter to you, perhaps?'

'Yes.' Mr Shand nods. 'I would.'

'But no such note was found, either in the property, or online, or with Richard's other very carefully arranged and easily found documents?' Mr Hamlin frowns.

'That's correct.'

'And he gave you no indication at all when you last spoke to him that he was preparing to take his own life?'

'None. I said I'd see him in the morning, he said he loved me, I said I loved him too and that was it.'

Having humanised Richard successfully, once Mr Shand has left the stand, Mr Hamlin swiftly picks the court up and drops them right back down at the beating heart of the drama by playing the recording from the first responder's body camera. Johnnie watches the jury lean forward with fascination as they see the police car door open and the two officers who have picked up the 999 request walk into the lobby of Richard's flat as if in real time. He sees the jury's eyebrows shoot up at how luxurious it all is, before they swallow with anxiety and expectation as the police hurry down a dim, still corridor before beginning to break the door in with ease.

The door shouldn't give way like that in a flat that posh, surely? And oh – what awaits them on the other side? The jury are tense, braced... but then they are in and there is a shape on the floor that is pixelated – Richard – and a *lot* of blood. A shocking amount of blood that makes one female juror gasp aloud.

Johnnie looks at Jude. She has her eyes fixed straight ahead as she hears herself on film flatly telling the officer that Richard has 'severed his carotid and jugular and he bled out very quickly' – as if she's doing handover notes to a colleague and has no emotional attachment to this patient whatsoever.

Mr Hamlin then 'accidentally' rewinds the recording and somehow manages to get stuck on the image of the pool of blood. He wrinkles his nose and pushes a couple of buttons hopefully but to no avail. 'I'm so sorry, My Lady. Perhaps this would be a good moment for the jury to have a cup of tea?' he suggests to the judge, leaving the usher to escort the horrified jury from the room, the lingering image of Richard's blood very fresh in their minds as Richard's father also gets up unsteadily and leaves the courtroom, pale with distress and in silent agony. It's been a good morning's work for Mr Hamlin already.

* * *

'Members of the jury' – Mr Hamlin is remarkably unruffled after his apparent technical difficulties when they return – 'if you could please open your files at item 3.'

It sounds so innocuous, thinks Johnnie, and yet item 3 is an image of the knife covered in blood. The actual item itself is then presented to court, sealed in plastic and held up to the jury by an officer wearing gloves. Mr Hamlin lets the blade itself talk and simply stands there in silence as they all look curiously at the weapon that did such deadly work. A medium-sized knife of about fifteen centimetres. Quite large for small hands to hold... some of them look coldly at Jude, hunched tiny in the dock looking at the floor again. Mr Hamlin gives a cough to bring them back to the room and calls his first expert witness.

* * *

'So DNA is unique...' Mr Hamlin shakes his head in amazement, as if he has not heard this answer a thousand times before. 'Thank you for that comprehensive explanation. The blood on the blade of the knife... did you find a DNA match for that?'

Johnnie almost rolls his eyes.

'Yes. It's Richard Shand's blood.'

'I see,' says Mr Hamlin gravely. 'And did you find any other DNA matches?'

'Not of blood,' says the forensics expert, a surprisingly young man who looks more like a lab technician's assistant in his jacket without a tie, but apparently he's the new boy wonder on the block, keen to make his mark and carve a niche for himself as the 'go to' forensics expert. 'But there was a DNA match on the handle which could have come from skin or sweat and which matches the defendant's profile.'

'Would the defendant have needed to have been holding the knife to leave this trace?' Mr Hamlin asks.

'Yes. We also found whole fingerprints on the handle that match the defendant.'

Mr Hamlin gives a well-rehearsed look of surprise. 'You'd have to be gripping a knife quite hard to leave such clear prints, surely? Hard enough to stab?'

The judge reminds about leading questions, and Mr

Hamlin apologises but looks down at his papers, quietly satisfied and ready to move on. Yasmin Curtis has yet to say a single thing.

'I'd like you to take a look at item 4, ladies and gentlemen, if you will.' Mr Hamlin waits a moment as they all find a picture of Jude's pretty dress splattered in blood, a sad reminder of a summer evening that ought to have been fun. 'Do these splatters of blood indicate anything?' Mr Hamlin asks, knowing full well they do.

Boy wonder nods eagerly. He's betraying himself as someone not used to being in court, thinks Johnnie. Will that make the jury doubt his expertise? With a bit of luck he might even forget that he's there to give evidence based on his scientific knowledge, not to support either side, and make his bias really obvious. 'Richard's DNA was in the blood spatter, and the high-pressure patterning suggests that the defendant was in close proximity to Richard at the time of the stabbing.'

'So the defendant was standing right next to him and at some point was gripping the knife as he was fatally injured. Thank you. If we move on to item 5...' Mr Hamlin is back at the remote control and this time transporting the jury to the police custody suite, where CCTV shows Jude slowly walking into the room wearing the bloodstained dress. Her hair is wet and straggly and there are faint smears of blood on her expressionless face. She looks terrifying.

'Jesus!' The custody officer captured on camera visibly jumps when he turns round and looks at her. 'All right, Carrie. Bit early for Halloween, isn't it?'

Mr Hamlin pauses the recording on the mad-looking Jude, her eyes wide and staring. 'Would you not expect there to be blood spattering all over the defendant's face, just as there is on the dress?'

'Oh you can see there was blood there,' boy wonder asserts confidently. 'It's visible around the hairline, but she's tried to wash it off. That's what has disturbed the original pattern on her face and created that diluted effect. If you look at item 6, however' – he is becoming bolder, enjoying himself and now even directing events – 'this shows the bloodstain pattern in the property, which was also compatible with the high-pressure blood exiting from a severed artery onto the defendant's clothing...'

'So the defendant was undoubtedly standing within close proximity to Richard as he died, his blood splattering onto her dress, face and hair and over the room.' Nods Mr Hamlin as if the pieces are slotting into place. Which they are.

Yasmin only manages to establish that there were no indications of a *fight* in the blood spatters and it was raining when Jude left the building, which accounts for the diluted blood – so nothing to suggest Jude 'tried to wash it off', merely that it washed off naturally. Had the night porter bothered to look up as she walked straight past him and out of the building, he would have no doubt seen the blood on her face that Jude was not attempting to hide.

* * *

'Well, "Yasmin" is utterly hopeless, isn't she?' Margaret concludes outside the building at the end of the first day. 'I didn't hear a single objection from her. I remember you telling me she had plenty of tricks up her sleeve – what very deep sleeves they must be.'

'Shouting "objection" only happens on TV,' Johnnie says.

'There was also a great deal of sitting around and everyone being asked to leave and then come back in, leave and come back in again...' Margaret rolls her shoulders uncomfortably. 'It was all terribly slow.'

'Again that's the reality of these things. There often need to be breaks so that points of law can be discussed. I can quite see it's tedious to watch though, so while I thank you for coming to support Jude today – and the gesture was appreciated – I would ask you please to refrain from—'

'Ah, here is Timothy with the car.' Margaret ignores him completely and simply limps away, leaving him hanging.

Johnnie looks up at the clear blue sky in exasperation. He doesn't want to have to request that she is banned from court: that would upset Jude, and no doubt Margaret would enjoy the attention of turning up and being barred. Perhaps she will have got her fill with just this one day. He watches the car pull away and mentally crosses his fingers. She is a malignant presence they can all do without.

* * *

The following morning, it is the pathologist's turn to provide his expert opinion. 'When I arrived at the scene, Richard Shand had multiple stab wounds to the neck and chest, arranged in groups,' he confirms. He is a well-fed man in his sixties, with neck bulging over his shirt collar and tie, but it's because the top button is smartly done up; and he exudes the weary experience of someone on the verge of retirement who has seen it all before and can be trusted. 'The post-mortem identified twenty-two sharp wounds. One of the wounds to the neck had severed the carotid artery and the jugular vein.'

Mr Hamlin whips round and looks at Jude accusatively, to remind everyone that's exactly what she said to the first responder! Well, well, well!

It's theatrical but Johnnie can see the jury are lapping it up.

'Would Richard have survived these injuries if the emergency services had been called immediately?' Mr Hamlin asks, and Johnnie hears someone give a slow sigh. Was that Jude herself? He doesn't want to look.

'He would have bled very quickly,' the pathologist confirms.

'There would have been significant blood loss within minutes and blood loss was the cause of his death. It's highly unlikely any intervention could have saved him.' This sounds at first like a bit of an own goal for Mr Hamlin, but he's not done yet.

'Oh, not from a lay person, I'm sure, but would the intervention of a trained medic – an A&E nurse, for example' – he glances at Jude – 'have changed the outcome?'

'Very unlikely, but possible.'

'"Possible", thank you.' Mr Hamlin grabs it and moves on. 'Did Richard have any other injuries?'

'Yes. A four-fingered cut to the right hand.'

'Why would he have slashed fingers?'

'Victims of stabbings often have defensive wounds to their hands where they have tried to grab the blade as it comes towards them, or to their arms as they put them up to block the blows of a knife.'

Some of the jury wince at this and cross their own arms as if they've made up their minds already, but Yasmin Curtis stands to cross-examine; unruffled, calm and ready to remove the clay Mr Hamlin has just carefully smoothed into position.

'Suppose Jude bravely intervened to prevent Mr Shand from trying to take his own life and grabbed the knife by the handle,' Yasmin suggests, 'only for Mr Shand to be so determined to finish what he'd started, he grabbed the knife back by the blade? Could that have caused the hand injury you described?'

The pathologist looks at her and blinks. He reminds Johnnie of a large frog. Benign but perfectly capable of opening his mouth, shooting out his tongue and gobbling Yas up at any moment. 'Yes, that's possible, but—'

'Thank you,' Yasmin cuts him off. 'And, of course, you'd have to grab the handle hard enough to leave prints if you were a female nurse of Jude's build, trying to wrestle a knife from a male former soldier.'

'Questions, not statements, Miss Curtis,' reminds the judge, and there is an audible tut from the public gallery. Johnnie closes his eyes. Shut *up*, Margaret! He turns and glares at her, but she refuses to meet his gaze, today draped in a vast silk shawl covered in a peacock print of teals and electric blues, her loose hair spilling in waves over her shoulders.

Yasmin sensibly ignores her and focuses on the woman who is actually in charge of proceedings. 'Apologies, My Lady.' She turns back to the pathologist. 'You mentioned the slash wound to the neck, but were there other potentially fatal wounds to the body?'

'Yes. One of the chest wounds had a depth of thrust of ten centimetres.'

'So either the neck or the chest injury would have killed Mr Shand. Would it be possible to establish which of these wounds was inflicted first?'

'No,' says the pathologist. 'It would not.'

* * *

'Professor Triding, you have published numerous studies on, and run regular clinics to treat, problems with sleep.' Mr Hamlin welcomes another expert witness, looking as if he himself has been sleeping very soundly indeed. Jude, on the other hand, looks wretched, thinks Johnnie. With every new day that she appears in court, she seems to be fading away a little more. It's as if her energy is leeching through to Margaret, who today is wearing a tightly belted pale blue trenchcoat and matching headband in what appears to be a deliberate two fingers to the 'discreet word about dress' Timothy was tasked with. Margaret is listening intently, her eyes scanning the jury.

'What are the effects of fighting one's body clock to stay awake at night and sleep during the day?' Mr Hamlin addresses the woman waiting patiently on the stand. The only nod to her off-duty personality is the brightly coloured designer frame to her glasses.

She considers the question for a moment. 'A fight is a good way of putting it.'

Mr Hamlin inclines his head graciously.

'Attempting to live nocturnally would, in the early stages, have the same effect as permanent jet lag. You're overriding the signals the brain is sending to your body. That leads to poor quality sleep at the wrong time and not enough sleep overall.'

Mr Hamlin shrugs. 'Why is it important to get a lot of sleep? Plenty of people manage on very little. Some of them lay claim to running the country successfully on no more than a handful of hours a night?'

The professor frowns disapprovingly. 'Trying to repro-gramme your body to sleep when the brain feels it should be awake – if it's light outside for example – has significant reper-cussions. You lose the ability to think rationally. Your judge-ments are affected and your ability to make decisions is impaired.'

'Goodness! So would one be emotionally unstable if severely sleep deprived over a period of, say, a few days or more?' Mr Hamlin asks.

'Yes. If you're chronically sleep deprived you can't process emotions properly. Your emotional hostility becomes heightened.'

'Would you expect someone to become irrationally angry very quickly and not be able to process that anger appropriately if they were suffering from severe sleep interruption or deprivation?'

'Yes, that would be possible,' the professor confirms.

'What about someone who has been sleeping during the day and working at night for a much longer period of time – years rather than weeks. Would you expect them to have the same difficulties regulating their emotions?'

The professor shakes her head. 'Studies have shown that permanent night shift workers have a greater ability to accommodate disrupted sleep, and they appear to report better sleep quality than rotating shift workers or someone new to working nights, so I would expect someone who has been working nights for a number of years to have much better control and management of their emotional instability than someone who has only recently started to work nights.'

David Hamlin takes his seat. Yasmin has no further questions. There is nothing she can dispute, and David Hamlin looks rather pleased with himself, as well he might, when he neatly concludes on Friday in time for lunch. 'Thank you, My Lady. That is the case for the Crown.'

TWENTY-THREE

It is a grey, heavy, unseasonably cold August Monday morning when Yasmin calls her first expert, another pathologist, this time with a well-cut grey bob, eyes that don't miss a trick and some extremely beautiful rings on her fingers. Fingers that have cut up hundreds of dead bodies in the search to discover what killed them. She reminds Johnnie of the headmistress of his prep school and, not for the first time, he finds himself glad he's a solicitor and does not have to question or cross-examine someone like her. What will the jury make of her opinion in contrast to the findings of the pathologist who actually conducted Richard's post-mortem? A jury who have lost the novelty of court... the practical inconveniences to their everyday lives now beginning to bite, to say nothing of the tedium of endlessly having to file in and out of a courtroom while yet more matters of the law are discussed. Yasmin has an uphill struggle ahead of her.

'Dr Avery. You've been a pathologist for forty-five years, involved in some very high-profile cases and have often been the first on the scene of national disasters,' she begins. 'You've examined the images of the stab wounds on Richard Shand's body.

What can you tell me about the groupings on the chest and neck?'

'They are all very similar to each other, almost all of them have a transverse orientation.'

'Oh?' Yasmin puts her head on one side as if puzzled, but Mr Hamlin remains expressionless. Certainly Dr Avery has the attention of the jury however, who are now looking intrigued. Some are even reaching for their pads and pencils. 'What does it mean if a wound has a transverse orientation?'

'It's referring to the angle at which the blade entered the body. If a person is being attacked, they will move around while trying to fight back or escape, leading to wounds that enter the body on different trajectories. When the trajectories are all the same, as in this case, it suggests that the person may well have been holding the knife themselves.'

Several of the jury look at each other, and Johnnie sits forward slowly, noticing their engagement. Yasmin definitely has their attention now.

'"May well have been?"' Yasmin nudges, to which Dr Avery raises a well-shaped eyebrow. 'Where does that sit on a scale of "likely versus not likely?"' she continues, and Johnnie sucks his breath in. Careful, Yas.

Dr Avery gives Yasmin a long, hard stare, but is a fair woman very experienced in giving evidence. 'It is my opinion that Mr Shand was holding the knife himself when the majority of these wounds were inflicted. Certainly one of the fatal wounds to the chest had a transverse orientation, and it appears to have been targeted deliberately into the intercostal space to avoid resistance from the ribs, which is a common feature of suicide.'

Yasmin lets *that* sink in, looking at her notes; and Johnnie glances up triumphantly at Margaret, who is sitting bolt upright in her seat, imperiously staring ahead while everyone whispers in the gallery around her. See? Yas can do this. 'Were there any other elements of note on the body?' Yas continues when they've settled.

'Yes. There are hesitation marks on the wrists.'

Mr Hamlin doesn't look up, only focusing on his notes as if unconcerned.

'What are they and what do they suggest?' Yasmin waits.

'Hesitation marks are the experimental marks someone will make on their body with a knife when they are building up to stabbing themselves with intent to do real harm. It appears from the images that the deceased had that evening started to practise on himself. They are fresh marks, and would have been made within hours of the fatal wounds.'

'Is this a feature you have often seen, throughout your forty-five-year career, in cases of people taking their own lives, this "practising"?' Yasmin asks.

'I have seen it often, yes.'

'Isn't it odd that the experienced pathologist who conducted the post-mortem didn't report on these marks?' Yas frowns then adds quickly, 'I'm not suggesting they were deliberately omitted, of course – rather just... missed?'

'In this instance they are very shallow cuts in the skin, not large slashes that would have been immediately visible,' Dr Avery offers candidly.

Yasmin half smiles. 'But you didn't miss them or omit them, did you, Dr Avery?'

'No, I did not. The deceased was also half-dressed when the incident occurred, his chest and neck bare. That is common with suicides, to allow them to see what they're doing and target accurately.'

Johnnie watches one of the jury members – a woman – close her eyes, distressed, as she imagines the scene.

'So this is all consistent with suicide?'

'Yes.'

'But one or two of the twenty-plus injuries could have been

accidentally inflicted by someone else, perhaps during a struggle for the knife, for example? Can you be certain which of the wounds was the fatal blow?'

'The cause of death was massive blood loss due to multiple stab wounds. There were several wounds to the neck which were fatal, most but not all of which had a transverse orienta-tion. The fatal wound to the chest had a transverse orientation. So the answer to your question is no. I could not say with certainty which one of the wounds was ultimately responsible for Mr Shand's death.'

'Thank you.' Yasmin sits down; but Mr Hamlin isn't letting that go without a fight.

'Is it common to find hesitation or tentative marks on suicide victims, Dr Avery?'

'Yes.'

'Presumably an experienced medic who has worked in the emergency services for a long time would know that too?'

'Yes, that's possible.'

'And you didn't notice any marks on the neck of Mr Shand in the photographs you looked at, just the wrists? Could they have been made *after* the fatal wounding? To appear consistent with a suicide?'

'Yes. That's also possible.'

'And are these hesitation wounds exclusive to people who have taken their own lives, or have you seen them on the bodies of murder victims too, in your capacity as a pathologist?'

'No, they are not exclusive to suicides. I have identified hesi-tation marks on the skin and bones of murder victims during my career.'

'So in your opinion it's possible that these hesitation marks could have been made by Mr Shand's attacker after his death, thank you. And would it also be possible that the first knife blow from his attacker could be fatal, Mr Shand then collapses to the ground and then the subsequent deep wounds could be inflicted by his attacker – deliberately all on the same orientation – because by that point, he was already dead and unable to fight back?'

Dr Avery considers him for a moment. 'You would have to know exactly what you were doing to create a scene that appeared to be a suicide to such a convincing degree, but it is theoretically possible, yes.'

'Thank you.' Mr Hamlin goes to sit down then changes his mind. 'Just one last thing for such an experienced pathologist as yourself to answer: what is the most common method of taking one's own life?'

Dr Avery looks at him rather pityingly. 'In this country, worldwide?'

'My apologies.' Mr Hamlin nods. 'You are quite right, that lacked quality. In the UK.'

'Hanging, strangulation and suffocation.' Dr Avery wastes no words. 'Which accounts for some sixty percent of suicides.'

'And stabbing oneself... in the UK?'

'Far less common.'

'And cutting one's own throat without hesitation?'

'Extremely rare.'

'You mentioned that Mr Shand was bare-chested, which is a feature of this uncommon method of suicide by stabbing. Mr Shand had just got out of bed. It was also a very warm, late-summer August night. Do you accept it's possible he was bare-chested simply because he was a bit hot?'

'That is, of course, possible, yes.'

'Thank you. Mr Shand had twenty-two stab wounds on his body. Is that a common number for a suicide case?'

'No. More than fifteen wounds is uncommon. However some cases have recorded more than ninety wounds.'

'How are most *murders* committed in the UK?'

'With knives or sharp objects. They account for about forty percent of all homicides.'

'Thank you.' Mr Hamlin sits down, satisfied.

* * *

Jude is staring at the floor again, worries Johnnie. What is she thinking? Is she even hearing everything that is happening around her? She doesn't appear to be. She seems increasingly disconnected, draining away in front of him. Margaret is today in a white trouser suit; Johnnie heard a woman walking into the press gallery excitedly describe it as 'very Bianca Jagger'.

When everyone – including the jury, he realises in dismay, watching them openly staring at Margaret – is more fascinated by the defendant's mother than your own next expert witness, you have a serious problem. She *must* now be persuaded to stop attending. This is becoming farcical. But after today that probably won't be an issue. He glances at Annalise, Timothy's reassuringly sensible wife, sitting next to Margaret, staring calmly in front of her, smoothing out her stone-coloured shift dress, no trace of the nerves she must be feeling.

No one has even noticed that the first witness of the day has taken her seat, getting comfortable with confidence as she looks at her watch as if noting what time to start billing from.

'Dr Schilling,' Yasmin addresses her. 'You are a well-known psychiatrist in the USA and now have an eminent practice in London. In the state your former practice was located in, recreational marijuana use was legalised in 2016. What effect did you notice this have?'

Dr Schilling snorts. 'Well, a lot more people started smoking it.'

There are a few titters from the press gallery, and Yasmin looks briefly irritated. 'Of course, but more specifically, once it became legal, was *what* everyone started smoking any different?'

'Yes,' agrees Dr Schilling. 'As recently as twenty years ago, we would be talking a joint containing a THC level of as little as five percent. Now it's much stronger.'

'I'm sorry,' Yasmin is back on track. 'What's THC?'

'It's the psychoactive ingredient of cannabis.' Dr Schilling warms up as she gets into her subject. 'Really high-potency cannabis has flooded the market. Today you could expect to find levels of ninety percent THC in a joint.'

'That must lead to substantially different effects with regular use then?'

Dr Schilling nods emphatically. 'Yes. The higher the content of THC, the higher the negative effects of regular usage.'

'And these negative effects would be?' prompts Yasmin as David Hamlin sits back and listens.

'Paranoia, psychotic episodes. A higher risk of anxiety and depression. It can cause insomnia.'

'Thank you. The joint recovered from Richard Shand's flat containing his DNA was analysed and found to contain a seventy-five percent level of THC. So that's high?'

'Yeah, you're going to get very high on that,' Dr Schilling says drily, and some of the jury smile.

'Could you have a psychotic episode like that after smoking it once?' Yasmin asks, 'Because my client's DNA was also found on the joint.'

Dr Schilling shakes her head. 'No. It's regular and sustained use over a period of time that causes the psychosis and mental illness. The official figures show the number of people taking their own lives in the state I worked in – and who had marijuana in their system when they died – has risen very significantly... and it's these incredibly potent products which are at least partially to blame for that.'

'So as a regular user – and the pathology report confirmed Richard Shand did indeed have marijuana in his system when he died – he would have been putting himself at risk of depression, psychosis, insomnia – and paranoia?'

Johnnie's fingers momentarily pause over his keyboard, but he has an immediate word with himself. No – Jude had detoxed herself. She wasn't smoking regularly any more. He starts typing again.

'Yes. That's correct. He would.'

Yas gives way to David Hamlin, who sighs as he stands, as if it's hardly worth his effort.

'Dr Schilling, have you ever had any of your papers withdrawn from a medical journal in the United States because of concerns regarding their content and conclusions?'

Dr Schilling looks very annoyed. 'Yes, but because of author consent, not efficacy—'

'*Thank* you, Dr Schilling. No further questions, My Lady.' David Hamlin sits down and returns to his notes. She has been dispatched.

* * *

Unusually for a defence witness, the next person Yas calls glares at Jude with naked, open hostility as he takes the stand and is sworn in. To the point that Yas has to repeat her first question to him.

'Mr Mills? You are a former soldier who served with Richard Shand in the army?'

'Yes.' Ed Mills tears his gaze away from the dock. Smartly dressed, and just like Richard's father, he stands with his hands clasped behind his back and legs planted wide. For a moment Johnnie wonders if Richard's father might have yearned for a military background too.

'When did you first meet Richard?' Yas waits for his answer.

'We signed up together when we were both eighteen. We

were twenty-three when he broke his back and was discharged. I continued but left the army myself three years ago.'

'You kept in contact with Richard after he left?'

'Yes, I did, but with respect, Richard didn't leave. He was discharged. It was everything to him. He'd have given anything to stay.'

'Thank you for that correction,' Yasmin acknowledges. 'And he did try *everything* not to leave the army, didn't he?'

As Mr Mills looks back at her his face unexpectedly darkens. Johnnie is surprised at the hostility to Yas now, until Mr Mills glances up at the public gallery, where Richard's father is sitting, and Johnnie realises he doesn't want to tell Richard's father something he doesn't know about his son and now won't be able to talk to him about.

'I understand this is difficult,' Yas persists, 'but could you please tell me what happened just before Richard was discharged?'

Ed Mills swallows and Johnnie watches the muscle in his jaw flex. 'Richard broke his back during active service. He worked hard at the rehab but he thought they were gearing up to medically discharge him after something one of the physios said. He was gutted and he took an overdose of the painkillers he was on.'

'He told you all of this himself, did he?' Yasmin said.

'He didn't need to tell me. I found him.' Mr Mills stares at Yas blankly. 'He was in one of the store rooms in the barracks gym. He'd been training and training trying to get fit again. Lucky for him he'd passed out face down because he'd been sick.'

'And how were you sure it was an overdose?'

Mr Mills frowns as if Yasmin is slightly dim: 'Because he had the empty pill packets on the floor all around him.'

'But there was no note telling you that was what he'd done?'

Yasmin pushes, and a couple of the jurors make some notes of their own.

'I didn't need one to tell me what had happened. It was obvious.' Mr Mills shrugs. 'I got him up. Richard came round and was confused and a bit tearful, like; he kept saying he was sorry. I put him to bed and that was that.'

'You didn't call for help? Didn't tell anyone what he'd done? Get him some medical attention?' Yasmin steps back, as if astounded.

Mr Mills looks at her steadily. 'You don't have much experience of the army, do you? I told the lads he'd had a few too many. No one asked anything else. He *was* discharged not long after that and we didn't talk about it again. Well... not until much later, after I'd left, too.'

'What did Richard say about it when you discussed it together?'

'Just – thank you for saving his life. We were having a few beers. I said I didn't do anything. He joked he hadn't even managed to get that right. I told him I'd have been pis— annoyed,' he corrects himself quickly, 'if he *had* done the job properly, because it would have messed me up. He said sorry and that was it.'

Johnnie shakes his head slightly at the desperately sad picture Richard's friend is painting but Mr Mills has turned out to be an unexpectedly decent witness.

'Thank you, Mr Mills,' Yas says. 'A couple of final questions. When did you last see Richard? Was he in a positive state of mind?'

'He was all right.' Mr Mills looks back at Yasmin defensively. 'No more or less positive than you'd expect given he had the trial coming up. I went to his flat about three or four weeks before he died. We had a takeaway, a smoke.' He shrugs. 'That was it.'

'When you say a smoke?' Yasmin asks. 'Do you mean ciga-rettes or something else?'

Mr Mills rubs his jaw and looks at Yasmin reflectively. It's quite clear that he doesn't like being questioned and doesn't want to be on the stand, but is a man conditioned to respect formalities. 'I smoked cigarettes. Richard smoked weed for his back.'

'Is that something you knew him to do regularly?'

Mr Mills gives a low chuckle as if she's predictable. 'He smoked a lot of weed. Yes, too much in my opinion – which is where you're going next – because it messed up his sleep,' he clarifies as Yasmin opens her mouth, 'but then I wasn't the one in a lot of pain all the time and it wasn't hurting anyone, so...'

'Well, except ultimately himself,' Yasmin points out. 'So it was a typical meet-up for both of you?'

Ed Mills hesitates. 'He gave me some money before I left. He didn't usually do that.'

'Had you asked to borrow some?'

Mr Mills glowers at her. 'No! Of course not. But Rich knew I was struggling. He said he wanted me to have something to tide me over for a bit, and I wasn't to worry about paying it back.'

'How much money did he give you?'

'A couple of grand.'

Yasmin pauses for a moment to let that sink in. 'What did you say to him?'

Ed Mills shrugs. 'I thanked him and said I *would* be paying it back, and he thanked me for always being a good mate to him. I told him to shut up and I...' He pauses and flushes red. 'I jokingly... half seriously... asked him if all this was his way of telling me he was dying or something?'

'Because it felt like a last goodbye?' Yasmin asks.

'Sort of, yeah,' Ed Mills admits.

'And you were understandably concerned by that, having found Richard after his first suicide attempt?'

Ed Mills hesitates but Johnnie frowns, spotting it and so does Yasmin.

'Mr Mills, that was his first suicide attempt – to your knowledge – was it not?'

Ed Mills sighs heavily. 'It might have been his second.'

Yasmin doesn't miss a beat, doesn't betray her surprise. 'When was his first?'

Ed Mills isn't looking at anyone now, just down at the floor. 'When he broke his back some people said he jumped from the watchtower, he didn't fall.'

'Were you there when this happened? Did you witness it first hand?'

'No. He'd had a bit to drink... I know that – and people who saw him do it swore he jumped, but genuinely being in the army was everything to him so I don't know... Rich could be a bit, impulsive.' He trails off and shrugs. 'It wasn't a good look for anyone either way, and we were told he'd fallen. He got flown back home, put together again and, like I said, afterwards, he tried *really* hard to make the rehab work. No one could have tried harder.'

'No further questions, thank you.'

David Hamlin slowly rises to his feet. 'Did you have a medical role within the army, Mr Mills? You seem to have a lot of medical expertise; you "knew" that Richard had taken an overdose. You "knew" that he was smoking too much cannabis?'

'No. I have no medical training.'

'Oh?' Mr Hamlin looks surprised. 'I see. So these accounts of Mr Shand's "overdose" and "fall" are merely your recollections of events that happened two decades ago. How old are you, Mr Mills?'

'I'm forty-three. Same as Rich.'

Mr Hamlin nods. 'That's young to have left the army. What do you do now?'

'I'm unemployed at present. As are a lot of veterans.'

Mr Hamlin nods sympathetically. 'How do you support yourself financially? Do you receive benefits of any kind? Ones that relate to your fitness to work because of your poor mental health?'

Mr Mills gives Mr Hamlin a long, hard stare. 'I have suffered from PTSD, yes.'

Mr Hamlin doesn't look up from his notes. 'Which can involve a difficulty concentrating and memory impairment. So it's possible your recollections might be impaired... or inaccurate. Did you leave the army because of poor mental health, Mr Mills?'

Ed Mills laughs suddenly. It's an incongruous sound, and Johnnie looks up quickly, his eyes widening in alarm. He spoke too soon, this is veering horribly off track now. Juries don't like laughing witnesses, it unnerves them.

'I'm not a nutter and like I said, I never asked Rich for a single penny, if that's what you're going to get at with this "how do I support myself",' Ed Mills flashes.

David Hamlin ignores that. 'Mr Shand contacted you and asked you to meet him at his property, which you were happy to do. That's correct? You said: "I went to his flat". This was at Mr Shand's invitation?'

Ed Mills hesitates. 'Well, we had made plans to meet but I showed up on the wrong night by mistake.'

'I see, you were – confused?'

'No,' Mr Mills retorts. 'I already said. I made a mistake.'

'Very well. But far from Mr Shand calling you out of the blue to set his affairs in order, what actually happened was you turned up unannounced at his property, having been confused, and left with Richard having given you two thousand pounds?'

'I don't get confused. My memory is fine. I didn't leave the army for health reasons, but because I'm gay and they don't like that much either, whatever they say otherwise.' He stares at Mr Hamlin defiantly. 'And before you ask about *that*, no, we were just friends. He was my friend. He was a kind, gentle man and I will miss him.' His voice shakes with energy and emotion. 'Sir.' He nods respectfully up at Richard's dad, shoots Jude another look of fury and, without waiting to be told he can leave, turns and marches across the court before banging out of the door.

Yasmin stands. 'I apologise to my learned friend and to you, My Lady, for the unorthodox interruption to that cross-examination.'

The judge nods. 'Thank you, Miss Curtis. Had you concluded, Mr Hamlin?' Her tone suggests she hopes he has.

Mr Hamlin stands. 'I have, My Lady.'

'Miss Curtis?' The judge nods to Yas, giving her permission to continue.

Johnnie, fully aware of what's coming next, raises his gaze to the public gallery.

'I'd like to call my next witness,' Yas speaks clearly. 'Lord Stratham, Timothy St John.'

The effect on Margaret is electric. She visibly jolts and turns to whisper furiously to Annalise, who leans towards her husband's aunt to listen, but says nothing in return, only placing a finger to her lips as one would when reacting to a cross child. Margaret looks utterly livid, but there's nothing she can do as Timothy walks into court, wide-eyed with anxiety. There are already dark, damp sweat patches under his arms, staining his new, pale suit. Margaret retrieves her vast glasses, jamming them on so her eyes are no longer visible, as Timothy takes his oath on the Bible.

'Lord Stratham, could you confirm your relationship to the defendant, please?' Yasmin asks.

'Yes, I am her first cousin, but she's more like a sister to me,'

Timothy says as Jude closes her eyes and, for the first time, Johnnie sees her give a faint smile.

'Thank you, Lord Stratham. Could I ask you to speak up, however?'

'Sorry!' Timothy nods rapidly. 'Of course. I said, she's like my sister.'

'You spent a lot of time together when you were growing up then?'

'Yes, we did. We were at different schools, obviously. We both boarded, but we spent a lot of our holidays together.'

'Where was this?'

'At Highcombe Hall. It's our family seat, property...' he adds. 'Jude lived there permanently with her mother and stepfather.'

Johnnie watches as Margaret jerks her head suddenly to look at Tim at the word 'stepfather', but just as quickly returns her gaze to the front again.

'I often visited because my parents lived in South Africa.'

'You say Jude was like a sister to you, does that mean you argued a lot? Or maybe that's just me and my sister.' Yas smiles at Timothy.

He swallows nervously and smiles back. 'No, we didn't argue at all. I meant I love her like a sister. We were pretty much left to our own devices most of the time, but it was fun. She's always been fun. And kind. She's always been very kind to me too.'

'So you were inseparable?'

'Oh no, there were plenty of times when I was at Highcombe on my own. My parents didn't always come and take me back to South Africa for shorter holidays like half-term, for example. I'd often go and stay at Highcombe, and sometimes Jude wouldn't be there because she'd be staying with friends. Particularly when we started getting older at around the age of twelve, thirteen.'

'That still sounds young to me?' Yas puts her head on one side, and Johnnie glances up at Margaret, who is now sitting bolt upright and staring out in front of her, like a statue. Annalise is watching Timothy intently, and Jude is frowning, worriedly.

Timothy shrugs apologetically. 'I was sent away to school at the age of seven.'

Johnnie glances at the jury. Several of them are pulling faces as if they think that's mad. Yes, it is. Johnnie takes a deep breath and turns back to his friend. Go on, Tim, you can do this.

'So who was at Highcombe while you were there without Jude?'

'The housekeeper, Mrs Brooks, her husband, my aunt Margaret and her husband, Benedict.' Timothy stops and looks up at the ceiling and blinks a couple of times. 'Benedict abused me sexually on several of those occasions. It started when I was twelve and it finally stopped when I was' – he frowns – 'thirteen. Quite suddenly. But I was pretty fat by then. That might have had something to do with it.'

The shock in the room is palpable. Oh, you brave man, thinks Johnnie. You brave, brave man. He lifts his gaze to the public gallery. Margaret has not moved, apart from one hand which is now gripping the rail in front of her, the ruby ring shining. Annalise has her gaze fixed on her husband, tears streaking down her face as she smiles at him and nods encouragement. Johnnie looks at Jude, who has covered her mouth with her hand, and he lowers his gaze.

'Did you tell anyone what had happened to you?' Yas asks. 'A friend? A trusted teacher?'

Timothy snorts. 'It wasn't exactly that sort of school. I would like to stress that I know no one knew at home, because they would have done something to stop it if they had. I say that as an adult obviously. As a child when someone says they will hurt you very badly if you tell anyone what's going on, you believe them. I didn't tell anyone until after Benedict and my grandfather died.'

'Who did you tell?' asks Yas.

'It was not long after Benedict's memorial. I was out on the estate first thing in the morning, it was only just getting light and I thought I saw someone walking down the drive. I drove up to see who it was and it was Richard Shand. I'd not seen him since I was fifteen, but I recognised him straight away. I asked him what he was doing and he said he'd come to "confront" my aunt. It was that word "confront".' Timothy stops for a moment and swallows. 'I didn't even know I was going to say it, but I said: "You know he died, don't you?" Shand said "who?" and I said "Benedict", and he just looked terrified and I knew, instantly. Or I thought I knew. I said: "Did he do it to you too?" Again – no idea I was going to just blurt it out like that.'

'What did Richard Shand say?' Yas asks.

'Um' – Timothy clears his throat – 'well, he rushed up to me, very suddenly, and he grabbed the front of my shirt. He leant right into my face and he said: "That's a lie! If you ever say that about me to anyone, I'll kill us both!"'

Johnnie scans the room briefly. No one is moving.

'That must have been very frightening?' Yas says eventually.

'Yes, it was. I just... started to cry and say I wasn't lying,' Timothy says. 'He was still holding the front of my shirt tightly, all bunched up in his fist and his face was very close to mine. He was saying "prove it, prove it" over and over to me, but he was crying, too. And then he just... leant his forehead on mine and for a second or two we cried together. Then he let me go and he just... walked off.'

Everyone continues to stare at Timothy, and Yas waits as he exhales with relief as if climbing out of icy cold water and wipes his eyes roughly.

'Did you see him again after that?'

'No. I didn't. I went back to the house and I finally told my wife what had happened to me when I was younger, but I didn't mention Richard. Partly because he'd said he'd kill me and he was pretty terrifying' – Timothy tries to smile – 'and partly because of what he'd said about killing himself.'

'You believed him?' Yas said. 'You thought he meant it?'

'There's no doubt in my mind that he meant it,' Timothy says. 'None at all.'

'Thank you.' Yas takes her seat.

David Hamlin stands slowly and looks at Timothy steadily. He is good man and a fair one, Johnnie has a great deal of respect for him. 'Lord Stratham, forgive me, but in the absence of Richard Shand being able to confirm or deny the allegations you have just made about him, do you have any evidence that they are true?'

Timothy glances briefly at the gallery and shakes his head. 'No, I do not.'

'So Mr Shand could have just been reacting angrily to your implied meaning? Some men, particularly those with a strong religious or military background – as we heard from an earlier witness – find the suggestion of sexual relations between themselves and another man very uncomfortable. Would you agree there is a possibility Mr Shand could have been reacting in that way?'

'Yes,' agrees Timothy. 'It's completely possible. But I know he meant it when he said he'd kill himself.'

'But don't we all sometimes say things in heightened situations that we don't always mean and aren't always true? *I just want to die; You're dead to me; You're the most beautiful person in the world; You're no child of mine; I love you* or sometimes: *I've never loved you.* Have you ever said something to someone that you didn't mean, Lord Stratham?'

'Yes,' Timothy admits. 'I have.'

'You're not alone. I think we all have.' David Hamlin smiles sadly at Timothy. 'No further questions, My Lady.'

Timothy can't leave the witness box fast enough, stumbling as he takes to the small steps. Johnnie is watching him being ushered to the door when there is a sudden crash from above. Margaret's glasses have slipped from her face while reaching to the ground for her stick. She scrabbles around for them and has to be assisted, rising to her feet unsteadily when they can't be found beneath her.

People offer steadying hands as she wobbles precariously. Her face is utterly ashen and she stares above the gaze of everyone looking up at her as if they are not there. Annalise stands and, with enormous kindness and dignity, offers Margaret her arm, leading her towards the door. Johnnie has never really appreciated the expression shell-shocked until now, but Margaret is, very publicly, exactly that.

Jude also begins to stands up in the dock as she anxiously watches her mother, but the officers either side of her put out a hand and one of them murmurs something to Jude, who sits down again.

Margaret is led slowly from sight by Annalise, walking past Richard's father, who is staring resolutely at the ground, looking at nobody.

Yasmin rises slowly, glancing at Jude uncertainly – who now has her head in her hands – but her voice echoes around the court, clear and true as she decides to go for it. 'I call my client.'

Jude tries to stand again, but begins to gulp with distress as if she's finding it hard to catch her breath.

'Ms Beauchamp?' Yasmin looks quickly at the frowning judge. 'My Lady?'

Jude simply dissolves to the ground as if she is made of water.

'My client requires urgent medical assistance, My Lady!' requests Yas as Johnnie jumps to his feet, catching sight of

David Hamlin calmly removing his glasses and folding his hands patiently as the circus begins around him.

The court officers are bent over their now unconscious charge. The judge begins to direct the clearing of her courtroom calmly and efficiently with the help of the clerk and ushers. The jury stand and file out. Plenty of them are frowning, some of them are peering curiously at the dock, but Jude is hidden from view.

* * *

'She's simply not going to be able to stand up in front of a packed courtroom with Lady Fawkes still in the gallery.' Yasmin is very unhappy as they stand outside the courtroom... not shouty, as that isn't her style, but unhappy enough for Johnnie to be taking her concerns very seriously. 'We're lucky that it's three o'clock now and it was easier to adjourn until tomorrow than drag everyone back in there. And the jury didn't like any of that. I'm not saying Jude collapsed on purpose.' Yas holds up her hands as Johnnie opens his mouth. 'But they thought she was faking it. So please, do whatever it takes but Lady Margaret needs to Fawke off and not come here in the morning if Jude's going to convincingly argue that she didn't do it.'

'Well, after today I doubt Margaret will even want to come—'

'Johnnie!' Yas interrupts and nods pointedly at someone behind him.

Timothy is waiting. Yas melts discreetly away, and Johnnie turns to look at his old friend. 'Hey. How are you feeling?'

'I don't know really,' Tim says, picking at his fingers anxiously. His nails are bitten back to the quick and look sore. 'I don't know if that was mine to tell. I just wanted to do the right thing.'

'It was definitely yours to tell. And you told the truth – you don't have the proof. Margaret destroyed it. So actually you've left the people who care about Richard with the possibility that it didn't happen, while explaining how he felt about it. I don't think you could have done any better than you did.'

Timothy nods. 'Thanks. Annalise is taking Margaret home now. We discussed in advance that I probably wouldn't want to go back in the same car as them, so I'm getting the train back. Is Jude OK?' He looks anxiously at Johnnie.

'She's being checked over, but she will be, I'm sure. I'll keep you posted.'

'Give her my love and I'll see you in the morning.' He turns to leave.

'Tim,' Johnnie hesitates. 'If Margaret says she wants to come tomorrow, could you—'

'She won't,' Timothy cuts across him. 'Not in a million years. I can promise you that. Not now.'

'But Jude is giving evidence so she might—'

Timothy shakes his head. 'The only thing that matters to Margaret is Margaret.'

'Just because she does have a habit of being contrary though, if she decides to come, could you do whatever it takes to keep her at Highcombe? I don't care what it is – a flat tyre, an ill horse – whatever. And don't feel you need to ring me and let me know why she's absent. I want Jude to have the best possible conditions to give her evidence.'

Timothy nods. 'Will do.' He turns to walk towards the door.

'Tim!' Johnnie calls after him. 'Well done.' Is that even the right thing to say? What do you say to someone who has so publicly exposed their life like that?

Tim doesn't turn back, just lifts a hand briefly in acknowledgement and walks from the dark atrium of the building, pushing uncharacteristically roughly past the waiting members of the press and out into the anonymity of a bright and busy London late afternoon.

TWENTY-FOUR

As the vomit splashes into the bowl of the downstairs lavatory, Margaret leans her hand on the cool, damp wall and waits. Her body heaves again but it's so empty now that nothing comes up apart from water. She wipes the spit from her mouth and limps into the kitchen, trying not to trip over the wide legs of her white trousers.

Fixing a tumbler of whisky, despite the smell making her want to gag again, she makes for the door, glancing at the bare table, only pausing at the last moment to set her glass on the sideboard before turning back and making her way over to the dresser. She manages to remove a mat and her napkin from the drawer, already tucked within its tarnished ring. Putting them at her place on the table, she returns to the dresser and stretches up with a moan to collect a cereal bowl, side plate and teacup, placing them down too. She has to pause to catch her breath. Finally it's the cutlery.

'How can you have known this for all these years and said nothing?'

She puts a spoon and knife down.

'Margaret, men like Benedict often "fall in love" with

vulnerable boys who just happen to be in their power in some way.'

Her hand grips the knife tightly for a moment as she swallows again, causing it to spin and sit slightly at an angle, out of place. She adjusts it back into position. There. Breakfast is laid. Standards.

'Lord Stratham, forgive me, but in the absence of Richard Shand being able to confirm or deny the allegations you have just made about him, do you have any evidence that they are true?'

Carrying her drink up the stairs requires considerable effort and she has to sit down on her bed stiffly, her stick slipping to the floor as she takes a moment before even contemplating tackling the bathroom for her ablutions. Little daggers of pain are shooting up and down her leg. She takes a tiny mouthful of whisky. A small bit of skin sticks to the glass and peels from her lip as she moves it away. She touches the exposed bit with the tip of her tongue and tastes blood.

Evidence

Evidence

Evidence

She places the glass down and, with a gasp, untucks her silk vest top from the waistband of her trousers, tutting as she looks down and realises it's got some marks on it. A water stain? Vomit? She'll see to it in a minute – she must do the phone first. She reaches slowly and slips open the bedside table drawer. Removing the mobile, she switches it on and dials into the voicemail. Betrayal. Nothing but betrayal, everywhere she looks. That Timothy could have stood up in court and told such awful, hideous lies for Jude's sake.

'You have three saved messages. First message received at...'

She closes her eyes and there is Jude.

'Hi Mum, it's me!' Her voice all high, trying to pretend she's not stressed. 'No news, I'm afraid. I'm at home but I'll try you again in a bit.'

Delete
Delete
Delete

She fumbles for the right button... and straightens upright in shock, her torso rigid, the sudden *pain* is excruciating! She gasps again, the breath sucking in and catching.

Delete.

TWENTY-FIVE

It's already a stunningly beautiful morning when Timothy knocks on the cottage door. The parkland is bathed in the apricot haze of the hot day that lies ahead, and the birds are busily chattering. He listens for a moment, then reluctantly knocks again.

Normally Margaret is waiting behind the door, ready to go... and springs it open before he even has a chance to raise his hand.

As he thought, she has no desire to go to court today, or to talk to him. He doesn't want to talk to her either, but it's going to have to happen at some point. He knocks for a third time and as he waits on the step, he turns his face briefly to the early morning sun and looks out over the comparatively new silhouette of the eastern parkland; the frames of the outdoor adventure playground and the barn that houses the soft play next to the gift shop and café. To the west is the new restaurant building that will double as a more cost-efficient wedding venue for people who can't afford to hire the main house, but still want the splendour of the formal gardens for their photographs. Annalise has worked wonders. She always does, but now that this next phase is nearly done, he'd like to walk away from it all. Someone else can take over now that it's a viable business. He just wants to go home.

He turns back and tries the door again. Nothing. Fine, be like that. He turns to leave but looks down, as with a scratchy yowl, Perdu appears from nowhere and begins to wind around his legs, leaving hair over his trousers. He hoofs her away gently with a foot but, undeterred, she returns to figure of eight around him again. She has never shown him this much attention and clearly wants feeding.

Why does she want feeding? He stares down at the cupboard-love cat. A cool misgiving whispers over him and he steps back and stares up at the blank windows of the cottage.

Pushing through the side gate, he makes his way to the back door and finds it locked. Peering in through the kitchen window he spies the table, still laid for breakfast for one. At – he glances at the clock on her wall – quarter to nine in the morning.

He immediately steps up into the garden onto the damp lawn to get a clear look at the upstairs windows. Margaret's curtains are drawn.

Marching quickly back round to the Land Rover he snatches open the glovebox and reaches for his enormous master set of keys. He eventually finds the right one, although his fingers are clumsy with mounting anxiety as he tries to slide it off the ring; but after what feels like forever he has let himself into the cottage.

'Margaret?' he calls. 'It's me, Timothy. Are you there?'

Silence, apart from the steady ticking of his grandfather's old clock from the kitchen.

He swallows. He doesn't want to go upstairs. He's afraid of what he might find.

'Margaret?' He calls up again and places a foot tentatively on the bottom stair. 'I'm coming up!'

He's halfway when he imagines Margaret furious and

hunched over, waiting in silence for him at the top of the stairs, holding her stick aloft. He quails and then rushes up suddenly, bursting around the corner, but feels faintly ridiculous when, of course, she isn't there. Her bedroom door is right in front of him, pushed to.

'Margaret?' he tries again and forces himself over to it, shoving it open quickly and stepping back – only to see that she is lying on her side on her bed, fully clothed, but with her legs hanging down, which is odd and doesn't look comfortable.

'Margaret?' he says, but she doesn't move. 'Are you all right?'

He walks around curiously to her front and leaps backwards. 'Shit!'

She is very clearly dead. Her eyes are wide open and her mouth is open too, almost in surprise as her soul was quickly yanked from her body before she could stop them from running away with it. He realises she is still in yesterday's clothes, her hair having fallen across her face without being moved, a knocked-over glass of what looks like booze on the rug, her hand hanging uselessly down... not crossed over her chest in readiness, as she was taught while a child. She didn't go out a good Catholic girl after all, when the Lord came for her.

Timothy fumbles for his phone, not taking his eyes from his aunt. He's not even sure if you phone for an ambulance if the person is already very much dead? Mrs Brooks will know. He pauses and wonders if perhaps he should phone Johnnie? Oh poor, poor Jude. This is the last thing she needs to hear just before giving her evidence, because they're hardly going to halt an expensive trial on the grounds her mother has died. And Johnnie did say not to call him... so he won't do that. He'll just sort everything out this end. It's the least he can do. Oh God, was it the shock of what he said yesterday? It literally killed her?

'Mrs Brooks? Could you come up to the cottage, please? I

need some assistance. Lady Margaret has passed away in the night. Thank you, yes. Dreadful.'

He hangs up and looks at Margaret again, shuddering. He will wait downstairs; he doesn't want to be in here with just her, like this. He turns away but as he does, he sees it sitting on the bed, close to her body, as if it slipped from her fingers. Her mobile phone.

TWENTY-SIX

'Why wouldn't an innocent woman want to tell her story? That's what the jury will think if you don't defend yourself. It's your opportunity to tell them that you did not intend to kill Richard or cause him serious injury, and you didn't lose your self-control. You were simply there and tried to stop him from doing this to himself.'

I nod because I'm too frightened to speak.

'One last thing,' Johnnie says, 'your mother and Tim aren't actually here today, so...' He trails off.

I'm not surprised to hear that. Of course she isn't. Not after yesterday. The reverberations of that bomb detonating will have been heard for miles around. There won't be any big black glasses or attention-seeking outfits today. A quiet retreat. Close the Highcombe doors.

'My father was going to come,' I manage, my voice trembling. 'He offered to fly over, but I said we should probably wait until this is all done before we meet in person. You don't want to see your daughter for the first time across a courtroom, do you?'

'No, not really.' Johnnie agrees. 'Not ideal.'

'We've written a lot though,' I say, starting to shake. 'Tim's mum set it all up. You know she's still out in South Africa? I wonder if Tim and Annalise will just sell Highcombe after this and go back there, too. Depending on what happens I could go and visit them maybe, meet my father that way. He seems a nice man.' I try a smile.

'That all sounds like a plan.' Johnnie hesitates. 'I'm really sorry your mum isn't here, Jude. Try to put it from your mind though, and concentrate on what you need to say and nothing more. Don't give David Hamlin an inch. You've got this. I know you have. Everything will be all right. Ready?'

* * *

I remove my hand, having sworn on the Bible, and glance at the jury. No explanation has been given for my collapse the day before and some of them are staring at me stony-faced. I know they think it was for effect but it wasn't. My body simply took over. I know the truth even if they don't believe me. I glance briefly at the public gallery too, which is a mistake. Lydia, Dom's ex, is sitting right at the front, staring back at me. She's chosen *today* to come?

'Ms Beauchamp?'

I realise Yasmin is addressing me, and I am already doing exactly what Johnnie told me not to do. 'Yes. I'm sorry.' I focus and clear my throat.

I see Yasmin's eyes flicker warily but she continues. 'Is this you, Ms Beauchamp?'

She clicks a screen and a CCTV still of me appears. I am running full pelt in my summer dress, in the dark, down the street towards Richard's, where he is still alive.

'Yes, it is.'

'And where are you going in such a rush?'

'To Richard's flat, at ten o'clock at night. I'm running

because I'm very worried about him and I think he's about to take his own life.'

'So you're running to *save* his life and get there before it's too late?'

David Hamlin mildly clears his throat. 'Really, this approach is not worthy of my learned friend's considerable capabilities?'

'Apologies, My Lady.' Yas looks at the screen. 'What was Mr Shand's mood like when you arrived?'

I remember Richard picking me up, carrying me into his flat. 'We were glad to see each other.'

'But this was a man who, ten months previously, had sought you out at the hospital you worked at – in the middle of the night while you were halfway through a busy A&E shift – so that you'd unwittingly give him information about your mother?'

'Yes, that's correct. I was in tears in the hospital café' – I look up – 'because it was the first anniversary of my partner's death. He came over and asked me if I was OK. He told me his name was Rik and that he was nocturnal. I'd never heard anyone say that before. He made it sound very appealing – a way of seeing a tired world in a different light. Quite literally. A sort of secret club. I was intrigued.'

'So you saw him again?'

I nod. 'We went for breakfast, but he ended up driving me from London to my mother's house in Berkshire. I thought he was being nice, that it was one of those extravagant gestures people make when you've just started dating. He dropped me off, had a look around her cottage but left very suddenly when he overheard that my mother had been arrested. I assumed it was because he didn't want to get involved in a family like that.'

'So when did you realise who he really was?'

'The Thursday before my mother's trial. I saw a picture of the person who had made the allegations against my mother and it was "Rik". I went to his flat to confront him, and over the next couple of days I began to realise that everything I'd been led to believe about him might not be true.'

'So that's why you're running to help the man that callously duped you, here?' Yas points at the image of me again.

'Yes. By this point' – I look at myself running – 'I know exactly who he is, he's not hiding anything from me. We've been honest with each other, but I'm frightened for him. I know he's not in good mental headspace and I want to check on him.'

Yas looks down at her notes again for a moment. 'That was at 10 p.m. What happened when you woke up at about midnight, after you'd both fallen asleep at his flat?'

'Richard wasn't in bed. I found him smoking a spliff on the balcony.'

'And what floor was his flat on?'

'Thirty-one. It made me nervous that he was out there, and it was starting to storm, so we came back in and we chatted again for a moment before I said I ought to leave. Richard was agitated and he showed me two photographs. One he'd stolen from my flat, and the other had been taken while we were at the Serpentine watching the moon set earlier in the day. It appeared to show us kissing. He told me his lawyers had wanted to use them in his trial, but he wasn't going to do that. He asked me if I would be prepared to show my mother the picture of us kissing. I thought it was weird that he'd mentioned my mother. Why would he care what my mother thought? Very quickly, I came to the conclusion that the photographs were just another part of whatever the real story was between him and my mother. I felt used.' I swallow. 'I felt like I was trapped in something I didn't really understand and I wanted to leave. I said: "It's over." I told him he disgusted me.'

That comment must have particularly hurt him, I realise, as I say it out loud, in the context of Timothy's revelations yesterday. I close my eyes.

'Richard became upset, he asked me to forgive him and then he reached for the knife. The one you've all already seen.' For the first time I address the jury directly, looking right at them. 'I shouted no and I reached for it too, but he got there first and he started stabbing himself in his chest and then everywhere.' I reach out my hands to the rail in front of me and hold on.

The only sound is Yas's footsteps as she walks up to the dock and places her hand over mine. 'Are you all right?' she asks, as if it's only the two of us in the room. 'Do you need to take a break?'

I notice Mr Hamlin roll his eyes. 'No.' I swallow. 'Thank you.'

'I'm sorry to ask you this, Jude, but it's important to be *very* clear. It was his chest that he stabbed first?'

'Yes.'

'Why did *you* reach for the knife?' Yas asks gently, removing her hand.

'To stop him hurting himself. I'm a nurse. That's my job. *Was* my job,' I correct myself.

'You didn't stop to think that this was a former soldier, much stronger than you, with a dangerous weapon? You didn't think he might have been about to hurt you?'

'No!' I answer without hesitation. 'Not for a second. Richard was a good, kind man. I wasn't thinking about having to defend myself; I wanted to stop him hurting himself. I managed to grab the knife by the handle at one point. We had our hands on it, but he pulled it back by the blade so I let go.'

'You just had to stand back and watch him violently hurt himself?'

'Yes.'

'He killed himself in front of you?'

'Yes. I've worked as an accident and emergency nurse for many years now and it's the most traumatic and distressing thing I have ever witnessed.'

'Your prison report documents that you have suffered depression while you've been waiting for this trial, alongside a difficulty with social integration, anxiety, significant sleep disturbances and nightmares. Is this because of what you saw Richard do to himself?'

'Yes. I keep seeing it happen again and again. I don't know how you "unsee" something like that.'

The court has fallen silent.

'Thank you.' Yasmin sits down... and Mr Hamlin sits very still as he appears to think deeply for a moment, fingers pushed together as if in prayer, resting on his lips.

He slowly raises his eyes and fixes them on me. I actually see the jury lean forward eagerly, wondering if he will break cover straight away or stalk me before giving chase. He stands slowly.

'Ms Beauchamp, you never met Mr Shand during the brief period he worked at your family home in 1994, is that correct?'

'Yes. I was away at school. He was gone by the time I came home for the holidays.'

'You told my learned friend that Mr Shand introduced himself to you in the middle of the night at the hospital café, in November 2021. How long had you been working nights at this stage?'

'About a week, I think? I was very new to it.'

'But you accept that Mr Shand was genuinely nocturnal? He lived a reverse life?'

Genuinely? So this is how it's going to go. I take a deep breath. 'Yes, I do.'

'After Richard Shand suddenly left you at your mother's house on the night of *her* arrest, you didn't see him again for another ten months, until you went to his flat the Thursday before his and your mother's trial was due to start.' Mr Hamlin looks at me evenly. 'Why did you go there?'

There is nothing at all to be gained by mentioning my

mother threatening to disclose her photograph... and everything for poor Richard's father to lose, because after what Timothy said yesterday it doesn't take a genius to work out what sort of photo it might have been.

'I went to see him because I'd just found out who he really was. That he tricked me,' I say.

'Tricked you in the sense that until this point you'd not realised he was Richard Shand? At least, you'd not explicitly discussed Richard's past with him?'

'He tricked me,' I say firmly. 'I confronted him about that and then I left.'

'You were angry with him?'

'Yes, I was,' I concede. 'And very hurt.'

Mr Hamlin considers this for a moment. 'When did you next see Mr Shand?'

'He came and found me after work the following day.'

'How did he know what time you'd be finishing work? Had you told him?'

'No, I suppose he assumed I was still working nights.'

'And fortuitously you were, weren't you?' Mr Hamlin looks up. 'When had you returned to working nights, Ms Beauchamp?'

'The week before.'

Mr Hamlin pauses. 'So for clarity, having not seen Richard Shand for ten months – during which time you were working a more conventional rota of mostly days with some occasional nights – the week before your mother's trial, you just happened to return to working nights and, four days before the trial, you discovered who Richard Shand was and, having confronted him, Richard then came to find you on the morning of Saturday, the 22nd of August, when he would have expected to find you coming off the night shift. You'd set everything up most conveniently, had you not?'

'I didn't set anything up. I was simply finishing a night at work.'

Mr Hamlin gives me a long stare then looks down at his file. 'What did Richard Shand talk to you about on that Saturday morning?'

'He wanted to go for dinner.'

'That evening?'

'No, then and there. I would normally be eating my main meal of the day at 8 or 9 a.m. and being nocturnal, so would Richard.'

'"Normally" for you being the habits of just a little over a week, of course. But you didn't go for dinner?' Mr Hamlin waits.

'No. I was meeting friends in the afternoon, so I wanted to go home and get changed and grab a couple of hours' sleep. He asked me to meet him the following day instead.'

Mr Hamlin stops short. 'Meeting friends when one would expect you to be asleep? So picking and choosing as it suited you?'

'No. I made a rare exception for my friend's birthday,' I explain and out of the corner of my eye I see one of the male jurors shake his head and note something on his pad.

'Did you meet these friends in the afternoon on Saturday?' Mr Hamlin removes his glasses and rubs his eyes.

'Yes, I did.'

'Did you have a few alcoholic drinks?'

'Yes, at about 3 p.m.'

'Which for you, is the equivalent of one of us popping out at 3 a.m. for a couple of vodkas. I see.' Mr Hamlin nods sagely. 'So by the time you met Richard Shand at the Serpentine at 6 a.m. on the Sunday in question, you'd been up for... how many hours? Consecutively?'

'About eighteen.'

'And off the back of a Friday night A&E shift too? You must

have been exhausted doing all of that on what, four hours' sleep and a few drinks?'

'I was OK,' I insist. 'Richard and I watched the moon set and then I went home to sleep.'

'But you decided to pay him another visit on the Sunday night at 10 p.m.? You ran to his flat, in fact?'

'I thought he was going to hurt himself.'

'So when you arrived you naturally looked for evidence of that assumption, of course. Did you identify any "hesitation marks" on his wrists?'

'No, I didn't. At least, I didn't notice any.'

Mr Hamlin frowns. 'You didn't "notice" any? So you weren't concerned enough to be looking for them, or they didn't appear to be there?'

'I didn't see any marks on his wrists that concerned me at that point.'

'So Richard Shand was in good health on your arrival. You had sexual intercourse, you slept briefly and you found Richard on the balcony bare-chested and smoking. Were you looking for or did you notice any marks or wounds to his body at this point?'

'No.'

'You then smoked some very strong cannabis together. Are you a regular cannabis user?' Mr Hamlin fixes me with clear eyes.

'No. I'm not,' I answer calmly. Not any more.

'You've never been to a rehabilitation centre for an addiction to it?'

'No, I haven't.'

'But you told your mother that you had, according to your police statements, did you not?' Mr Hamlin looks up at me.

'Yes. I told my mother I had been to a rehab facility when I hadn't.'

A member of the jury audibly tuts.

'You lied?'

'Yes, I lied to my mother, but yesterday when you talked about the things people tell each other that they don't always mean, you said that's something everyone does.'

Mr Hamlin puts his head on one side. 'Ms Beauchamp, have you just lied to the jury about what happened on the night of Richard Shand's death?'

'No, I have not.'

Mr Hamlin puts his glasses back on. 'So you smoked some cannabis with Richard and then he presented you with some photographs. I'd like to refer directly to your police statement. The interviewing officer asks you if the photographs made you upset?'

'"JB: Yes. I told him it was over.

IO: And were you angry? Did you mean it was over because you were about to kill him?

JB: No! I meant... our relationship was over. He asked me not to go and to forgive him then he looked at the knife next to him and reached for it.

IO: Why was a knife next to him?

JB: He was cutting a lemon.

IO: You saw him reach for the knife?

JB: Yes. I reached for it at the same time.

IO: Why?

JB: Because I thought he was going to hurt himself.

IO: You didn't think he was just going to cut the fruit?

JB: No, it wasn't like that. He asked me to forgive him and it was a quick movement, a sort of panicked one to grab the knife. I said "no!"'

'So Richard begged for your forgiveness, according to you,' Mr Hamlin says, 'to which you responded "no" having already reached for the knife?'

'Not "no" I didn't forgive him,' I say quickly. '"No", don't do this to yourself'. He was asking forgiveness for what he was about to do to himself, which is why I reached for the knife to stop him.'

'And you struggled?'

'Yes! He was trying to stab himself! I was trying to stop him!'

'While you were holding the knife – a fact that is not in dispute – were you looking at your hands on the handle while holding it?'

'Yes.'

'You are certain of that? Just as you're certain that the first wound to Mr Shand's body was to his chest?'

'Yes.'

'How was Richard holding it both by the handle – you said: "our hands" were on the handle – *and* by the blade at the same time?'

I hesitate. The room falls so quiet I can practically hear the low warning hum of energy, like standing next to an electric fence. I take a deep breath and grab the wire. 'I meant my hands. Not our hands. Richard stabbed himself in the chest,' I insist. 'I put my hands on the knife handle. I did not see the blade enter Richard's body while I was holding it. I was looking at our hands on the handle. One of his hands moved from the handle to grab the blade. I let go of the knife.'

'So *that* is the version of events you'd like to stand by, is it?' Mr Hamlin's voice is clotted cream with a skin of flint dust.

'Yes.' Is all I can say. 'He stabbed himself again, he collapsed and died.'

'You said a moment ago that you're certain the first wound was to Mr Shand's chest and yet you didn't mention that at all to the first responders, did you? You told them that he'd severed his carotid and jugular – as if that was the main injury site and the wound *you* were sure was responsible for his death. And that's the wound that does *not* have a transverse orientation.

Why do you think you specifically mentioned that wound and not the wound to Mr Shand's chest, Ms Beauchamp?'

'I don't know,' I say. 'Because it was most visibly distressing, perhaps? And the largest cut? It would probably have been my immediate assumption that was how he died, because I obviously wasn't able to see how deep the stab wound to his chest was.'

'So after Richard died, what happened next?'

I waver on the stand, I feel almost punch drunk and I think of Timothy again, what he had the courage to do yesterday and how in trying to protect Mum, because I felt so guilty about sleeping with Richard, I've obfuscated the truth, something she's spent her whole life turning her back on and how she isn't even here to see me do it.

She isn't even here...

'Truthfully?' I say, and I see both Yas and Johnnie swing round in alarm.

David Hamlin stares at me. 'Yes, of course truthfully, Ms Beauchamp.'

I take a deep breath. 'I was in shock, I'd smoked some strong cannabis and I panicked. I called my mother because I had some unkind texts on my phone from her and I didn't know what to do about them. I waited for her to call back. No more than a minute, I guess? But I smoked some more while I waited. She didn't call me and I decided it would be sensible to get rid of the phone. I sent my mother a text telling her to get rid of her phone. I went downstairs and I threw my phone in the Thames. Was that stupid? Yes. Did I go back up and call the emergency services? Yes. Could I have saved Richard? No.'

I can feel the whole room staring at me. How did Timothy do this yesterday? He's amazing.

'What did the "unkind" texts on your phone say?' Mr Hamlin asks.

'That my mother wanted Richard to disappear. She called

him a cunt...' I ignore the shocked gasps from the jury. We can talk about violent stabbings in graphic detail but I can't say 'cunt'? 'She was not kind about Richard when he was alive,' I admit, 'but she played no part whatsoever in his death. It just didn't look that way and I panicked.'

'I'm going to read you your police statement, Ms Beauchamp.'

Of course he is.

'"IO: You're a nurse, but you left someone bleeding out, with multiple stab wounds, only returning to the victim to call for help when you made sure you had first disposed of your phone?

JB: I told you, Richard was already dead. There was nothing I could have done to save him and I was in shock. I wanted to get away from that room. I went downstairs and it was raining. I tried to phone my mum, got frustrated and threw the phone away.

IO: Is your mother frightened of her case going to trial?

JB: She's in her seventies! What do you think? Yes!

IO: What was on that phone, that you didn't want anyone to see?

JB: Nothing.

IO: No incriminating messages? Admissions you needed to get rid of? Messages confirming you'd done what you and your mother had decided was the best way to end this?

JB: There was no plan to hurt Richard.

IO: If I ask your mother for her handset, will she still have it, Jude?

JB: You'll have to ask her that, not me."'

'So you lied to the police, Ms Beauchamp?' Mr Hamlin looks right at me. 'There were, in fact, messages on the phone?'

'I was trying to protect my mother. That's all.' I look down at the floor. 'What I did after Richard's death is not relevant to how he died.'

'Is that what you told yourself as you made the hesitation marks on his wrist to make his death appear consistent with suicide?'

'No. I didn't make those marks. He must have done it himself and I just didn't notice them.'

Mr Hamlin eyes me steadily. 'You are a habitual liar, aren't you, Ms Beauchamp?'

I shake my head. 'No.'

Mr Hamlin closes his eyes and rubs his brow as if tiring of my façade. 'You lie to people you've just met, you lie to family members, you lie to the police... yet you insist you've told the jury the truth. Why should they believe you? Ms Beauchamp, you have given evidence that Richard Shand produced two photographic images that "upset" you. You admit you shouted. You were tired of being caught in the middle between these people. He "disgusted" you. And yet you want the jury to believe Richard Shand stabbed *himself* over twenty times?'

'I didn't kill him! I would never hurt someone. I have nursed people my whole professional life. I make people better, I look after them!'

'You would "never hurt someone", Miss Beauchamp?' Mr Hamlin lifts his calm eyes again. 'That's not true either, is it? When the police found you in your car outside the house of your ex-partner's new girlfriend, in November 2020 – she'd called them because she felt "threatened" by your presence – what did they find in your car?'

Here we go. Just as Johnnie and Yas said, he was inevitably going to arrive at this point. My heart thumps and I don't look at the public gallery. 'Plenty of things,' I reply, my voice starting to shake. 'My phone, my—'

'Did they find a rope, a saw and plastic sheeting?' David Hamlin talks over me to more shocked gasps.

'It was my cousin Timothy's car, and he'd been using those items for the general maintenance of the estate.'

'Did the police find rope, a saw and plastic sheeting in your vehicle, Ms Beauchamp?' He repeats.

'Yes. They did. But my partner voluntarily came back home to our flat with me that night, so he can't have been that frightened, can he? He was perfectly satisfied that the items you mention were self-explanatory. And just for the record, it was the home of his childhood sweetheart that he'd gone to; she wasn't a new girlfriend. She'd been very important to him for a very long time.' Still I don't look at Lydia.

Mr Hamlin looks up at me and I know what he's going to say next. Here it comes.

'This is the partner who died the week after returning to your joint home at the age of thirty-nine, is that correct?'

'Yes.' I brace myself.

'How did he die, Ms Beauchamp?'

I hang my head like a single rose wilting in a vase on a windowsill in too bright sunlight. 'His name was Dominic. He took his own life.'

The fireworks of more shocked gasps sound all around me.

'He jumped from Waterloo Bridge,' I carry on. 'There was nothing to suggest he was going to do it. He had no mental health issues that any of us were aware of. I was in the very early stages of an unexpected, unplanned pregnancy and perhaps he'd not wanted to come back to me, but felt he ought to and had then become very overwhelmed... that's all I have to explain it.' I still don't look at Lydia. 'His death was a total shock to everyone that knew him and for the avoidance of *any* doubt, I wasn't with him when he died – as my mother told the police, she was with me that night.'

'Were you angry with him?'

'For taking his own life?' I ask. 'I think anyone who loses someone they love in that way will tell you at points you feel very angry with them, yes. I miscarried after he died.'

'In November 2021, around the first anniversary of this

deeply tragic event,' David Hamlin continues, 'the transport police were called to an incident where you physically assaulted a male passenger on a train. Wer—'

'Oh no. Please don't do this,' I cut in, begging him. 'Don't make it look like this. The male passenger called me a "stupid bitch" because I didn't want to talk to him. When I tried to move carriages to get away, I accidentally threw a *salad* over him. At most a fork brushed his arm. Women and girls are out there every day being murdered and assaulted by men, often their partners or boyfriends... sometimes random males they just had the misfortune to walk past in the street. These aren't encounters any woman goes *looking* for!'

'Some of these women you would have treated first hand as part of your work as an A&E nurse, is that correct?' Mr Hamlin interrupts.

'Yes. I was part of a team who tried to save the life of a four-teen-year-old girl who was stabbed by two sixteen-year-old boys in broad daylight the weekend Richard died, in fact.' I hold his gaze. 'But by all means, ask me about the salad.'

'Were you angry about the incident involving the stabbed fourteen-year-old girl when you went to see Mr Shand at his flat on the night in question?' Mr Hamlin's voice is quiet.

'How could I not be?' I exclaim, exasperated. 'A young girl with her whole life ahead of her had it taken away! Her family had her taken away from them! But I wasn't angry with *Richard* about that, just like I wasn't angry with the man on the train.'

'But you gave the man on the train some money after you lost control and assaulted him? You admitted liability?'

I exhale. 'I didn't lose control. I didn't assault him. He was given some cash to pay for having his suit cleaned, yes.'

Some of the jury actually make a note of that. It was a salad! Fuck's sake!

I realise too late that I've said that out loud.

Mr Hamlin looks up immediately. 'Have *I* now made you angry, Ms Beauchamp?'

'No,' I insist. 'You really haven't.'

'Well, I think we all heard that you appear to have taken exception to what I just said.' Mr Hamlin looks around him. 'You have a history of taking exception to the way men "behave", it seems. I'd like to read you part of your mother's statement to the police: "Jude has always had a complex relationship with men. She puts them on a pedestal and becomes terribly sad when they let her down."'

I shake my head. 'That's just not true! There are two men in particular who have been a hugely positive influence in my life – my cousin Timothy, who is pretty much my whole family and a man I couldn't be more proud of... and I also have a male friend who I've known since we were fourteen.' I look at Johnnie's very upright back as he faces away from me, but I know he's listening carefully. 'He's always been there for me, and I've loved him for a very long time now. There's no record of any professional complaints against me or made by me about *any* of the male members of staff at work, so no, I don't hate men or have unresolved anger issues with them, which is what you're trying to suggest... but that doesn't mean I can't still be angry about what is happening to women at the same time. It's not a binary one thing or the other, just like lying about something to protect my mother doesn't mean I lie about everything!'

'And yet here you are, someone who rightly identifies that women are simply not safe alone on the streets in broad daylight, making the utterly extraordinary choice to return to working at night. *Choosing* to walk the streets in the dark, alone...' Mr Hamlin clicks onto the image of me running to Richard's flat again. 'Except you're not walking here, are you, Ms Beauchamp? You're running.'

'Of course I'm bloody running!' I start to cry. 'Because I'm thinking it's about to happen all over again! I'm going to be too late to stop someone else who is vulnerable from hurting himself!'

Mr Hamlin shakes his head. 'You're clearly not comfortable with being on the streets alone in the dark, and no one can blame you for that at all, Ms Beauchamp. They're not safe – no one disputes that. So what possible justification could you have for making such a choice to return to working nights and exposing yourself to risks you were well aware of, just days before you re-entered Richard Shand's life, I wonder?'

I exhale. 'There is an uplift for working nights. You get more money. I needed the money. That's all.'

'Oh, come now, Ms Beauchamp!' Mr Hamlin regards me. 'Your mother, Lady Fawkes, was quite prepared to give you generous amounts of money, according to your police statement. Wouldn't that have been much easier and a *safer* solution to your financial difficulties?'

'I've financially supported myself for many years now,' I answer.

'Yes, all while living in a generously sized Zone 1 property owned by the family trust, quite,' Mr Hamlin remarks drily. 'You returned to working nights just before appearing back in Richard Shand's life as part of a carefully orchestrated plan to hurt Richard, didn't you?'

'No.' I shake my head. 'I knew that my mother was going to struggle in the last few days before her trial, and she'd be phoning me constantly. It's selfish, but I went back to working nights at that precise point so that I would be legitimately asleep during the day and she wouldn't expect to be able to reach me.'

Mr Hamlin shrugs. 'You couldn't have just turned your mobile off during the day while you were at work? That's not unreasonable – and would have achieved your goal with far less inconvenience. Ms Beauchamp' – he moves on before I can answer – 'the police seized a number of items from your property after your arrest, one of which was a laptop. The laptop contained numerous searches on suicide, methods of suicide, outcomes of suicide, studies on suicide. You searched "signs of suicide" two days before Richard's death.' Mr Hamlin looks up at me. 'How do you explain that?'

'When someone you love takes their own life, you never stop thinking about them and the things you could have said, the *signs* you could have seen that might have made a difference. I was an A&E nurse, I searched lots of medical terms to offer my patients the best care I could and, of course, given my personal experience, I have a special interest in suicide prevention. I never want that to happen to anyone else.'

'Are you aware that one of the studies in your bookmarked documents discusses hesitation marks? Like the ones Richard Shand was identified as having?'

'I'd expect it to. It's a really important warning sign for all health care professionals to be aware of.'

Mr Hamlin pauses and removes his glasses again. 'At midnight, on Sunday, the 22nd of August last year, you got into an argument with Richard Shand and you reached for a knife.' He lifts his gaze. 'I put it to you that you stabbed Richard's throat and, while one might at first be led to think this was a "red mist" response to his betrayal – a loss of control and that anger again – you knew exactly where to aim. He tried to grab for the knife by the blade to stop you and sliced his fingers, but collapsed. You then proceeded to stab his body again and again and again, didn't you?'

'No!' I shake my head, determinedly. 'No.'

'—and without calling even 999,' Mr Hamlin raises his voice over me, 'you calmly walked down to the river and called your mother to let her know, *it's done...*' Mr Hamlin gently closes the file on his desk. 'He wasn't a threat to your mother any more. You admit you then threw your phone into the water to cover up damning messages between you and your mother about Richard Shand, something which you had denied to the police. Your mother's phone has never been recovered. You are an adept manipulator and self-confessed liar who gives a little truth here to hide the lies over there, except we see the whole picture now, Ms Beauchamp.' He actually pauses to put his glasses back on. 'You deliberately and painstakingly created the circumstances to make this crime possible. It was entirely premeditated because you were *angry* with Dominic, *angry* with the man on the train, *angry* with those boys who took the life of that fourteen-year-old girl and *angry* with Richard Shand. Are you still "nocturnal", Ms Beauchamp?'

'It's not possible for me to be able to live like that while I'm in prison, so no.'

'Of course you're not.' He looks at me calmly. 'Because there is no need to be, is there? Not now that Richard Shand is dead. I have no further questions, My Lady.'

* * *

But he seems to have all of the answers.

As he closes his case, Mr Hamlin again reminds them that I am an established liar. My story has changed repeatedly and yet what remains clear with each version, is that I had the motive and the means for murder.

'This was not a tale of two people who were always destined to meet, finally finding each other by moonlight, rather the darkest stuff of nightmares. There is no dispute that Jude Beauchamp was with Richard Shand at the moment of his death. His blood is on her dress. Her fingerprints are on the knife. But this was not suicide by an extremely unusual means, as Miss Beauchamp would have you believe. Richard Shand had spoken to his father only hours earlier, insisting he would see him in the morning. There was no suicide note to be found.

The first lethal cut to the neck that severed the jugular and carotid did not have a "transverse orientation".

'The police have attended two other incidents where Jude Beauchamp has been warned about her threatening and violent behaviour, where she lost control. On the night in question she was already severely sleep deprived, which as our expert explained makes it very difficult – if not impossible – for someone to control their emotions. Someone sleep deprived is quick to anger. She had also smoked strong cannabis; she was upset with Richard Shand. They argued and he asked for forgiveness, but she reached for the knife and she stabbed him. Her background as a nurse meant she knew exactly how to make it appear a suicide. By her own admission she smoked some more cannabis, didn't call for help and calmly disposed of any incriminating evidence, only then returning to the scene of the crime to tell the 999 operator and first responder that she had witnessed a violent suicide. Another lie...

'There was no tragic romance here.' Mr Hamlin sweeps his gaze around the entranced jury hanging on his every word. 'This was not a girl, standing in front of a boy, trying to save him. At best we might see this as a total loss of control on Ms Beauchamp's part. She had been betrayed *again* and she stabbed and killed him. But the evidence points to something far more sinister than that. It shines a light on someone with a cold-blooded plan, an intention to manipulate, deceive and murder... a habitual liar and part of a family that didn't like Richard Shand. As a fifteen-year-old child, Richard Shand innocently walked into their home, and twenty-eight years later, he paid for that mistake with his life.'

I look at the coat of arms on the wall as Yasmin stands up.

She clears her throat before the hushed, expectant court.

'Jude bore witness to the horrific sight of a man in a state of such desperate emotional pain and paranoia he was prepared to stab himself multiple times with a kitchen knife. But that's all she is – a witness.

'Her prints were on the knife handle because she bravely tried to stop him. Yes, they struggled, Mr Shand was a former soldier and much stronger than her, but regardless of that, she immediately acted on her nurse's instinct to preserve life, no matter what.

'Except this was a very determined man who had attempted to take his own life twice before at moments of crisis, when, just as on the night in question, he simply snapped with no warning, no note... On the night in question, however, Jude wasn't able to stop him from succeeding. How very tragic that is, but it's not Jude's fault. Richard Shand had indicated to another member of Jude's family on a separate occasion of his intention to take his own life. This was a threat he'd already attempted to carry through and, ultimately, he made good on his promise.

'In the moments after his death, Jude's thoughts immediately turned to her mother – protecting her mother. She made some choices in the aftermath of what Richard did to himself that perhaps you don't agree with. Perhaps you think they seem callous. They were certainly misguided, but she had just watched someone kill themselves in front of her; she admits she'd smoked some very strong cannabis. She acted to protect her mother and then she went back to Richard. She waited with him. She has waited in prison for the last year to tell you what she saw. Jude Beauchamp cannot be punished with a prison sentence that will swallow up the rest of her life for failing to prevent someone from taking *his* life. Young men are increasingly taking their own lives, and we might wonder how on earth they are to get help if we're not even prepared to acknowledge it's happening or talking about it for the huge problem it is... The Crown have insisted my client is responsible for Richard Shand's death, and that her honourable attempts to correct the record mean you can't trust anything she says, but that position is simply not supported by the science and the facts.

'Almost all of the stab wounds on Richard Shand's body had a transverse orientation. It was the sworn testimony of an expert witness with over forty-five years of experience in her field that these wounds were inflicted by Richard Shand himself. Even if you were to consider that one of the wounds may have been inflicted by my client, neither pathologist you heard give evidence was able to determine which was the fatal wound, so it is simply not possible to say, beyond all reasonable doubt, that Jude Beauchamp is guilty of murder. It was not her fault that Richard Shand died.' Yas turns to look right at me. 'It was not your fault.'

I am grateful to her, I really am. I know I've reduced her entire defence to the angle the knife entered Richard's body. As I look at the jury, some of them are scribbling on their notepads furiously while the judge begins to sum up, directing them towards the requirements of the law and reminding them that it is only *their* view of the evidence that now matters, that they must work together and listen to one another to reach a unanimous verdict. It's very clear that some of them have already made up their mind about me.

But there is nothing more to be done.

The jury is out.

TWENTY-SEVEN

Yasmin practically runs towards him, her gown billowing behind her and her wig slightly askance.

'Three hours?' she exclaims at Johnnie, who is waiting for her outside the courtroom door, also slightly breathless, from having run up from the cells below. 'Are they taking the actual piss? I've had tractor theft deliberations last longer. I thought they at least felt sorry for her.' She pauses. 'They don't like her, do they? How can you possibly give fair consideration to that much evidence in three hours? It should have taken them at least that just to wade through their directions document. *How* can they have a verdict already? Bloody juries.'

Johnnie gestures helplessly. 'It's much, much too quick. I don't like it either.'

'She's absolutely fucked.' Yas looks up at the ceiling and exhales deeply, puffing her cheeks out. 'I thought we might get manslaughter but... three hours. How can juries think they see things so clearly?'

'Because they are not cynics like us,' David Hamlin remarks, calmly sauntering past them back into court with the air of a man about to win his case.

Yas rolls her eyes. 'Let's do this then.' She frowns at Johnnie. 'You OK?'

He nods, but he isn't OK at all. He's terrified.

'Come on then.' She jerks her head at the waiting court-room and walks in, but he lingers outside a moment longer. Up until now there has at least been hope – but what happens when that too is removed in a moment?

'Johnnie!' He hears a shout and turns to see Timothy running towards him, pushing through the throng. Word has got out about the verdict and the galleries will be full.

'What are you doing here?' Johnnie exclaims. 'You didn't manage to keep Margaret—'

Timothy raises his hands. 'Stop! I need to tell you something.'

Johnnie looks over his shoulder. 'Now's not really the time. The verdict's in!'

'Johnnie, please! For once shut up and listen to me!' Timothy orders. 'Margaret died last night. She'd been ill. Cancer apparently – her heart gave out. I found her this morning, and on the bed next to her was her old mobile: the so-called lost one. There are still three messages on it. I started to listen to it.' He lowers his voice to a whisper. 'The first really is from Jude. It starts: "Hi Mum, it's me..." but I couldn't listen to the rest of it, Johnnie! Or the others.' His eyes fill with tears. 'I just couldn't do it. Margaret must have been saving them every couple of days for the past *year*.'

'Where is the phone now?' Johnnie frowns, 'because you can't have brought it in here? You're not allowed to. Did you leave it at Highcombe?'

'No,' Timothy says. 'I left it at the travel agent around the corner. They said they'd keep it safe for me. There isn't any storage here, so that's what everyone does, apparently.'

Johnnie lowers his voice in disbelief. 'You left a phone with a possible recording of a murder at a *travel agent*?'

Timothy looks at him, confused. 'What else was I supposed to do? I've got a ticket?' He holds up a small scrap of paper.

Johnnie exclaims aloud, then looks at everyone filing slowly back into court, torn between proceedings possibly resuming without him versus the very real risk of the phone being lost, stolen, or worst of all, handed back to someone else with a ticket by mistake. If there is even the slightest chance Margaret was telling the truth and someone else listens to that message... he shivers. He, of course, as part of the defence, is under no obligation to disclose whatever *might* be on the phone even if it is incriminating. If it falls into the Crown's hands via the police, however...

Except what is he thinking? There will be no such message. This was just another one of Margaret's hideous lies. 'We'll get it afterwards,' he says, his voice brusque. 'There's nothing on it. We agreed as much at the time.'

Of course Jude didn't murder him! Have they actually met Jude? She couldn't say boo to a goose.

Even Margaret herself knew that Jude would never... wait though. Johnnie stops dead. He has sifted through every single detail of the evidence, the statements, over and over again in case there is something he's missed. He knows it all inside out and back to front. Jude only left two voicemails on Margaret's phone that night so how are there *three* messages?

'Tim!' he calls and beckons his friend quickly. 'Give me the ticket and show me where this travel agent is, now!'

* * *

They burst out onto Newgate Street, pushing past workmen and rushing across the crossroads, narrowly avoiding a bus turning left, and past the pub on the corner, heading in the direction of Bart's hospital. 'This way?' Johnnie shouts, alarming several passers-by as Timothy starts to puff and fall back.

'Yes! Over the road,' Timothy calls, hands dropping to his knees as he bends, trying to get his breath back. 'Further up! On the left.'

Johnnie picks up speed, spying the shop window. Slamming in through the door so hard that it bounces off the wall, he cannons in and stumbles into a sea of thick carpets and images of luxury destinations. Several people instinctively jump up from behind their desks in alarm as the one lone customer with a small dog on her lap shrieks and the dog begins to yap.

'I'm sorry,' gasps Johnnie, holding out his small scrap of paper, 'but who do I need to give this to so I can have my phone back?'

The staff visibly relax. 'Oh,' says a man, serving the affronted dog woman. 'I see. If you can just give us a moment, sir, someone will be right with you.' He sinks back down into his seat and smiles at the lady. 'So we were—'

'No!' Johnnie watches them, amazed, as they all start to drift back to their business as if he's popped in on spec for a trip to the Maldives. '*Now!* Get the fucking phone for me NOW!' he roars, for once using his height and build to its full advantage.

They all leap back to attention, visibly frightened, which even given the circumstances, he regrets, as a middle-aged woman wearing a wedding ring and a gold 'mum' necklace rushes over, snatches his ticket and quickly returns, passing an old android to him with shaking hands.

'Thank you,' he takes it, and she immediately recoils.

'I'm sorry I shouted,' he shouts as he bangs back out onto the street and, with fumbling hands, turns it on. It has no passcode but he's not even sure how to access the voicemail on a phone as basic as this. 1? 150? 'Fuck it,' he shouts as he pushes buttons desperately; and Timothy arrives alongside him, scarlet in the face with his chest heaving. 'Here.' He reaches out for it, dials and hands it back.

Johnnie stands still and listens intently, unseeing, as Timothy dry retches next to him with exertion and anxiety, not noticing a passing black cab, a cyclist, just concentrating.

'You have three saved messages. First message received at—'

'This is just Jude, like you said. Saying she'll call back,' he announces after a few seconds. 'Come on, come on... next message. I thought that maybe...' He looks at Timothy, his shoulders sagging, 'but it looks like – wait. Wait!' He puts a hand out in mid-air, freezes and listens.

Timothy looks at him nervously. 'What is it?'

Johnnie slowly draws his hand in and covers his mouth, his eyes widening. 'Oh my God!' he whispers. 'Oh shit! SHIT!' He looks around him desperately, then at Timothy. 'We've got to stop them. They need to hear this!' He shoves the phone at him like a relay baton. 'Save the message!' he orders, 'and don't let *anything* happen to that phone!'

He turns and sprints back towards the court, tie and jacket flying behind him, arms properly pumping, dodging around people stepping into his path, speeding up across the road. His muscles are on fire but he doesn't stop as he pounds up the steps.

'I have to get back into Court 14 immediately,' he gasps to security, holding his arms up to be searched. 'I'm part of the defence and I need to halt proceedings. Hurry! Please hurry!'

Hurtling down the corridor he pushes open the door to find a quiet, packed courtroom. All eyes swivel to look at him, Yas, David Hamlin, the judge herself, all staring at him in astonishment, apart from Jude, already standing in the dock, eyes closed, hands clasped behind her back. Dear God, even the *jury* is in... the foreman is rising to his feet.

Yas quickly returns her gaze to the front and no doubt her silent prayers that by some miracle the jury will have arrived at manslaughter... David Hamlin looks respectfully back at the bench in front of him as well, far too dignified for the open confidence he is undoubtedly feeling. Johnnie pushes through to take his seat behind Yas and begins to whisper to her as the clerk addresses the foreman of the jury.

'What did you say?' says Yas, twisting round to look at him.

'You've got to stop it, now!' Johnnie begs. 'Quick!'

'Mr Foreman,' the clerk's voice is confident and clear against the rest of the room collectively holding its breath. 'Answer my question: yes or no.'

'What do you mean "stop it"? I can't just—' Yas looks at Johnnie like he's mad.

David Hamlin is now frowning and looking at them, pushing his glasses back on his nose.

'I have proof of her innocence!' Johnnie insists.

'Have you reached a verdict in respect of the defendant upon which you are all agreed?' asks the clerk.

'Yes.' The grandfatherly type on his feet nods uncertainly, glancing at Yas and Johnnie and the judge, who is looking increasingly annoyed.

'On the count of murder—'

'STOP!' shouts Johnnie, and murmurs of disbelief and excitement ripple through the galleries as he whispers more to Yas.

'Miss Curtis!' The judge looks, as well she might, absolutely furious.

'Apologies, My Lady, for this very exceptional interruption,' begs Yas, looking incredulously at Johnnie, 'but might I have a moment with my learned friend?'

'Now?' The judge removes her glasses as if she can't quite believe what is happening.

'Yes, My Lady.'

The judge sighs and briefly pinches the bridge of her nose, no doubt reflecting on this extraordinary turn of events just as she was settling down to review some papers peacefully.

'Mr Hamlin?' she says.

David Hamlin frowns, looks at Yas and Johnnie pleading with him silently and, because he is a decent man, nods. 'Very well, My Lady.'

Johnnie instantly slumps down onto his seat, limbs rubbery with relief, closes his eyes and sees fifteen-year-old Jude lying on the grass by the Highcombe fountain, giggling helplessly at something he'd said – his delight at having made her happy – and looking so beautiful in the dusk. His heart stopping as *she reached for his hand*. Staring at her, knowing he was going to kiss her... and his own total joy and bliss when she kissed him back. He wanted to give her the world.

And now he has.

TWENTY-EIGHT

'Margaret, this is Richard Shand speaking. I know you won't pick up this call. I've just read your text that you'll be switching your phone off for the rest of the night. It was the text where you called your own daughter "fucking selfish" and a "deeply unpleasant burden". Not to be confused though with the one where you call me "an evil cunt". Or the one where you say all Jude had to do was make me "disappear".

'So I'm leaving you this message to say you don't need to worry about me. I won't be in court tomorrow. I'm done. This has gone on long enough.

'You should know though, that after I asked you for help and you literally burnt everything down around me, I went on to have a good life. I loved being in the army. I fucked it up like I eventually do most things, but it was good while it lasted and I did all right after it too. A lot of kids will benefit as a result of that, which makes me really happy.

'But I'm also tired now. Constant physical pain is exhausting – as you know, I think. I can't do a lot of the things that keep me sane any more. I increasingly miss my mum these days. I'm stuck *in the past basically and that's no good for anyone. I'm the burden – not your daughter.*

'I don't want to be that person any more. You shouldn't want to be that person either, Margaret. Do something about it.

'And just please, destroy that photo. It's the last thing I will ever ask of you. I don't want my father ever seeing me like that. It wasn't a fucking affair and you know it. Your husband abused me, more than once, and you did nothing. Do this now for me, at least.

'I am on my way. I'm nearly there.'

TWENTY-NINE

'You heard the message yourself?' Jude sits rigidly in the cell. 'You're sure it's Richard?'

'Well, that's why we would ask them to adjourn deliberations now – so the Crown could assess the validity of the recording,' Johnnie explains eagerly as Yas stands back. 'But when they do determine it, I hope they'll offer no evidence.'

'It means they have no case,' Yas explains. 'And when they offer no evidence the jury will be directed to deliver a not guilty verdict and all of this will be over.'

'How will the judge determine it's really Richard?' Jude asks.

'They'd ask someone that knew Richard to listen to the recording.'

'Like his father?' She shakes her head. 'I can't let that happen.'

'Jude, he says he's "done", that he won't be in court in the morning, that he's "on his way", he's "nearly there!"' Johnnie gestures widely with his arms. 'That's a clear demonstration of intent to take his own life.'

'But he also says why, right?' Jude says, 'and he didn't want anyone to know that. He desperately didn't want anyone to know. Particularly his father. You can't ask a father to listen to the first bit of his son's last words – to identify him – and not listen to the rest of the message... but if he does, it'll destroy him. I don't want to use this message as evidence. Do we have to disclose it?'

Johnnie straightens up. He can't believe what he's just heard. 'You don't want to use it?' He rubs his jaw with his hand, tries to calm the roaring frustration flooding his head. 'OK, so this is not how trials usually go, Jude. They're much more mundane. I've never known a client go off script as you did when you gave your evidence; I've never seen a jury come back in that quickly for a trial of this nature. I hope to God I never have to stand up and yell "stop" like that as a verdict is being delivered ever again. I've also never had evidence surface like this at the last moment which turns everything on its head in a *good* way for my client' – he swallows – 'only to have the client say they don't want to use it. It would be mad not to use this message.'

'I do feel pretty odd, actually.' She leans forward and puts her head in her hands. 'My apparently very ill mother, who I've just found out died last night, has been sitting on evidence for a year that could have freed me, so that she could have the best of last times...'

Neither Johnnie nor Yas say anything to that. There is nothing they can say.

Jude sits up again. 'While it looks like Mum was possibly going to do the right thing eventually, because she kept on saving the messages rather than deleting them, I think we can all agree this is taking the piss a bit, in terms of leaving it to the last minute. And no, I don't know what the hell to do with that, to be honest with you.' She pauses for a moment and clears her throat. 'I also don't understand how Richard saying he intended to take his own life proves he definitely did?'

'Well, it doesn't but you remember what I said?' Johnnie frowns. 'We don't have to prove that you're innocent, just show that there is sufficient reason for doubt that you are guilty – and this message is that.'

'But Richard did not want people to know what had happened to him, especially his family,' she repeats and takes a deep breath. 'I've given up so much already. I have to destroy that last part of him, just to cross the finish line?' Her eyes fill with tears. 'I'm instructing you as my solicitor not to use the message.'

Johnnie looks up at the ceiling. 'And I'm telling you as your lifelong friend,' his voice wavers a little as he starts to speak, 'that the jury came back in under three hours with a possible life sentence. Shand's dead, please don't try and be noble about this. There's no heaven he's watching you from and saying: "Hey! Thanks for honouring my wishes!" He doesn't know what's happening to you right now, but this is *your* life. The rest of your life... a life to spend with the people who love you!'

'Johnnie,' says Yas, quietly.

'No!' says Johnnie. 'You know what I think happens when you die? You don't get to see the people who you loved and lost. You don't get to hug them again. That only happens when you're *alive*. You've got that chance *now*. You could have another fifty-odd years of a life – which is such a privilege, and I know you know that better than anyone – but you want to risk that for someone who is already dead?' He shrugs incredulously. 'Please don't do this, Jude!' he begs. 'Please! I can even cope with the prospect of you going to South Africa forever as long as you're happy, but don't waste this chance! Tell me – what would you do, if you walked away from here, free, today?' he demands, trying to get her to see what's within her grasp.

'I would go back to Highcombe. I might think about going away for a bit. I would legally change my name back to Rachel. Being Jude was never my choice and I'd like to put it behind me... but Richard's family have suffered enough.' She looks at the ceiling as she wipes the tears away. 'This is about how he's remembered forever!'

'Then he shouldn't have left that message, should he?' Johnnie exclaims.

'He wouldn't have thought for one moment my mother would keep it. I know he wouldn't. I can't use it. He has a right to privacy, even in death, surely?'

'You don't think,' Johnnie insists, trying to calm down, 'that you're in shock because you've just found out all of this stuff about your mum... which brings a lot of complicated feelings into play and might also be making you behave in ways that you normally wouldn't?'

'There is nothing normal about any of this. But I can't use that message.' She looks down at the floor. 'I really can't.'

'OK,' Yas cuts in. 'Then I'll go and tell the judge that it was a false alarm, we'll be back to where we were just before Johnnie burst in, and the only thing that'll be different is I'll probably never work again.'

'I'm sorry,' Jude says. 'I really am.'

Yas yawns and stretches. 'Don't sweat it. I still get to go home tonight. My work here is done.'

Johnnie frowns in surprise, and Jude looks up at her quickly.

'Johnnie's right though, you should grab your chance,' Yas concludes cheerfully. 'Don't leave it up to the jury to make this call. All juries are mad. It's the best we've got – but it's a shit system, nonetheless. Use the message.'

* * *

'Wow.' Yas turns to Johnnie as soon as they're out of earshot of the cell.

'I know,' Johnnie says. 'While it was very noble of her to want to do that, I'm extremely glad that...'

Yasmin eyes him. 'You bought that spiel?'

'Yes! Of course!' Johnnie says instantly.

'Hmm.' Yasmin ponders that. 'Hamlin's right, I can't think of a single one of my female friends who would be comfortable to walk around at night, let alone choose to do it. Ask any woman roughly our age, she'll tell you she's tucked her keys through her knuckles while walking in the dark at least once in her life.'

Johnnie crosses his arms. 'You think she's guilty?'

Yas shrugs. 'Sometimes it's obvious when they're telling the truth, sometimes it isn't. That's all. Humans are programmed to want complete certainty – proper *justice* – but the only two people that will ever know for sure what happened that night are Shand and Jude.'

Johnnie nods. 'True, but the timing doesn't fit for it to have been part of a plan, does it? She went back to working nights before she even knew who Shand was... because she needed the money.'

Yas grins. 'You might be doing this work for free, I'm certainly not; and if she can afford my services, she didn't need the NHS "uplift" for working nights. Unless she's going to sell her flat to fund it, which must be worth at least a million... the kind of fallback *all* A&E nurses have, of course.'

Johnnie shakes his head with a smile. 'Not her flat. Belongs to Tim – the *man* of the house. But you're right, how are nurses supposed to work safely in the capital? Beats me.'

Yas pauses and steps a little closer to him. 'Last night my boyfriend went for a run at 9 p.m., so it was dark. He just pulled on his trainers and went. Didn't give his personal safety a single thought. Lucky him. A woman would never do that.'

Johnnie nods, as if considering her point. 'Fair. It shouldn't be like that, it sucks. But just so I'm clear, Jude going out after dark makes her guilty of murder?'

Yas shrugs again, eyebrow raised, amused. 'It doesn't matter what I think anyway. We just present the evidence to the best of our ability. All that said, despite her truly humbling desire to protect Richard's privacy, it's really great news that the Right Hon Jude is reluctantly prepared to use the message after all, thanks to your genuinely impassioned speech... So all's well that ends well. Unless you're Richard, of course,' she adds wryly. 'I've liked working with you, though. If they ever let us, after that total shitshow earlier, we should do it again.' She holds his gaze for a moment then turns her back on him. 'Come on. Let's go and face the music.'

THIRTY

'Tell me what you see.'

'The coffee shop girl wiping tables and looking back at us like we're crazy.'

'Yeah, her,' he said. 'But I also see us. Our reflections, standing next to each other. You wouldn't see that if I wasn't real... and you wouldn't be able to feel this either.'

I keep my eyes closed but I clasp my hands together, as if he's holding mine in his.

'You are full of surprises.'

'I'm really not actually.'

'I think you are. This all suddenly got a bit art-house film, didn't it? Hopefully any second now a single red balloon is going to blow past symbolising all is not lost... although we're a bit high up for that.'

In my mind I see Richard sitting on the balcony, legs crossed, smoking his spliff, staring out over the night sky, the moon hidden away behind the clouds.

'Mr Foreman. Answer my question: yes or no. Have you reached a verdict in respect of the defendant upon which you are all agreed?'

'Yes.'

My breathing starts to speed up, and I imagine Richard slowly turning to face me.

'On the count of murder, how do you find the defendant, Jude Beauchamp? Guilty or not guilty?'

Richard reaches a hand out to me...

'Not guilty.'

I catch my breath. Richard's face is expressionless.

'Members of the jury, do you find the defendant guilty or not guilty of manslaughter?'

'Not guilty.'

The cry that escapes me is such a strange sound. Richard vanishes in an instant and the room is suddenly full of people staring back at me. The judge and clerks. Timothy, smiling. Yas turning to David Hamlin, who is leaning across to say something to her... Johnnie with his back to me, bolt upright, his hands on his head.

I sit down heavily as the judge begins to speak. I can't hear a single thing she says, but the jury are already filing out of their places, and my life, and, moments later, so does she.

I am free to leave.

I did it.

I glance up at the emptying public gallery one last time. I half expect to see Mum there, in her enormous glasses, but the first eyes that catch mine belong to Lydia.

She looks away first, gathering her things and quietly leaving alone. Someone else waves hesitantly and I realise it's the beautiful girl from Chinatown who was sick at Richard's feet. I haven't seen her since the night I put her in the ambulance for my colleagues to take care of.

She stands up, in a pretty 1950s-style dress and, tucking a clutch bag under her arm, she makes a heart with her fingers and thumbs, gives me an uncertain smile and with a swish and a flick, she's gone.

I hadn't really appreciated how many people will have been following the trial. Everyone else is starting to leave; no one else I recognise or know. Just one person remains seated.

Richard's father.

I put my hands in my lap and I wait. I see Johnnie notice what's happening and, respectfully and politely, he ushers the remaining people out until we are the last two left.

Eventually Richard's father stands. He takes one final glance around him then looks me right in the eye. I hold his gaze. I am so much stronger now. I meant it. I will never let anyone inside my head again. Everyone will see only what I *want* them to see. He gives me a stiff nod and leaves the court for the last time.

I wait until it is quiet and still... and close my eyes. I think of Dominic and the photograph of us laughing, on the side at the flat, lit up by the bright sun shining through the window. I see myself walking with Mum, down the hill towards Highcombe at dusk and feel her arm slipping around my shoulders, the swifts swooping and calling, ready to begin their long journey home. And finally I picture Richard sitting down in the coffee shop, telling me to trust in time, that it won't always feel like this... before his arms gather me up, in the lift... but just as quickly it all melts away and instead I see a wide, very bright blue sky and a blood-red balloon rising higher and higher until it becomes a tiny speck, absorbing into the vast beyond of stars and the dark, part of everything and gone.

A LETTER FROM LUCY

Dear reader,

I want to say a huge thank you for choosing to read *The Night She Lied*. A long time ago, I did jury duty and ever since I've been fascinated by how people can view the same evidence very differently. It will be very obvious to anyone with a legal background that I've gone for the drama rather than real-life accuracy, but I hope the point stands up to scrutiny; there are still cases, even in this day and age, where only the people involved know what happened for sure. To that end, I also apologise if you wanted to know categorically if Jude killed Richard or not. I decided to write it as if I wasn't sure myself, so I could make it as convincing as possible. Feel free to message me if it really bugs you – I always enjoy hearing from readers – and I'll tell you what I think, but no spoilers here...

If you did enjoy the book, and want to keep up to date with all my latest releases, just sign up at the following link. Your email address will never be shared and you can unsubscribe at any time.

www.bookouture.com/lucy-dawson

And lastly, if you have time, I'd be very grateful if you could write a review of *The Night She Lied*. It makes such a difference in helping new readers discover one of my books for the first time.

My thanks again for reading *The Night She Lied*.

Lucy

www.lucydawsonbooks.com

facebook.com/lucydawsonbooks
x.com/lucydawsonbooks
instagram.com/lucydawsonbooks

ACKNOWLEDGEMENTS

My thanks to Tony Kent, Neil Lancaster, Wanda Whiteley, Rebecca Bradley, Cally Taylor, Jen Blackhurst, Jo Dickinson, Erin Kelly, Sarah Hilary and Colin Scott. Claire Simmonds and the Bookouture team have as ever made the actual publishing bit easy, as have Ellis Moore and all at Bolinda - I am very grateful for your support. Last but never least, to Eli Keren and Sarah Ballard at United Agents, who went above and beyond, thank you.

Made in the USA
Middletown, DE
02 December 2023

44486460R00196